Pious Rebel

Jory Post

For Karen Wallace,
who has always been my Pious Rebel

ACKNOWLEDGEMENTS

ADMIRATION FOR

- The hard work of property management workers
- KDFC for their dedication to filling the airwaves with classical sounds
- Linden Street for existing
- Santa Cruz poets and printers for their creative energy
- Santa Cruz and Berkeley and Point Reyes Station for providing unique opportunities for nesting
- Anyone who's ever mounted a Harley
- Folks who eat smoked sockeye salmon on stoned ground wheat thins
- Bloggers everywhere willing to share their thoughts and lives to help others thrive
- The healing power of Land of Medicine Buddha
- The raw bliss of Nisene Marks
- The Spanish for inventing paella
- IBM for inventing the Selectric
- Vino Cruz and Soif for keeping us in fine wines
- Dog slobber and cat purrs

ACKNOWLEDGEMENT OF

- Scott and Sabrina Ellis who have gone above and beyond in their support of my writing and the medical teams who have helped me over the past two years
- Julia Chiapella for the original creation of the notion of a pious rebel
- Karen Wallace for listening to me read new sections every morning and providing me with ongoing critique
- Kathy Chetkovich for our weekly meetings where she would cut to the bone and remind me to stay consistent, and for her multiple copy edits
- Jon Franzen who told me to cut every occurrence of "always" from my work
- Clifford Henderson who "prompted" me to open my brain and fingers on the keyboard
- George Merilatt for introducing geodes into our lives
- C & J for their inspiration about and knowledge of hemp seeds
- Every Santa Cruz Restaurant that made an appearance
- Lydia Davis for her piercing wit
- Robert Pirsig for his quest of quality and value
- Richard Powers for entwining us in the lives of trees
- Carlos Castaneda for expanding our consciousness
- Gemzar and Abraxane for modifying the structure of brains and keeping the monster at bay
- Hannah Hutton, my granddaughter, for proofing the final edition and being a thought partner
- Elizabeth McKenzie for being my literary muse and mentor
- Karen Ackland, Cheryl Brothers, Karen Conley, Kathy Chetkovich, Janie Crabb, David and Maria Culver, Scott Ellis, Peter Ferry, Jon Franzen, Elizabeth McKenzie, George Merilatt, Sarah Rabkin, and Karen Wallace, for being my first readers and providing invaluable suggestions

1

THURSDAY
11-14-19

L ISA HARDROCK NEEDED THIS OFFICE. She needed to see and hear the cars buzzing by outside the window on River Street. Needed to have proof of existence. To watch the woman walk by carrying a purple orchid in one hand, cell phone in the other, talking to someone she cared about. Maybe a sister in a rest home on the other side of the country. Or a daughter in a rehab facility down in Monterey.

Lisa wondered if she might get to know the woman. Maybe she'd walk by the window three times a day. Maybe after 120 days they'd wave to each other. Maybe the woman would leave an orchid outside her window. This was how relationships formed. How living occurred. How loving started. At least she thought she remembered it like this. Living in the woods for so long had cocooned her thinking, wrapped her in soft filament that didn't allow touch, very little sight.

Cars stopped at the red light across the street. Right in front of Lenz Arts. Purple and teal letters spelling it out on the side of the building. She needed to walk over there, buy some pens, some Post-its, two erasers, a box of Kleenex. Other things would come soon enough. Wall hangings. Maybe a heater. She was used to logs crackling in a fireplace, two big dogs curled up next to her on a throw rug keeping her warm. A cat. Eloise.

But what she needed now was this office, this reason to drive fifteen minutes to town and force herself into an identity. She had seen the sublet space on Craigslist, had written the check to secure it within twenty-four hours. She had brought in one banker's box full of five manuscript boxes she had never opened, had never shown anyone — not even Gregory. A water bottle. Her cell phone, which she knew was a mistake. She had watched the Joyce Carol Oates' *Master Class* and the first thing Oates had said was "Interruption is the writer's worst enemy." She didn't know if that was true, but figured this office would allow her to bury herself in the experiment. The cell phone was clearly a source of interruption. She should leave it home. Not that she was a writer. But she was a reader. Had been an avid reader. Which is why the final item she set on her new desk, always carried in her pack, was a copy of *To the Lighthouse*. She loved Virginia Woolf. Everything about her, except the stones in her pockets.

During the first half hour in the open-space office, one of the four employees in the property-management business played music that drifted over her no-ceiling walls. There was a door, but it didn't help. Not a big deal, though. It wasn't too loud, not heavy metal. But when one of the partners sat at the conference table with a walk-in colleague, used the Polycom Sound Station to initiate a conference call with what sounded like board members, they talked so loudly and vehemently about the new legal issues facing property managers and whether or not to send something out to a revote, she felt like she was sitting at the table with them, engaged in a conversation she cared nothing about, would never care anything about, and she knew she had made a mistake by not insisting to sit in one day to test the environment. Now she'd have to dust off the Bose noise-cancelling headphones, recharge the battery, begin the next test tomorrow.

2

FRIDAY
11-15-19

P USHPINS AND POWER STRIP IN HAND, Lisa arrived downtown the next morning after stopping at McDonald's for two sausage burritos and a large orange juice. The parking spot just outside her window she had looked forward to capturing was not available at 7:57. She breathed deeply, not a big deal, there were others. The deep breathing was not new, but had been long forgotten these past few years. Disappointment had chiseled its way into her life, had successfully disengaged the breathing, the quiet depth it had once helped her achieve. While she was now hunting for something new, she was also hoping to retrieve some of the old, some of the way-back stuff that had helped to create her power, establish her presence.

Inside the office, music was already disrupting her need for silence, lyrics working their way into one ear, melody the other. She stuck pages onto the walls, varied the color of pushpin depending on the content of the pages. After plugging in her laptop and phone, she slipped the Bose headphones over her ears. The chatter was still loud. She switched to the Beats Solo. A little better, but not much. The check she had written yesterday for $618.35 covered the prorated rent for the rest of November and her obligation through December 31. Her savings account would handle rent for a couple months, long enough to help her focus, figure some things out, a fresh place with life and traffic and orchids walking by. But disappointment was creeping in, finding an entrance when she took a bite of the sausage burrito. She had never eaten anything from McDonald's, not even an offered French fry. At least forty-five more days in this office, this place she was hoping would be the catapult to spring her forward into a new life.

The journal she had purchased online from the handmade-book artist she found in Chicago was sitting on the desk. It was laced with literary quotations throughout. She had trusted the book artist to use her own judgment, include ideas she thought might inspire her. Lisa hadn't opened it yet, hadn't read any of the quotations, authors' names, looked at any of the books mentioned. She didn't know the woman whose image graced the cover. She flipped it open, read the dedication on the inside:

> *For Murasaki Shikibu, who opened a door for women*
> *authors over one thousand years ago.*

From a zippered flap of her pack, she removed an Ohto Graphic Liner pen with pigment ink, removed the cap and touched the nib to the Somerset Book paper the book artist had used to make the journal. She didn't move her wrist into a cursive flow, wasn't ready yet, instead watched as what started as a small mark spread into a pea-sized circle, soaked through the page to the back side. She attached eight legs, grew it into a spider, and finally touched fingers to keyboard:

> This black widow from nowhere appears simply because it
> chooses to, takes its form from accident, from a resistance to
> move forward, from an expanding disappointment that
> began at birth and continues through the creation of these
> sentences, having nothing of value to say, to think about, to
> share with anything except a one-dimensional spider that
> won't even expose her deadly red dot.

She noticed as she typed, in the silence after periods and commas, that a jackhammer had been pounding at concrete somewhere up the street. She hadn't heard it when it was pen on paper, had allowed the noises of the city to inhabit their natural space, had let go of the me-first behavior that had had its claws at her throat for so long. Her ears hurt, like a boxer who had sparred for days in a row. She removed the headphones, the jackhammer blasted louder, the volume of the music bounced off walls, the conversations amped up. She looked at her reflection in the mirror on the back of her door, ears puffy and red. But the rest of her looked relatively good. Her whole life folks had told her she looked younger than her age. It was still true at thirty-seven. The auburn waves of hair flowing over her back and shoulders. The long sinewy body, strong cheekbones, not inherited from her five-foot-one mother. The coaches at Piedmont High had recruited her to play volleyball, hounded her for the better part of her sophomore year. But she was a reader. Didn't have time for the serious practice required to become a star. They told her it didn't matter. She was a natural. But she had been in the middle of *War and Peace*, had just started with *Infinite Jest*, had a dozen other thousand-page tomes lined up for her spare time.

Lisa took her hand off the keyboard, held it in front of her eyes, rolled it from the back to the palm. She remembered holding it up to her mother's hand as a young girl, her twelve-year-old fingers dwarfing those of her mom. Alice had never given her information about the other half of her DNA, simply said her father could have been any one of five friends who had helped her out. She didn't give her the full turkey baster explanation until she was older. Alice had taken Lisa and her adopted sister, Cody, to see the world premiere of Sam Shephard's *The Late Henry Moss* at the Theater on the Square in San Francisco in November 2000. For two seventeen-year-old girls, seeing Nick Nolte, Woody Harrelson, Cheech Marin, and Sean Penn on the same stage would have been enough to satisfy them for months. But for Lisa, the added attraction occurred when Sam Shephard entered the theater from the stage, waved at the cheering audience, walked up the stairs, and sat in the empty seat next to her. For two hours, Lisa was not able to look at the stage, her eyes trained on Sam's hands, hands that were identical to hers. Could her mother have hooked up with Sam Shephard eighteen years ago? He was a mainstay at the Magic Theater back in the '80s, and her mom was a theater groupie.

It was on the trip home over the Bay Bridge when Lisa said, "I think Sam Shephard's my father," that her surrogate sister Cody had laughed uncontrollably, that Alice had smiled and said, "Five of my male friends came over one night and filled a turkey baster for me. They are all long gone. You will never know your father." Lisa ignored them. She had seen Sam's hands.

•   •   •

The content of the dialogue in the outer office pounded into her head over the open ceiling.

"Hey. This is Bianca over at the property management office. Did you find a bag of wet clothes at 108 Pine?"

Lisa heard the other voice on speaker phone, didn't know who was talking.

"I did," the male voice rang in.

"Yeah. We got a call about it. The former tenant left it in the washer. Hasn't been seen in days."

"I'll pick it up when I go back. What should I do with it? Toss it?"

"No. We'd probably be liable. Let me get back to you."

Under her spider picture and words Lisa drew a line down the middle of the page. She labeled the left side "Disappointments," the right side "Accomplishments." Under Disappointments she wrote "Making too quick a decision about this office." Across from it under Accomplishments she wrote "Finding this office." Another Disappointment was "Eating at McDonald's." She added, "Remember to eat something at home for breakfast." Another Disappointment: "The loudness of the office noise." Its counterpart was "Learning something about property management." This activity reminded her that her whole life had been lived out in a series of paired beliefs that opposed each other, sitting on the middle of a fence, "Yes, but" as a constant mantra.

3

SATURDAY
11-16-19

MOTORCYCLE ENGINES ZOOMING BY. A car alarm. No employees there on Saturday and Sundays, so distraction was less of an excuse for lack of productivity. What could pose as an excuse was that she had no idea what she might produce. At home the night before she had done research on noise pollution, noise cancelling, white noise, discovered pink noise, and a well-known author who first put in earbuds, then headphones, and finally found ten hours of pink noise on YouTube. It did block out extraneous noises from the street, but it was grating, sounded like the crash of a waterfall against granite boulders.

She opened the notebook to the spider page, touched the same pen to paper just above the black widow, drew her a mate that she could devour, placed it close enough to attract the original one to jump off the page and claim her lunch. Again, the new arachnid inspired ideas, words began to drip through the ink.

Why is it that one mate feels the need to devour another? Maybe it's not really a need, but rather an instinctual requirement, not triggered by the brain, but dormant in the blood, just waiting for an opportunity. Had it been that way with Gregory? Did he have no control over the way he treated me, the obsessions, the need to be right about everything? It was one reason why we slipped away from each other, or never slipped toward each other, that understanding I came to about being right. That it was not so important to always be right, even when you knew you were, but sometimes more important to let it go, rightness belonging to folks who would die too soon from heart attacks. I'd rather be eaten by a lion on a trail behind Chaminade, have it leap from behind a boulder, grab my neck with a tight jaw, rip out a jugular vein, blood flowing, bright and red and hungry.

A key opened the front door. The bell rang twice, the indicator that someone had entered. So much for the no-weekend work schedule.

"Hiya. I'm Bianca," a voice barked over the wall. "I'm only here for about forty-five minutes. Showing a townhouse." An apologetic tone, a disclaimer, a hurried breath she carried to the bathroom. Lisa packed her bag, headed for the front door when Bianca appeared.

"Oh, hey. Hi." She shoved her tiny hand at Lisa, a firm shake. "You must be Lisa." She was built like a fire hydrant, probably under five feet tall, solid, as if she'd been teaching Zumba classes seven days a week. Black hair just below her ears, a slight Hispanic accent. "We manage all these townhomes. I've got to hurry out and show one now. I look forward to getting to know you. Bye."

4

SUNDAY
11-17-19

L ISA HAD DONE THE MATH, A FEW TIMES. Sixteen dollars a day was all she was paying for the office. She could afford not to show up for a day. Pretend like Sunday was religious, meant something to her other than the day between Saturday and Monday. She could afford not to show up at all. Simply disappear until New Year's Eve, the final day of her temporary sublet, remove the two wall hangings, the papers she had scattered around the desktops, dive into 2020 with a different vision of her life.

Coffee made and second cup warming her hands, she sat in her overstuffed chair in front of the fireplace. Gregory's chair was occupied by Eloise, claws digging into the fabric. Gregory had split the aged oak logs the day before the incident. She stared at them now, could see the ax high above his head swinging down and smashing through the wood, him scooping it up and piling logs on the hearth, November turning colder than usual.

"Damn global warming," he had said. "Changing everything. Fucking up our planet. We'll need a lot more wood than this." She

9

knew better than to argue with him about politics, wood, the rising price of gas, impeachment. It was her role to placate him, nod her head, keep food on the table, make love with him when he wanted it, tend to the greenhouse. She knew her missing him was more a brain thing than a heart thing, but she did have some pain in her chest, a dull ache that coincided with his death.

She set the empty cup down on the table between the chairs, ran her hand across Eloise's back, felt the purr rising under the orange fur, walked to the hearth and traced the steps Gregory went through to build the fires. As long as she had lived here with him, he had never allowed her to build one. She checked that thought. She had never tried to build one, relied on him to keep her warm. She scrunched up a sheet of newspaper into a tight ball, set it on the grate, along with four more. Six pieces of thin kindling on top. She placed two of the oak logs on the pile, just like Gregory would do. She snapped the long match against the side of the box, the flame hissing at her, touched it to the paper.

As the fire began to crackle, she lifted Eloise out of Gregory's chair, sat herself down, pulled her feet up under her thighs, placed Eloise on her lap, motor now running full speed. Eloise was *her* cat. She had gone to the SPCA and picked her out of the line-up, knew she was a match by staring into her eyes. They both missed his presence.

Gregory had been good at most everything he tried, such a fast learner, able to wrap his brain around any problem, come up with more than one solution, apply just the right one. Except that last thing. He told Lisa he was concerned about wood for the winter, took the chain saw and ax with him, the dogs at his feet. He left Lisa inside with Eloise purring in her lap. She was reading an article about the Snohomish Indians, headset hugging her ears, Erik Satie caressing keys in the background.

When she heard the dogs scraping at the front door, she knew, threw off the headphones, raced outside barefoot straight for the stand of oaks he had slowly been culling this year. The chain saw was still growling, held firmly in his left hand, a sharp branch of the fallen tree sunk into his forehead, a puddle of blood soaking into the ground around his head.

It was October 1, Halloween on its way. She remembered his pranks of years past. Just like him to pull some trick like this to freak her out. She waited a few seconds, hoping he would jump up, say

"Surprise!" and lick the ketchup off his lips. But no. She screamed, couldn't control her stomach and threw up all over his boots. She reached for his wrist, no pulse, screamed again, knowing no one would hear, acres surrounding their place, his place.

When the EMTs arrived ten minutes later, the dogs were cuddled up next to her, cowering, one under each arm. By the time they cleaned Gregory up, lifted him into the ambulance, Lisa had drifted, wondered who would worry about global warming and impeachment now? How would the planet survive without him? How would she survive without him?

5

MONDAY
11-18-19

7:43 WAS STILL NOT EARLY ENOUGH to secure the parking spot. The partner with the yellow-and-black Mini Cooper got it again. Maybe tomorrow. The computer table Lisa ordered from Levenger's was on the porch when she arrived home yesterday. It took her most of the morning to put it together. The instructions were in German, but the pictures weren't. Gregory had taken care of this stuff, assumed she couldn't handle it. But here she was. A metal chair she'd brought from home. The new table was perfect to hold a phone, a glass of orange juice, her laptop.

She looked out the window at Lenz, jumped up, walked through the lobby, and found herself pushing the button at the light. Once inside, she lost herself for a few minutes. She had lived in this town for seven years, had never been in this store. The decorative papers made her salivate. But the pens weakened her knees, sent her back to Point Reyes Station where she had first met Gregory, his fluid body, walking up to the counter in the bookstore she co-owned with Ryan, placing three used books on the counter — a rare copy of Jack Gilbert's *Views of Jeopardy*, Rilke's *Letters to a Young Poet*, and the *Kama Sutra of Vatsyayana*. She was not usually impetuous, but when he handed her cash for the books and said, "Can I take you to dinner?" she quickly said, "Yes. We close at eight."

"I'll come back then."

And he did. She had been watching the clock, expecting him not to show, thought he was toying with her because she was just a clerk at a bookstore, not the entrepreneur, lover of books, master gardener that she was. But there he was. She'd texted Ryan, told him she was working late. *Again*, he answered. *Don't wait up*, she fired back. The town shut down at eight. No restaurant of merit open.

· · ·

She placed six pens on the counter, found the easel pads and bought two. A package of no-odor marking pens. Back in the office she ripped off two sheets of paper from one of the pads, stuck them to the mirror on the back of the closed door, wrote out a larger version of her T-chart, one she could easily see without having to flip through pages of her journal, and copied the disappointments and accomplishments she had written the other day. She added another entry:

Disappointment : McDonald's again today, buttermilk-fried-chicken sandwich and fries. Accomplishments : Ate some protein. Helps with the albumin levels.

Guilt about the lack of time she was spending in the office filled in around the disappointments and white space that occupied her brain. To make the best use of her resources — money, time, energy — she felt she should spend at least six hours a day here, figure out who she was, what she wanted, find the best way to dig out of her self-imposed lethargy. Find ways to keep her mind off not only the disappearance of Gregory from her life, but also of her lovely slobbering bull mastiffs, Turks and Caicos, that Gregory's brother Michael had swooped in and removed from the property. The dogs loved it there. She loved them there. It had been abrupt, rude, no conversation, as if he held her responsible for G's death. Or maybe was pissed that they had co-inherited his possessions, property. It made no sense. But not much around the behavior of men did.

She checked her phone. She had only lasted two hours and sixteen minutes today. Too bad. She had to get out, go breathe some fresh air. She added 2:16 minutes to the Disappointments side, 2:16 minutes to the Accomplishments side, walked out the door, ignoring the office mates as she passed through the lobby.

6

TUESDAY
11-19-19

E LOISE HAD SWIPED HER THIS MORNING, the orange claw slashing the inside of her left arm. Although she thought about smacking her, she didn't, never had, wouldn't start now. Lisa cuddled her instead, surrounded her, wrapped herself around the body that reminded her of the astronaut drink, tang. They were both suffering through the changes in their lives. They'd adapt, eventually. Lisa grabbed a pair of scissors, snipped a leaf off the aloe plant, squeezed the goo onto her arm, let it seep in, work its magic. She filled her sixteen-ounce coffee mug, ignored Eloise as she left.

At the Crow's Nest she parked, walked out to the jetty, worked her way along the rocks until she was at the entrance, early enough to see fishermen in their boats, a few taking the time to wave at her. Why wouldn't they? They were their own bosses, probably owned their boats, maybe even slept on them, having identified the life they wanted to live. She was an attractive woman sitting on the rocks watching them head off to their solitary lives on the water. Of course they'd wave.

Coffee gone, Lisa walked back to the Crow's Nest, ordered a large steel-cut oatmeal to go, drove downtown, found the Mini Cooper in its coveted spot. 6:59. Damn! How early did she really get here? Or did she sleep here? Her name was Rhonda. So far, she had worn the same pair of shoes every day, short leather boots that left the top of her slender ankles bare. Lisa imagined her as a tennis player, wearing coordinated outfits, backhand stronger than forehand. She was the business partner of Sarah, who had rented her the office. Maybe she had no social life. She wore a wedding ring, so there was a husband or wife, but maybe one of those spouses you wanted to spend as little time as possible around. Even though Gregory hadn't been Lisa's husband, her time with him had started to feel like that near the end. The end. It felt so strange to talk about a tree through the forehead as the end. Like a song by the Doors. Like a Cormac McCarthy novel.

She thought she had needed this office but wasn't so sure now. The noise had persisted. Deliveries of light fixtures and bathroom sinks and mailboxes. More conference calls. Tenants calling with complaints. Out-of-town owners with questions about contracts. And the music. Which was not terrible, but which was not hers. Mostly soft country, women singers. Always the same, singing about unrequited love and loss. The one time she had needed to use the bathroom, it was occupied, the light and fan on, the receptionist not at her desk. But fifteen minutes later when nothing had changed, and her bladder was ready to leak from her navel, she knocked lightly twice on the door, and was met with a rather snarly, "Just a minute." It was five more minutes before she got in.

Five hours so far. She'd reach the six hours today. Not that she had accomplished any more than that, but it was a start, maybe even a breakthrough. At noon she walked to the little Mexican restaurant across the street, ordered a chicken taco, crispy, and a soda water. With the free chips and salsa, just enough.

After lunch the series of one-sided calls she heard went like this:

"Hey, Bianca over at MP. There's some water leaking onto the floor. Great. Thanks."

"Juan? Just talked to Carlos over at 2011 and he'll get on the leak within an hour. Right. Talk later."

"Yes, we do manage properties from Watsonville to Boulder Creek, and as far east as Gilroy. What have you got? Uh-huh. Yes, that's the kind of work we do. I can't quote you a price right now, but one of the partners will get back to you later today. Let me have your email and phone. Uh-huh. Okay. Great. Thank you."

"Good afternoon, Bianca. Oh, hi. So, hey is it curved lavender? Are you working with them? I have something at 2:00, so 11:30 would work better for me. Okay. Cool. Let me know. In the meantime, I'll add you to the calendar. Two showings. One up, one down. Great. Talk later."

Lisa went to the wall chart, used the purple marker to write "six hours" under Accomplishments. And it was. Lasting six hours was huge. She might have to celebrate. But what would that look like now? That first meal with Gregory reappeared. She had put the CLOSED sign up and they walked to his truck. He drove her to the Olema Inn. When they entered his room, the candles were the first thing she saw. Then the elegant plates, silverware, cloth napkins, delectable food.

"How did you do this?" she asked. "You've only been gone for ninety minutes."

"Just clever, I guess." She should have known right then. Who says that about themselves? Ryan never said that, felt the opposite about himself. Not clever. Boring. Not enough for anyone. Which is part of why she stayed with Gregory, why she didn't immediately call a cab and get away from this cocky character. And when she tasted the food, she melted, fell straight from the crème brûlée into his bed, his arms, his long and strong arms that caressed and cuddled her, made her feel like she mattered, like she was more than the co-owner of a fledgling bookstore.

•   •   •

At the car, she imagined Eloise occupying her chair. She couldn't wait to get home, pet her, unleash the purr, tell her she loved her.

7

WEDNESDAY
11-20-19

"WE'VE HAD A LOT OF INSECTS LATELY," Rhonda said. No one answered. Lisa wondered if she was talking to her, through the open space above the eight-foot wall. She laughed, loudly, at her absurd thinking, loudly enough she imagined to make Rhonda and the others wonder what she was laughing at. Time to dig the headphones and earbuds out of her pack.

"I know," Bianca finally answered. "The cold weather driving them inside."

"Yeah, I've got ants all over my kitchen."

Lisa turned on the pink noise. She grabbed a red marker, went to her T-chart, wrote "Lack of tolerance" on the "Disappointments" side, "Release of anger and tension" on the Accomplishments side. It had happened again last night at home. One of those phone calls came in, the 800-Service kind, where a recorded voice tells you this is the last chance to take advantage of discount credit card rates. She had ignored it, stayed in Gregory's stuffed chair with Eloise. But the second call couldn't be ignored. She heard a female voice announce, "Call from

Gregory Daniels." She flung Eloise off her lap, ran across the room and grabbed the phone.

Out of breath, she managed a "Hello! Who is this?"

"Hi there. Is this Mrs. Daniels?"

"Who the hell are you? How do you manage to have my phone tell me that Gregory Daniels is calling me? This is his phone! Was, his phone. He's dead! How dare you? What the fuck do you want?"

The caller hung up. Lisa leaned her head back, screamed at the ceiling, Eloise darting out of the room into the kitchen.

•   •   •

The pink noise was getting on her nerves. She thought about that. How does something actually "get on" nerves, attach itself to nerves? She didn't know the science of it. But thinking of the gall of telemarketers, the continual annoyance of property-management talk, was definitely causing something to crawl inside her nerves and ruffle them up. What would a nervous breakdown feel like? She went back to YouTube and found "Gentle relaxing sounds for deep sleep, positive meditation music, peaceful sleep music." Better than all the rest of it. She thought it would annoy her before long. But for now, it was better than pink noise and the other alternatives.

Laptop tilted at the perfect angle on the new table, she rested her fingers on the keyboard. This was her seventh day in the office. She had accomplished nothing so far. Part of that was due to having no definition of accomplishment. She didn't know what it looked like. Gregory would wake up every morning with a long To Do list, accomplish everything, strike through every word, every phrase. She stood, grabbed the green pen, green with envy, she thought, envy for Gregory's ambition, his ability to stick to a plan, wrote "No plans for accomplishment" on the chart. Across from it she wrote "Plenty of free time." She opened Google, typed in Disappointments and Accomplishments. There were dozens of them, mostly blogs, several with clever titles like "The Good, Bad, Ugly, and Me." She typed in "websites for bloggers." Maybe she could blog. There wasn't much to say right now. She could write about her life with Gregory, about that first meal at the Inn, how she overslept the next morning, couldn't unwrap herself from around his limbs, as if she had grown into them, like the branches in the *Jumanji* house. Overslept was a simplification. She had not gone home to Ryan. He would have been waiting for her all night, waiting for some fabricated excuse. No. She wouldn't write about that. Not yet.

There were hundreds, probably thousands of listings for WordPress websites, for blogging options, one called *The Daily Dish* purported to be best for chefs, writers, artists. Not that she was a chef, writer, or artist. She liked the looks of it, liked how designers had used it to showcase their clients' skills, had used the typography options to their advantage.

She saw the long Aramark van pass by her window on River Street. She had seen it every day so far, had no idea what they did, who they were. She opened a second browser window, not wanting to leave her list of blog options, and typed in Aramark. Uniforms and Apparel. Were they delivering uniforms to downtown businesses? Maybe to the Boardwalk. Seaside Company t-shirts with logos. Or the university. No. That made no sense. Service stations. Auto repair.

Back to blogging. She could write about whatever came to mind. It didn't matter that nobody would read it. Cody would read it. She had called yesterday before Lisa got home, left a message asking how she was doing. If she was hanging in there.

"I'm okay," Lisa said later, when she was home sitting in front of a hot fire.

"How okay? Okay I'll survive? Okay I'm hanging on the edge? Okay I've got Eloise to comfort me? Come on. Open up. Give me more."

She had smiled. Leave it to Cody to inject a little perk when needed. "Some of each. I have an office."

"You what? What do you mean you *have* an office?"

"Just what I said. I went onto Craigslist, found a space down on River and Pacific —"

"River and Pacific! Right across from Lenz Arts?"

"Yes. I stare at their sign every day."

"I love that place. The purple and teal. But wait! You have an office!" Cody needed to compare, negate, know all there was to know, about everything.

"I do."

"What are you doing in your office?"

"Not much yet. I'm thinking of blogging."

"About what?"

"I don't know yet. Exploring my options. How's Aspen? When are you coming to town? I need to see your cheery face."

"Aspen's a lot like Santa Cruz. Great art and literary scene. But colder. I had to buy new clothes. My Bay Area garb was good for wind, but not bone-slicing chill. I'll be in the city for Thanksgiving. Need to see my attorney. Pack a few more boxes to send to my classroom."

"What color's your hair these days?" A natural blond, Cody had changed her hair color twice a year since middle school.

Cody laughed. "Jet black with a slice of blue across the front."

"Are you liking the new school?"

"Love it. They love me. The younger kids are different than the uppers, but I've taught it before. School is school, wherever you go. But these guys are not administrative assholes. They're supportive and let me do it my way."

"Cody's way. The only way."

"You know it, girl. My plan is to see the attorney on Friday morning then head down to you. Are you still staying at his place?"

Funny to hear it said like that. *His* place. It was his place when she moved in seven years ago, but she liked to think it had become their place. She thought about Turks and Caicos. Missed them. Their incessant mastiff slobber.

"Yes. I'm still there, here. Can't wait to see you."

"Okay. Got to go. Someone's at the door. See you soon. Love you."

Lisa was too slow with the return '*Love you.*' Dial tone. Eloise on her lap. A fire in the fireplace, that she had made, with G's kindling, his oak.

•   •   •

Maybe she'd write the blog as a way to communicate with Cody. She'd pretend nobody else on the planet would read it. Would imagine she'd written it in a made-up childhood language that no one could understand. Lisa had yet to have a conversation of merit with anyone in the office, her door closed, not inviting anyone to engage with her.

21

She looked at the growing T-chart hanging there. The meditation music had been mildly successful, took her mind off the noises, the office chatter. She took out the earbuds, opened the door, and walked into the lobby, looked at the four folks sitting in their respective chairs, Bianca and the receptionist at regular desks in regular chairs, the two partners working from stand-up stations. She remembered someone talking about spinal problems and how the adjustable desks helped.

Without addressing anyone specifically, she blurted out, "Anyone here familiar with blog sites?"

"I've got one," Bianca said.

"Me, too," said the receptionist.

"We've all got them," Rhonda said. "And one for the company. You've got to have social media these days, especially in this business."

8

THURSDAY
11-21-19

S HE WOKE EARLY, ELOISE WRAPPED AROUND HER NECK like a boa.
While eating a toasted English muffin with chunky peanut butter
breakfast, she listened to four messages on the answering machine,
Gregory still the greeter for every call that came in. It was eerie to hear
his voice. Almost made her cry, which she hadn't done yet, hadn't
allowed herself to burst out, hadn't allowed herself much of anything.
The thought *hadn't cared enough* pushed its way in. No, it wasn't that.
She cared. Maybe too much. Maybe stuck in that place between way
too much and way too little.

The first three messages were from Gregory's brother, all the same.
"Lisa, we need to talk." Click. By the time she reached the third, she found
she was listening for the breathing of Turks and Caicos in the
background. She didn't want to talk to Michael, had nothing to say to him.
She wanted her dogs back. He probably wanted to talk about a memorial,
which Gregory had been adamant he didn't want. Or more likely, what
their relationship would look like moving forward — landlord and
tenant, or whatever it would become. She and Michael were fifty-fifty

inheritors of the house, property, possessions, as per Gregory's will. She wondered if Michael was okay with that. The house — ranch-style with four bedrooms, the one she shared with Gregory, one for his office, a guest room, and a spare room crammed full of boxes piled on a bed. Two bathrooms, the big one in Gregory's room with the only shower. The property was twenty-five acres of wooded land, with a greenhouse and a private workshop that Gregory had kept locked. They'd figure it out. How to split things, but not the dogs. She missed them. Might have to bargain things away to get them back. The fourth call was odd. Nobody spoke directly into the phone. In the background, a woman's voice said, "Is she there?" Then a muffled "No," closer to the phone. The woman's voice again, "Just hang up. No message." *Click.*

• • •

Bumblebee hadn't gotten the parking spot this morning. Instead a light blue Tahoma truck inhabited the space outside her window. Maybe that was the other partner's car — Sarah. That would make sense. In and out a lot, delivering materials to properties.

Lisa stared at the cluster of homeless folks huddled against the wall of Lenz Arts as she opened her laptop. Three men and a woman, sharing a bag of potato chips. Passing a jug of what looked like murky water. Maybe lemonade. Last night she had viewed a hundred more blog sites, WordPress themes, getting more confused with each, talked her "Yes, buts" out loud. "I like the colors but not the fonts. I love the sample sites — Junot Diaz, Deborah Cramer, Gabriel Urza — but hate the menu options." It went on like this for every feature she found, though the hates were stronger than the loves. She clicked again on the Daily Dish Pro link, ready to make the decision, but looked at two dozen more example websites before returning to the page. Her finger hovered over the mouse pad, the cursor floating above the link to BUY the theme.

After talking with Bianca about blogging, she had mapped out the steps for Lisa:

1. Go to host and secure your domain name, e.g., *lisahardrock.com*. But be prepared with other names because there may be 3,000

24

Lisa Hardrocks out there, and you might want to be a little more anonymous.

2. Sign up for web hosting. You can get it for as cheap as $2.95 a month, but I prefer to use the $4.95 plan that comes with a few more bells and whistles. If you get it for three years, it's about half price.

3. Go out to your themes website and purchase it, e.g., Daily Dish Pro.

4. Download the theme folders and upload them through FTP to your Bluehost *wp-content/themes* directory. (You'll probably need my help for this part.)

Wait. She reread Bianca's steps. She was supposed to secure the hosting and domain name first. She opened a second browser window, worked her way through the Bluehost process. She hadn't given a lot of thought to a domain name, but one appeared from her past. One of her mom's favorites. She typed in "piousrebel.com" for her domain name, and it came back as "Available". She was a bit lost, but giving a credit card number was easy. She signed up for three years. *You never know,* she thought.

Back at the Daily Dish Pro site, thumb against the mouse pad, she clicked it, entered her credit card info. *Success!* the page read back to her. She would definitely need Bianca's help for step 4.

She opened her office door, walked toward Bianca's desk. "When can you help me set up my blog site? I'll buy you lunch."

"Lunch hell! Let's do dinner. How about tomorrow? Five o'clock."

"Great. Your pick."

"Oh, no question. If you're buying, we're going to the new place, Barceloneta, where Bento used to be on Pacific. You like paella?"

"I love paella!" Gregory used to make it on Thanksgiving instead of turkey, a huge pot they would snack on for days. Jumbo prawns, codfish, chicken, chorizo, fresh peas, saffron. She'd miss it this year.

9

FRIDAY
11-22-19

S HE SPENT MOST OF THE DAY FRIDAY piddling with the WordPress web site. Studying YouTube tutorials. But she was distracted. Looking forward to dinner. Paella on the brain. She knew G's was better than what she'd taste tonight. On the T-chart she wrote "Barceloneta" on the left, "G's paella" on the right, question marks next to both.

She'd sit at the counter at home and G would hand her tasks, never let her get close to the paella pan, the one he'd ordered online from Spain. He would allow her to work on the herb blend, place the olive oil, parsley, garlic, and lemons on a wooden tray he had carved one afternoon while feeling somewhat unproductive. The parsley and garlic came from her garden. The olive oil purchased from friends who had their own grape and olive vineyards somewhere near Santa Ynez. He never took her on those trips. Left her home with the animals and the greenhouse, which was okay with her.

While she chopped parsley, cut and squeezed lemon juice, minced garlic, G would attend to what he called the "real" business of the meal. It didn't look that difficult to her, but he swore it had to be him preparing it for it to turn out correctly. Sometimes she snickered as he measured out the cup of water, opened three cans of chicken broth, dumped them into a saucepan, added a teaspoon of saffron threads. She imagined him paying tuition for some high-end culinary institute in San Francisco where they taught him how to open cans, measure water, use a teaspoon. As the mixture simmered, he'd peel and devein eight to twelve jumbo prawns he'd purchased fresh off the wharf before she'd even gotten out of bed.

"You've got to keep the tails intact," he said, as he placed each one on a paper towel to drain. "It's not authentic if you don't." Being authentic was a phrase he carried with him throughout every thought, every action. She had trouble with that. She thought about being creative, experimental, trying new things, which seemed like it might tangle with authenticity, tradition, making sure it matched the results of famous chefs. The special pan took its heralded spot across two burners on the gas stove. One tablespoon of olive oil dripped into the center, swished around with a gentle wrist flip until all metal surfaces were glazed over medium-high heat.

He used the knife from Japan to debone the chicken thighs, slice them in half, sauté them for two minutes on each side, remove them to another paper towel. The same process for the chorizo and prosciutto. Two minutes, paper towel. Then the prawns. Same thing. By this point in the procedure, she'd be finished with the herb mix, lean her elbows against the huge wooden chopping block that sat in the center of the kitchen, watch him work. It was time to reduce the heat, drop in the finely chopped white onion and red bell pepper. Eloise would vault to the chopping block, rub her tail against Lisa's shoulder, brush her whiskers against her face. Lisa would grab her, set her gently on the floor before Gregory found her there. He'd taken that big pan and knocked her to the floor at least a dozen times, and it made Lisa hate him for an evening, maybe into the next morning, eventually dissipating with good sex. The good sex complicated things.

She didn't want to write this one on the T-chart. She didn't want the janitors reading it, or the women in the office who might very well snoop when she wasn't there. Nobody should know how the sex prevented her from staying mad as long as she thought she deserved. How it was so good with Gregory she couldn't imagine ever being with anyone else.

Thinking about it now was not helpful. She wanted to work her way through the end of his paella prep, but the thought of him now was seeping in like it hadn't done in the past few weeks since the accident.

She backed up. The Inn at Olema. Ryan texting her. Lisa waiting for Ryan to open the bookstore, having G take her to their farm, her packing up everything that was hers, leaving a terse note: *Sorry. Had to leave.* She and G driving down Dramamine Drive, past the lighthouse, a short hike up Mount Tam, what seemed like a magical drive over the Golden Gate Bridge, ending up at G's property on Porter Gulch Road in the foothills of the Santa Cruz Mountains. Turks, then Caicos, greeting her with wet jowls, drenching the front of her dress, making her jolt back to Ryan who would have seen the note, would have opened the bookstore by himself, would be wondering about how to survive without her. Disappointment = Ryan. Accomplishment = The bookstore. She had expected Ryan to come looking for her. He didn't. No email. No phone call. Cody was still working at the school in Point Reyes Station, so she had been the mediator, passed contracts and other papers of importance between the two. Lisa gave Ryan the store. All she wanted was her black Saab.

•   •   •

The thought of G's paella made her hungry. She left the office and walked up River to the Los Pericos Mexican restaurant on Water Street. Something else she had never done. Eaten at this place. A small interior, the place was buzzing, every chair full, at least a dozen folks in line. She waited at the end. The man taking the orders was fast, efficient. There was one chef who handled all the grilling, the beef, the pork, shrimp, and fish. Lisa wondered if he was on drugs. But his co-worker, the one who filled plates with rice and beans, filled tortillas with lettuce, tomatoes, and salsa, he was bouncing around, dancing to mariachi music in the background, smiling, happy to be alive. The fourth employee was blasting through dirty dishes, carrying up tubs of clean ones. She was impressed. Could stand here watching this show for hours. Well, at least until her order came up, which it did within ten minutes.

She carried it back to the office, shut her door, opened the laptop and searched for popular blogs. After reading *Green Living Guy,*

Humans of New York, Convince and Convert, and *I Have Cat,* she stopped. I have a cat, she thought. No. She would not blog about Eloise. Even cats had their right to privacy. She thought about switching it from piousrebel.com, something catchier. Cody would help. She was good with acronyms and project names. Didn't Lisa now qualify as a project? Wouldn't Cody treat her like one? Cody who seemed to care about people, made it her side job to make sure people were having a good time. Cody, who she'd heard from mutual friends had helped Ryan through the rough times after Lisa left, had moved to the farm, Lisa's bed, offered Ryan her mothering embrace.

Lisa opened up a blank document in Word, titled it *Blog.* She wasn't ready to be creative, come up with clever names. Cody would help. Cody would cuddle with her, help her fall asleep in that big empty bed with dog slobber on the bedspread. She wrote:

•   •   •

How far back to go? Do we begin at the beginning? And does the beginning take me back to before there were planets, black holes, desperation, and disappointment? Maybe not that far. Maybe just up the coast to Point Reyes Station. To a time and place where I met a man. Two men. She folded her palms behind her head, massaged her neck with her thumbs, read what she had written. Did she really want to start this thing by talking about Ryan and G? Probably not. But at least she was writing. Here she was again. On that fence. This one feeling electric, like riding it could cause injury, could cause permanent damage to her skin, her mind. The other thing she decided about the blog was that it shouldn't sound suicidal, because Cody would find it, try to provide what she thought would be a safety net. But there was no safety net. So keep it to yourself, she thought. She started again:

> I once co-owned a bookstore. Could buy and sell whatever I wanted. Read books all day long. Had customers who loved me, whom I loved. Held readings for local authors on Thursday nights. Made hot chocolate, spiced apple cider, blueberry muffins from scratch. Had a niche I thought I filled nicely. But things happen, and continue happening whether

29

you want them to or expect them. What they are is not as important as the fact that they just are. We are lucky to find compatible folks to accompany us on the journey. They may very well disappear, and if we are able, we'll rise up, find others, make do, make a new life.

Now who in their right mind would want to read that trash? She laughed, remembered where she was, the open space eight feet up, the four others over the walls who could hear her just as easily as she could hear them. She laughed again, this time with intent.

10

SATURDAY
11-23-19

MAKING THE SIXTEEN DOLLARS A DAY COUNT creeped into Lisa's mind when she found herself still at home under the covers, the hours ticking by on her tenth day as an office dweller, as it approached 5:30 p.m. She couldn't remember the last time she'd had a hangover and wasted the day away. Eloise was whining, hadn't eaten all day. Lisa opened her a can of salmon. Not cat-food salmon, but real sockeye salmon that a friend of Gregory's brought him from Alaska every year, a case of it. The guilt for leaving Eloise alone for so long was partially appeased.

Seventeen minutes later she was inserting a key into the door of the dark downtown office. She had never needed to learn how to turn on the lights and didn't know how. But she didn't need them now, the light from her laptop and the constant flow of headlights zooming by her window was plenty.

She felt good about showing up at all today, wrote it on the chart under Accomplishments, but quickly added, "Drank too much, slept too long" to the left side. It was Bianca's fault. No. It was her own fault, but Bianca had been a more than willing accomplice, a spiritual guide on the tour of fine Spanish wines.

Barceloneta had been packed when they walked in at 5:00. They waited at the bar for over an hour before they were seated, Bianca ordering a bottle of a Samso Garnacha blend, the cheapest one on the menu at fifty-eight dollars. Lisa had not had a drink since Gregory died. Hadn't really had much to drink since she left Point Reyes Station. Gregory wasn't much of a drinker, preferred his homegrown sinsemilla instead to get his buzz. Sometimes she joined him. He said the sex was better with it. She hadn't noticed. The sex was good anyway.

"Okay. Let's talk about this blog thing. Are you totally sure you want to do this? It's a serious commitment. At least to do it right. I'm probably online an hour in the morning, another hour at night, occasionally through the day, getting myself out there in the world."

Lisa listened, nodded, didn't want to interrupt her, slow her down. She wanted to gather everything she could from Bianca's social-media mind.

Bianca asked again. "Are you really sure?"

"Well, I've got the time. No job at the moment. I need to do something in the office. I'm paying for it. I need to make it count." Lisa was feeling the warming in her blood by the time Bianca ordered the second bottle, the Mencia Raul Perez. This one was seventy-eight dollars. Lisa had a credit card, but could see that this consulting she was getting from Bianca would probably end up costing her $150 an hour. She couldn't keep spending like she had when cash was flowing in. Bianca also dominated the ordering of food — the Pulpa, grilled Spanish octopus, and the Pinchos Morunos, grilled lamb skewers with cumin yogurt and chermoula. Lisa had never heard of chermoula, but didn't ask. There was a thirty-minute wait for the preparation of the seafood paella, which Bianca had ordered in advance at the door. They were halfway through bottle two when it arrived, in a huge pan, not unlike G's, but not nearly as big. It looked great. She took a picture of it with her cell phone, just in case she might end up blogging about this meal, but she might not do that, might not want to say anything about the conversation with Bianca that could be seen by others in the office, that theoretically could be seen by Michael, by Ryan.

"Did you decide on a name yet? You going with *lisahardrock.com*?"

"No way," Lisa answered quickly. Ryan was the type of guy who was probably searching her name daily on the Internet tracking her movements. Luckily, until now, there had been nothing to track. She didn't use Facebook, rarely sent emails, was not listed as an occupant under Gregory's address, rarely received snail mail addressed to her. She was still dealing with the dozens of letters addressed to Gregory each week, tossing most of them, dropping what looked to be important ones into an empty Costco box, thinking that eventually Michael might want to collect them. She'd need to answer his calls soon. He'd be banging on her door if she didn't. On Gregory's door. Maybe on his own door depending on how things proceeded.

They both heaped rice and seafood onto their plates, Bianca's portion twice as big as hers.

"That's good. Something different. Catchy. Keep them off guard."

"What's your site name?" Lisa said approaching her mouth with a forkful of paella.

"HotMama. They definitely remember me. Lots of repeat offenders, if you know what I mean."

Lisa didn't know what she meant, but guessed it would come out by the time the bottle was empty. Lisa hated the paella. Too much salt. Way too much saffron. The rice was greasy. The seafood was edible, but not like G's jumbo prawns, the herb flavoring nowhere near as good as hers.

"You come up with any ideas yet?" Bianca said as she scooped another pile of food onto her plate.

"I was thinking something like I Can't Get No, or maybe We Don't Need No."

"You like the music stuff, huh?"

She actually did. Loved riffing on lines from songs. When she was a teacher's aide in a sixth-grade classroom, she used a lyric when giving definitions for spelling test words.

"Yes. I do. But I'm thinking Pious Rebel makes most sense."

"Oh! That's a good one. That's the best. Stay with that one. How'd you come up with that?"

"Alice, my mom, loved oxymorons and we kept a list of them. I'm pretty sure this one was on it."

•   •   •

Fingers on keyboard, she typed. A fast typist — but not a very fast thinker at this point, so typing speed was moot.

> I went to Spain last night. With my new best friend. What started as a friendly meal at a downtown restaurant quickly veered out of control after the second bottle of wine when one of us called for an Uber ride to take us to the San Francisco airport. After a two-hour stopover in Miami, we skipped over the Atlantic in the dark and landed in Madrid at dawn. By noon we found ourselves in Bilbao, and by 1:00 were paying the entry fee to the Guggenheim Bilbao Museum. I read to my new friend from the program for Jesse Jones: Tremble Tremble, as we made our way to the exhibition. "While made under conditions of heated abortion-related debate in Ireland, and referencing also the Italian feminist protests during the 1970s — in which crowds of women sang the motto "Tremble, tremble, the witches are back!" — the work functions as a portrait of a timeless archetype beyond national or ethnic identification. The powerful witch in Tremble Tremble may in fact be perceived as an incarnation of magical thinking, a figure of radical transformation of the real and a trigger of cosmic chaos." As the last drop of Mencia Raul Perez slid across our tongues, I had convinced her we had to get on a plane, and see this exhibition now. That it could change our lives. That we could get hit by a car crossing the street for lunch tomorrow. And it did. I'm writing this post from a small villa near Playa de Las Catedrales, Galicia. I will stay here until my money runs out.

Thinking about money brought her back. The bill at Barceloneta had topped $350 with tip. She thought about the theoretical blog post. What would Bianca think if she did post it? And what would it matter? If she posted something like this, she might need to clarify that it was fiction, fantasy, inspired by expensive wines.

11

SUNDAY
11-24-19

T HE DRIVE TO WORK WAS ALMOST FEELING TOO SHORT, the quick fifteen minutes without traffic before 7:00 a.m. She had discovered the radio station KDFC FM by accident. She was looking for some light jazz and stumbled across it at 103.9. The station was dedicated to making classical music a more important part of people's lives. Every time she turned the engine on, some classical piece made its way into her ears, made for pleasant rides to the office, even more pleasant when coming home through a bit of congestion on Soquel Drive.

Today she had spent time with Eloise, stayed in bed with her past noon. Yesterday she had decided to read at least one book every week, which was nothing compared to her output at Point Reyes Station. She was halfway through Rookery by Traci Brimhall by noon, hadn't eaten yet, hadn't fed Eloise either. A review she had seen on Goodreads said the book was "fraught with madness, brutality, and ecstasy." She agreed, thought it mirrored her own life fairly closely. By 1:30 she had reached the last poem, "Prayer to Delay the Apocalypse." Was it that easy? Lisa thought. A simple prayer. Maybe not. Maybe it had to be a very complicated prayer, a lengthy one cited in two-part harmony with a close friend. She'd have to wait for Cody to show up. Lisa was not so good with harmony in her own life, but Cody could sing, could guide them through this prayer, skirt their way past death and mayhem and darkness.

No time for a shower now if she planned on making it to the office by 2:00, which would give her a little over an hour and a half before she had to be at the Horticulture Center at Cabrillo College for a poetry reading by a friend of G's, a man who used to be a physicist and was now a retired-physicist-poet.

Even though the office was empty, a typical Sunday, she closed her door so she could see the T-chart. She had avoided eating at McDonald's for a few days, was over that phase, she hoped, but today she had come down Ocean Street and stopped at Ferrell's Donuts. It was empty except for one employee. She ordered a cinnamon roll and a maple twist, ate them now as she added the disappointment to the chart: Ferrell's Donuts, sugar on sugar.

Back at her computer table, fingers resting on the keyboard, she was comfortable, didn't need the headphones or earbuds or pink noise or meditation music. It was mostly quiet, no management chatter or tirades going on over the wall, just the steady flow of traffic out the window, soothing in its consistency. Especially when they stopped at the light and she could look in through their windows undetected, a voyeur. Maybe she could incorporate voyeurism into her blog theme. "I like to watch," said Peter Sellers as Chauncey Gardiner in *Being There*. That was one regret. She had left her movie collection behind with Ryan when she hooked up with Gregory. All her favorites. When she saw a movie she loved, she'd watch it two more times to make sure, and when positive, she purchased it for her home library. She imagined Ryan watching them without her, laughing at all the funny parts by himself, or maybe with Cody. Or someone new by now, given Cody's departure to Aspen a few years ago.

The stoplight next to Lenz Arts turned green, didn't give her too much time to stalk. Now there were no cars, silence, no visual spinning of tires on pavement, no engines whining, just the couple walking on the sidewalk in front of her window, his arm around her shoulder, kissing her cheek, her hand in his back pocket. The woman turned, looked at Lisa through the window as they passed, nodded, smiled.

When she thought about the Bilbao piece, she laughed, loudly, realized there was no one there to hear it. So she laughed again, a total of three times, just because she could, just because she noticed that humor and smiles and a lightness of being had left her since Gregory died. Had left her long before he died. Maybe even when she left Point Reyes Station and Ryan and Cody and the bookstore.

She wanted Turks and Caicos back. She'd call Michael when she got home. But now, blog site activated, empty, waiting for content, she needed to write something, say something, anything. It didn't really matter. No one would read it. Except maybe Bianca.

Get the humor back. Put the tongue into your cheek. Come on! Go for it.

12

MONDAY
11-25-19

L ISA COULDN'T FIND THE HUMOR, wrote one bland opening line after another that didn't sound like her, erased each one, finally gave up. Under the Disappointments column she wrote "Me" before getting in the car and driving home.

No messages on the machine this time. Just Eloise waiting for her can of salmon. There were a few left. She'd have to look through Gregory's things to find Zack's email or number in Alaska and ask him to send a couple more cases. Later. She hadn't gone into G's office since his death. He was private about his things, his projects, his ideas. It felt like she had to pry things out of him. She stayed out of his office, his computer, and especially the locked workshop where he spent a good portion of the day, locked from the inside when he was working, a clear sign for her to keep out. But this was no longer about Gregory. It was about Eloise and her addiction. Eloise was still here, still hungry, still purring.

The one thing Gregory had allowed Lisa to participate in was the work in the greenhouse. He had perfected a growing system, had secured some of the finest seeds on the West Coast, and he needed her in every phase of the project. Even though they were lovers, partners in a different sense, he paid her like an employee for her work with the pot. The greenhouse was also locked, but he had given her a key so she could work whenever she wanted, when she couldn't sleep, when he took trips out of town to deliver product. She planted, watered, culled, snipped colas off branches, cleaned them, bagged them, removed the old plants, rejuvenated the soil, readied it for the next growing cycle. She walked out to the greenhouse, slipped the key into the lock and entered this space that had occupied so much of her time and energy for so long.

Everything looked the same as it had after the harvesting in October, the week before G died. The soil was empty, fresh. The room was clean, the way she kept it. She walked to the back where the safe stood, locked. They kept the seeds in there, the cash Gregory would bring home from the Central Valley trips and from Michael's local clients, the bagged pot ready for sale. They had harvested fifty pounds, thirty-five that G had planned on taking with him on his trip south. She hadn't been out here since. She twisted the dial, but the combination didn't work. She tried it three more times. Nothing. She hurried back to the house, picked up the phone, called Michael.

No hello from him, just "It's about goddamn time. Are you hiding from me?"

"Why would I be hiding from you?"

"Because we're co-owners of that albatross of a piece of property you're currently living on."

"Currently?"

"That's one of the things we need to talk about."

"We also need to talk about the safe. Why the combination no longer works."

"That wasn't me. That's you trying to cheat me out of my fair share."

"Fair share?"

"Fifty-fifty now. You read the will."

"Yes, I read the will. Speaking of which, what makes you think you can walk in here and steal my dogs?"

"*Your* dogs? I figure at least one of them is mine. But it's better for them if they stay together, so I took them both. But I got to tell you, I had no idea they could eat so much and slobber so much over everything.

Pamela's not too happy about that." Lisa hadn't thought about Pamela in quite some time. Lisa thought Pamela was not too happy about much in her life, the marriage to Michael, that Gregory had been his brother, that Lisa had moved into the picture. She wasn't sure now if that had been an original thought, or one that Gregory had planted, like so much of her life since she moved here. Lisa was now thinking that Michael's calls were more about the dogs than money or property. "But let's talk about this safe thing? I figure we're fifty-fifty on the business side as well. What's in it?"

She was reluctant to tell him anything, especially given that neither of them now had access to it. It must have been Gregory who changed things up before the tree smashed his forehead, left things to be sorted out by the will. But she didn't want to piss Michael off. His temper could waver moment to moment. But that had usually been related to some issue with Gregory. Lisa hadn't been the recipient of it until now. She wondered if he was unhappy that she was getting half of everything that had belonged to his brother. She'd take it slow, approach him carefully. Yes, the money and pot and seeds could be important to her future, but right now she wanted Turks and Caicos back.

"I helped G load it the week before the tree hit him."

"I figured that much. What was there?"

"Fifty-plus pounds of our high-end buds. Maybe ten thousand dollars." She decided not to tell him about the seeds. He wasn't savvy about such things. Michael repeated what she said. In the background she heard Pamela's voice.

Michael said, "What about the seeds?" How the hell did Pamela know about the seeds, and why would she even care? She started to worry about the Pamela factor.

"Oh. Yeah. Two bottles of seeds." Gregory hadn't talked about Pamela much, but what he did say had always been negative. There were a lot of things Gregory didn't share with her. She knew he lied to her, as if it was truth, as if she was the one with a problem for even delving into the lies, seeking truth. It didn't happen for the first four years. Check that. She didn't recognize that it was happening. Of course it must have happened. The first time she realized it, it had to do with a menial task in the kitchen. It wasn't a paella feast, just a vegetable stir-fry with fresh mushrooms she had picked on the property. After dinner, Gregory was holed up in his room as she washed dishes, set them on a towel to dry. Gregory preferred the dishwasher, was concerned about germs, way too concerned about them from Lisa's perspective. She had gone out to the greenhouse to trim some plants. When she came back in, all her dishes were gone from the towel.

They had a running joke about correcting each other, related to when they both read Jonathan Franzen's *The Corrections*. Gregory was sitting at the kitchen table peeling an orange, his thick fingers dwarfing it, Warriors cap covering his short, black hair.

"Did you just correct me?" she asked.

"What do you mean?" She opened the dishwasher, all the dishes she had just washed stacked neatly on the racks.

"Oh, that. I didn't want to dry them by hand, so I set them in there to dry." He was usually half-way decent about his logical explanations about actions, but this was a terrible lie.

"Are you kidding me?"

"Okay. Sometimes I rewash things you leave on the counter."

"God damn it, Gregory!" She walked out, didn't know what to do, where to go, grabbed the dogs and took them out for a walk. The actual correction was not what bothered her. It was the lie. The blatant lie that rolled off his tongue so easily and eloquently. It was so easy for him to do. She now wondered about everything he had ever said to her. About that first meal at the Olema Inn. How did he get that food in his room at 8:00 in the evening, a room with no kitchen, no way to prepare anything? Where was he really going when he took the road trips out of town? Who was he staying with? Did he really dislike Pamela as much as it seemed?

That's when things changed. She never again trusted or believed anything he told her. To keep herself from going crazy about it, she didn't ask him about anything after that, never posed questions to which his answers might have been truthful or false. Conversations became minimal. The sex was still great. That wouldn't change. The money from her role in his business was more than she could have made at the bookstore or any other job. So she stayed, dug in, relied on Eloise and Turks and Caicos to be straight with her about their needs. When they were hungry. When they needed to go out for a walk or to pee. That they preferred one food over another. Salmon. She

41

needed to get Zack's info, finally walk down the hall to G's office and dig in, to whatever she might find, whatever mysteries or treasures or lies might be there. Including hopefully the key to his workshop. Either that or she'd have to call a locksmith to open it for her. And maybe something about the safe.

"Why did he change the combination to the safe?" Michael said.

"Is that you asking or Pamela?" She heard the tone in her voice, regretted it, tried to hurry away from his response. "I'm as baffled as you are. He's lied to me about everything forever, and you as well, from what I understand, so why should we be surprised about the safe?"

"He was a compulsive liar, ever since we were kids. We were amazed it took you so long to figure it out."

"Yeah. Well, I did. Now we have to dig in and figure what's true and what's fabricated and how to maintain a relationship that's beneficial to both of us." She surprised herself. Without Gregory around to keep her in check, she could say and think what she wanted. She thought about Michael's blue eyes, the structure of his cheekbones. It would be hard to look into them. They were Gregory's. He was a slightly smaller version of his older brother.

•   •   •

At the office, she got the spot next to Lenz, the one where she could see her car the whole time she sat in the ten-dollar chair she'd picked up at Grey Bears. It fit perfectly with the table from Levenger's. She felt comfortable, like she belonged here. To the right side of the list she added "Physically and mentally comfortable, today."

The comfort of being able to look out and see the constant view of her car was not something easily understood or explainable. She had owned the black Saab for over ten years, bought it just before she bumped into Ryan at a book festival in Marin, hadn't seen each other since college. They walked out of one of the workshops together and before he knew the car was hers, said, "Look at that gem! I love Saabs! Especially black ones. And this one is pristine." It was certainly not the firm foundation of a three-year relationship, but it worked for a while, got them into the same house, opening the bookstore together, both loving to read. The Saab was the one thing she could count on, so to see it across the street as she tried to think of a topic for a blog post, was soothing. She touched the keyboard, opened up.

> I have never really had a strong feeling about cars. In high school, my dad bought my first one, a classic Ford Falcon. All my friends thought it was cool, wanted to ride with me. I didn't think it was so cool. It ate gas. The interior was torn and faded. The turn signals didn't work. This is how I started with cars. Same with the Pontiac LeMans, the '57 Chevy, the '67 Camaro, the 2002 BMW. They all had that level of classiness that I should have appreciated, but I didn't. They were simply a means to an end. But when I found the 2005 black Saab, I instantly drooled, fell in love unexpectedly, and have never regretted a day since. She has lasted longer than boyfriends, girlfriends, being a vegan, and my passing admiration of Ryan Gosling. I look out at her now, see leaves blowing by her down the street, wonder about the next PG&E warning regarding a power outage. If you don't see another blog post from me for a while, you'll know I have no power to my computer, but you'll also know that I'm out on the road in my Saab having some fun somewhere!

She reread the post three times. She looked out the window again. The big blue truck was pulling in behind her car, this time carrying a motorcycle on the back. It was Sarah. Got that one right. It made sense. She could see Sarah, her thick Swedish body mounted on the bike, digging in around a mud track, her muscular arms and legs manipulating the bike. She copied and pasted the blog post into her website, hit Publish, made her first post without worrying she had offended anybody that mattered.

On the ride home, she thought about G's lying to her. How much of it was a compulsive response to the world, to her, as Michael had suggested? Had it been a sense of accomplishment for him to lie to her successfully? Or was it something completely different? Had he lied to her about the dishes because it was simply easier to fabricate something than it was to have the conversation that would ensue about his belief that her dishwashing skills were limited and required correction? Was he so afraid of her reaction to the truth? She could have understood his desire to wash the dishes again, using his preferred dishwasher method, given the numbness in her fingers that had started a few years earlier. Her fingers didn't work the way she wanted them to. Maybe he was right about washing dishes. They were definitely off in keyboard skills. She could still type fast, but not always so accurate, a bit of neuropathy settling in. Her left little finger missed the "A" key way too often and swiped the Caps Lock instead, which would quickly become apparent. And when she needed two l's, for some reason three would appear. She looked at her post, was proud to see it in print online for the world to read. Except for the typos. She quickly moved into Edit mode, removed some extra l's, cleaned up a few other lazy-finger issues.

13

TUESDAY
11-26-19

S HE WOKE UP WITH STOMACH CRAMPS. It had happened occasionally since Gregory's accident. The stress, the constant reliving of the events, finding him on the ground, chain saw rumbling, the EMTs and ambulance, all of it could easily be having odd effects on her digestive tract. She hadn't paid much attention to it, other than finding G's Compazine pills in his bathroom. The bathroom was just one more thing that had been off-limits, with him having no intention of sharing a toilet seat with her. He'd let her use the shower, because it was the only one on the property. She was fine with that, occasionally stuck her head in to see how clean it was, how the towels were folded in thirds, hung neatly on the racks, color-coded with the tile and paint. The Compazine had seemed to help, but made her drowsy. She took two before the trip downtown, stopped at the Buttery for their famous muffins to keep the office crew happy, handed them to the receptionist — whose name she still didn't know — before stepping into her own space. The cramps were approaching pain. She closed herself in the bathroom, turned on the fan, and sat. Fifteen minutes. A bit of movement that she hoped would lighten the cramps. Back to her office, but had to turn around immediately and head back. Four times she did this. The pain increased. Dizziness set in and her shoulders ached.

Calling Michael to pick her up would be a mistake right now. Pamela was not even a possibility. She could call Uber, but she hadn't done it often so figuring out how to do it while feeling this badly wouldn't work well. She took a sip of water, breathed in deeply three times. After a few minutes, she packed her things, walked by the front desk, said, "Sorry. Not feeling well. Have a great Thanksgiving if I don't see you."

It would probably be smarter to head down Soquel Drive, stay on streets with slower speed limits, in case she passed out and needed to bump into a curb. But the Saab was pointed in the other direction and she didn't feel like maneuvering the turnaround. On the freeway she stayed in the right lane, drove fifty miles per hour, made it to the Park Avenue exit and up Porter Gulch to their driveway. Their. Natural thing to say or think. But it was no longer their driveway. Unless Gregory's share had now been transferred to Eloise. Lisa slipped into bed fully clothed, no energy to kick her shoes off. Eloise jumped up, tried to snuggle in under her chin, but Lisa twisted so much in the sheets, looking for the least compromising position, hoping for a little relief, that Eloise gave up and left the bedroom.

After two hours, the pain subsided to light cramps. She had started keeping a clipboard with blank paper and a pen on the bed, rested against G's pillow, so if she had ideas during the night she could track them. Maybe they'd work their way into a blog post. Writing about the cramps might help, might move her mind away from them, into a realm more mental than physical. Maybe a title first this time, to pull her through, guide her into something meaningful. The iPhone also rested on G's pillow. She set it for the meditation music, ten hours of it if she needed. She laughed, which was a good sign. The phone would probably die before the ten hours of music played out. It was relaxing. She should do this more often. Sideways. Because that's what the day had done to her so far. Turned her away from the task at hand and tossed her into bed.

> Have you ever had one of those days where you feed your
> cat, have your two cups of coffee, head out to start your day,
> and it goes sideways?

On cue Eloise entered, sprang onto the bed, brought her whiskers and tail into Lisa's face, as if she had read her mind, knew what she was writing, thinking. Lisa reached over and revved up the purr.

> Sideways in that you get to your office, ready to do whatever
> it is you do there, and something happens. Maybe because of
> the crazy fall winds and the instability of PG&E, the power
> goes out and your computer slowly runs out of charge.
> Maybe the other inhabitants of your open-space office have
> another conference call that is too loud and there is no way
> you can think your way through to what is next. Maybe when
> your partner is found dead under a fallen oak tree everything
> melts into a puddle that seeps into the earth and disappears.
> Or maybe because of all the other maybes you develop a
> severe case of cramps that debilitates you, makes you
> wonder if you have diverticulitis or colitis or stomach cancer
> or a dozen other possibilities. Makes you drive home
> unsafely, crawl into a hole under your hot sheets, wait for
> something to change, for the pain to drift away, for your life
> to return to some sense of normalcy.

She wasn't sure she'd be able to post this one. She hadn't talked to anyone about G's death other than the EMTs, the cremation service, and Michael. And Cody, briefly. And now she was considering a post that would make it visible to the whole world. Though her whole online world consisted only of herself, and maybe Bianca.

Eloise was making her hungry sounds, light growls, prancing on the tips of her paws. Lisa followed her to the kitchen, opened the salmon. It smelled good. She thought of dipping the fork in for a bite, but she wouldn't dare do that to her stomach right now. With Eloise's head buried in the can, she walked back down the hall toward the bedroom, stopped at the closed door to G's office, turned the knob, pushed it open before walking in. She had only been inside twice since she lived here, times when G was out of town and needed her to find something. He gave her detailed instructions about what to do and what not to do. Find the item, get out, close the door. It made her want to go back in when he was gone and look at everything, open every drawer, envelope, his computer and all the files. But she didn't. She wasn't the type who looked in someone's wallet or purse just because she was curious, just because she wanted to know more about a person than they were willing to give. She liked to know about people, but through conversation, through what they were willing to share. Honesty packaged in a willingness to connect.

This was new, walking in without an assigned task, entering of her own accord because she wanted to, needed to, for her own sanity, to reduce her stress, to deal with Michael, and Pamela, and get on with her life, however sideways it might take her.

14

WEDNESDAY
11-27-19

W HILE MOST OF HER TIME YESTERDAY had been spent in bed or trying to figure out what would suffice as comfort food — rice pilaf, Campbell's chicken-noodle soup, French toast, or maybe her mother's favorite, poached eggs on white bread with butter and pepper — she had spent a good portion of her waking hours thinking about the day she was missing at the office. The sixteen-dollar day had been wasted. Even though she had written the post yesterday, she hadn't published it yet, couldn't wait to get into her space, read the post one more time, make a decision.

When she had walked into G's office, she had been overwhelmed. The tears finally appeared, a waterfall that knocked her off her feet, sent her to the carpet, an Iranian rug he had traded pot for in 2016. Plush, colorful, soaking up her sorrow. It was so confusing to her, not easy to separate the sorrow from the disappointment, the hatred from the love. It was too soon to dig through his stuff, to uncover the real Gregory that she had never known. The mysterious nature so prevalent, and the lying. She had no idea what she'd uncover in there, was not sure she wanted to. Maybe she should leave this part to Michael. Let him come in and see what he could find. But he'd probably bring Pamela, and that wouldn't work. Eloise didn't like her, had scratched her more than once, which was okay with Lisa. It had kept her away. Had kept Michael away, too, which was not so okay, for two brothers to be estranged because of one's wife. She wondered if Michael felt the same way about her, if she got in the way of his bond with Gregory, if her short time in G's life had superseded his lifetime as a brother.

• • •

In the office, she closed the door, took the purple Crayola marker from its box, wrote on both sides of the chart: "Cried in G's office."

Rice pilaf is what she'd decided on for comfort food. Gregory made large batches, kept a huge supply frozen and ready to nuke. They both loved it. She had eaten a big bowl last night and brought the leftovers with her for lunch today. It was an Armenian recipe that G's father had gotten when he was in the hospital for a bleeding ulcer. His roommate, an Armenian from Berkeley, would eat it almost every day instead of hospital food, his wife bringing enough for the whole family and for G's father and his friends and family. Lisa wasn't sure if it was the browned vermicelli or the cube of butter that made it so good. The white pepper and onions also helped. She liked adding some freshly picked mushrooms when he'd let her.

She reread the post she had written yesterday. Talking about G so publicly bothered her. But it was just one line. The title was good. The idea of life going sideways on its own, like a landslide in winter, slipping down a mountainside, interested her, not just because she was living it, but because everyone was probably living it to some degree. That it was a universal. She remembered studying cultural universals when she worked in the classroom, how every culture used the same list of eleven or twelve universals to identify themselves, to be identified by others. Going sideways was clearly a universal, whether one was willing to admit it or not. After a few minor corrections — the word made her think again about the dishes G had slipped into the dishwasher — she hit the Publish button, and the post was live. Maybe his correction had been warranted. Maybe she didn't scrape the crud off the dishes. Maybe the dishwasher was healthier. There she was again. On that damn fence. "Yes, but."

She couldn't wait for lunch, popped the pilaf into the microwave and wolfed it down, along with a leftover piece of pita bread she had brought. It felt like her stomach was handling it okay.

The banker's box full of manuscripts she had brought in two weeks ago hadn't been touched. She looked at it now. On the top it read, "For my eyes only," in her mother's handwriting. Alice had been secretive. Spent hours every day pounding on her IBM Selectric typewriter. Locked the door to her home office when she wasn't in there. Lisa had no idea how much she had written or what the content was about. When her mother died, Lisa had found the banker's box tucked in the corner of a storage shed behind Alice's garage. That was a year ago. Lisa hadn't brought the box into the house, was fearful that G wouldn't respect her or her mother's privacy. She left it in the trunk of the Saab, covered it with a blanket, had never even lifted the top.

Maybe she wasn't ready to tap the secrets of G's office, but she was ready for this. Cody would be here Friday, and they could attack the office together. For this box, though, she thought it would be better to do it without Cody, Cody who had been such a big part of her life and listened together with her for uncounted hours as the typewriter behind the locked door clacked away. Lisa removed the lid, leaned it against the wall, where she could see her mother's handwriting.

While she had never opened the manuscript boxes, she had peeked in the banker's box before, counted the five interior boxes, no writing on any of them. She picked up the top one, set it on the desktop, did the same with the other four. Side by side, it looked impressive, what her mother had accomplished. But she didn't trust looks much anymore. She opened the first box, recognized the Courier 12-point font from Alice's typewriter, read the top page:

The Baker's Quintet

Book 1: <u>I Really Knead You</u>

By Alice Hardrock

January 1990

Lisa had been five in 1990. She opened the second box:

The Baker's Quintet
Book 2: <u>Rocks and Rolls</u>
By Alice Hardrock
June 1995

Lisa's tenth birthday happened in June 1995. A red velvet cake with white icing her mother had taken the time to bake. A trip to the Conservatory of Flowers in Golden Gate Park, with Cody, Mom, Mom's friend Anita.

The Baker's Quintet
Book 3: <u>Love Muffins</u>
By Alice Hardrock
September 2001

Sweet sixteen. Mother still typing away. Boys. Lots of boys swarming around Cody and her. Box four opened to reveal:

The Baker's Quintet
Book 4: <u>Waiting for Good Dough</u>
By Alice Hardrock
January 2005

Lisa was a sophomore at Cal by then. Double major in psychology and English literature. Had either of those things helped her so far? Too soon to tell. The final title:

The Baker's Quintet
Book 5: <u>This Site Uses Cookies</u>
By Alice Hardrock
January 2008

Second year of grad school at UCSC.

Lisa hoped there was real writing inside the manuscript boxes. She remembered hearing Terry Tempest Williams tell a story at a Tomales Bay writers' conference about how her mother had shelves full of journals in her office, and how she made Terry promise to never read any of them until she was dead. When her mother died, Terry opened one journal at a time and discovered they were all empty.

Lisa opened Alice's boxes one at a time. The pages were full of writing. All five boxes. She picked up *I Really Knead You*, laughed out loud at her mother, who was the queen of puns, making sure every title contained something a little askew, sideways.

She read the first paragraph:

> I was foolish to marry a baker, had no idea about the long hours, the struggle for economic viability, the issues with weight and diabetes, that I would become the bookkeeper for a futile profession and an overgenerous man. My life may be a blueprint for why you should not marry for love, should instead seek stability with someone you could get by with for most of a lifetime. But that's not what I did. I needed him too much.

Lisa closed boxes two through five, pulled out the 400-page manuscript from box one, and continued reading.

15

THURSDAY
11-28-19

I T WAS THANKSGIVING. Not that she had much to be thankful for. Was that really true? She tended toward the negative, would choose to look for the unhappy things first. She sat in the Grey Bears chair looking out the window. The property management folks were off for the day. Lenz Arts was closed, as was its neighbor, Outdoor World. She switched it up, looked for happy first. These weren't really accomplishments, so no need to add them to the chart. She was happy that her gut had quit acting up, that the pain had disappeared. The phone call with Michael had not necessarily been pleasant, but she was happy to connect with him finally, happy to hear that the dogs seemed to be too much for him to handle. It was probably Pamela who was too much for him to handle, which also made her happy. Cody had arrived in San Francisco last night, sent her a text:

I'm here. Off to see the esquire this afternoon. Hope to reach you by noon tomorrow. You need anything?

She needed a lot, but nothing Cody could bring her from San Francisco.

Wait. There was one thing.

Salmon. Canned salmon for Eloise. She's hooked.

That Cody was back on the West Coast for a few days made Lisa happy. That Lisa had walked into G's office made her both happy and sad. She added it to both sides of the T-chart. The yellow marker, which was harder to see, wouldn't remind her so much of her inadequacies if it blended into the yellow Post-it pad.

It was strange sitting in the cold empty office, listening only to the tires of passing cars, the heater blowing in the outer office. She was getting used to the meditation music, opened YouTube, brought the site up, plugged in the earbuds.

Her cell phone buzzed, lit up. Michael.

I'm coming over this afternoon. Will you be there?

She ignored it, picked up her mother's manuscript for Book 1. She read fifty pages before setting it down. Another fence-sitting excursion. Happy to learn something about her mother that she never knew. Sad to have not known the woman who was able to put thoughts like this down on paper, spend hours of her life every day pursuing a passion that she kept private.

It was freezing in this office. She needed a scarf, a pair of gloves, maybe a heated jacket with coils that lit up. Even a heater from Home Depot or Costco, two other stores she had never been in since living in Santa Cruz.

A man walking by Lenz Arts stopped in an alcove, reached down, picked up a bag that looked like a Goldfish-cracker container. He didn't look homeless, maybe a little with the backpack strapped to his shoulder, but when he shook the bag, looking for crumbs, she knew he was hungry, would eat most anything he could find on the streets or in trash cans. How many degrees of separation between her and the man? Was her involvement in a lucrative yet illegal growing culture the only thing that kept her off the streets, from hunting for food where she could find it, from living in the back seat of her Saab?

The phone lit up again.

Are you ignoring me? My plan is to be there by 2:00. I hope you'll be there to greet me.

Michael was pushy, inappropriate at times, just like Gregory. She texted back:

I'm in my office right now. I'll be serving Thanksgiving lunch at the Veterans' Hall until 2:00ish.

She didn't want to completely ignore him, piss him off, or piss off Pamela, who was probably the architect of this visit. She wanted to ask if Pamela would be there, but chose not to.

Another ping.

Office? You have an office? Where? Why? What do you do there?

She laughed. Typical Michael, posing question after question before you had a chance to respond to any of them. And she wouldn't. Would keep him guessing, just enough to drive Pamela a little crazy.

I'll be there when I get there.

As if he were in her head, he sent:

It'll just be me.

Alice Hardrock was turning out to be more than just a mother. She was also a writer, a thinker, an unpublished author who had a way with words, with at least 2,000 pages of material that Lisa knew of. She would need to head back up to Berkeley soon and revisit the storage unit where she and the movers had placed all her mother's belongings last year. They had hurried through it, a last-minute move that had been a shock to Lisa, having discovered that her mother never owned the house, had been leasing it from a professor for over thirty years. She had never spent much time thinking about an inheritance, but had assumed there might be something there. Lisa had rented a large U-Haul, loaded everything up, found the storage unit on the way out of town, dropped it off, and locked it up. The banker's box and a box of geodes were the only items Lisa had brought to Santa Cruz with her.

She read another twenty pages of the manuscript before she stopped, placed it back in its box, felt the need for some productivity before she showed up at the Veterans' Hall for her 11:30 shift.

Tingling fingers on keyboard, she made a point of pounding the keys hard so she could quit losing letters, having to retype and edit so often. She rambled on for a bit, knowing she'd come back and cut what felt extraneous. She typed the title first:

Who Do We Really Know?

She continued:

We pretend to know ourselves, believe we have predictable habits and actions that can be replicated day to day, but it's all a façade held up with mirrors and ceiling wax. I thought I knew my best friend Cody better than anyone on the planet. Planet. She was using that word too much. There were other ways to say it, and she had to find them. I thought I knew my best friend Cody, thought I knew everything about her, thought there was nothing we would ever hide from each other, until I discovered she was living with and sleeping with my former lover and partner. Yes, it was me who left, an impetuous departure that took me 100 miles south, but that's not the point. I did not know her at all. And my mother, whom I lived with for the majority of my life--it turns out I knew very little about the woman who hid inside the role of mother. I'm finding out too late. Finding out who and what I missed. Then there's G. The mystery, the secrets, what is and was hidden everywhere. I feel like someone has taken a melon baller and scooped out my insides, everything that had its proper place in my body and mind removed and replaced with foreign matter. I'll see G's brother today, a man I know very little about, a man with whom my future is so connected. I doubt I'll learn much, but as Joan Armatrading once said in a song, "I'm open to persuasion."

She went back to the title, erased it, and replaced it with:

I'm Open to Persuasion

There was no way she could post this one. Way too personal. Way too public. Revealing. She hit the Publish button, packed her things, walked to the car outside the window, drove to the Veterans' Hall to serve up large scoops of stuffing to men and women who relied on this event, relied on her.

16

FRIDAY
11-29-19

IT HAD NOT GONE WELL AT THE THANKSGIVING DINNER. The volunteers argued over who got to serve what. The clients they served ranged from full-of-thanks to dripping-with-attitude. Lisa scooped thick gravy onto piles of mashed potatoes and stuffing for over three hours, longer than she expected, after two of the volunteers squabbled, took it out to the street, and never returned. On top of it she was starting to have stomach cramps again, sweating.

She pulled into the property at 3:30. Michael had not waited for her. But, to her astonishment, he had left Turks and Caicos in their pen. She laughed. Pen was a gross understatement. Gregory had built them a run that measured a hundred yards by fifty yards, including a ten-by-ten-foot house with mastiff-sized cushions and food dispensers and a door big enough to allow them entrance to the house when they wanted it. When they saw her, their noses were jammed through holes in the wire fence, tails wagging. She had missed them so much. For a moment, her elation negated her physical discomfort. She went into the house and unlatched the door that allowed them into the kitchen.

Eloise raced down the hallway for safer ground. It would take her a while to get used to them again. They did all like each other, but Eloise had been spoiled since G's death, had Lisa and the house all to herself. Turks and Caicos romped through the rooms, reacquainting themselves. The sweat reappeared on Lisa's forehead. In the kitchen, she poured herself a glass of ginger ale, grabbed a sleeve of soda crackers, and headed for bed. Before she got to the door, she saw a plate of food wrapped in plastic, with a note from Michael:

Sorry I missed you. The dogs will be happier here with you. Pamela will also be happier they're with you. Let's talk soon.

Nice, she thought.

In the bedroom, Turks guarded one side of the bed, Caicos the other. Lisa grabbed the electronic thermometer from a drawer in the nightstand, rolled it from temple to temple. It blinked at her, gave her no reading. Damn this thing! She never remembered to take the protective cap off before rolling it across her forehead. The second time it read 100.1. She took a swig of ginger ale, ate two crackers, grabbed G's pillow, and snuggled with it like it was his back, his wide shoulders.

She tried to meditate, invoke her go-to mantra, but she couldn't clear her mind, was experiencing those fever dreams that came to her with a high temperature. The face of one of the clients at the Veterans' Hall, gnarled and grizzled from living outdoors so long, his jacket filthy, holes in his shoes with dirty toes protruding, a plate in each hand. "One's for me and one's for my buddy Harvey." She knew Harvey. Jimmy Stewart had played Elwood P. Dowd in the movie where the imaginary rabbit was named Harvey. The name tag on this man read James. He shoved the plates in her face, said, "To the top. Harvey ain't eaten in a week." She ladled three scoops of gravy on each plate. The man snorted, didn't thank her, moved down the line toward green beans and cornbread.

A text message was dinging on her cell phone. No way she was moving out of this bed. No way she was letting loose of G's big shoulders. Eloise crept up to the open door, glanced in both directions at the sleeping dogs, padded her way to the foot of the bed and made a graceful leap, snuggled up to Lisa's legs under the blanket. No way was she moving. She may never move again. More ginger ale, another cracker, two Ibuprofen, and she could feel herself disappearing.

It was still 99 degrees in the morning. She forced her achy legs out of bed and onto the floor so she could refill her glass, get another sleeve of crackers, scoop up her cell phone and laptop and return to bed. Turks and Caicos had already headed out for food and a romp in their playground. Five text messages from Cody.

Where are you? I'm coming tomorrow. Not sure what time yet.
I mean seriously, you have no life, how can you not be answering me?
It's looking like early afternoon for me tomorrow. Details with the lawyer.
Okay. It's Friday and you haven't responded. I hope you're not out cutting oak trees. Sorry. That was bad taste. Hope you're okay.
I'll be there closer to 5:00.

17

SATURDAY
11-30-19

C ODY HADN'T SHOWN UP UNTIL AFTER MIDNIGHT. A couple more texts had appeared first.

Still having drinks with the lawyer. Leave a key under the mat. I'll sleep on the couch.

Lisa hadn't responded. She had curled up in her bed with Eloise and continued reading her mother's first book. She wondered if the story was pure fiction, fabricated out of desire and lack, or if she had based it on someone's life, a great-grandmother or friend of a friend. Or could it have been her own life? Maybe the turkey baster story had been a lie. Maybe there was a baker, or a banker. Maybe Alice really had been capable of loving someone earlier in her life.

It didn't really matter. The story was good. The characters were multi-dimensional, steamrolled into conflict and love, drama and mystery. And it was written by Alice Hardrock! Her mother! Lisa fell asleep at page 101, woke in the morning to find both dogs and Eloise huddled together at the foot of the bed. She found Cody on the couch, buried under the big stack of blankets that G had kept there when he couldn't sleep. Which was often. She had never heard him leave, but would find him there in the morning, empty Coke cans and bowls of half-eaten popcorn surrounding him, the TV still on.

As she reached the kitchen, she realized it was Saturday morning, that she had stayed in bed all day Friday, had wasted another sixteen dollars and some good blogging time by staying holed up and under cover. Damn it! The only good news was she had another disappointment to enter, if she ever made it back into the office, which was questionable now that Cody was here. They often found ways to get into or cause trouble when they were together, possibly attributable to Cody's love for Patron tequila. And she refused to drink alone. Lisa wondered if Cody had already researched the Santa Cruz hangouts that might fit her needs. Lisa had never been anywhere in this town. The more she counted the places she had never been, the more she realized how much Gregory had cocooned her on his property, created nonstop projects for her in the greenhouse. She loved the work, which she guessed is what he was counting on, that he didn't look like an ogre, that she had opted into this lifestyle, had left a milquetoast boyfriend behind for this promising adventure he offered her. Still, she was feeling the effects now of having been secluded for so long.

But she had an office now, was learning how to blog, how to think about topics that were important to her, write them down, have no fear in clicking the Publish button. Well, a little fear, but learning how to overcome it.

In the kitchen she found a bag full of Wild Planet wild pink salmon, non-GMO. *Thank you, Cody!* The woman usually came through, eventually, if sometimes she took a skewed pathway, a twisted foray into some wild and crazy activity. As soon as she placed a can into the electric can opener, Eloise came running, rubbed up against her legs in a frenzy. Lisa walked down the hall toward the closed door to G's office. She opened it, left it open, for the first time in seven years. She walked back to the living room, sat on the couch at Cody's feet, hoping to stir her. There was no stirring. One of Cody's feet stuck out from G's blanket. Lisa put her hand around it, searched for a pulse and found one. She snugged the blankets up to Cody's neck, covered the exposed foot, made her way outside to the playground. Turks and Caicos were at the far end, slapping paws against each other, rolling in the dirt. They were puppies when she first got here, puppies bigger than any other dog she'd ever seen. That made them close to eight now. She had done some research. The breed lived to be between six and twelve years old. She was banking on twelve for these two. Didn't really want to lose anything else in her life. A mom and a couple of boyfriends was enough.

She passed through the kitchen, saw Michael's note still lying next to the plate of food, grabbed a fork, scooped it into the stuffing and put it in her mouth. It tasted like G's. She wondered if the brothers had a secret recipe of their mother's they used every Thanksgiving and Christmas. Or was it Pamela's? No matter. She was hungry, poured a glass of ginger ale, walked down the hallway to G's office and sat herself down in his chair, plate resting on her lap, filling herself up with homemade cranberry sauce, moist turkey, mashed potatoes, sweet potatoes with marshmallows and pecans on top. She finished with the chocolate pie, whipped cream having lost its puff, drizzled off the sides. But it was good. She sat back, spun the Herman Miller Aeron chair slowly to each side, took in the view as she did, one she had never seen before, photos of his family on one wall, letterpress broadsides given to him in trade by some local poet friends on the other wall. There were file cabinets on both sides of the desk. The desk itself was large, handmade, mahogany, brass corners neatly fitted. His MacBook Pro sat in the middle of the desk, top closed. A Rolodex next to the computer. A landline phone. It made her think about his cell phone, attached securely to his body, zipped into the front pocket of his Patagonia jacket. She hadn't remembered seeing the jacket since the accident. She didn't think he was wearing it, knew he wasn't wearing it, because her semi-photographic memory had emblazoned the image of him on the ground with the tree on his forehead, saw the boots, the blue jeans, a long-sleeve plaid shirt, the orange chainsaw, heard its rumble. The blood. But no Patagonia jacket. It had to be somewhere. She'd try to call it later, have Cody help her track it down. Might be some important message on it. She lifted the lid of the computer, saw an image of the interior of the greenhouse in full September bloom as his background image. In the center of the screen was a password field. She had no idea. Had no interest in playing this game right now. Cody was good at this stuff.

Cody stayed comatose on the couch until it was time for dinner. Lisa thought about driving downtown to the office, maybe taking a photo of the Lenz sign and Outdoor World to post with her next blog entry. She had a good camera if she could find it buried among G's things. No, the cell phone would be fine, which made her think again about G's jacket, his Patagonia pocket where he carried everything that mattered. She wanted in there. While she wasn't a snoop, she was a widow of sorts now, and she wanted answers. Wanted to know everything there was to know that she had never taken the time to discover, or had never been given the opportunity. Like with Alice.

Lisa still had a light fever. She should stay home and rest. She could never remember the old adage — "Feed a fever, starve a cold," or vice versa? Maybe because she was rarely sick. Alice had taken care of her. And of Cody. She opened her computer, Safari, and typed piousrebel.com in the address field. The site appeared. No photos. A home page and a blog link. Very spare. Like her life. Isolated. Hidden. Mysterious. She clicked on the blog link, needed a more interesting title for this page. She reread the previous posts. It was a little embarrassing what she had said, sharing her thoughts with the world. No clue what she was doing yet, she dug into the guts of WordPress, found that there had been six visits to the site. She checked the IP addresses. They had all been her. The old tree-in-the-forest adage. If no one has ever read your words, did you really say anything?

Back in bed, she propped herself up on a pile of pillows. Gregory had loved pillows, bought them while on the road, traded for them. MacBook open, ready for some pithy new post, she thought about the plate of food Michael had left her. Should she have worried about whether or not it contained poison? If Pamela had been the one to prepare it? No. Michael was not a terrible person. Right now he was scared, angry. His big brother who kept the world spinning, attached to its axis, who acted as if he knew the answers to everything, was gone. She and Michael were both newborns, working on keeping their eyes open, reaching and feeling for something out of reach and unexpected every day. Regardless of why, he had brought her Turks and Caicos, the plate of food, the note, possibly all of it a peace offering, a request to move forward through this thing together. She picked up her phone, typed him a text. *Thank you for the food!* She questioned whether or not to leave the exclamation point at the end. It ramped things up a bit. Made them a little more dramatic or important than they really were. Was it Elmore Leonard who said you only get one exclamation point in a lifetime? She couldn't remember. Some great writer, though, who seemed to know what he or she was talking about. She left the exclamation mark there. Had truly been glad to find the food, glad the note was written in Michael's handwriting.

Cody is in town. Remember her?

How could he forget? She had been all over him after a raucous drinking bout at Margaritaville on the Esplanade in Capitola.

> We're going to try to solve some of the mysteries around here. I'll keep you posted. Let's talk soon. And thank you so much for Turks and Caicos! They are so happy here! By the way, in addition to an office, I have a blog. Nobody has seen it. Feels like it isn't real yet. If I give you the link, will you take a look? Not tell anybody else about it? Especially Pamela? Okay. Here's to trusting you: piousrebel.com. Knowing you might be reading this may help me to not blab too much about things too personal to post. If you know what I mean.

She pushed Send.

18

SUNDAY
12-1-19

O N SATURDAY NIGHT, LISA HEARD THE DOOR HANDLE TURN. Cody ran in, dived onto the bed, Eloise jumping over Lisa to miss the landing. She wormed her way under the covers, worked her way into a spoon position. Lisa placed a palm on Cody's firm thigh. Lisa dwarfed her. Wrapped her up like a fetus. The younger sister. The twisted sister.

"I have missed you so much," she said.

"Me too you. I guess your time with the lawyer was more than you expected."

"Ben. Let's call him Ben, not lawyer. I'm tired of lawyers and the lawsuit and that whole other lifetime."

"But you're not tired of Ben?"

"I don't think so. We had a nice time. He told me to forget about the suit. He'd handle everything. I'd get some money. Get my name cleared. All I ever wanted. He took me to Quince for dinner!" Lisa shook her head, didn't know about it. Didn't know much about any restaurants except those that Gregory had gotten takeout from, or the few he'd taken her to. "Quince! Michelin three-star! Where have you been hiding yourself? It's an eight-course tasting menu at two hundred ninety-five dollars per person. Not counting the wine pairing for an additional two seventy-five. Michael Tusk is the chef. Turns out Ben is his attorney, so Michael comes over to the table, brings us a special bottle of wine he's been saving. We ended up at Ben's penthouse with a three-hundred-sixty-degree view of the city. I told him I couldn't spend the night, that you were expecting me, but we did spend some quality time under those satin sheets of his. So, what about you? What's up? What's new and exciting?"

Lisa had forgotten how fast Cody could talk when she was revved up, and a new man never failed to rev her up, especially one like Ben, who could treat her the way she thought she deserved. Not really forgotten, but it had been a few years since they'd spent live time together. There was catching up to do, questions to sort out.

Turks and Caicos lumbered into the bedroom, one thrusting into Lisa's side of the bed, the other into Cody's.

"Ooh, ooh, ooh!" she said. "When did you get these monsters back?" Cody had never liked their slobber, stayed far away from them. Gregory would lock them out in the playground when she came to visit.

"Thursday. A Thanksgiving gift from Michael. Or more likely a demand from Pamela to get them the hell out of her house."

"And how is psycho woman handling all this stuff?"

"I don't know. Michael is strange. We're in this awkward position of both being in the will. Gregory changed the combination to the safe, and that's a critical piece. There's the key to his workshop. Access to his computer files. Lots of buried treasures."

"What? Well, that's fun! This calls for a scavenger hunt."

"I agree."

"Oh, I can't wait. Can we start now?" Before Cody got her teaching credential, she had been an assistant to a private detective in Berkeley. She had loved the intrigue of the work, the costumes, dark glasses, long-distance photography, wiretapping. For a while she'd thought about changing directions, becoming a private eye herself. Until someone shot at her boss one night when they were both on a case. She backed away, changed her mind, chose the more refined pathway.

"No. I need a shower and food first."

Cody was in the kitchen whipping up a breakfast-for-dinner concoction with a scrambled- egg base, a cup of Yukon Gold sliced potatoes, a can of artichoke hearts, a scoop of salsa fresca, black olives, and tomatoes when Lisa entered, dressed fresh, wet hair. She sat at the kitchen table, let Cody serve her the scramble, a large glass of freshly squeezed orange juice, and toasted English muffins with blackberry jam that Lisa had canned last year from the patch on the other side of the dogs' playground.

"Thank you. And thank you so much for remembering the salmon."

"That was Ben. I mentioned it to him as we were sorting through documents. He pulled out his phone, sent a text, and on the way to the restaurant we stopped by Fisherman's Wharf and there was a bag waiting for us."

"Sounds like a find."

"We'll see. Oh, I forgot to tell you. You will actually see. He's coming down tomorrow."

"Down where?"

"Down here."

"What?"

"I invited him."

"You gave him my address?"

"What's the big deal?"

"Did you forget what I do for a living? The greenhouse?"

"Don't worry about Ben. He's cool. Who knows, he might even be able to help sort things out for you."

"What things? I don't need any sorting!"

"Oh, really. Computer password. Lost combination to the safe. The locked workshop. No, you're just ducky, aren't you?"

"Do not start with this."

"With what?"

"Taking over my life. Controlling things. I'm just not in the mood right now."

"Taking over your life? What the hell?"

Lisa had waited a couple years to bring up the Ryan thing, had felt like it was probably none of her business, but it had burrowed under her skin like a tick, had festered. Now seemed like the right time. Before she let Cody help her with uncovering what might be hidden in this house. Gregory's house.

"I heard through the grapevine —"

"Let me stop you right there. Grapevines are usually unreliable. Especially if this has to do with me. I would prefer that you'd be more precise with details than some rumor-mill tidbits."

"Right. A mutual acquaintance of ours —"

"'Ours' meaning you and Gregory or meaning you and me?"

"Quit interrupting me and let me complete a sentence, goddamn it! Did you or did you not shack up with Ryan when I left town?"

Cody chuckled. "Oh. That. Certainly took you long enough to bring that one up. And how dare you? How can you think you have any right to know or judge anything about the boyfriend you walked out on with zero explanation, and the best friend you left behind with a terse text that said, 'Sorry. I can't do this anymore'?"

"Sorry. I couldn't. But we've been over that. We've had that discussion. What about you stepping in to be Ryan's savior?"

"That's what you think happened? Naïve you. I was devastated. He, however, didn't give a shit. Had been over you for a long time. Was seeing at least two other people when you left. The guy you like to call Casper Milquetoast. He swooped in and comforted me. We'd talk all night, trying to figure out what had gotten into you. He didn't mind that you walked out, left the bookstore to him. He had new folks ready to help within days. Other people liked him, loved him. It was you who didn't appreciate him. We hit it off because we had you in common, could commiserate, though it was mostly me doing the complaining and crying."

Lisa took a bite of her scramble. "Thank you for dinner."

"It's breakfast. You're welcome. Are we done with the Ryan thing yet?"

"Maybe for now. Probably not forever."

"I agree. You were a total shit and we've kept it tamped down for way too long. Time for atonement soon."

Lisa's cell phone buzzed. Text from Michael.

You're welcome. Want my help on the hunt?

"Who's that?" Cody asked. Lisa stared at her. "Not controlling! Just curious."

"Michael. He wants to help."

"Michael. He's much cuter than Gregory. Love those curls that twist around his ears. More real than Gregory was."

"Yes, I remember. Margaritaville."

"Jeez. That wasn't me. That was Patron. I thought Pamela was going to run me through with that steak knife."

"That would have solved two of my problems. Put her behind bars. Teach you a lesson."

"We don't need him for this. Keep him out of it. At least for a while. You may not want him to know about whatever we might find."

Cody and I are taking some time to catch up. I'll let you know if we find anything useful.

"What'd you say?" Lisa pointed the phone at Cody's face. "Good. Are we caught up yet?"

The phone buzzed.

I'll bring tequila! :-)

Lisa showed it to Cody.

Talk soon. Lisa responded.

19

THEY'D SPENT TWO HOURS IN GREGORY'S OFFICE, Cody at the computer, Lisa hunting through two desk drawers that weren't locked. Very neat, organized. Typical Gregory. In case the auditors showed up. In case the police knocked the door down and rifled through the place.

The first password they tested was 'Lisa'.

"No," answered Cody. "What else?"

"Turks. Caicos. Turks and Caicos."

"No. No. No."

"Eloise."

Cody laughed. "Not a chance. He hated that cat."

"He did not."

"Give me more."

"Weed. Pot. Greenhouse."

"Keep going. More creative than those."

"You think G was creative?"

"Sometimes. You finding anything in those drawers?"

"Checkbooks. Invoices. A Swiss Army knife too big to fit in anybody's pocket. A harmonica. Never heard him play it. First time I've ever seen it. Receipts from Moore and Sons where he gets his Harley repaired. He's got one stashed in his workshop. I've never seen him ride it, though. Never even seen it, just heard him talk about it on the phone with his friend Zack."

"We've got to get into that place. Could be some real fun stuff in there. I'd jump on that hog."

"I'm guessing that'll be Michael's."

"Right. More passwords, please. What was important to him? What did he care about? Other than you."

"I'm not sure how important I was to him. Try 'Michael'."

"No 'Michael'."

"Try 'Cody'."

"No."

"Try 'Codyrocks'."

"What? That's crazy."

"Try it. That's what he liked to say about you. That you rocked." Cody took her hands off the keyboard, squinted her eyes at Lisa.

"Why the hell would he say that?"

"We both said it. Talked a lot about your energy. Your sleuthing abilities. 'Cody rocks' was a common mantra around here, especially when we were stoned. Go ahead. Try it." For just a second Lisa locked on the image of Cody maybe rocking Gregory, his world, maybe that's why he said it. A little clue about him and Cody, more buried secrets that he figured would never be uncovered. Cody still hadn't put her fingers back on the keyboard, stuck her hands between her thighs, curled her fingers under her legs.

Cody looked at her watch. "Hey! What time does SNL air out here?"

Lisa thought it was probably a rerun, was curious about Cody's sudden interest.

"Eight thirty. Why?"

"It's eight twenty-three. I'll make some quick margaritas, meet you at the TV. We'll work on this tomorrow morning."

It was a rerun. David Harbor from *Stranger Things* with musical guest Camila Cabello. Cody made a pitcher of margaritas that took them through the Weekend Update.

"I'll go make some more," she said.

"No. I'm good. Come to bed."

Cody got under the covers. Lisa switched the TV to a rerun of *The Big Bang Theory*, her favorite way to fall asleep.

She woke up close to midnight, reached her arm over toward Cody, but found Eloise instead. She craned her neck, looked around the bed, the room. No Cody. She padded down the hall barefoot, saw the light on in G's office, Cody with fingers on his keyboard.

"Hey. What are you doing?"

"Oh, hi. Couldn't sleep. Thought I'd try a few more guesses. I'm in. I haven't dug into any files yet, but I made it in a few minutes ago."

"What do you mean you made it in? With what password?"

"You're not going to believe this."

"Try me."

"I don't think you'll like it. Are you sure you want to know?"

"Don't be stupid. That's why we're doing all this. The hunt-and-gather patrol. Come on. What is it?"

"Okay. It was 'Pamela'."

"Pamela? No way. Why the hell would he use 'Pamela'?"

"Don't know. You tell me."

"I have no idea. Log out. I want to try it."

"I changed it already. Figured you wouldn't want to have to think about what that meant every time you logged in."

"You know, you need to talk to me before you make decisions that affect my life."

"How did this decision affect your life? Jeez. What is wrong with you? The new password is 'lisahardrock', lowercase, all one word." She stood up, relinquished the chair to Lisa.

Lisa logged out, typed in the new password, and the computer popped open.

"What now?" Lisa asked.

"I don't know. Are you still pissed at me for solving your access problem?"

Lisa breathed deeply. "Sorry. Why the fuck did he use 'Pamela' as his password?"

"I'll assume you don't really want me to answer that question, but I'm guessing once we dig through his files we might find some answers, to that question and others I'm sure we'll want to pose."

Lisa turned off the computer, put her arm around Cody's shoulder, led her back to the bedroom. "I'm so sorry. Thanks for busting through. I just can't believe the Pamela thing."

"Why not? I've always thought he was a bit of a horndog." They crawled back under the covers, Eloise jumping between them, the dogs nowhere to be seen.

"I never thought he was a horndog. But his trips out of town raised a bit of suspicion. I'm tired. You want the TV on to sleep by?"

"Sure. I like *World Series of Poker*."

"Seriously?"

"Absolutely. I'm addicted. There's a casino just down the street from my school. I spend a fair amount of time there."

"You'll have to teach me."

"I'd love to. Good night."

In the morning they brought their granola and bananas to G's office. Lisa was feeling guilty again about not showing up at her downtown space. She hadn't even thought about writing a blog post in a few days. She vowed she'd get one out, soon.

"Let's go to Documents first," Lisa said.

"He's too smart for that. Would bury important stuff elsewhere. But let's start there."

"Was."

"What?" Cody said.

"Was too smart for that. Not too smart to avoid a fucking falling oak tree. By the way, how do I change the password if I want?"

"Why would you want to do that? I thought *lisahardrock* would be perfect, easy to remember."

"Yeah. Too easy. I might keep it. Just show me how." Cody walked her through the steps as Lisa took notes on a pad G had kept on the desk. Random notes. Doodles. Out-of-town phone numbers. Local cell-phone numbers.

As they opened the Documents folder, Lisa wondered if they'd find manuscripts in there. Novels G had written about their lives together. *No. Not his style.* The thought brought Alice back to mind.

20

TUESDAY
12-3-19

"ALEXA. PLAY VIVALDI."

Alexa's stiff voice said, "Shuffling through songs by Vivaldi."

They spent all day in the office. Vivaldi. The Beatles. Eric Clapton. U2. Annie Lennox. Nothing earth-shattering had popped up in the Documents folder. They did find a file titled "2019 Passwords" that Lisa printed. She'd come back to that one later.

"I'm starving," Cody said. "How about Mexican?"

"Okay. Let's get it delivered. I want to keep hunting."

"I'll go down to Tortilla Flats, pick up some rice and beans, tacos," Cody said.

"Sounds good."

Cody hadn't been gone ten minutes when Lisa heard a knock. The dogs, resting on the living room rug, reacted first, rammed their heads into the frame trying to bash it open. Lisa hurried to the door. "Turks. Caicos. Back off." Another thing G had done well. Trained the dogs to obey specific commands. They backed up three feet, sat down. A stranger was there. Over his shoulder she saw the cocoa-colored Porsche Panamera.

"Can I help you?"

"I thought your mastiffs were going to have me for lunch. Or drown me with that slobber. Sorry. I'm Cody's friend. Ben." He held out a hand, didn't offer what she thought was a typical lawyer's grip. Not too firm, not limp. Lisa ran through a mental card catalog of all the men Cody had dated, and this guy didn't fit. He was short, maybe the same height as Lisa. Short blond hair on the sides, but mostly bald on top. He looked fit. Dressed in business casual. Neat. Tight. Sailing shoes. A little out of place on Porter Gulch Road.

Ben. Ben the lawyer. The penthouse guy. Now a Panamera. He must have a yacht somewhere. Maybe a vacation home in Pasatiempo.

"Yes. They're a little rambunctious when they think a playmate has arrived. Come on in. Cody went to get some lunch. She'll be back in a minute. I'll text her that you're here if you want to add to the order."

"Thanks. Already did. Rice, beans, and tacos, as I understand."

"Right. Have a seat." The dogs hurried over and each stuck a wet jowl on his lap. She wanted to get back to the computer, especially to have some free time without Cody looking over her shoulder. But she thought that might be rude, though she was caring less and less about being rude, and more and more about uncovering the mind and inner world of Gregory P. Daniels. She sat across from Ben, decided to dive right in.

"So how's it going with Cody's battle?"

"God, I love these dogs. Wish I was in one place long enough to own a couple. Care for them properly. These two certainly look well loved."

She looked at Turks and Caicos, thought about Ben's observation. It was true. They had both been loved, by G and by her. She didn't know about Michael, and especially Pamela, the past month while they babysat them. Or had absconded with them, depending on how you looked at it.

"Nice diversion tactics," she said.

"What's that?" He cupped his hands and ran them over the dogs' ears.

"Avoiding my question by focusing on the dogs."

76

"Oh. I do absolutely love dogs. And I do absolutely love my work and would hate to get sued by a client for divulging attorney-client information. So, yes. Two birds, if you will."

"She won't mind. We're like sisters. Siamese twins. Attached at the …" She paused.

He finished her sentence. "The cerebellum, so I've been told."

"That's about right."

"I will tell you that your *sister* will no longer have to worry about her tarnished reputation at the hands of that bozo admin."

"And she'll walk away with a hundred thousand dollars?"

He smiled. "You are relentless. Probably more."

The first impression suggested Ben was okay, might make someone a good partner. Lisa guessed he probably had more than just Cody dangling, each of them hoping to be identified as that good partner.

"I understand you're dealing with passwords and combinations and locked workshops and more."

"So much for *my* client-attorney privileges."

Ben chuckled. "I'm betting you haven't signed a legal contract with Cody, yet, but you are correct in assuming that she has been loose-lipped with your private matters since," he paused before continuing a bit more cautiously, "Gregory's passing."

"It's okay. You can mention his name. But let's not skirt around things by saying it was a passing. It was bloody. It was ugly. He didn't pass. He was mauled."

"Sorry."

Another knock. The fickle dogs raced toward the door. Michael walked in without waiting for an invitation.

"Oh, sorry. Didn't know you had company," he said.

"Seriously. You thought that car you just passed in the driveway was mine?" Lisa laughed.

Ben stood, offered his hand to Michael. "I'm Ben. A friend of Cody's."

"Hi, Ben. Michael. I'm Lisa's … I mean my brother was her …"

"No worries, Michael. I know who you are."

Lisa didn't like "no worries," hated "no problem." So had Alice.

"You do? How's that?"

"Do you *know* Cody?"

Michael chuckled. "Good point."

Lisa moved back to the couch. "Have a seat. Too late to add you to the order."

Michael put his hands up, shook his head.

When Cody entered with food, the dogs lunged for the bags she was carrying, which she lifted over her head. "Hey, Ben. Great to see you!" She turned to Michael. "What are *you* doing here?"

Lisa didn't want to hear him say he owned half of everything here, so changed things up. "Come on, Cody. Let's prep the food."

"It's already prepped. What are you talking about?"

Ben said, "I'm happy to share my portion with Michael."

"Very sweet of you," Cody said as she and Lisa unpacked the food.

The dogs nestled into Michael's legs. "Yeah, I know. I missed you, too."

"So sorry to hear about your brother," Ben said.

"You guys want salsa?" Lisa asked. They both nodded.

"Yeah. Thanks. Nice car."

"Thanks. You know the Panamera?"

"Not specifically. I know six figures when I see it."

Ben laughed. "Mine's a lease. The six figures are amortized monthly over thirty-six months. Helps some."

"What do you do that you can afford that kind of monthly payment?"

Ben watched Michael and the dogs, was slow to answer. "I'm an attorney."

Michael sat up, pushed the dogs away, as Lisa and Cody brought the plates of food, a six-pack of Dos Equis. Lisa handed a plate to Michael, Cody placed Ben's on his lap.

"Thanks," Ben said.

"I hear you've brought in an attorney," Michael said to Lisa.

"What? Where'd you hear that?"

Michael nodded toward Ben.

"Did you say that, Ben?"

"In fact, I didn't. As with you earlier, I didn't divulge any information protected by attorney-client privilege."

"He's Cody's attorney!!"

"Michael, I am Cody's attorney. But today I'm here to visit. We have … been dating. That much I'll divulge."

Lisa laughed. "Been dating? A one-night fling in your penthouse?"

Ben looked at Cody. "Now who's been divulging information?"

"I had fun. I like to share things."

Michael grinned.

"What?" Cody said to him.

"I'm just surprised you didn't bring tequila to go with the Mexican food."

"Who says I didn't? Alexa, put on Los Lobos."

"Shuffling songs by Los Lobos."

"Gregory has one of these devices in every room," Lisa said. "All night long he'd be talking to her. Sometimes I got a little jealous."

"Really?" Ben said. "I don't know how things are going with your hunt, but you should check out the Voicegram website."

"What do you mean 'hunt'?" Michael asked. "How does this stranger know that you're hunting for something?"

Cody hid behind a pillow before saying, "Truly, tequila did play a big role in that discussion."

"Five margaritas, to be exact," Ben shared.

"Is that information you can share?" Michael asked.

"More than happy to, given the awkward circumstances we find ourselves in."

"Tell me more about Voicegram," Lisa said.

"You mean tell *us* more about Voicegram," Michael said.

"Yes. Sorry. That's what I mean."

Ben took a bite of his taco, washed it down with a swig of beer. "It's an app that lets you record your voice on Alexa."

"You're kidding."

"I don't spend much time in the kidding department. Especially when it comes to ownership and possession, which I believe the two of you are steeped in at the moment."

Conversation stopped as they all dug into their food. The dogs sniffed around the plates.

"Turks, Caicos. Out!" Lisa said. They jumped up and headed for the door to their playground, clearly happy to do so.

Cody smiled. "Does that work if you say it to Michael?"

"Fuck off, Cody," Michael said.

"No, thank you."

"Wait, Ben. Are you suggesting that G may have kept some of his secrets on Alexa?" Lisa asked.

"It's a possibility. You say he's got an Echo or Dot in every room. Why? Just for music or weather? I doubt it." Ben took his plate to the kitchen. Cody followed.

"Come on, Ben. These two have things to talk about. Let's go for a ride."

Michael and Lisa continued to eat.

"So?" Michael finally asked.

"So what?"

"You've hired an attorney?"

"No! He's Cody's attorney. She got hassled by a bully administrator at her school in Point Reyes Station, walked out the door, and hired Ben to sue them on her behalf. Do I *need* an attorney? Do you have one?"

"Too soon for all of that. I did bring the dogs back, if that means anything."

"It probably means Pamela threatened to leave you if you didn't get rid of them."

Michael ignored the comment. "Any luck with the safe or computer?"

"Not the safe. We did get into the computer, however."

"We?"

"You know Cody's background. She's a whiz at this stuff."

"So what's the password?" She paused, not sure she was ready to deal with Michael's reaction. "Why the hesitation? Are you planning to keep secrets from me? Should I ask Ben to represent me?"

Lisa grabbed their empty plates, headed for the kitchen, over her shoulder said, "It was *Pamela*. Any idea what that's all about?" Michael followed her.

"What? Why are you saying that? What's wrong with you? Just stirring up problems?"

"Not me. Why would Gregory use 'Pamela' as his password?"

"He wouldn't. Never. He didn't like her much. Told me she was weighing me down. But I don't get it. What's in it for you to lie to me about the password? You find stuff in there you don't want me to see?"

"I have not found anything in there I wanted to see or didn't want you to see. And I didn't lie to you. We hunted last night for a while, gave up and watched SNL. I woke up and Cody was at the keyboard and had figured out the password."

He laughed. "Oh! Now it makes more sense."

"What does?"

"Who was lying to whom. The password to Gregory's computer was absolutely not 'Pamela'. Trust me."

"What are you talking about?"

"Gregory gave me the password a few weeks before he died. Thought somebody should have it other than him."

"You've known this since before he died and never told me? Talk about trust. You made us jump through hoops to figure it out on our own?"

"I'm trying to understand whether or not we can work together."

"I'm pretty sure we can't if you're going to withhold things from me. For now, I occupy this house and I need to figure things out about Gregory. What trails he may have left behind. How to move forward."

"And we need to do that together. Once we have a mutual understanding of each other's needs."

"Or greeds."

"I have no need or interest in greed."

"What about Pamela?"

"Let's leave her out of this."

"Why? You haven't convinced me about the password, about anything."

"Okay. I'll tell you the real password. But you won't like it."

"Try me."

"Codyrocks."

"What?"

"You heard me," he said. There was no way Michael could have known about the Cody-rocks conversations she and G had shared.

"Wait a minute!"

"Yeah, starting to make just a little bit of sense to you. I said you wouldn't want to know."

"This is getting way too twisted." Lisa pounded her palm against the table, not sure what to believe anymore.

Michael stood, looked out the window, changed the subject. "Have you seen the car Ben drives?"

Lisa was not interested in small talk or skewering Cody's attorney. "Please don't tell Pamela about the password fiasco," she said.

"Why would I? You don't really understand the nature of the relationship she and I have."

"How *would* I? You've never talked to me about it. And if you confided in G, he never shared anything with me."

"He didn't know either. Someday I'll tell you. Probably not important now as we dig deeper into this thing."

"This thing?" Lisa said.

"This tangled web Gregory has left behind. I got to go. Good luck with the Ben and Cody show." He put his hand on the doorknob.

"Wait!" Lisa shouted. "Why did he give you the password?"

"Don't know. Must be something in there he wanted me to find. Or you. Good luck." He walked out.

It was beginning to feel like Gregory was still controlling her life. Maybe she should take the ashes off the mantle over the fireplace, sprinkle them somewhere that mattered to him, lose him from this process sooner than later.

21

WEDNESDAY
12-4-19

BY THE TIME CODY AND BEN STAGGERED THROUGH THE DOOR, Lisa had passed out on the keyboard. Lisa felt Cody's hand on her shoulder, heard the whisper in her ear, "Wake up. It's two o'clock in the morning. You learn anything new?"

"Oh, yeah."

"Tell me."

"Later. Too tired. You guys have fun?"

"Do I smell like I had fun?" She parted her lips and breathed a mouthful of tequila-laced air in Lisa's face.

"I'm going to bed. See you in the morning. Take your pick of guest rooms."

"Ben's making breakfast tomorrow. You won't want to miss it."

"I'll be here."

In bed, she muted the sound to the episode of *The Big Bang Theory* where Bob Newhart was the guest as Arthur Jeffries, better known as Professor Proton. She didn't need to hear the words, knew the scene by heart.

She wasn't sure whom to trust anymore. Maybe she needed to toss them all out of her life, start fresh, like she was doing in the downtown office. Which she was missing. She hadn't been there since Thanksgiving. How were the property managers surviving without her? She hadn't written a blog in over a week.

Cody was an enigma. She drank way too much, and it affected her ability to think straight, to function as a caring human being. Lisa thought about the trip they had taken to Chicago a few years ago. Cody had wanted to go to the Art Institute to view the Joseph Cornell boxes. She had taken control of every aspect of the trip, booked the tickets on Alaska Airlines for a Saturday morning, return trip the following Wednesday. In addition to the Art Institute, the itinerary included a meal at Oriole's Restaurant the first night. A friend of Cody's would pick them up at the airport and act as tour guide, except he couldn't drive after dark, something about a brain hemorrhage and a subsequent surgery, but he could guide them well as long as one of them drove. The plan included the Poetry Foundation building, the American Writers Museum, the Midtown Athletic Club, a play at the City Lit Theater, a jam-packed five-day trip. Except that Cody got so shitfaced at Oriole's that the rest of the trip catered to her hangover and side effects from vomiting all day long. Lisa had played nursemaid the whole trip, stuck inside at Cody's friend's place, watching reruns of shows she hadn't seen in decades.

It was always something with her. And now this. This Ben character. Another bad influence? The password caper. There was some degree of logic about why G would have used 'Codyrocks' as his password, based on their jokes about her lifestyle, her devil-may-care attitude about life, men, art, work. But why did Cody lie to her about the password? Why had she implicated Pamela?

While Cody and Ben were out partying, Lisa had spent four hours in the bowels of G's computer. Most of it was boring. His bookmarked files on Safari the most extensive thing she found: his obsessions, some of which she knew about, like the lakes of Canada, the train routes from Vancouver to Newfoundland, a few other Canadian things like Whistler and Banff, the fimo art of Jon Anderson, the soft porn sites they sometimes watched together. Bed-and-breakfasts of Lake County, a number of Facebook links to clients who lived up and down Highway

99, Facebook messages, mostly women she had never heard of, an apparent fascination with slot cars. Most of this was trivial, didn't matter much to her in relation to how her life might move forward.

She finally found one folder, buried ten levels deep, folders nested within folders, an intentional hiding with no sensible pathway to uncovering its existence.

The folder, LeChaim, was locked, required another password. She went to Google and searched, discovered that it was a Russian magazine founded in 1991, most content having to do with Jewish studies, memoirs, culture. What was G playing at with this stuff? After another half hour of searching, she went to Anagram Solver, which she sometimes used when she played the *New York Times* Spelling Bee. She didn't consider it cheating to use it, instead thought of it as a learning tool. She typed in L-E-C-H-A-I-M. The first word that appeared was *Michael!* She typed 'Michael' in the password field and was inside the folder reading three file titles:

For Lisa

Client List – Local

Client List – Central Valley and beyond

She opened the first file, a note from G:

Lisa –

If you're reading this, something terrible has gone wrong
with my plans, most likely at the hands of my
less-than-organized crime customers in the Central Valley, or
some other mysterious unknown.

And if you're reading this, you've somehow 1) figured out the
password to my computer (ideally you've talked with
Michael, who knows the password, and the two of you have
decided to play nice given my apparent demise), and 2)
found your way into this buried folder and will now discover
more than you ever wanted to know. (I'm guessing Cody may
have helped you solve this puzzle.) More puzzles to come.
I'm hoping you take the lead instead of Michael or Cody. I

don't see any need for Pamela to be involved. By now you'll have discovered that the combination on the safe has been changed. Michael knows what's in there, so don't try to cheat him out of it. I've kept him updated. He's liable to test you, so beware. Here you go: 3 – 36 – 29. Key to my workshop is hidden under the turtle's left front paw. Are they called paws on turtles? Anyway, as I'm sure you've expected, there's more to uncover out there. I apologize.

Print out a copy of the Client List – Local for Michael, who I'd like to have a continuing relationship with those folks. Leave the Central Valley list nested in this folder. Not sure what your plans will be, but if you choose to move forward in my place, be careful. Some of those folks are ruthless, greedy. You know the greenhouse cycle better than anyone. Couldn't imagine anyone doing it better than you. But, you and Michael may decide to sell the whole place and move on. Maybe back to Point Reyes Station for you.

Again, I apologize. Didn't think it would go this way. Sorry for being such a controlling bore.

G

P.S. About my workshop. I know you'll be surprised. Take some time before you go in there. Deal with the computer, the safe, Michael, first. Plenty of time to sort out the rest.

•　　　•　　　•

She ran to the greenhouse, went to the safe, and was in. Ten thousand cash still there, fifty pounds of sale-ready buds still there, two jars of seeds still there. She closed it and tested the combination one more time. Still good.

•　　　•　　　•

Newhart had been a great addition to *The Big Bang Theory*. That dry wit still going strong at age ninety. Eloise had snuggled up to her cell phone. She ran a palm across her back, waited for the engine, then slid her hand under her belly to grab the phone. She typed in Michael's number, texted:

> Great news. Found the combination. All is good. Let's talk about next steps soon.

22

THURSDAY
12-5-19

L ISA HEARD NOISE IN THE KITCHEN. Ben was up early. She turned off the TV, *The Big Bang Theory* still blasting away. She slipped into a robe, some boots, stuck her head unnoticed into the kitchen as Ben was slicing vegetables, squeezing oranges, stirring eggs, all at the same time, like he had done this many times for many women.

Michael had not texted or called yet. That surprised her. She thought he would be over first thing. Maybe Pamela had access to his phone, had blocked him from seeing the text. Lisa didn't have a clue about the Pamela connection, why Cody would lie about the password. She didn't want to think about it now. Knowing that the safe was in order, that she could appease Michael, she shifted her consciousness, brought her focus now to the turtle's paw. She lifted it off the step of the workshop and removed the rusted key. As G had suggested, she wasn't ready to go in yet. Back in the house, she smelled Ben's work in the kitchen. Reminded her of G, his masterful concoctions.

After securing the key to her keychain, she breathed deeply, kicked off the boots, stepped out of the robe, and for the first time in weeks felt a hint of relief, a little more in control of her life. In the shower she stared up at the stained-glass window she had designed last year. G had installed it, and it let in the perfect amount of light for a morning shower. How had she gotten here? Standing in this handcrafted shower stall, perched in the middle of twenty-five acres of secluded land on a semiprivate road? Yesterday she had been with G, a week ago with Ryan, a month ago just a kid in a college town with a mother, no father, a kind-of-sister named Cody.

She followed the odors to the kitchen.

"Hey," Ben said as he flipped pancakes in G's copper frying pan.

"Good morning," Lisa answered. "No Cody yet?"

"No. I guess she's a late sleeper."

"That's right. I imagine you're still in the guessing stage."

"Yeah. I like to play it by ear for a while, see which way the wind will blow."

She had mostly liked what she saw in Ben, until that comment. She didn't appreciate people who spoke in clichés, Alice sitting on her shoulder. Preferred folks who were able to think on their feet, come up with new descriptions, new ways to think about their observations and thoughts.

"And when I say which way the wind will blow, what I'm really trying to say is how the hurricane that surrounds her will whip things into a frenzy and rip up landscape and buildings wherever she walks, might eventually ebb, sink into nearby lakes and streams, stir up a current that will eventually wane."

There it was. That was more what she expected from a lawyer named Ben with a penthouse in the city and a Panamera sitting in her front yard.

"Yes, that's Cody, all right. Tornadoes and toadstools and whatever else she can stir up along the way. I'm waking her up."

"Good. Would you set the table first? Not sure which silverware you'd like to use." The real silver was in a hand-carved box G had made, sat on the kitchen hutch they had found in Monterey at the Cannery Row Antique House. She didn't like being told what to do by a stranger in her house, but she liked that he was thoughtful enough to be inquisitive about the silverware. She laid out four placemats, used the handmade plates she had bought at Many Hands Gallery, the ones with glazed fish, birds, elephants, used the cloth napkins held together with brass rings, the silverware from G's box, and Waterford crystal glasses for the orange juice.

Ben carried bowls and plates of food to the table from the kitchen.

"Why four place settings?"

Lisa looked at the table. Why, indeed? She couldn't tell if she'd been thinking of G joining them, or maybe Michael.

"Good question."

In the spare bedroom she grabbed the blankets from the foot of the bed, yanked hard, and uncovered Cody, who lay naked with a pillow over her head.

"What the fuck?" she grumbled, grabbing for the heat and comfort of the blankets.

"You slept in. Breakfast is on the table."

"I'm not hungry."

"Yes, you are. You're going to want to eat this. Trust me."

"Oh my god. You are such a pain."

"Up. Get up. Or I'll get the ice cubes next."

"Okay. Okay." Cody rolled out of bed, stepped into a pair of jeans crumpled on the floor, tossed on a t-shirt that must have been Ben's, as it hung off her shoulders and down to her knees.

Back at the table, Ben passed bowls, announcing the contents of each with a flourish.

"Herb-fried potatoes with a splash of truffle oil." He'd found G's truffle oil? Lisa didn't even know where he kept it, off-limits to her.

"What herbs?" Cody asked.

Ben smiled. "Thyme, sage, a little oregano."

Turks and Caicos came running through the house, side by side, sliding across the wooden floor, bouncing their heads into the front door, even before they heard the knock.

"There's your fourth," Ben said, grin wide on his face.

Lisa could see it was Michael. He could wait. He hadn't been invited. She might have to say something directly to him about just stopping by whenever he wanted. But he was half owner now. She scooped potatoes onto her plate. "What's next?" Lisa said. "The potatoes look great."

"How about if what's next is we answer the door," Cody said. "Come in!" she yelled.

Michael entered, saw the fourth plate, took off his coat and sat down. "Hey, thanks for thinking of me."

"We weren't thinking of you. At all," Lisa said.

"Didn't you get my text?" Lisa reached in her pocket for her phone, pulled it out, slammed it a little too hard against the table.

"It's dead."

"Well, it must have been ESP, then. I am hungry." He picked a potato off the platter and tossed it into his mouth, looked at Lisa. "Is this G's truffle oil?"

"Ask him."

Ben passed the next bowl. "Sautéed spinach with pearl onions and gruyere. Truffle oil was in the back of the fridge behind the mango chutney."

Lisa plugged her earbuds into the phone, into her ears, turned on the meditative music, tired of listening to Cody's wit, Ben's accomplishments, Michael's lack of accomplishments. She ate more potatoes, each bite drifting her back into G's arms, bed, life. This whole thing she was living now had been carved out of his thoughts, his plans, his desires. In addition to the oak tree to the head that had forced a new way of living and thinking, his note buried on the computer pointed to something unexplainable yet sensible, a new way of her being in the world. Cody and Ben would head back to San Francisco after breakfast. Lisa was glad, couldn't wait. Too much of Cody led to too much of Cody, and the unknown Ben factor spun it out even more.

Not that she was looking forward to alone time with Michael, but it had to be done, she had to move forward to figure out what was next.

After Ben cleaned up the kitchen mess, washed and dried all the dishes, returned G's truffle oil to its designated spot, he and Cody packed their things, and he carried suitcases to the Panamera.

Lisa noticed the maneuver. "What's happening here?" She looked at Cody.

"I'm driving back with Ben. Leaving my car here. If that's okay."

"What do you mean?"

"I mean I'll be back for Christmas break and I plan on spending the whole time here with you. Thus, my car, here, in your driveway, waiting for me when I get back. Ben will bring me down."

Lisa smiled one of those glued-on grins, bent over and whispered in Cody's ear. "How do you know this guy will last?"

"Oh, he will."

Lisa continued, "Either you're going to dump this guy after he settles your suit, or he's going to dump you when he figures out how fucking crazy you are." Cody laughed out loud, hugged her hard.

"Yeah, but look at me having wild fun along the way to finding out."

"Finding out what?" Ben said as he ducked into the Porsche.

Lisa looked at him. "Whether or not you're a fraud like the rest of them."

Ben smiled. "Oh, there's no question. Just as fraudulent. But I do have the attorney's gift of knowing what to say when."

"Right," Lisa said. "Thanks for the nice breakfast."

"Thanks for the nice hospitality."

"Are you two lovebirds done cooing yet?" Cody said. "We've got paperwork to shuffle, statements to make. See you in ten days."

Lisa leaned in again, kissed Cody on the lips, held her cheeks in her hands. "Why did you lie to me about the password?"

Cody shook her head. "Oh. That. It's complicated. We'll talk."

Michael sat on the porch steps watching, listening. Lisa felt his presence through all of it, like the hawks that gathered in the oaks, or a fresh FBI agent looking for evidence, truth, justice. Ben didn't rev the engine or toss gravel from his tires as most Porsche drivers would do. He backed out softly, gave a one-finger wave to Lisa, a nod to Michael, drifted onto Porter Gulch and disappeared down the road.

Lisa beckoned Michael to follow her as she slipped the earbuds back in. At the safe, she ripped a page off a notepad and wrote the combination down before handing it to Michael.

"Try it. Twice. Memorize it." He opened the lock on the first try, tore the note into tiny pieces.

"What have we got?"

She didn't like hearing him refer to them as we. But that's the way it was. At least for now, until they could work out the details. Figure out who'd become the alpha male. A role that neither of them were suited for.

"I'm not sure what you mean."

"In the safe."

"Just what I told you before."

"Right. The ten-k. The fifty pounds. The seeds. But that's it?" He stuck his head in the safe, and it made her think of Hansel and Gretel. Could she hit him over the head with a shovel, stuff him inside?

"What else are you looking for?"

"Something from Gregory. Instructions. His idea for the future."

"His idea for the future was that he'd still be here. That none of this was happening."

"But it is happening." She pulled up G's note in her head. Her semi-photographic memory came in handy sometimes. There was nothing in it that Michael couldn't read. It was probably a good idea to let him take a look.

"Lock that thing. Come on."

Michael shut the safe door, spun the lock to reset it.

She drank a third cup of coffee as Michael read the printed note from G. The mug was one her cousin, Leta, from Chicago, had given her two Christmases ago, that read, "My cousin has the best cousin in the world." She laughed.

"What? What's funny?" Michael asked.

Of course he'd wonder that. A me-first thinker. She held up the mug. "Leta gave me this. It's funny. Makes me miss her. Makes me think I should go to Evanston for Christmas. Skip the shit-show that is sure to arise with Cody and Ben. And you."

He set the note down, picked up the list of local clients Gregory had left for him. "Why do you expect a shit-show with me?"

She didn't know how candid she should be with him. Should they jump right into this stuff and get ugly now, or take their time to drift into it? Sand through an hourglass. "Sometimes you can be high maintenance, Michael."

He nodded. "I see. This is a relative thing, I'm guessing. I mean, as opposed to you being so low maintenance." She *was* low maintenance. She didn't know if he was being sarcastic, suggesting that her maintenance was at least as bad as his, or if he truly believed that she wasn't much of anything, someone who never pushed back, never required maintenance. "Or are you thinking just because I'm with Pamela I've earned a maintenance badge to match the one you think she has pinned to her chest?"

They could dig this hole for way too long. "What do you think of G's note?"

"First thing I'm thinking is that there's probably a lot more buried in that computer."

"But isn't this what you want? Control of the local clientele?"

"I'm not sure I like hearing the word *clientele,* or my name used in conjunction with it. This was Gregory's thing from the beginning. He just sucked me into it. Kind of like the way he sucked you into it seven years ago."

"What's that supposed to mean?"

"What? You don't think he sucked you into this life, his life, his kingdom?" She shifted, took another sip of coffee. "You don't think he went to Point Reyes Station looking for someone just like you he could tempt into a new life, a steady income, offering a salary better than that of a fledgling bookshop owner?"

23

FRIDAY
12-6-19

I T FELT GOOD TO BE BACK IN THE OFFICE. Bianca's loud voice blasting over the top of the walls, negotiating with a client. Even though it was a monthly sublet, it was the closest thing she had to something she could call hers, something that didn't include Gregory's stamp of approval. She was glad to have Cody back in Colorado, Michael at arm's length, figuring out how to deal with the local customers without Gregory's management and intrusion.

Time to get back to Pious Rebel. A new blog post. Watching the regularity of traffic racing by in both directions, in and out of town. Earbuds twisted tightly into her ears, she heard only the echo of music, the bass of voices worrying about who would clean what when, and how much should be paid by whom. She placed nine of her fingers on the keyboard, the only exception being her left thumb, which she had successfully and neatly sliced open with a paring knife while trying to remove the peel of an orange at breakfast. The fresh juice had been worth it, but her thumb now stuck out from her other digits, wrapped in gauze and bright green tape to hold it all together. She hadn't realized before that she never used the left thumb on the keyboard, just the right to hit the Space Bar. She had no excuse not to dig into a new post and make her presence known to the world once again, even though that world didn't really exist yet outside her head. But the key word was *yet*. There were rumblings in her brain that *yet* was a temporary condition that would soon be modified. She hunted for a title, typed in *The Search for Yetis*, smiled, erased it. Then *Point Reyes Redux*, quickly erased it, thought of Ryan, of Cody and Ryan, or a Ryan who was not as madly in love with her as she had once imagined. She shrunk her viewing audience down to its true size — Michael. Maybe Michael. But only if he was trying to figure her out, gain access through this slit of a window she had provided him. Pamela didn't know about the blog, would most likely never see it, so what the hell. New title: *The Trouble with Laws and In-Laws*. She had no plan for what might get said in a piece with this title, but she thought it had potential. No words came. She switched to the Spelling Bee on the *New York Times* website, found the pangram within ten seconds: *outgrown*. She tried *towngown*, now living in a university town where such words were made up and tossed around. The *Times* didn't like it. She stopped after keying in *wrong, wrung, grunt*, a series of negative words that brought her back to Pamela, Michael.

> When a significant other walks outside to chop down trees
> and never returns, the trees instead chopping him down,
> flattening him into a lifeless lump of hardening flesh, what
> remains, what detritus blows about in the wind, what
> memories force their way into restless dreams, what fills one
> day after another, what occupies a mind that had grown
> used to routine and what seemed like comfort? Laws and
> in-laws come to mind. Laws that govern real property and
> possession and intellectual property and who gets what and
> who deserves what. Seven years and the statute of
> limitations and lawyers named Ben. She paused, thought
> about Ben, Cody. She had told neither of them about the
> blog, so it wouldn't matter. Left thumb pointed toward the
> ceiling, she continued. And in-laws. A brother ... you know
> who you are. How you are? Where you are? Trying to figure
> out what one cares about, what is legal, what is sensible, not
> that any of this or anything will ever make sense again.

96

A man on a bike wheeled past the window. The basket behind the seat was full, scarves, spare shoes. The handlebars were wrapped with torn shreds of blankets. A carrier pulled behind the bike, crammed with every possession the man owned: a sleeping bag, a lightweight waterproof tent, dishes, mugs, a couple of joints in a baggie to keep dry, with a lighter. She imagined. More. Things she never had to worry about. Things the in-law never needed to consider. Nor his wife. Or whatever she was. Back at it. *Are you paying attention? Are you watching me?* The notion of stalking, or watching, came to mind. Would Michael be paying attention? And if so, why? Calculating his next play in this larger-than-life game of Go they were engaged in? Or just for fun. To see what might happen next. Or to predict what might happen next. *Are you a seasoned watcher? Are you any good at it? Do you care what comes next, or are you willing to accept anything?*

Lisa reread the post, disjointed, awkward, no topic much less topic sentence. She clicked on the Publish link and it was gone. Live. In the world. In Michael's world. She heard Bianca cackle on the other side of the wall. She wanted to run out to the lobby, look at her computer screen, see if Bianca had figured out her presence, her handle. She let it go. Picked up *I Really Knead You*, cackled over the wall herself, remembering her mother's penchant for puns, every chance she got. She reread the first paragraph and thought about the continuum beginning with stability and ending with love, or vice versa. Or two separate continua, intersecting each other, one moving from no love to way too much love, and the other moving from no stability to way too much stability.

She slipped back to the Spelling Bee, found *tong*, just one point. She was at 38 now, needed 74 to achieve Genius status. This one would be tough. She gave up and went back to *The Baker's Quintet*, Book 1, page 102. The narrator's name was Celia. Lisa snorted. Mother and her anagrams, needed some kind of wordplay to spice up their lives. Was Alice Celia? Not if the turkey baster story was true. But who knows? She'd never really know, had to make it all up. Historical fiction. Mix the truths with the desires. But if Celia's baker was Lisa's father, that would have changed everything. The baker loved Celia. Celia loved the baker. This continuum they rode had very little to do with stability, regardless of whether it was parallel or perpendicular or existing in separate universes. They rocked each other in bed, drenched each other in sweat, carried it into the kitchen and made sweet rolls and buns that their dedicated customers couldn't resist. But by page 120 it was feeling like it might not have been enough for Celia, that something was missing, that the crates of sugar were clogging their arteries, raising their blood sugar, a silence running through their bodies that was maddeningly loud.

Wont. One more point. 39.

It was nearly noon. More folks were walking past her window. A woman in high-heel shoes. A man wearing camouflage pants and a backpack. A woman with earbuds plugged into an iPhone in her tight rear pocket. Everybody probably on their way to lunch. She was hungry, needed to take a long walk down Pacific Avenue and find some food.

Another man pushing a bike. All his possessions tied on a handlebar. A whole life bundled up as if it mattered. And did it really? She closed the computer, put a bookmark on page 120 of Alice's first manuscript, walked through the lobby and waved goodbye to Bianca and the no-name receptionist, headed down the street. Friday on Pacific Avenue was busier than usual. Especially on First Fridays, when the downtown community prepped itself for the literary and art and foodie crowd who flocked in to find out what was new, to bump into friends, to find excuses to party and drink and smoke.

As she walked through El Palomar's wooden doors, she flashed on the seven letters in today's Bee, an "n" in the middle, along with "w-r-t-g-o-u." *Runt*, she thought. She needed a five- or six-letter word to bump up closer to 74 if she wanted to be a Genius today. She wanted to be a Genius every day. Amazing was second best. No good. Gregory had never played with her, thought it a silly game, wasting one's time on words and thinking about words when you could be out in your greenhouse or workshop. A waitperson showed her to a table. She was irked that G had never played with her, had never allowed her into his workshop. That was about over. She'd go in today. First read a few more pages of *Knead*, find a couple more words, then take the newly found key and open up the shrine. She had no idea what she'd find in there, except the Harley that she envisioned Cody and Ben hopping on, heading up the coast toward Davenport.

"Can I have the Burrito Michoacana?" Lisa asked. "And a lemon Crystal Geyser." She was trying to eat less meat, for the sake of the planet, for the sake of her body, and mostly for the sake of the animals who were raised to feed an all-about-me world. Today she'd eat veggies, but tomorrow she might very well order the chicken kebab at Carpo's. Or pork sliders.

Waiting for her food, she gave up the purity of becoming a Genius using only her brain. She opened Anagram Solver, typed in two sets of the letters, quickly found *gorgon, turnout, untorn, wonton, unwon,* and *unworn.* 76 points. Genius!

•   •   •

Back in the office, she closed her eyes, realized she wasn't disappointed about anything yet today. The lunch had been excellent. The walk was good. She had read another ten pages about Celia and her baker husband while waiting for the burrito. She plugged into the meditation music, laid back in her chair, envisioned the T-chart.

A light knock on the window behind her head pulled her out of a rare nap. It was Pamela. Lisa wasn't exactly sure if she was still buried on the edges of a bad dream. No. The scrunched- up face without a smile was real, nose against the window, heat flaring against the pane from her nostrils. Red glasses resting on the tip of her nose, brown hair wrapped up in a bun. Lisa waved her around to the front door of the office, slipped the open manuscript into its container and dropped it inside the banker's box, ripped a blank page off her easel pad and covered up the T-chart before opening the door to Pamela and closing it behind her. Damn that Michael! Couldn't keep his mouth shut.

"Well, hello," Lisa offered. "Haven't seen you in forever."

"Five weeks." She sat down before being offered a seat.

"Right."

Lisa drifted back to the front row at the cremation center. There had only been the three of them watching. As they walked to their cars, Pamela had asked, "Why no memorial? Didn't he deserve at least that much?"

In unison Lisa and Michael had replied, "He didn't want one."

"What does that matter? He's dead. Memorials are for the living. To give the grievers their venue."

"And who do you think would attend a memorial for G other than the three of us?"

"Oh. They'd show up. Write up an obit. Put it in the *Sentinel.* Post it on Facebook."

"Maybe put up a sign on telephone poles like a missing cat," Michael had added, a grin trying to work its way around his lips.

"Hilarious," Pamela said. "Zack would show up. Clients from town. Maybe even some from down south."

"Great!" Michael said. "Just what we need is to be seen in public with clients."

"Probably Cody. Isn't she your best friend?" Lisa had ignored the question, knew it was laced with the bad taste of tequila from Cody's foul mouth.

The discussion had ended with them all leaving in separate cars, heading in different directions.

•　　•　　•

"Hello?" Pamela said, "Anybody home?"

"Sorry," Lisa said. "Just remembering the last time we saw each other." Pamela nodded.

Lisa didn't want to ask her how she knew where her office was, instead watched her as she nosed around the walls, checked out her wall hangings, tried to read through the paper covering the T-chart.

Finally, Pamela spoke. "Nice poem by Joe Stroud. He's wonderful."

"How do you know him?" Lisa asked.

"I took a poetry class from him straight out of high school. Cabrillo had all those great writers back in the day."

Lisa hated when people talked like that — back in the day. As if they were seasoned and wiser than everyone else. As if she had a leg up because she had shared her poems with Joe Stroud. She paused her thoughts, shook her head at herself for using the leg-up cliché, even if it was just a thought. Didn't like it when others used them. Disliked it even more when they crept into her own thoughts. Stay fresh, crisp, pay attention. Thank you, Alice.

"By the way," Lisa pointed at the wall, the lack of ceiling, whispered, "they can all hear everything."

"How do you know that?" Pamela frowned.

"Because I hear everything they say."

Lisa's phone clinked. She quickly grabbed it, held it close to her face, away from Pamela. It was Michael. Of course it was Michael.

Hey! Wanted to warn you. Pamela is headed downtown, looking for your office. For you.

Lisa smiled, thumbed in Too late. What's she want with me?

Lisa looked at Pamela. "Cody. Lunch break in Colorado."

No clue. Good luck.

She replied, Thanks. I think., before zipping her phone away in her purse.

Pamela stood. "Just thought I'd stop by and check out your new office. Thanks for reminding me about Joe Stroud." She turned and left.

Lisa shook her head, had no idea what that was about.

24

SATURDAY
12-7-19

O N SATURDAY MORNING ELOISE STRETCHED when the phone pinged. Alice's manuscript was spread across the bedspread, Eloise rattling the pages with her paws. Lisa reached for the phone, thought about how this electronic extension of her life, her brain, demanded such attention. She should take a hammer to it, never answer it again. But Cody was so far away. It was her only way to keep in touch. Until next week, when she'd be here way too much. It was Michael. She didn't want to engage with him right now, was still thinking about *I Really Knead You,* wondering how much of Celia had come directly from Alice's life rather than her imagination. She'd never know the truth, so it wouldn't hurt to speculate, shape it to fit her own needs, the way she wanted to remember the past.

Went to Nutcracker in San Jose last night. Did Pamela drive you crazy yesterday?

She turned the phone off, rubbed Eloise's back to get her to move off the papers, scooped them up, put them back together in the right order. She removed the last chapter, propped herself up on three of G's pillows, and read.

It had been a mistake, a mistake of passion, like the whole marriage had been. For six months, they had managed to pay most of the bills on time, or at least eventually. Celia's dreams of making costumes for the local theater put on hold as she worked side by side with William to perfect his art, the braided bread loaves, the decorated cookies, the wedding and mitzvah cakes, the potato rolls and garlic cheese twists, to continue to grow their dedicated clientele with fresh goods, friendly faces, caring about the customers and their families.

Now this mistake. They had tripled up: the rhythm method, condoms, and a diaphragm. No way would they allow a wayward sperm to make its way to its frenzied goal and change their dreams, William's dreams. But the visit to the gynecologist's office last week had confirmed her suspicion that on Valentine's Day, which by all accounts fit into the appropriate rhythm, it was possible that the diaphragm was placed too quickly and maybe crooked, without the proper amount of gel, that they had used only one condom instead of two, and that because of the passion that overcame both of them, there was a slight chance the condom had broken while he was inside her.

"Good news!" Doctor Johns had announced, big grin on his face. "You're going to have a baby."

"When?" was all she could muster.

"Late November, early December."

"Damn!" she was surprised to hear herself say out loud.

"Why 'damn'? Are you not happy about this pregnancy? You and William seem like such loving people, I'd think you would welcome this Christmas gift from God."

It was a small town. The doctor and his wife bought all their baked goods from them, picked up two boxes of food every Sunday morning, one to take to church, the other to drop off at the Homeless Project.

"Oh, sorry. No, I'm very happy," she lied. "We're just so busy for Thanksgiving, Christmas, all the holidays. New Year's, Valentine's Day. I'm just thinking about how a big belly will get in the way of all my tasks."

"Think of it this way. In fourteen or fifteen years, you'll have a kid who can stand by your side and help you out."

Celia had to get out of there before she hit this kind-hearted man who didn't have a clue. Before she took her fists and pounded on his chest, kicked his shins, left bruises, made him understand how much she did not want to bring a child into her current life with William.

"Did you say daughter?"

"Oh, sorry. These new-fangled sonograms. I just assumed you'd want to know."

Celia grabbed her coat, picked up her purse, and ran out the door into the street without looking, without thinking of anything except the disruption this accident would cause in their lives.

By the time she reached the bakery, the line was out the door and wrapped around the front window. She peeked in, head buried beneath a scarf and dark glasses, saw William busily waiting on one customer at a time, a big grin on his face, putting a hand on a shoulder, shaking a hand, placing a loaf in a bag. She really did love him, more than she loved herself, more than she loved the thought of being nominated for a Tony for costumes she had designed and sewn for the Broadway hit of the year. She didn't know yet what the show would be, if it would be a revival or something fresh and new. But she had imagined herself on stage, looking out at an audience on their feet, clapping and whistling, William in the front row, jumping up and down, tears dripping down his face.

She couldn't tell him. Not now. It was too soon, and she couldn't wait fifteen years for the help. She'd take care of this. Her friend Margie knew someone. Inside, she tied her apron across her back, thought about the tiny life growing inside her, wanted to curl up in the back room and wail. Instead, she rubbed William's back, kissed him on the cheek, pushed him back to the kitchen, which is

where he really shined. She grabbed a sugar cookie from
the case, broke it in half, shoved it in her mouth as she
helped the next customer.

"What's wrong?" The customer asked.

"Nothing," Celia answered. 'Why do you ask?' she said,
as she bagged a half-dozen francese rolls and handed
them to the woman who showed up every other day.

"You just looked so disappointed."

Lisa put the chapter down. *It must be genetic,* she thought. Alice, as Celia, unable to keep feelings of disappointment from invading her life, changing her mood, altering the ways she lived.

She took the rest of the day off from Alice and Celia, from the office, from responding to texts from Cody and Michael, from thinking about blog posts, from anything that forced her to pay attention to things she should be paying attention to. She hiked up to the end of Porter Gulch Road with Turks and Caicos, had to decide whether to head into the Forest of Nisene Marks State Park, or veer over to the Land of Medicine Buddha. She'd only been to the dharma retreat once. G had taken her there, wanted to buy something for a friend from their store. It had been pleasant enough, people who seemed to care about the world and other people more than themselves. But she didn't want people right now. Just wanted the dogs and the massive expanse of Nisene Marks to wear her body down, to empty her mind.

She had found one of G's packs in the closet of his office. She filled it with oranges, dry-roasted cashews, apples, dog food, and enough water for all of them. She had never hiked here before, liked that it was all new to her, that she had to look ahead to figure out how to navigate a canyon, a ridge, a thicket too dense to pass through. She did bring her cell phone, in case she broke an ankle or something else that would strand her. It was in her shirt pocket, resting just over where she thought her heart was. It kept buzzing, made her think she was having a heart attack or a-fib. She ignored it, them, whoever they were. She needed not to be needed, to be on this solo journey with her two friends who didn't speak, who romped through the forest as if it were theirs, as if they'd been here every day of their lives.

By the time she reached home it was dark. Eloise was waiting to be fed. *Saturday Night Live* was almost on. Lights were flashing on the message machine. She placed her cell phone upside down on the kitchen counter, microwaved the last frozen container of G's Armenian rice pilaf, put it in a big bowl with a big spoon, slipped under the covers of her bed, flicked on the remote, and was happy to see Jennifer Lopez in the middle of her monologue. She loved Jennifer Lopez, one of those women who did it all, who could do anything she ever tried, could probably have been an astronaut, a senator, a blogger. She wanted to stay awake for it, but her muscles ached, and she fell asleep to the chorus of snores led by Turks and Caicos.

25

SUNDAY
12-8-19

W HEN SHE WOKE UP, LATER THAN USUAL, she had forgotten Gregory was dead, expected to find him in the bed, his bare back pointed at her, her legs scissored around his, a warm embrace. She smashed her fist into his pillow over a dozen times until her wrist throbbed. "Goddamn you! Goddamn all of you!" Eloise and the dogs disappeared, left her alone with her rage. After a quick shower she went straight to G's office, didn't think of feeding herself or the animals, typed in *lisahardrock* and watched the desktop appear, inviting her in, G smirking at her, saying *Let's see what you can find today.* She spent hours digging inside every folder, opening every file, finding nothing of use. She did a search for Pamela — nothing. She did a search for Cody Rocks and Codyrocks — nothing. She dug into the computer settings. Cody had taught her how to change the password from *lisahardrock.* But what? Something to do with none of them. Something none of them knew anything about. For a minute, the phrase *'none of them'* stuck. The *them* had to be anyone from her past or present that could identify her, track her, know anything about her.

A fresh phrase, plunging forward into this new future. *Blogbaby*. She hated it, but it would work for now, would keep Cody out of her business. She knew she'd need to change it again soon, maybe even before dinner, which reminded her she hadn't had breakfast or lunch, hadn't downed her usual three cups of coffee yet, and what about Eloise? The dogs could take care of themselves, but Eloise would be pissed by now. The electric can opener brought Eloise in a hurry.

Back at the keyboard she dug in, finally found Zack's email address, sent him a message:

Zack,

I'm sorry to be sending this from G's email, but I'm on his computer and so it goes. How's Sarah Palin's view of Russia today? I need a big favor. You remember my cat, Eloise? She has become addicted to the canned salmon you gave Gregory. I need to order more. Cases. Maybe four. If you could FedEx them ASAP and let me know how much I owe you, I'll send it through PayPal.

I hope all is well with you and the family. I'm trying to hang in and figure out what's next for me.

Warmly,

Lisa

• • •

By dinner she was fried, her back hurt, she had a pain shooting up her leg that felt like another attack of sciatica, which she hadn't had for a couple of years, and she was hungry. So far there was very little of interest on the computer. She could start sending off emails to everyone on G's list, but that might be dangerous given the nature of G's work, and she had no idea about the depth of his relationships with them. And it was difficult to tell whether some were men or women, diverse names such as Dreamweaver and Goldenrod.

She grabbed Cody's keys off the kitchen counter, ready to head to the driveway to start her car, drive it into town to get some Thai food, when the cell phone pinged. She had intentionally left it in the kitchen to avoid having to deal with anyone today, barely dealing with herself. Michael. If she kept this phone, she needed some new friends, some pings she'd look forward to, not feeling disappointed every time it beckoned, knowing it was Cody or Michael wanting or needing something from her.

How's your life today?

That was better than she expected. Not leading with a request for a progress report.

She continued walking to Cody's car as she typed.

Bad day. Woke up thinking G was still alive. After nine hours buried in the guts of his computer, I'm pissed, and glad he's not here. Glad Cody's not here. Glad you're not here.

There was no immediate response. She opened the car door, sat down, typed some more.

Sorry. Not happy today. I'm about to start Cody's car and take it down to Sawasdee to order some of that great chicken satay they've got.

Saliva filled her mouth just thinking about it. The pieces were so plump, moist.

Lisa could see the three dots bouncing on her phone, letting her know Michael was in the middle of typing something back to her.

That peanut sauce is the best! I tried to get their recipe once, but no chance they'd give it out.

She nodded, even though there was nobody there to see her affirmation. There was a long pause on both ends of the thread.

Finally another message appeared.

Pamela is with her mother tonight. Binging on The Crown. Olivia Coleman as the older queen.

She smiled. He had stopped short of inviting himself to meet her at the restaurant. Left it open for her to do so if she chose. So far he seemed more like a normal human being than usual. Though what did she know about normal human beings? She wasn't one herself. Hadn't lived with one the past seven years. And Cody was far from normal. Ryan may have been the last normal human being she remembered spending any time with.

What about this? she finally texted. You meet me at the restaurant and we'll split an order of the satay. Extra peanut sauce.

The quick response said: Only if we can order garlic shrimp eggplant and fresh spring rolls as well.

Of course. she answered. On my way.

When she walked in, Michael was already seated at a table, two bottles of Singha waiting.

"Look." She threw up her palms. "You can't be doing this!" She stayed on her feet.

"What?" Michael asked.

"Making decisions for me and assuming that just because you like Singha beer that I'm going to like it as well!" She sat down. "I am just so tired of living other people's lives, living up to their expectations. Digging through their fucking computer for cryptic clues to their pasts. My future."

Michael took another sip of beer. "I thought you liked Singha."

"That's not the point. Is it?"

"I'm not sure what the point is."

"Right. Me either." She picked up the beer, took a swig. "Yes. I do like Singha. But I can take care of myself. You know?"

"Yes. I do know." He opened the menu.

"But thank you. For ordering it."

"You're welcome. Shall we get what we texted about, or go wild and crazy with this menu?"

"I can do without wild and crazy right now."

When the waitperson came to their table, Michael pointed at Lisa, and she placed the order. "Oh, and we'd like an extra portion of the peanut sauce."

They sat quietly for a couple of minutes, watched a line of people backed up at the counter to pick up take-out orders.

One irate man was yelling at the clerk. "I've been waiting here over an hour! This is ridiculous. Your website said it would be ready in fifteen minutes. This is irresponsible! You guys should be shut down." Three more takeout customers entered before he finished his tirade.

Michael leaned forward. "Glad we're not in a hurry."

"Aren't we?" Lisa answered.

"Good point. I'm not."

"I guess I'm not either. But I haven't eaten all day. Trying to find something of value in that damn computer."

"What is it you're looking for? You think he's hiding something?"

"I'm just trying to understand the implications of the little note he left. Suggesting there was more."

"The way I read it said he was more interested in your reaction to whatever's in his workshop."

"Yeah, there's that."

"Have you gone in yet?"

"No. I want to finish with the computer first. Dig deep and make sure there's nothing else there. Aren't you interested in that? Aren't you thinking about the goddamn secrets and mysteries hidden around the property?"

"No. I'm not."

"Not sure I believe that. And even if I did, don't you think Pamela's thinking about it?"

"You should believe what I tell you. I have no need or interest to lie to you or anyone else. And this is not about Pamela and her thoughts."

"There are just so many unknowns around this life that Gregory built, around me, you, around himself. I'm a bit tired of it all."

"Why don't we just sell it all. Liquidate everything and rid ourselves of it and him."

"Is that what you really want?"

"Not necessarily, but it sounds like it might be what you want, or what's best for you."

"Again, don't go thinking you know what I'm thinking or want. You can't have any way of knowing when I don't know myself."

"Fair enough. All I can really know is what you tell me now, or what you might be implying in your blog posts."

The waitperson delivered the five chunks of chicken satay with two bowls of peanut sauce.

"Oh, jeez, this looks good!" Lisa took two pieces, set them on her plate, and used the tines of the fork to pull the meat away from the skewer before dunking a piece in the sauce and dropping it in her mouth. Michael did the same.

"You've read my posts?"

"Of course. Did you think I wouldn't? You told me about it."

"Just didn't think you'd care."

"Now you're the one putting thoughts, or lack of them, in my head."

"Sorry. I don't know yet what I'm doing with this blog thing. Don't know what I'm saying or why I'm saying it."

"To be honest with you, neither do I, but given that we're trying to sort out Gregory's business, figuring out how it affects our lives, if the only access I have to your brain and thoughts is through a few online posts, I'll take that. I read everything you put up there."

"So you can critique me?"

"So I can know you a little better."

"After seven years of, what, being in the family, you don't think you know me?"

"No way. First of all, Gregory kept you hidden away from the world. And then there's you, also keeping yourself hidden away from the world."

"That reminds me, how did Pamela just happen to figure out where my office is and just happen to show up knocking on my window?"

"Oh, that. She snoops. She wakes up in the middle of the night, checks my phone, my emails. A very good detective."

"And you allow her to do this?"

Michael shrugged. "How is it any different than what you let Gregory do to you?"

Michael took his knife and cut the fifth skewer of chicken in half, took his piece, dipped each end and ate it.

"I don't know that it is. We don't know each other well enough to be able to dive into each other's psyches and make sense of ourselves or each other."

"I will tell you that I look forward to your blog posts, at least for now. So, please, keep writing, keep thinking."

This man was so different than Gregory. How did they both fall out of the same mother?

26

MONDAY
12-9-19

I N THE OFFICE WAY TOO EARLY. Couldn't sleep. Woke up and fed the animals, jumped into Cody's car and drove straight to the Buttery, where she ordered a double oatmeal with brown sugar and bananas, a large San Pellegrino, and two Russian tea cookies. She got the prime parking space, could stare at the dirty fenders and windows of Cody's car twelve feet away. The oatmeal was good, hot, just what she needed. Sliced bananas, brown sugar. The heaters in the office weren't working, her feet and hands were almost numb. She pulled out her computer, opened it, clicked on her journal, and started typing a new entry — not so much for the content of the sentences, but to warm her hands, to get blood moving, up through the fingers, the arms, across her heart and into her brain.

She didn't go straight to the website and open a new post, knowing now that Michael was really out there, paying attention to what she was posting. In the journal, she wrote:

> I'm falling behind with my intended output. Not that I even understand what my intended output is. More blog posts.

Solving at least one of the many mysteries of my life. Saying
something that I think my audience of one might want to
hear. Know that I am thinking about you, my audience, and
am therefore consciously holding back on the nature of my
content, typing these sentences now before 7:00 a.m. mostly
to warm myself, to break loose solidified plaque from
arteries, to ignore things that I should attend to, things that
I'm unwilling to share right now. Maybe later. Maybe
tomorrow.

The two bells at the front door went off. Even though her office
door was closed, she heard Bianca yell, "Hey there, Pious Rebel. Found
you! I like what you're doing. Keep it up." Damn. Now she had two
audience members to worry about. Opening the door, she walked to
Bianca's desk, saw the Pious Rebel page up on her computer screen.

"How long have you known?"

Bianca smirked. "Since your first post. Did you forget about those
two bottles of wine we had at Barceloneta? You spilled everything."

Lisa hadn't remembered much from that night, except for the
large quantity of wine.

"Damn! Now I'll need to change it."

"What the hell? Why? You don't want me reading it? What the
hell's it for, then, if you don't want people reading it? Or maybe it's
just *me* you don't want reading it. Is that it? You can be honest with
me. I can take it."

"No! Of course that's not it." Lisa wasn't sure if this was a lie or
not. In a way, she didn't want Bianca reading it. Just another filter
clogging her words. But she'd need to get over that. Or take the blog
down. "It's just strange for me. Doing this at all."

"Get over it. It's no longer your life. You're a shared commodity.
Get used to it. How many followers do you have?"

"I don't know. I guess two, counting you."

"You guess? Come on. Sit down. Let's check the statistics." Bianca
gave her a brief lesson that showed her where she could view all the
analytics, know how many people were following her, how many hits
per day, if the hits were coming from the same or different IP addresses.

Lisa stood up, said, "That's kind of scary."

114

"What?"

"I don't know. The details. The lying in wait. The stalking."

"It only feels like stalking," Bianca said. "That's your fault. You didn't turn on the Comments sections of your pages, so you have no idea what people are thinking about your posts. Turn them on and you'll get an earful. Well, at least from me and the other guy who's following you. Who is the other guy?"

She wasn't sure how much she wanted Bianca to know about her life. "Gregory's brother."

"Oh, that's fun! What kind of guy is he?"

"I don't know yet. Still trying to figure that out. Thanks for the help."

Lisa went back to her office, shut the door, expecting the other three office mates to appear soon and for the noise level to ramp up to its usual din.

She lifted the bulk of papers her mother had titled *I Really Knead You*, straightened the pages, set them back in their box. She wasn't ready yet to dig into the second book, still needed some time to think about what life had been like for her mother, what it was in her life, or missing from her life, that inspired her to write about Celia and the baker. She opened Safari and searched for "Is disappointment hereditary?" Nothing. Just an article written in 2005 talking about disappointment in the Genome Project. She already knew that depression was hereditary, that if your parents suffered from it you were three times more likely to suffer from it yourself.

She typed in "Is disappointment a cousin to depression?" The first article listed was titled "When Is Depression Not Depression?" The first line read "Depression is not depression when it's disappointment." It was a *Psychology Today* article and she read the whole thing. The line that stood out was "Pessimism thrives in the wake of disappointment."

She hadn't really felt much pessimism in Celia, her mother's character, just the disappointment that crept in by the end of the first book. She opened *piousrebel.com*, a new post:

I've never thought of myself as a pessimist.
Merriam-Webster defines pessimist as "a person who is inclined to expect poor outcomes." That doesn't really describe me, though I guess that's what most of us would say

about ourselves. I think back to my mother, Alice, and I don't remember her ever calling me a pessimist. There were other adjectives, but that's another post. I've had two exes in the past ten years, and neither of them referred to me as a pessimist. So when I read in *Psychology Today* that "pessimism thrives in the wake of disappointment," I have to reevaluate my tendency toward disappointment. Just because partners or mothers haven't attached labels may not tell the whole story. I tend to keep my disappointments tucked away, out of eyesight or earshot of others. In my new office, where I'm typing this potential blog post right now, I keep a T-chart indicating my disappointments and accomplishments. I haven't written anything there in the past couple of weeks.

She stopped typing, turned and looked at the chart, stood and picked up the purple marker. Under 'Accomplishments', she wrote, "Haven't added to the chart in two weeks." Under 'Disappointments', she added, "Haven't added to the chart in two weeks."

"See how you are," she said out loud.

"What?" Bianca yelled from the other side of the wall.

"Nothing," Lisa yelled back.

"Doesn't sound like nothing. Sounds like you're writing on your T-chart."

Lisa didn't ask her how she knew about the T-chart, made the assumption that Bianca was a snoop, checked out her office when she wasn't there. She should introduce her to Pamela,

Back to the post:

There are not a lot of people in my life at the moment. Fewer than ten. Only one of them whom I consider a friend. Most of them disappoint me one way or another. It doesn't disappoint me that I know so few people here. For now, it's probably easier, until I figure a few things out. But that will all change. Soon. Watch for it.

She reread the post, found it mostly boring, but published it anyway.

27

TUESDAY
12-10-19

O N PAGE 10 OF *ROCKS AND ROLLS*, Lisa read how Celia hid the pregnancy from William for the first two weeks, wrapping the bulge in muslin. Hiding the need to vomit by making too many trips to the trash bin. She didn't sleep nights. Slipped out of bed and worried herself all night long. She didn't want a baby. Didn't want an abortion. She didn't want to be staring at the ceiling all night long while William snored in the bedroom, sleeping soundly so he could get back to the kitchen by 2:00 a.m.

Lisa's cell rang. Cody. "Hey! How's the snow?"

"Stupidly cold! I love everything about this place, when it's warm. What's up on the West Coast?"

"The same. Mostly."

"Now that's an enticing word. Tell me more about the *mostly*."

"You know. You know how I am."

"Oh, that. If that's all the mostly refers to, I don't need to hear it. Your propensity toward disappointment never sat well with me. I mean, if you're going to waste the time burrowing in, then go for a full-on depressive low that keeps you in bed for a week. Why fritter around the edges?"

"So nice to talk to you. What do you want?"

"I want you to be glad to hear from me. Standing here watching these kids freeze their noses off playing in the snow is just crazy. But here I am, calling you."

"What's your plan?"

"I fly in to SFO on the seventeenth. Ben will pick me up."

"Then what?"

"We have what may be the final meeting with the district. Ben is great at what he does. But I'm glad he's on my side. Then we head your way. I've got three whole weeks. This school believes in winter ski break."

"So, you're here on the nineteenth."

"In that neighborhood, yes. I'm wanting to keep things loose and open with Ben. You know, in case he wants to surprise me with something wild or crazy."

"Like what?"

"Sorry. Got to go. Recess is over. See you soon."

There was a frenzied emptiness that rushed in after a call with Cody. A small blizzard that left things in disarray but without much visible damage. What if she told Cody she didn't want her staying here that long? If at all. Right. What if a small earthquake shook Porter Gulch Road off the map? More likely. Maybe she could intervene. Let Ben know what really makes Cody happy. Big Sur. That high-end resort up Carmel Valley, Bernardus. Help him whisk her away, a disappearing act that would be good for all three of them.

She opened *Rocks and Rolls*.

Celia would force herself off the couch by midnight, find her way to the kitchen and prep the dough for William's now-famous rolls in advance so she could take an unnoticed break in the morning. On the wall in the kitchen next to the walk-in, she kept a calendar she'd picked up from Fred's Auto on the corner, big red X's crossing off days, William never asking questions about it, her marking time, how much longer she had to decide about whether or not to show up for the appointment with the doctor her friend had made for her.

Had Alice been struggling with whether or not to abort Lisa? Or maybe it was an older sister she never knew because she was never born. Lisa was mixing art with life, which she tended to do way too much, fiction aficionada that she was. Making things up that might or might not be true. She was certain that's what all authors did. Very few of them outlining from front to back, instead telling stories straight from family albums, or twisting every word and thought into existence from flour and water, on the fly, as they walked by on the street, made their way into brains.

She knew Alice loved her, in her own way. And of course Celia would love her own daughter.

The can of sockeye salmon sat on the kitchen counter next to the opener. She began to open it, and Eloise made a gymnastic move onto the counter and stiffened her tail in Lisa's face. After scraping the can clean into Eloise's bowl, she opened her computer and sent Zack a fourth email. He had responded to the first saying, "Don't worry. I got it covered." But the two subsequent emails to remind him had gone unanswered. Zack's salmon was not available in stores outside Alaska. And if it had been, the prices would be absurd. Zack and G had worked a trade every year. Which reminded her, Michael would be there soon. He wanted to talk business, had said the two of them needed to make some decisions about their futures. At least he hadn't said about his future. And he had stopped short of saying Pamela had anything to do with it.

Lisa had promised him lunch, but hadn't shopped since Cody had left. She refused to resort to the freezer and eat any more food Gregory had created. She knew Michael loved the salmon on crackers, but that wasn't an option. In the fridge she found tortillas, a triangle of Brie cheese, a white onion, a few other veggies. Quesadillas were her specialty, making use of whatever was available. Ryan had loved them. Would have eaten them every night if she were available to cook them. Ryan wasn't that terrible. He wasn't terrible at all. They just didn't love each other. Gregory had felt like a savior at the time, allowed her to escape a mind-numbing existence for something new, something two hours away from the same daily customers who sat in cozy chairs and read books for free, from Ryan who never cooked and ate too much, drank too much.

When Pamela's Jeep pulled into the driveway, Lisa was carrying a tray of food toward the greenhouse. She couldn't see the driver. She worried that Pamela was again reading Michael's texts, taking what she wanted from the world. It was Michael. He nodded his head, smiled. She nodded back, no smile. She bumped the greenhouse door open with her elbow, carried the tray to the table they used for cleaning and packaging weed. Michael followed her in, shut the door behind him, went straight for the wood stove and stacked kindling and wads of newspaper and dried oak logs for a fire.

Michael looked over his shoulder at her. "Your famous quesadillas?"

"More like infamous in this case. Our cupboards are a bit bare at the moment." She thought about correcting herself, saying "my cupboards" instead of "our". But it would seem too strange to bother with making a correction that didn't matter. What mattered is that the two survivors were here right now, ready to talk about their futures. "But, yes, quesadillas indeed." She handed him a plate and a glass of cran-raspberry mixed with sparkling water. She took a bite. It was good. Even with Brie cheese instead of something a little firmer that held things together better.

"Wow! Just wow!" Michael said. Lisa flinched, worried that his obsequious behavior had more to do with his future needs than it did with his taste buds. "Slivered almonds. Roasted. Sautéed mushrooms and white onions. Some of Gregory's truffle oil. Brie. Cauliflower. Sesame seeds."

She allowed herself to smile. "Got it all. Good job." They both cleaned their plates, finished most of their drinks, without bringing up business. Until now. "How do you want to do this?" Lisa said.

"I don't know. This part was Gregory's domain. I pretty much followed suit."

"I wouldn't call my part following suit. The greenhouse, all the growing, the detail work, cleaning, bagging, that was all me." She thought about it for a minute, let it sink in. Had never really thought about it like this before, but said it anyway. "All of this was all about me. What you and G did wouldn't have worked without me."

Michael leaned back in his chair. "Why are you saying this? I've never heard you talk like this before."

"That's because I've never thought like this before. You know that. Gregory did the thinking for everyone in the room. But now, there's nobody here to negate my thoughts. Unless you plan on taking that role over."

"You mean, taking Gregory's place?"

"Oh, we both know that'll never happen."

"I'm not sure whether I'm being dissed or lauded."

Lisa laughed. "Sorry. To be honest, probably a little of both."

"I have customers waiting for product," he said.

Lisa pulled her chair closer to the table, propped her elbows up, stared into his face. "How much product?"

"Five pounds to start with."

"These are all loyal, known customers?"

"Yes. All folks I've dealt with since we started. They come to my house for dinner. We go to theirs."

"The use of 'we' suggests that Pamela is in on this as well."

"She *is* my partner. We do socialize together. She has nothing to do with the money or the exchange, though."

"If we continue to do this, maybe you should keep her as far away from the business end as possible."

"Two things bother me about what you just said. The obvious first one is your concern with Pamela."

"Aren't you concerned with Pamela?"

"I don't think any concern I have with Pamela is any of your business."

"It is if my livelihood has any chance of being at risk. What's the second thing?"

"You said 'if we continue to do this.' Don't you think we'd better deal with that rather hefty 'if' before we consider any additional future?"

Lisa nodded. "Yes. That makes sense. You mentioned the other day selling everything and getting out of this life, starting fresh."

"I don't think I said anything about starting fresh, but getting out of it is a real possibility that might be the best thing for all of us. Especially you."

"Why especially me?"

"You lost a partner. The grief. Devastation. I'm guessing you might want to leave it all behind."

"You lost a brother. What about you?"

"That's different. In many ways, we weren't very close. Just business partners."

"And you think that's different with me?"

"Well, the intimacy part comes into play in your case."

"Sure. But it doesn't define me. That part was never a question. But what you said the other day, about G coming to Point Reyes Station to find someone like me. That's stuck with me. Wondering a lot about that."

"I spoke out of turn. Heat-of-the-moment kind of thing. One question. Do you want to stay in the illegal pot-growing business? Risk going to jail for a little financial comfort?"

She had never really thought about it like that. G had promised there was no legal worry, that he owned the property, it was his big idea, he'd be the one headed to jail, not her.

"If we sold everything, the property, his truck, the Harley, I figure we could cash out at over two million," Michael said.

Lisa listened, watched his eyes.

"Or we could split the twenty-five acres into five-acre parcels. It would take some time. Maybe two years to jump through the county's legal hoops. And some money. But five lots, some with buildings, one with the house, probably brings in just under five million."

She took a big swig of her drink. This didn't sound like the Michael she had come to know over the years. Felt like Pamela was hiding in his pocket, tugging on some strings, making him speak.

Michael went on. "Or we can continue like this."

She leaned forward, pointed at his empty plate. "You want more?"

"I do. But I'd rather keep talking. We need to figure things out. I'm losing sleep over this. So what about our options?"

"Sounds like you've been thinking a lot about this stuff."

"Sure. Haven't you?"

"Not much. Maybe just a little about next year's crop. It's not like I have a partner who's keeping me awake asking me questions all night long. What does Pamela want you to do?"

"What difference does that make? Do you think she's mapping my life out for me?"

"I've never been in your house, have never paid too close attention to discussions you two have, but the little I've engaged with her, like showing up at my office, I feel she's a little headstrong, demanding, pushy. There are more adjectives, but I'll stop there for now."

"I don't want to talk about her. I want to talk about you and me. What we're going to do. Come to some agreement."

"Like I said. I haven't thought much about it. Been doing other things."

"Right. The office. Your blogs. I'm waiting for more."

Lisa leaned her chair back against the wall, balanced herself on the back two legs. "Mostly I've been thinking more about today than tomorrow. In answer to one of your questions, I don't like the idea of running an illegal operation without Gregory here to take responsibility for it. No offense, but I don't think you're cut out for that part. And neither am I."

Michael stood up. Walked over to the growing pots, ran a hand through the soil. "I'm fine with the local stuff. But I don't want to have anything to do with the Central Valley folks. Do you?"

"No way. Scares the hell out of me. I've had a few hang-up calls and I wonder if it's them. I mean, we've got the lists, the names and numbers. If one of us, or both of us, didn't want to deal them, we could bring in a third party."

"Oh, jeez. That's when we get in trouble. The fewer people who know about this, the safer we are."

"And yet, we really aren't safe at all, are we? Without G's big brain to think it all through, to map out how to avoid the pitfalls."

"No. Not really."

"But I don't like the idea of selling everything. I like it here. The dogs love it here, were born here. And then there's Eloise. I'm guessing Pamela would like you to get your million-plus and coast the rest of your lives."

"I told you to keep her out of this. This is my life. My decision. Our decision. So, if you had to make a choice right now, this very second, what would it be?"

"That's absurd. I couldn't do it."

"I'm not talking about reality. I'm talking about 'what if.' What if I gave you one minute to decide?" Michael stared at his watch, waiting.

"Okay. I'll play. I don't want to sell the whole thing. I don't want to risk going to jail. The splitting it up into five lots is interesting. I had never imagined anything like that."

"To be honest, that was Pamela's idea." He smiled.

"But like you said, that would take time, and money. If we're not making money selling weed, we are most likely not making money. Although I did have one sparkle of an idea pop into my head. Rather, it walked by my office window and it's made me wonder."

"I assume this is something I'll never guess, so I won't try."

"Okay. Here it is. The first day I sat in my downtown office, a woman walked by with an orchid in her hands. It was lovely. Halfway between purple and pink. I wanted her to walk through our doors, into my office, and present it to me. Of course that didn't happen, but I wanted one anyway. I went onto Yelp and found that Ferrari Florist had some, so I drove over there, bought one for close to a hundred dollars, and brought it back to my desk."

"You should write a blog about that."

"You think?"

"I do. I'd love to read about that. Even though I'm guessing I just heard most of the story."

"Right. But what you haven't heard is what I've been thinking every time I'm in the office looking at that orchid."

"I'm waiting. Because it doesn't feel like this is helping us come up with a solution to our issues."

"Why have we been successful at our little venture over the past seven years? I mean other than Gregory's genius for developing the master plan."

"Regular customers. A steady income stream."

"Yes, there's that. But before we get to customers and income, there's the growing. There's me. Not bragging, but I've become kind of a master gardener."

"That is kind of bragging."

"But is it true?"

He sat back down. "Yes. We'd be nowhere without your skills."

"Thank you. And we'd be nowhere without yours. You have the local connections, know how to attract and keep clients happy. Know their schedules and needs."

"Still. I don't get it."

"What if we get legal? Grow something that keeps us out of jail, but has a high-end market and return customers who want more?"

Michael twisted in his chair. "Orchids?"

124

"Yes, orchids."

"Do you know how to grow orchids?"

"Not yet. I didn't know how to grow pot either when I started. But I'm a quick learner."

Michael's cell phone kept buzzing him all afternoon and evening as he and Lisa pulled out the easel and pads, mapped out strategies, one full sheet containing items they'd need to research: the growing cycle, whether or not the Santa Cruz County environment was conducive to growing, the related expenses, fertilizers, culling and trimming procedures, replanting, wholesale versus retail marketing, which stores in Santa Cruz already sold orchids, who their competition was.

Lisa pointed to his cell phone. "Are you going to answer any of those?"

"She can wait. This is important. We're onto something here."

They worked through dinner. Large Post-it sheets stuck to the inside walls of the greenhouse. Michael called Doorbell Dining and had turkey burgers and fries delivered from Carpo's. He cut two slices from his burger, gave them to Turks and Caicos.

Lisa fell into bed exhausted, forgot to turn on *The Big Bang Theory*. Forgot she had planned on opening G's workshop, to check out the big mystery, prepare for whatever his controlling mind had left behind. Tomorrow. She promised herself to get in there. Right after she spent a few hours downtown. Right after she conducted some orchid research.

28

WEDNESDAY
12-11-19

A T THE OFFICE — FIRST ONE IN — she started by admiring her orchid, then sending another email to Zack. "Are you there, Zack? My cat needs you! Help." She opened a new blog post, started typing:

> A friend told me I should share this story with you.

She stopped, read the sentence. First, Michael wasn't really a friend. But he would like reading that she said so. Second, she was using *you* as if her audience was larger than Michael and Bianca. Again, no one would see it. Get on with it.

> In my downtown office, the first day I came in and sat in my chair watching the cars and people go by, a woman holding an orchid. She looked regal. A big smile on her face. Either someone had given her the plant, or she was on the way to give it to someone else. Regardless, she was happy. Being in the presence of the orchid was giving her a feeling of joy.

Yesterday I had one of those aha moments that changes
lives. I'm a good gardener, have been perfecting my craft for
a long time now. I have a large greenhouse on my property
that is currently lying fallow. Not anymore. I've decided to
grow orchids. So keep a look out here on the blog. Sometime
in the future you'll be able to buy orchids from me, right here
in my downtown office. More soon.

She expected an immediate text from Michael, but it didn't
happen. She remembered he was a late sleeper. The double bell of the
front door buzzed, Rhonda yelling "Hi" over the wall.

"Hi, back," Lisa said. The bells rang again and the other partner
entered, no greeting, grumbling about something on her phone with a
client. One more time with the bells.

"Hi, hi!" Bianca said. Within a few seconds, Lisa heard the
knuckle knocking against her door.

"Come on in."

Bianca entered and shut the door behind her, grabbed the spare
chair and slid up to Lisa. "Look! Your post this morning was cute. But
now that you're taking this thing somewhere else, you need to turn on
Comments, so folks can start responding to your posts. Especially if
you plan to use it to sell orchids. I've told about a dozen of my friends
about you and your site and your dead boyfriend, and I'm telling you,
you've got a following. Right now a hidden following, until you turn
on the damn Comments. You understand?" She stood to leave, put her
hand on the doorknob, waited until Lisa responded.

"I understand. I'll think about it."

"No. You will not think about. You'll do it. Before you leave
today. It's simple to do. Trust me. It will change this boring life of
yours." Bianca left the door open. Lisa shut it, went back to her
computer, and looked up "cultivation of orchids in California."

As expected, she found hundreds of listings for growing orchids
on Google. She opened a new bookmark folder and titled it "Orchids."
The first site she bookmarked was called "Orchids Made Easy," written
and maintained by a grower named Ryan Levesque. The site was a
good first landing point. He provided a chart with ten different orchid
names, their grow seasons, bloom frequency, and bloom length. What

she focused on was Ryan's combination lists, showing how to maintain year-round blooms. Year-round product. That would be the key if this venture was to work out. She signed up for his free Orchid Tips newsletter, ordered a copy of his book and DVD, and became a member of his Green Thumb Club, which included "weekly step-by-step training and tips." It made her think briefly about the other Ryan, the farm they shared, the blackberries she tended.

She searched Amazon for books on orchids — dozens of great finds. She wanted to order four that looked promising but remembered Gregory's rantings about the evil empire of Jeff Bezos and how he was attempting to control every aspect of marketing, of thinking, of everyone's lives, including the destruction of local mom-and-pop stores. She held off, would go to Bookshop Santa Cruz on her way home, see what they had on the shelves, order what they didn't. She was trying. She'd given up plastic a few weeks ago. Not that she'd ever have kids of her own, but she thought it would be a good idea to leave the planet in as good shape as possible for the sake of others' kids and grandkids.

Lisa decided to look at Bianca's website. It was plastered with information. Tips on property management, restaurant reviews, two to three new blog posts per day. Each post was accompanied by a Comment section. Some posts had up to fifty comments, especially the ones where Bianca was loose with her opinions, especially the thousand-word essay she had posted on the town-gown relationship between UCSC and the city of Santa Cruz. Lisa read through the comments, trying to convince herself that she should not add comments to her own posts. It didn't work. The posts were mostly intelligent, thoughtful, respectful, and provided points of view that were often overlooked, offered opinions that represented all sides of the issue.

A knuckle-knock on her door again. This time Bianca didn't wait to be invited in. "Look. I can see you on my page, looking at comments folks have left. I know your IP address here. The analytics tracks it. Here's how I do it. I have all comment privileges turned on for my whole site. But they have to come through me first. I vet them. If I don't like them, I don't let them go live. Got it? Do it!"

Her phone pinged. Michael.

That was fast! Suddenly we're in the orchid business and you're
selling them from your office? Am I a partner or just a casual
observer?

She wanted to ignore this one. Let him stew. She didn't like the
tone, the neediness. The tendency toward greed or control. Like his
brother.

She texted back.

Doing lots of research on the business of orchid growing. Lots of
online help out there. More soon. Got to go.

She didn't want to deal with him today. Their session yesterday
had drained her.

Another ping.

Are you unlocking Gregory's workshop today? I'd be happy to come
help.

In her current mood she didn't want to see the name "Gregory"
pop up in Michael's text. In his brain. In juxtaposition to her life. Just
leave her alone. Give her room to breathe.

Thanks. Got it covered.

She turned the phone off.

She read the final comment on Bianca's town-gown piece before
returning to the guts of her own site. It was a simple check box. One
click of the mouse pad. She did it. Comments were now on, to be
vetted by her before being posted.

To avoid Michael, to avoid waiting for comments to appear on
her site, she needed to lose herself, not in the street traffic and parade
of misfits coming to and from the homeless enclaves up and down
River Street. If she spent too much time thinking about the individual
lives of every backpacked person walking by, of every couple that
looked like they had slept in some muddy pit up near the freeway, it
would wear her down. Make her wonder why this problem had still
not been solved. Wasn't it easier than everyone made it seem? Weren't
there solutions they could implement today? Wasn't it all about greed
and need and willingness to tilt the planet at the proper angle for
everything to fall into place and serve?

No. Not today. She couldn't do it. Needed to focus on her own
survival. Needed to bury herself in some fiction. Or was it historical
fiction? Or maybe fictography? She picked up Alice's *Rocks and Rolls,*

turned her chair away from the window and began reading from where she had left off.

> William was removing a tray of hot cinnamon rolls from the oven when Celia entered the kitchen.
> "Slept late again today."
> "Yeah. A bit of a headache."
> "You been having those a lot lately. Maybe we should get you to the doctor."
> "No, I'm fine. Just need to drink more water."
> "Your boyfriend came by already." He nodded toward the cash register.
> "Stop that!" Celia said, a light grin on her face. She went to him and put her arms around his wide shoulders. "You know you're my one and only boyfriend."
> William bent over and kissed her. "I know. Just razzing you. I love you. Some nice ones there today. I traded him a half-dozen cinnamon rolls."
> Celia walked to the register where a new collection of three rocks awaited her. Justin was fifteen. His family were rock hounds. Took semiannual trips to the Hauser Geode Beds near Blythe. He brought Celia samples when they returned. Mostly geodes. Other fascinating rocks they found in the desert.

Lisa set the manuscript down, remembered the day she had gone to the shed in Alice's backyard after her memorial service. She had removed only two boxes, the one with the five manuscripts, and a heavier one full of Alice's geode collection. Lisa could see the collection that had grown over the years, most of them lining the edge of Alice's desk behind the typewriter. Eventually they moved out of the office into the living room, the dining room. There were so many. Maybe there had been a real Justin who brought them to Alice. But Lisa had never seen him, had never met a stranger bearing gifts.

She needed to add this to her long-term to-do list: 1) Get back to Berkeley and check out the storage facility. 2) Find out where Gregory had hidden the geodes, so selfish about his space, his property, his things.

Over the wall she heard Bianca's voice. "See! I told you! You just got to trust my judgment. We'll get you on the map yet."

Damn her! She wouldn't bite. Left her computer closed and read on.

> Celia was sorry she had missed Justin, sorry she
> spent the better part of the morning with her head stuck
> in the toilet bowl. She knew Justin had a crush on her,
> but it was harmless. Eventually one of the girls at his
> high school would discover him, his big heart, and he'd
> move on and give his geodes to her. But for now, she
> cherished the gifts. Lined them all up on the shelf in the
> back room where they kept the cans of baking powder.
> Last time in, Justin had been so excited with his new
> collection. "So this time my dad takes us east on
> Interstate Ten until we get to the Coachella Valley. We
> see the sign that says Hauser Geode Beds and we
> immediately know we're there, hundreds of geodes
> scattered everywhere." That time Celia had given him a
> dozen cheese buns, her favorite, as well as William's
> favorite, the honey buns.

Alice used to make honey buns for Lisa and Cody on Saturday mornings, before she buried herself in her office to write for the weekend. She had loved the buns, not quite as sweet as a cinnamon bun but sweet enough. Heated in the oven for a few minutes, sliced open and spread with butter. Alice wasn't much of a cook, but Lisa bet the few recipes she used existed somewhere in a box in Berkeley. She remembered that fruit-cocktail thing she made that baked so long it tasted like the churros they bought at the flea market on the weekends. The whipped cream piled high on top. Chicken and dumplings, every Thursday night. Celery, carrots, a thick gravy it all stewed in, thighs and breasts, all perched on top of a pile of buttered white rice. Cody preferred the Tuesday-night minute steaks. Browned on both sides, placed between two slices of Kilpatrick's white sandwich bread, slathered with mayonnaise on both slices. With some frozen French fries. Lisa remembered how Alice would always make too much food. Or maybe it was just the right amount, as Alice packed up the leftovers in tinfoil and the three of them would drive over to street corners occupied by what Alice said were "good folks who were a little down on their luck," and distribute the packets of food.

• • •

"Wow! You go girl. *Pious Rebel*'s getting some new nicknames!" Bianca's voice cackled over and through the walls.

Lisa wanted more of Alice, more of Celia and Justin and William and buns in the oven. But she couldn't resist. She put the manuscript back in its box, dog-eared the current page, and opened the computer to piousrebel.com. There were over a dozen comments on this morning's post, waiting for her to vet them.

> I keep an orchid in bloom on my office desk. Keep me posted. I'll buy some!" - Nutty Buddy.

> Orchids for sale! Yes. Sign me up! - Claire C.

> Any friend of Bianca's is a friend of mine. Danna Rosanna.

> Maybe you should change your site name to Little Orchid Annie. Hammerhead.

> Do you know that the scientific name is Orchidaceae? From Ancient Greek translating to "testicle" because of the shape of the double tubers in some. Mard E. Grass.

It went on. This was hilarious. All these folks must be Bianca's online friends. Except the last comment, posted ten minutes ago.

> Seriously? Is this how we're going to do business together? Surprising each other with random posts online for the whole world to see? Peter Rarebit.

Well, at least Michael had hidden his real name, had brought in his Welsh background to this pseudonym. She accepted all the comments except his.

On her way home, she stopped at Bookshop Santa Cruz, purchased The Orchid Whisperer: Expert Secrets to Growing Beautiful Orchids, The Book of Orchids: A Life-Size Guide to Six Hundred Species from Around the World, and Understanding Orchids: An Uncomplicated Guide to Growing the World's Most Exotic Plants, and ordered two more.

On the drive to Aptos she listened to Vivaldi's *Four Seasons* on KDFC. She imagined playing the music for the orchids in the greenhouse from gestation to full bloom. Who wouldn't want to thrive listening to that? She had planned on heading straight to the greenhouse and G's office to search for Alice's box of rocks, but there was a large blue truck in her driveway, with those monster tires that made it nearly impossible to climb into the cab, trails of mud on all surfaces of the fenders and grill. She heard muffled noises coming from Turks and Caicos' playground. In the back of the truck were at least twenty cases of sockeye salmon. Holy shit! She walked around the side of the house and saw Zack in the pen playing with the boys.

"Hey!" she yelled.

Zack let go of the dogs and came toward Lisa, opened the gate and hugged her. "They still remember me," he said. "How about you?"

"To be honest, if I hadn't seen the cases of salmon, I wouldn't have had a clue."

"Yeah, I look different, and we only met those few times."

He had put on twenty pounds, well over two hundred now, had a cleanly shaved head and face where long frizzy hair and beard had been. Levi's. Long-sleeve plaid shirt. Red Reeboks.

"But wait. You drove here from Alaska to deliver some cat food?"

"Not just any cat. This is Eloise. Gregory's cat. And not just any cat food. Least I could do."

She wasn't about to tell him Gregory didn't like Eloise.

"Come inside. Let me fix you something to eat." She still hadn't gotten to the store yet. It'd have to be quesadillas again.

"No need for food. Just ate. But getting a load off my feet will help."

Inside he went straight for the fireplace, lit a couple of Gregory's logs, kicked his boots off, settled into Gregory's easy chair. Zack had curled up in front of the fire, eyes closed within minutes, snoring deeply. He'd stayed awake long enough to tell her the drive from Alaska took fifty-six hours over four days.

29

THURSDAY
12-12-19

L ISA SKIPPED HER MORNING SHOWER and found Zack in the same position on the couch. She didn't know what Zack's plans were, but figured he might want to spend a night or two. The door to the guest room had been closed since Cody and Ben had departed. She had no idea what to expect when she opened it. If it had been Cody by herself, it would be a mess. Cody, who kept a classroom full of antiques and toys and puzzles and books, from floor to ceiling, to inspire her students, their parents, herself, and who didn't care much about order and categorization. Creative, yes. Organized, no.

The room was unusually clean and straightened, more so than when Cody had arrived. The books she kept on a small bookshelf had been alphabetized by author name. The clock on the wall whose batteries hadn't been replaced in years was humming with the current time. She couldn't be sure, but it appeared the sheets and pillowcases had been washed, the bed made neatly, corners tucked in the way she liked. This had to be Ben's work. Even at a distance, she was growing fonder of him. Maybe this one would stick. Maybe Ben could solve the riddle of Cody.

In the kitchen, she ripped a page from the back of her journal, wrote Zack a note, set it next to him on the couch:

The spare room down the hall is ready for you if you like. I'm outside dealing with salmon. Eloise and I thank you so much for the salmon, and for the hand delivery.

Warmly, Lisa.

She went out to his truck, brought in one case to the kitchen, opened a can and fed Eloise. She stacked the remaining cases in a corner of the pantry.

Zack was gone from the couch when she returned. She'd brewed a large pot of coffee, scrambled eggs, fried bacon, dropped bread into the toaster. Zack appeared, wet hair, wearing sweats and a t-shirt reading *If Juneau What I Know.*

"Coffee?" she asked, as he passed through the kitchen to the living room.

"No thanks. Gave up caffeine. Juice maybe." He dropped to the floor and began a yoga routine.

"Breakfast will be ready in fifteen minutes."

"Perfect. So will I. Is that bacon I smell?"

"Straight from Corralitos Market."

"Thanks, but I'm a vegetarian now."

"No problem. I'm trying to be. Turks and Caicos aren't."

They were both quiet during most of the meal. Finally, Lisa said, "What are your plans?"

"Good question. These days I don't worry much about plans. Four days ago, I planned on having my crew load up my truck then I'd head south for a few days. Here I am. That plan worked. I've got folks at home working my boats, prepping the fish, canning it, getting it out to market. They do fine without me."

"Right," Lisa said. "Thanks again for bringing it down. So much of it!"

"My pleasure. This is nothing. We sell close to a thousand cases a month now."

"You manage to do this year round?" She was thinking about the orchids now, if she could create a cycle that would harvest and provide income all year.

"Oh, yeah. We go down southeast and keep ourselves busy with wild trout, halibut, lingcod, all five varieties of salmon. Never lets up."

"And you've got that cycle all mapped out?"

"Uh-huh. Why do you ask?"

"Just trying to figure out the next stages of my life. What to do out in that greenhouse now. That reminds me. What do I owe you for the salmon? I can manage a trade if you like."

"Gave that stuff up, too. No fried foods, no drugs, no alcohol. Looking at this body as a temple I'd like to keep intact as long as possible."

The extra weight looked good on him, as did the shaved face and head.

"But the salmon. How much?"

"Not a thing. If you all had had a memorial service, I would've brought it down for that. Instead, Eloise reaps the benefits."

"That's crazy!" Lisa said. "That's valuable stuff."

"And there's enough there to last the two of you until just about Labor Day. There is something, though."

Here it comes. She thought he'd take a little more time to bring it up, but he was probably in a hurry, needed to head back up and tend to business.

"I love this town, my visits to see Gregory, our rides out to San Juan Bautista and the Pinnacles. Love all those tarantulas out there. Anyways, I was thinking I might hang around town for a while. Maybe crash here if you've got room."

A night or two was what she'd expected. Not an indefinite stay. She watched him clean the eggs off his plate with a dab of toast. This life thing was never predictable. She'd have bet money that he'd want the Harley. That would have been easier. She assumed Gregory would want Zack to have it. She wouldn't touch the thing, had never agreed to hop on the back and accompany him on any of his rides. Michael wouldn't want the bike but would probably want his fair share of the $10,000 value. Cody would be the one to complain. "Hey! I've got plans for that hog. Me and Ben, up and down the coast, maybe all the way to Puerto Vallarta."

"Right. I'll have to talk to Michael about that. We kind of share the property, the expenses now, trying to figure out how we make decisions together."

"I understand. No rush. I can hightail it down to a motel in the meantime."

"No, of course not. Michael's coming over today to talk business and I'll bring it up."

"Great! Then there's the Harley."

Ah. There we go. She was getting better at predicting the future, at reading people. She made a mental note: *Accomplishment, knew what Zack wanted. Disappointment, potential disappearance of G's bike.*

"Oh. I haven't seen that old thing in ages."

"It's out in his workshop, isn't it? That's where he used to keep it."

"Yes. I believe it is. I've been avoiding opening that room since he died."

"I understand. I'd be happy to do it for you."

"Strange coincidence, I was hoping to get in there today, but I'm not feeling it right now." She sidestepped it. "Michael and I are thinking of growing orchids. Get out of the pot business. Keep ourselves out of jail now that the mastermind is gone."

"The way I heard it you were the mastermind, the master gardener. Pot, orchids, whatever those pretty little hands touch, it's going to thrive." This sounded like he was looking for more than a temporary place to stay, a bike. Maybe someone to keep his shaved head warm at night. That wouldn't happen. Or would it? She did not have a good handle on her needs or desires right now, especially as she was beginning to think about self-sufficiency and survival. Zack clearly had money, was clever in an entrepreneurial way like Gregory. But she couldn't picture intimacy with him. Probably because it had been so perfect with G. Their thirty minutes or so coiled together under sheets caused her to drift outside her body. She thought it was the only time that Gregory had actually loved her, or at least liked her. And mostly it had been enough.

Zack pulled a folded piece of paper from his pocket, set it next to Lisa's plate. She opened it, found an email from G to Zack, read it to herself:

137

Zack buddy,

Took the bike out for a spin today. Missed having you next to me flying up 395. I want you to know, if anything ever happens to me, you know, like one of those bad dudes down in the Valley gets up on the wrong side of the bed one day and decides to mess with me, my bike is yours. It's not in the will or anything, but I figured this email would suffice, as far as legality and all go.

I don't think either Michael or Lisa would mess with you on this one.

Be well, my friend.

Hope to see you soon.

Gregory

It was jarring seeing Gregory's name, not as bad as hearing his voice on the answering machine. Still, weird. She reread the note, hearing G's voice in her head rather than her own.

She handed the note to Zack who folded it up, stuck it back in his pocket.

"Like I said, I'd be happy to help you with the workshop thing. I know these things can be difficult for folks."

"What things?"

"Oh, you know, the stuff that triggers old memories, makes you wonder what the truth really was or is, what comes next. The normal things you go through when death smacks you over the head."

"You're saying you went through these things when you heard about Gregory's accident?"

"Oh, yeah. Friends since grammar school. But not just him. Lost three crew members last year to a monster wave out of nowhere. Lots of canned fish at those memorials. Two other friends to cancer." He paused, took a drink of orange juice. "My daughter."

Saying "I'm sorry" didn't feel quite right. Saying nothing felt worse. "Wow," she finally said. "Those kinds of things."

"Yep. So I'm here to help."

"Thanks. I've got to do the workshop by myself. It's been one of those things I keep avoiding every day. I'm not quite sure why. The only thing I expect to find in there is his bike. I should say your bike. I'm fine with that, by the way. But I do have to run it by Michael."

"I completely get it. A whole new person suddenly in the mix. Happens to me all the time as I expand my humble little northwest empire. Hey! Speaking of that, what about this for an idea?"

"I'm listening."

"Next time I come back to town to deliver more cat food, I can take a truckload of orchids to sell up in my neck of the woods. Or better yet, I might give them away as gifts to my customers."

Lisa smiled, kind of liked the idea, having a known market for product distribution and income. As long as Zack didn't want or expect more from her, as long as Michael stayed in line.

"Interesting idea. I'll run it by Michael."

"Gotcha. Though if you don't mind me saying, you need to quit worrying about Michael so much. Gregory was all too aware of his limitations, and of your strengths."

"I'm headed downtown to my office and will stop and get some groceries before I come back." She left Zack in the kitchen to clean up.

·　　·　　·

When she walked in, Zack was asleep on the couch again. After unpacking the four bags of groceries, she tossed a blanket over him, grabbed her computer and went to her bedroom where she was greeted by Eloise, Turks and Caicos.

She propped the computer up on G's pillow and went to the orchid man's website, carefully avoided Pious Rebel, not wanting to deal with vetting any new comments tonight. Not wanting to see more complaints from Michael. Especially not wanting to hear any mention of the locked workshop she still hadn't managed to open. Now with Zack here, she'd have more excuses to avoid digging in. She wouldn't want him nosing around, checking out the Harley and whatever else might be buried out there. She created a spreadsheet of supplies for growing orchids: humidity trays, rubber grids, sphagnum moss, general-purpose orchid mix, orchid pots, fertilizer, misting bottle, grow lights, pest-control supplies, pruning snips, and orchid mounts. She priced each item at OrchidSupply.com. Much of it she already had from the marijuana operation. She printed out two copies, ready for her scheduled meeting with Michael tomorrow afternoon.

More lists. Not just for orchids, for everything that was creeping into her life, demanding space in her head. She opened a blank Word document, wrote *To Do* at the top. A Gregory thing. The man of action who took care of business. Her turn. She started her list:

To Do

- Meet with Michael tomorrow about orchids.

- Read up on medical marijuana.

- Ben. What about Ben? Hadn't he said something about Alexa and Voicegram?

- More blog posts.

- OPEN THE GODDAMN WORKSHOP!

- Find Alice's rocks.

She jumped up off the bed, hurried down the hall to G's office. She had been through the desk, the boxes piled in stacks against the wall, but hadn't looked in the closet yet. She hunted. It was a white banker's box just like the one Alice's manuscripts were in. It would be heavy, filled to the top with rocks. There were a few boxes on the floor, a couple on the shelves, but none of them with Alice's rocks. She sat down in G's chair, tired, brain still a little on fire. She leaned forward, saw Ben's name written on a pad, followed by a note. "$150,000 minimum. Cody."

The settlement amount. Ben was shrewd, might be a keeper. She remembered his comment about Voicegram, turned to G's computer and logged in, searched it. She was redirected to a website titled Sayspring, where she was told "Sayspring is now part of Adobe." The mega-monsters continued to buy up everything of interest, make themselves pop out of their skins, like the Hulk, angrier and much more dangerous with each iteration. There was a link inviting her to "Request an Invite." She didn't want to slide into this muck. Couldn't imagine that G would have done so either. She searched for "record my voice on Amazon Echo." A list of options appeared: Notes, Voice Capture, Daily Log. After fifteen minutes of research, she turned to the Echo, said, "Alexa enable Daily Log." She was successful. Alexa was now speaking with her. Tomorrow she'd dig a little further, find out if G had used this fairly simple method to track ideas, business transactions, anything he wanted to keep a secret from her, Michael, anybody.

Back in bed, she turned on The *Big Bang Theory* episode where the character played by Billy Bob Thornton has an interest in Penny. She laughed, hadn't had a good one in a while, but let it roll out tonight, from deep inside, the kind that ended up with sobs into her pillow. Jeez, these writers were good. Maybe they could write her blogs for her. She dozed off for a bit, and opened her eyes to see that Billy Bob was finally understanding that Penny was with Leonard, was not available to him. They all laughed. The audience laughed. She laughed.

30

FRIDAY
12-13-19

W HEN MICHAEL APPEARED IN THE AFTERNOON, Lisa watched him in the driveway, cocking his head at Zack's truck, kicking the tires, running a finger through the dusty fenders. There was a cordial exchange between him and Zack, but a distance, a distance Lisa had felt with most of G's friends. More like acquaintances. Zack may have been the only friend. At least this awkward moment was short, as Zack hopped into the cab, drove off down the road.

Lisa and Michael spent all day and most of the night in the greenhouse. He stoked the fire. She made tuna-melt panini sandwiches with sharp cheddar. He researched the local markets for orchids. She unrolled the Post-it pages, typed the notes into a file, printed it out, tacked it to a bulletin board that still contained schedules for their last growing cycle.

At some point, Lisa said, "By the way —"

Michael cut her off. "I really hate that opening. It tends to lead somewhere dark and weird."

Lisa turned to the next page and kept typing, restarted, "By the way, Zack opened up to me a bit. Thought you'd like to hear it sooner than later."

"Sorry," Michael said. "That's a Pamela thing. She tends to open with that a lot, then knock me up the side of the head with some wacky idea or something I've done wrong. Talk to me. Tell me about Zack. By the way," he paused, smiled, "old Zack looks quite different these days."

"Yes, he does. In a good way or a bad way?"

"Looks pretty good to me. Healthy."

"Yeah. Doesn't eat meat anymore. Gave up pot and alcohol. And he brought twenty cases of his salmon for Eloise."

"What? That expensive stuff? You're feeding it to Eloise?"

She ignored the jab. "No charge. He doesn't even want pot in trade, so we don't have to dig into your local needs."

"That stuff is like two hundred a case. That's over four thousand dollars."

"I know. He showed me an email from Gregory. Talked about the Harley. G told him it was his if something happened to him."

"Well, something certainly happened to him. Didn't we kind of know this?"

"Probably. But it's ten thousand we could use toward the orchids."

"I've been thinking about the orchids."

"I would certainly hope so. Did you bounce it off Pamela?"

"No. I'm wanting to act like it's none of her business."

Lisa grinned. "But, you know that's not the case. She wants everything to be her business. Or so it seems to me."

"My point is I'm not sure how much income we can make through orchids alone. There's some pretty stiff competition out there. Big farms up in Half Moon Bay. Quite a few within the county as well."

"Right. With big overhead. We don't need big overhead. I can handle most of it on the growing side. You can help if you want."

"Of course I'll help. But we might want me to be more on the distribution side."

"Yes. I agree. Here's another thought by Zack related to distribution."

"One day he's in town and you're already talking business with him. We don't need another partner."

"Agreed. But listen to this. He says he'll drive back down with more salmon next year. He says he'll purchase orchids to take with him to Alaska to either sell in his networks or give as gifts to his big clients."

"Really? I like that idea. As long as he pays cash up front before he loads them into his truck for a three-thousand-mile drive."

"Yeah, the details still need to be worked out. Hell, the plants still need to be grown."

"Back to how much money we will or won't earn. I have another little idea."

"Okay."

"One of the main reasons we're even considering this direction is the legality part. What if we still grow some pot, but in a legal way?"

"Tell me more. I thought the laws were pretty restrictive now."

"Unless you're a medical marijuana patient. If you have a card, and anybody can get a card these days, you can legally grow six plants, theoretically for your own consumption."

"Not sure I like the 'theoretical' part of this idea."

"Right. That's still the tricky part. They can't keep us from growing it as long as they don't know we're selling it."

"And you would keep selling it to your handful of trusty friends?"

"Right. There's another piece. They also can't keep you from forming a collective with up to five people. That's up to thirty plants."

"You're talking about a hybrid operation. Part orchids, part pot."

"Mostly orchids. Maybe seventy percent of the greenhouse. Just use the back end for the pot. We need to get clear about the laws. Make sure we're not at risk."

"How about if I keep working on the orchid plan? You on the pot plan."

"Sounds good."

"There is one more thing."

"Always is."

"About Zack."

"Of course it's about Zack."

"He likes Santa Cruz. Wants to hang out for a while. Here. You okay with that?"

"It's your house."

"Technically ours. But you don't mind?"

"Why would I mind? I'm thinking it's more about whether you mind."

"I know. I'm not sure yet. Not exactly sure what he wants. How much he wants."

"I'm guessing you're getting a little lonely by now."

"What? It's been less than two months. That's crazy."

"Not at all crazy. It was never much of a secret how unaffectionate Gregory was. To you, or anybody."

"What do you mean, 'anybody'?"

"To you, me, Pamela, every girlfriend he'd ever run through. Zack was the only one he seemed to truly care about. So I say go for it. You do owe him for the salmon."

"I know. I'm a little worried about what he expects in return."

. . .

Through the kitchen window the next morning she saw Zack's truck was gone. There was a note on the counter, a plate of food — salmon scramble, toast with blackberry jam, freshly squeezed orange juice. She read the note:

L-

Found a party at Moe's Alley last night. Wasn't sure if you'd had a chance to talk to Michael yet, so I stayed away for a bit. Today I'm headed down to Big Sur for a few days. See you when I see you. Here's my cell number: 1-555-555-1515.

Z

. . .

She made it to the office by noon, had snapped a photo of Eloise eating salmon straight from the can before she left home. She and Michael had agreed to give each other some space, do their research separately, come back together on the weekend. Inside her cubicle she stared at the orchid, imagined them sitting on desks in every office throughout downtown, the county, the central coast. She hadn't done the math yet, didn't want to delve into the naked reality of what it would take to survive on orchid growing. Michael's idea had potential. If he could guarantee they could stay legal.

Fingers on keyboard she typed:

I don't generally believe in fairies, angels, elves, pixies, or ghosts. But someone arrived in my life yesterday who may be a subtle blend of all of them. A magician who appeared in my driveway with 480 cans of salmon his company caught off the coast of Eastern Alaska and canned for their northwest customers. For me. Not really for me. For my cat. (Thus the attached photo.) Her addiction has become my burden. I should say the burden now of the magician, who has supplied her with her heroin of choice. Eloise, the heroine of this story, of my story, of my life. Today I believe in magic, tomorrow I probably won't.

She didn't think or worry about this one, or bother to edit it. Hit Publish and was done with it.

"You've got to be kidding me," Bianca yelled over the wall. "This is precious!" Lisa was aurally reminded how thoroughly tuned in to social media Bianca was, how quickly she got alerts to new posts. She logged in and there were over fifty comments, most repeat visitors, friends of Bianca, who appeared to be becoming friends of hers. Three from Michael. A dozen new folks. Nothing too radical, nothing she'd need to hide from the world. No need to hurt the feelings of commenters who were willing to take time from their schedules and post a comment. She accepted them all.

Bianca shouted over the wall. "I'm headed to Zoccoli's. You want something?"

She didn't, but she should eat. She'd lost ten pounds since the accident, and she didn't have that much to lose. "Vegetarian lasagna. Perrier. A blondie. Make that two vegetarian lasagnas, please"

"Big appetite! You got it. Back soon. Let's talk." Sounded like a lunch date. She grabbed *Rocks and Rolls* from its box, turned to the dog-eared page, could probably get fifteen to twenty minutes in before Bianca got back.

Justin's family continued to strip California deserts of their precious rocks. The Grapevine Mountains. The North Black Hills. Potato Patch Geode

Beds. Cinnamon Geode Beds. Celia was given detailed
descriptions of every trip, every locale. William
listened from a distance. Shook his head, a slight grin
wriggling from his face. Celia knew what that meant. A
bit of jealousy, but not really of a fifteen-year-old boy.
More a remembrance of what it was like to be that age
himself, to have what seemed to be a life-threatening
crush on someone older, wiser. Hers had been Timothy
Whalen. He was the manager of Cody's Bookstore on Euclid
Avenue, managed it when Fred and Pat Cody weren't there.
He knew everything about everything, about every book
on every shelf. Could quote authors from their <u>Paris
Review</u> interviews. She had held that crush for the
better part of her fifteenth year until one day she was
hurrying over from school and saw Timothy behind the
bookstore kissing an older man, hands all over each
other, a passion she had rarely seen, never seen in her
parents, maybe only on movie screens.

When Justin left, William said, "Baking-soda shelf is
full. Need to pick a new one." She moved to the coffee
shelf. They fit perfectly there. The X hadn't been placed
on today's calendar yet. After swiping the marker across
the day, she counted the days left. Three. Her friend
Margie would pick her up early, before 6:00. They'd drive
the two hours to the small town east of Berkeley. Margie
said the procedure would be quick, as long as there were
no complications. Hers had only taken a little over an
hour. Margie would drive her home, put her to bed, tell
William she had the flu and to leave her alone for a few
days, stay away from her so he wouldn't get sick.

As they reached Tracy, headed southeast toward
Vernalis, Celia started shaking her head.

"What?" Margie said. Celia kept shaking it, thinking
about William, about how they talked to each other about
everything, "attached at the hip," he used to joke to her.
He had told her about all the women who wanted him to
teach them how to bake. "After hours," they'd say. Or,
"Come over to my kitchen." Was honest with her, never lied
about anything. And she with him. Told him on their

wedding night that she'd had one boyfriend who went a
little too far, passed third base. He had laughed, said,
"No details please. You're mine now." And she was. Was all
his. And he was all hers. But if she did this thing?

"Tell me what you're thinking, Margie said, gently
and firmly combined. Celia stayed quiet. "This is your
choice, you know."

"That's what I'm thinking about. How it's my choice,
and it's William's choice. I haven't given him a voice in
it. It's not like either of us to silence the other. Not
even have a conversation."

"I know this nice little diner around the corner.
Let's go get a coffee." Celia made her decision and they
headed home.

When Margie dropped Celia off behind the bakery, she
slipped inside the bathroom, removed the muslin wrap,
turned the <u>Closed</u> sign around, locked the door.

"What are you doing?" William asked. "We've got two
more hours." She grabbed his hand and took him upstairs
to their living room, sat him down on the couch, told him
everything. William wept first and she quickly joined
him, soiling aprons and blouses and tablecloths.

But Alice hadn't had a William in her life to commiserate with. To
help her make the sensible choice. Maybe Anita. Or maybe Alice hadn't
been completely straight with her about things. People lie. People are a
disappointment to each other. Can't live up to others' expectations of
them. Whatever had happened, Lisa was still here, had been her mother's
choice. That she didn't know who to thank for that didn't really matter.

Knuckles on the door, Bianca back with lunch.

"Two veggie lasagnas. Perrier. Blondie. And I decided you needed
two pieces of garlic bread with that lasagna. Am I right? Am I right?"

It had been years since she heard someone use that double
question to assert themselves. The answer was never a real answer. A
head nod was all that was expected. Anything more was way beyond
what the asker wanted to hear. Lisa nodded, stuck her plastic fork in
the lasagna, still warm. The garlic bread was a perfect complement.

"Thank you," Lisa said. She reached in her purse and handed Bianca twenty-five dollars.

"Oh, please," Bianca said. "After Barceloneta, this one's on me."

Lisa saw a familiar couple sitting on the sidewalk against the Outdoor World sign. "Back in a minute," she said to Bianca. She grabbed one of the lasagnas and pieces of garlic bread, stopped in the office kitchen for two plastic forks. She crossed at the light, handed the food to the woman, who blessed her.

Back in the office Bianca was on her, seemed like she hadn't even noticed she was gone.

"Open up Pious Rebel. Let me show you something. Good. Click on Statistics. See there. These are your commenters. Some will show up who you never want to let post to your page. You can add their email addresses and IP addresses to a list that you never allow in."

"Thanks. What else?"

"So far you've got about fifteen individual commenters. I lead the pack with ten comments myself. It looks like Peter Rarebit is next. It's clear he's got some hidden issues. You'll probably have to vet his comments individually, not grant him carte-blanche access. Unlike me, who you should just let in as I wish. Click here to do that." Lisa looked at her, grinned.

"And why should I trust you?"

"Because what I say is going to increase your traffic, make you a household name. I am somewhat of a figure in the social-media community, if you know what I mean."

"I'm guessing you mean you are the HotMama and I should never forget that."

Bianca laughed loudly. "Yeah. Something like that. Trust me. You're going places. Pious Rebel. Orchids. To the moon, Alice!"

Lisa thought about her mom, about Celia and Justin and William. About Jackie Gleason threatening to send Alice to the moon, in his playful way that wasn't really so playful. But her Alice, mom Alice, probably deserved to go to the moon. In a private spaceship. Maybe Lisa could reserve a flight, take Alice's ashes, sprinkle them on the surface.

"I haven't said much about your content yet."

"Yet?" Lisa cocked her head.

149

"You know me. Eventually I'm going to tell you what to do, right? Because I know. Been around the block with this stuff. But not yet. You're fresh. People like fresh. Like ideas that fall out of your mouth and heart clean and mean without much editing or rethinking. Just give us what you've got. What's raw and means most to you. I'm already seeing it, feeling it. You're on a roll."

"Thanks, I think."

31

SATURDAY
12-14-19

A T HOME THAT AFTERNOON, Lisa found a series of excuses to keep from opening G's workshop. She found the journal designed by the Chicago artist, the one with literary quotations and photos, sat down on the couch, G's perfectly cut logs roaring in the fireplace, Eloise on her lap, Turks and Caicos at her feet, and worked her way through page by page, quote by quote. Anaïs Nin: "We write to taste life twice, in the moment and in retrospect." She had never really thought much about her writing, mostly because she hadn't written much. That was different now. She was writing a lot. And yes, half of it was for now, for watching and feeling the words fall out of her head onto the screen, a creation happening in front of her eyes. But the second half was becoming more fascinating to her. The retrospective part. To look at her words again, through the eyes of others, through the comments posted by others. She hadn't read Anaïs Nin in a while. It was time to dust off her book collection, unbury it from wherever G had hidden them. "Books are a distraction," he had said to her when they started the growing cycle. "We need to be focused on the goal, caring for our girls, bringing them through to perfection." She wasn't sure where the books were now. He might have tossed them on a burn pile when he cleaned up the slash from his oak harvesting. Maybe they were locked in his workshop. Maybe in the other spare bedroom that was crammed full of more of Gregory's "treasures."

Henry David Thoreau: "How vain it is to sit down to write when you have not stood up to live." She didn't understand that one. The vanity part. Maybe it was more like how dare you try to write about anything before you had actually lived it? That made more sense, made sense given the life he had lived. She wanted to walk over to the Land of Medicine Buddha retreat, get a feel for the land, stand up and live in a way she hadn't tried before. She didn't know if they allowed dogs on the property. She'd need to visit soon. Find out.

The quotation by Sylvia Plath echoed Thoreau's thoughts: "Let me live, love, and say it well in good sentences." Same idea. Live it. Tell it. Although Plath's outcome was not what Lisa had in mind. But living it and telling it was making more sense all the time.

One more quote, then she'd take Turks and Caicos out with her to romp outside, force her way to the workshop, take care of business.

Franz Kafka. She had read *The Metamorphosis* while at Berkeley, but it was a long time ago. Gregor Samsa, who woke up as a monstrous vermin. She thought about Gregory, sometimes had imagined him as evil, but never as a Gregor, never monstrous: "Don't bend; don't water it down; don't try to make it logical; don't edit your own soul according to the fashion. Rather, follow your most intense obsessions mercilessly."

But she didn't jump up and head outside. The next item in her series of distractors was digging through the other spare room to look for her books. She hadn't been in there in years. Another one of those domains G had claimed as his own. She hadn't been explicitly prohibited, but it was clear he hadn't wanted her in there, messing with his things.

Most of it was his. Cases of motor oil. Wooden boxes stacked in piles to the ceiling. What he had called "treasures" reaped from the Saturday flea markets. Old dolls, creepy dolls with scary faces, missing limbs and eyes and hair. She hated them. She'd come in from the greenhouse late after tending to the plants, to find doll heads in the freezer, under the toothbrush bowl in the bathroom, perched on her bed pillow. She was glad they were hidden away in this spider-infested room. She looked in every box, found dozens of old games that he had never played with her. She loved games. It pissed her off to know they had been sequestered away in here, never played. That was one thing she and Ryan had done well, game playing. Canasta, spades, chess, Connect Four, two-handed pinochle. It may have been their only source of fun, that and talking about books. Thinking about it now, she wasn't sure what she could label as fun between her and G. The lovemaking could be classified as fun. But not really. It was frenzied, hit the roof, drained them for a half hour, and then they were back at the grind, her in the greenhouse, him locked away in the workshop.

In the back of the room was a closet blocked by piles of boxes. When she finally cleared a pathway, she found them. Ten boxes full of her books. She wasn't about to pull them all out now, had no idea where she'd put them. But she reached in the box closest to her, pulled two books off the top, not looking at the titles until she got back to the couch.

Notes to Myself: My Struggle to Become a Person, by Hugh Prather. In her twenties, she'd thought she'd read pages from that book every morning for the rest of her life. It lasted a couple of weeks before she got bored and wondered if she'd ever become a person. The second book was *The Teachings of Don Juan: A Yaqui Way of Knowledge* by Carlos Castaneda. She had read all his books. He became her next temporary guru. He lasted longer, the better part of a year as she worked her way through his altered states of consciousness. She didn't think she'd read either of these books now. But it was nice to know they were here. At hand. Able to help trigger her brain back to a different time in her life, pre-Gregory, pre-Ryan.

Something else to look forward to. Something that was all about her, without Gregory, Michael, Ryan, Zack.

Her next diversion was to open the computer to start a new blog post. She ignored the Comments section for now, started writing

> If you were ever lucky enough to have been or to have become a reader at some point in your life, I mean a dedicated reader who might start a book after work and dinner one night, maybe crawl under the covers by 6:30,

unencumbered by a man who'd distract you, and read
straight through for ten hours until reaching the last page at
4:30 in the morning, then you know why I'm writing this one
today. I have found my old books, buried in a closet, in a
room I wasn't allowed to enter. It's a long story I don't want
to go into. The important piece is that I found them. They're
mine. I may build an altar to and for them. I haven't bought a
new book in years. She thought about the orchid books, the
three sitting on the kitchen table, the two on order at
Bookshop. Let me correct that. Last week I bought some
books about growing orchids. I love them. I love the pictures.
I love the nonfiction that created the engine that drives
them. But I want some new fiction. I've been away from it for
so long, I wouldn't know where to start. But I will. Help me
out. Give me some ideas.

This is the first time she'd solicited comments from her audience.

Lisa reread the post, ignored Kafka's advice and edited, just a
little, mainly the line where she had talked about "a man who'd distract
you." She was limiting her audience in that phrase, to women, or gay
men. She changed it simply to "a mate who'd distract you." There.
Now she could appeal to the whole world. She laughed out loud at
herself, said, "Ah, delusions of grandeur abound." Turks rubbed his
nose against her hand.

The phone pinged. Michael.

Are we meeting tomorrow?

What day was tomorrow? The days were all beginning to blur into
each other. If she made it into the office and there were people there,
she knew it was somewhere between Monday and Friday. Right.
Tomorrow was Sunday. The day they had agreed to meet. Another
ping.

Have you made it into the workshop yet?

Kafka jumped into her brain, her fingers.

Fuck you! Leave me alone. By the way, I found my old books, buried
away in the spare room. What treasures!

His response was slow, came in spurts.

Didn't know you had books? I'd love to see them some time.

A two-minute pause as she watched the screen.

Why fuck me?

A shorter pause, before his next text appeared.

Let's skip tomorrow. Lisa typed. Sorry, Did I hurt your feelings with the fuck you? Don't take it personally. It's kind of a story. I'll tell you when I see you. Mostly I'm feeling guilty about the workshop.

A quick answer.

No worries. I don't take much personally these days. Pamela wants me to take her to a SF Jazz concert tomorrow. Her boss gave her tickets.

Her boss? Lisa didn't even know what Pamela did. She couldn't imagine her bossed by anybody.

They agreed to meet Monday afternoon.

32

SUNDAY
12-15-19

S HE WOKE TO A TEXT FROM CODY.
Hey. Are you ready for Ben and Cody? We have news! More soon.
Hope to see you sometime between the 17th and 19th.

A few more days before Cody would storm the West Coast. Lisa
had work to do before her arrival. Needed to get back into *Rocks and
Rolls*, write a few more posts, get into the workshop. Today for all three,
she promised herself. Made a to-do list and filled it up. She added "More
research on orchid production" to the list. Michael was working on the
legality and realities of growing pot for individuals or in a collective. She
needed to build a spreadsheet for the orchids, start pricing all the
materials and getting a handle on whether such an operation made
sense. If it could make any money. One more item for the list: Open G's
snail mail. She had avoided it for five weeks, had dropped it all into a
Costco-sized box that used to hold toilet paper. At the time she thought
it was fitting. Now it was just amassing, getting closer to the top.

She toasted an English muffin and added peanut butter, washed it
down with orange juice, and drove downtown, listening to Edward

Elgar's "Salut d'Amour". She pulled over in the Temple Beth El parking lot to attend to the piece. It may have been the most beautiful music she'd ever heard. She wanted to hear it again, as it had only lasted a few minutes. She hurried to the office, found it quickly on YouTube, and listened to it four more times. This music changed something in her, like an infusion, a refreshing of red blood cells. It was not easy for her to explain, or even think about. Music appreciation was on a longer to-do list, one she hadn't started yet, but it would be near the top. Maybe Cabrillo College offered a night class. She searched for Music Appreciation, found it quickly, a document downloaded to her desktop. She opened it, read through the grading criteria, thought it was just what she wanted, except it was offered from 9:30 to 10:50 on Tuesday and Thursday mornings. And the syllabus was dated 2012. Had they used the same syllabus for seven years, or was it really just that out of date? She'd have to call, or stop by on the way home.

She added "Call Cabrillo College" to the To Do list. Elgar's music invaded her sensibilities. She went back online and searched "Salut d'Amour," learned that Elgar's girlfriend, Caroline Alice Roberts, had given him a poem titled "The Wind at Dawn" for their engagement, a piece he set to music. His response was to compose "Salut d'Amour" as his engagement present. Lisa searched for the ten most romantic classical pieces ever written and saw that it topped three of the lists. She wrote a quick blog entry about it, posted it, moved on to Rocks and Rolls, lifted it out of its box, ready to continue where she'd left off. But her brain drifted, took her to Justin in the last piece she'd read, to the rocks Alice had scattered around her office and their house, like little trophies with no explanations, Lisa having no idea where they came from. She had loved them, loved seeing the new ones appear. She remembered now that Alice would make up stories for each of them, wild tales about how they were found or who found them or how they were formed from magic and mystery. She hadn't remembered those stories until now. Why was that? What was missing in her life? With her mother? Now she wanted the rocks, like her boxes of books. Maybe they were buried in the closet with the other things Gregory didn't like. Her things. Her clutter. The small amount of her life she had brought with her from Point Reyes Station. She imagined Ryan and Cody having a bonfire with the rest of her stuff, hauling it out to the beach, dumping gasoline on it, starting a huge blaze, finishing it off by toasting large marshmallows on coat hangers.

Back to Celia:

> William and Celia talked with each other every
> morning before they got out of bed, in the shop before the
> customers came in, in the evening once closed, made sure
> they talked honestly and openly about everything,
> everything that Celia had been afraid to share with him.
> He absolutely wanted the baby! The daughter. The
> daughter they had made together. And he was honest that
> it would be difficult for the business as she got bigger,
> became more tired, had the baby, had to spend time feeding
> and caring for it, though he promised to help, promised to
> work harder and get up earlier to bake more rolls and
> products to sell to cover the cost of diapers and cribs
> and toys and bright paints for the baby's room.
>
> Their passion and compassion for each other reached
> a new dimension. This truth-telling had hidden values.
> Once having worked through the pains of it, it expanded
> them, made Celia worry less about the way-too-much-love
> compared to the way-too-little-love scale, and how it
> crossed or merged with way too much stability versus way
> too little stability. She had to quit thinking that way
> now. They had a daughter to look after. To raise. To
> teach how to be and live in the world.

Lisa's life with Gregory had been stable. She had worried some about police breaking the door down and hauling him away. But she had the dogs, the cat, ate well, loved her work in the greenhouse. And, of course, the income. She still had a small savings account, never having spent much. No lunches or dinners or movies that G would be quick to point out as extravagances. At least stable if not at all loving. It made her think of Michael and Pamela. Where did they fall on the grid? It didn't appear like they were either loving or stable. Cody and Ben? Too soon, really, but at least temporarily stable and temporarily in lust or love. How about Zack? She didn't know much about him. Remembered him mentioning losing a daughter. Losing children quite often was connected to losing spouses. The inability to suffer through the grief together. The constant reminders that are easier to push aside and bury if you're alone.

Not digging too deeply into any of her to-do list items, but checking them off, nevertheless. Next up was orchid research. She spent an hour online, opened a new bookmark folder and added ten sites, dealing with everything from the cost and size of greenhouses to appropriate pesticides, fungal treatment, and once again, to the page about which combinations to build for year-round income. The more she read, the more discouraged she got. She moved on from the sites of those folks who were dedicated orchid growers, mostly as an avocation, a few trying to make a living, and found herself reading the pages of agricultural reviewers who knocked current-day small farming ventures. Corporate jaws were gobbling up everything that looked like it might make a profit. The monster farms that worked strictly on volume and could undersell every small farm.

She switched her strategy for a while. Went to the Santa Cruz County website to look at the requirements and timelines for lot splits, permits, licenses. She ran a double-strike line through each of the items on the list, felt a sense of accomplishment, which she added to the T-chart.

The only unchecked items on the list were Cabrillo College and the workshop. In the car, she drove to Cabrillo while listening to "Finlandia" by Sibelius. At the administration office they told her the Music Appreciation class was still being offered on Tuesday and Thursday mornings, and the syllabus was current. She wanted to mouth off, say something like, "I guess if it's classical it never changes." But she didn't. Maybe there was more truth to that than she thought. Before she left, the clerk said, "Or you can take the online class. One hundred and nine dollars." She picked up an application, took it with her, the class not starting until the third week of January.

•   •   •

The animals were hungry, lonely, waiting for food and affection. As Lisa pulled into the driveway, the boys ran to stick their noses through the fence, Eloise, at the living room window, padding back and forth across the sill. Lisa was on a roll. One more item to check off her list, she should head straight for the workshop, get it over with. But she didn't. Went inside to feed Eloise, thought about Zack down in Big Sur hiking through some wilderness. Unloaded the better part of a fifty-pound bag of Iams dog food into Turks and Caicos's food bins. Found a bottle of red wine in the cupboard, poured herself a glass. Found a partial joint in the silverware drawer, probably left over from Thanksgiving. She never smoked without G. This would be the first time since he died. She took two hits, which was more than enough, given the high quality of her weed. Phone in hand, earbuds in ears, she walked to the workshop, located Elgar's salute to his fiancée, plugged in the earbuds, set it to loop and listened.

The rusted key fit in the lock. It hadn't been used in so long that she had to jiggle it, pull it in and out a few times before it clicked to the left, opened. The room was dark. She had never been inside. It had been locked when she arrived seven years ago, had stayed so ever since. Off-limits. To everybody but G. He didn't even let the dogs in. Zack had been here twice over that period and he was the only one G let in. Last time was a year ago.

She fumbled for a light switch along the walls. Nothing. The building was so old she wasn't sure about electricity. She remembered G working out here during the night occasionally, but had he brought a flashlight? Standing in the doorway, she remembered sixth-grade science camp, the night hikes, the naturalist telling them to wait a few minutes before walking down the trail, give their rhodopsin a chance to kick in and help them see in the dark. Cody had laughed out loud, the only noise in the quiet, dark forest other than the naturalist. "What a stupid word that is!" she had whispered in Lisa's ear. "How do you even spell it? R-O-A-D-H-O-P-S-O-N?"

It had worked then, and was working now. Lisa recognized outlines of desks, file cabinets, chairs, the Harley, easels and pads, more. Stuff hanging on the walls, jammed into every corner. There was a small brass lamp on a table. As she made her way there, she took small steps, bumping into boxes and tables as she went. She flicked the switch. The lamp gave off enough light to get a better look at the room and what was in it, at least on the surface. This was worse than the spare room, or maybe better, depending on what she'd uncover. It was a large space, close to fifteen by twenty feet. On the small table she found a flashlight and another Amazon

Echo. Damn things were pervasive. In the world and on her property. She recalled G's ranting about Jeff Bezos again. She removed the earbuds, said, "Alexa, loop Edward Elgar's 'Salut d'Amour'." Alexa answered. "Playing Edward Elgar's 'Salut d'Amour'." Lisa didn't know if the loop command would work, but didn't want to restate the command every few minutes to replay the short piece. She bumped into a table and the lamp fell, light flicked off. She turned on the flashlight. The ray was dull, giving a muted view of the room's contents, just a hint into G's mind, a guest, rarely invited in. The Harley was covered with a blue tarp.

The flashlight flickered, went dark. She bumped it with her hand, brought the ray back briefly, pointed it at an easel pad that read, "Hemp Seeds. $1.00 each." The light disappeared. She backed out of the room, said, "Alexa, stop," before she locked the door. It would take daylight to do this correctly. And maybe different music, something that didn't evoke romance and love and the good parts of living with G. Maybe some Metallica or Led Zeppelin instead. In the morning. First thing. Before anything else slowed her down.

Inside, all her electronic devices were demanding attention, as were Eloise and the boys. She started with the landline, pushed the button in front of the blinking light. The first message was one of those fake IRS messages where an electronic voice threatened fines and jail. Which reminded her about the box of G's snail mail. Damn! The second message was Zack. "Hey, Lisa. Hanging out here in the wilderness. Clearing my head out really well. My plan is to stop back by your place on Tuesday, find out what you and Michael decided. Talk soon." Now for the cell phone and computer. But first, she placed two ham-and-cheddar hot pockets into the microwave, poured a glass of red wine, went to G's office, and added today's mail to the box. She wasn't about to deal with this in his office, lugged the box down the hall to the bedroom, went back and brought G's shredder into the room, plugged it in next to the bed. She stopped to cuddle the boys' ears for a couple of minutes, elicit a purr from Eloise, then brought her dinner to bed with her. She poured the contents of the box onto the bed, Eloise quickly finding a spot on top of it.

This was crazy. Why wasn't he here to take care of this himself? She wasn't sure how much of what she was feeling was anger and how much sadness. The wine and pot affected her judgment. The huge pile of envelopes and packages reminded her of her teacher's aide job. The principal had been a curmudgeonly kind of guy, friendly, a continual smile on his face. But when he was finally fired, the secretary found all the mail from the previous six months stuffed into bags under his desk, unopened.

She ran back down the hallway to G's office, grabbed a letter opener off his desk, came back and sliced open the first letter, a reminder about an upcoming subscription deadline for *H.O.G. Magazine.* For a second, she thought about Zack, maybe he'd want it. But no. She couldn't do this for every piece of mail. She dropped it in the shredder, changed her strategy, started culling the pile by looking for everything that was obviously bulk mail and crap. The shredder ate them all up, quickly filling up its container, and she had to empty it into the toilet-paper box. Three times. Eventually the pile narrowed to about thirty pieces of mail in envelopes that might or might not have been important, and a dozen packages sent through USPS, FedEx, and UPS.

G had brought his mail straight to his office, never let Lisa see what he was receiving. She was told to stay out of the mailbox, that he'd give her anything that was hers, which had rarely happened over the years. Told her to stay out of the office. In some ways this was like Christmas, opening packages, even if they didn't have her name on them. The next envelope she opened was a letter with no return address for G. Daniels. Inside was a single sheet of paper, no heading, no greeting, no closing, simply one typed line that read: "Same as always. See you in January." There were no clues anywhere about who the letter was from. How would G have known? She turned the envelope over, saw that it was postmarked Clovis. Maybe that was enough. One customer in Clovis who expected product delivered in January. She didn't shred it.

The next six envelopes contained bills, bills that she assumed were now past due. G had handled all the bills, all in his name, never giving the world a clue of her existence on his property. But now there was a utility bill, a Waste Management bill, the property taxes that were due last month, a large amount now past due. There was money in G's bank accounts, but neither she nor Michael had dealt with access yet. She opened her computer and created a new to-do list for tomorrow, added "Talk to Michael about bills, accounts." For today's list, she struck through "Cabrillo College" and "G's workshop." If she were at her office, she'd add it to her accomplishments list. It had been a good day. No disappointments at all. While on the computer, she went to Pious Rebel. There were over 100 comments to vet! That was the first disappointment of her day. But it shouldn't be. She should assume that all 100 comments love her work, love her. Don't drift to the negative just because it feels comfortable, because you expect it. She decided to wait on the comments, closed the computer, back to the shrinking pile on the bed.

She slid open another envelope with no return address, writing that looked like a woman's. Inside, again a single sheet of paper, no date, nothing but the one line, this time written in green ink, tiny hearts dotting the i's, that read: "Missed you last time. I'm ready. Hope to hear from you soon." She shook her head. Of course she had known. But to have evidence in hand made it too real. And maybe it was just about the pot. A client. Not a lover. What did it matter now? He was gone. Three more letters like that, all with different handwriting, that she put in a pile to share with Michael. Back into the computer again for the to-do list, to which she added: "Write and publish an obit for Gregory P. Daniels." They had avoided it. Didn't want to publicize G's demise, especially if they were to continue with the business. But these letters would keep coming if they didn't let people know.

The packages were easier to handle, less personal. A book about Harleys sent to him from Zack. Magazines. One package contained catalogues and price lists for feminized hemp seeds.

Hemp seeds? Twice in one day. She needed to get back into the workshop early in the morning. She shredded three more letters, got off the bed, hauled the box of shredded paper to the trash bin outside, returned the shredder to G's office, turned on *The Big Bang Theory*, opened the computer, accepted every comment without reading them.

Her cell phone buzzed. Michael.

Is tomorrow still good for you?

Nice of him to ask. Or was it no longer good for him?

She typed: Late afternoon is good for me.

She had to spend time in the workshop, do a little more research on the orchids before meeting with him. Think about an obit, how to deal with the Central Valley women, maybe hemp seeds, whatever other surprises she might uncover in the workshop.

33

MONDAY
12-16-19

G HAD ASKED HER ABOUT HER DREAMS. Was quick to tell her everything about his, which she found odd. He never shared anything about his personal life, his thoughts, what he did out of town, but he was happy to share the fantasies that came to him in the middle of the night, the contents of dreams that would often wake him and send him into the living room on the couch in front of some late-night reality motorcycle show.

He would push her to talk about hers. She'd shake her head, say, "I never dream. Never remember them if they exist. My whole life. Nothing." But since G's death, something was going on in her head at night. She wouldn't label them dreams, because they felt more real. They weren't narratives, no beginning, middle, and end. Words would appear. Phrases. She didn't believe in mysticism, seances, connecting with the dead, but for some reason the words had been popping into her head the past few weeks.

They'd roll around in there, in that state between sleep and wakefulness, trying to pretend they were part of a dream, but they weren't. When she wanted, she'd pop open the computer, add them to her journal. She usually didn't make the effort to do so, but this morning her eyes widened, and she opened the journal. She wrote down "construction, destruction, instruction, obstruction." No clue why. But anything and everything these days was fodder for her blog. She added "hemp seeds." She turned to the Dot sitting on the nightstand on G's side of the bed, remembered about Voicegram. "Alexa, can you record me?" Alexa answered with a rambling answer about privacy and contacting Amazon that Lisa didn't really want to hear about or follow up on. She tried again. "Alexa, can I add a list?" Alexa said, "What would you like to call the new list?"

If G had hated the idea of Amazon and Bezos so much, why would he use Echos and Dots all over the property and house? He *was* an all-about-me kind of guy, so if it was to his benefit, why worry if others were suffering at the hands of the evil monster's ideas, strategies, life-style? One more question: "Alexa, what are my lists?" Her quick response: "You have seven lists. Shopping. Hogs. Zack. For Michael. For Lisa. Hemp seeds. Just in case."

"What the fuck!" Lisa said out loud, as she shifted herself up and out of bed. This was the third occurrence of the hemp-seed topic, even if one had been fabricated by her brain. Not a dream, she reminded herself. Just a follow-up to the easel-pad jottings in G's workshop. She wanted to ask Alexa about the contents of every list but wasn't exactly sure how to proceed. She started with the shopping list. "Alexa, what's on my shopping list?" Alexa said, "You have three items on your shopping list: Staff of Life five-nine-two granola, bananas, and almond milk." G had loved the 592 granola. Wouldn't eat anything but. Wouldn't shop anywhere else. Complained about the conglomerate that Trader Joe's had become, not to mention that Jeff Bezos now owned Whole Foods.

Even though she thought it would make more sense to be completely prepared for her meeting with Michael, listen to the contents of all the lists before he arrived, she decided to wait. Do it together, act as if they'd be business partners into the future, even if it failed. After a quick shower and tending to the animals, she went to the cupboard and found G's container of 592 granola. She filled a bowl, sliced up a banana, added a dash of vanilla, a teaspoon of psyllium, and a tablespoon of protein powder, just the way G liked it, filled the bowl with almond milk, used the large spoon like he did, and took one bite after another. It was good. It was G. She picked up her keys and headed toward the workshop.

It was freezing in there. First thing she did was wrap herself in an old blanket. In daylight, she could see the Harley was covered with a layer of dust after being unused for five weeks. She found a pile of red shop rags on top of a tool cart, picked one up and wiped it down. Zack would appreciate it. So would G.

Another Herman Miller swivel chair sat behind a desk. G certainly knew how to take care of himself, if not those around him. She took a seat, slowly turned clockwise like the second hand on a clock, propelling herself with one foot, looking at the 360-degree view of the room. Walls completely covered, mostly with large cupboards, floor to ceiling, posters of concerts, broadsides of poems. She stopped abruptly when she saw a bookshelf in one corner, got up, mouth open, and made her way to the collection. Every one of Alice's rocks had been mounted on a fine piece of hardwood. There were over a hundred of them. She took one off the top shelf, ran her hand across the crystalline surface of the geode, turned it over, and saw a hand-carved narrative about the stone: "Discovered by Lisa's mother Alice on a day trip to Death Valley in 1956." Total fabrication. There is no way G knew anything about Alice, her rocks, any excursions she may have taken, because she never took any. But he had done this thing. Without ever mentioning it. She wanted to fall down and bawl, but she didn't. She was pissed. Why had she never seen this side of him? Why did he need to be so secretive and mysterious? She wasn't sure she wanted to share this room with Michael. Not sure it was his business. But she'd only just begun to uncover what was hidden in there. She wasn't sure who all's business might be there. She had only been a small part of G's life. For the better part of an hour she stood in front of the bookshelf, read every story, every fabricated narrative G had etched into the bottom of mahogany, cedar, maple, zebra wood, koa, dozens of other varieties of wood she didn't recognize.

Most of the cupboards had locks on them. She was getting a little tired of G's constant mysteries and hoops that had to be jumped through to discover what he had left behind, what he had been working on and thinking about in secrecy for so long. She didn't know what was most important, what things mattered in terms of moving forward with lives, hers and Michael's, and what things were more sentimental, or unsentimental, things like other women spread across other counties. This workshop was going to take some time. The locked cupboards. And the lists on the Echos and Dots. What else? The greenhouse. The safe. Nested folders on the computer. If he had only spent a portion of the time on her that he spent in juggling his secrets.

Too much to take in. She focused on the easel right in front of her, the one with "Hemp Seeds" written on the first page. She stood up, flipped the page, found a handwritten drawing of their greenhouse, thirty feet by hundred feet, 99 twenty-five-gallon squat pots equally distributed throughout the space. G had never talked to her about these ideas, never talked to her much about anything except the problems with the world from his perspective. She continued flipping. There were pages on the 18-hour x 6-hour growing cycle, the switch to a 12 x 12 cycle in the final month. Much of this was similar to what they did now, but there were modifications. She knew nothing about hemp seeds. But if G had, she'd better learn fast. Other pages talked about the 2018 federal legislation that legalized the growing of hemp, both for fiber and seeds, regulated by the amount of THC in the plants, less than 0.3%. This was another whole field of research she didn't have time for right now. Her life was getting busy, too busy on topics that cost her money rather than made her money.

She needed a vacation. Needed to get away, find a place to hide and think. Write blog posts. Maybe vet a few comments. Get away from people and mail and cell phones and even hungry animals.

Back inside Lisa made a tuna sandwich, the kind of tuna she liked: mayo, red onions, diced dill pickles, not that god-awful version G demanded with sesame seeds, honey, Greek yogurt. She covered whole-wheat bread with the tuna, dropped on a slice of sharp cheddar, buttered the outsides, and put it in the panini maker. She had come to love the panini, the melted cheese mixed with the tuna and a slight crunch to the bread. Michael texted.

See you in a couple of hours. I'll bring food. Want anything special?

Nice of him to offer, but she was full now. No appetite. But it could be a long session.

She typed: Dos Equis.

He typed back: No Patron?

She rarely used smiley-face icons, but did now.

Cody will be here soon enough. Probably by Friday. With Ben. Then you can bring your tequila. And Pamela, if you want a real party.

A frowny face appeared, followed by: Hilarious! See you soon.

On the far edge of a nap, words paraded through her head. But she couldn't make them out, nonsense words made up wholly of vowels or consonants. Behind the words came a steady flow of Alice's rocks mounted on life-sized slabs of wood, bikinied beauties perched on them, waving at some crowd, congregating in the parking lots of Temple Beth El and Cabrillo College.

She heard the soft whoosh of carbonation pushing its way out of a bottle, twice, opened her eyes to see Michael moving her way from the kitchen, setting a Dos Equis on a coaster next to her, taking a seat in G's easy chair. She had to stop thinking like that. It wasn't G's easy chair anymore. It was just a chair. That anyone could sit in now. Michael didn't barrage her with questions and small talk, took a sip of his beer, laid his head back, closed his eyes. This was new, nice. Could she learn to relax with him, let loose of her prejudgments? Probably not, but this was something. She closed her eyes, found herself on one of the rock floats, not waving, but trying to read the scrambled words marching behind her. It was no use. Now it looked like someone had printed the words flipped horizontally. It was disconcerting, made her a little dizzy, but she wasn't sure if the dizziness was inside the nap or truly inside her body. She opened her eyes, sat up, took a sip of beer, stared at Michael, who was strangely serene.

"Thanks for the beer," she said.

"You're welcome," he answered, eyes still closed, head still rested.

Eloise jumped into Michael's lap, made herself comfortable. His hand gentle on her back, he pulled at her tail. "This is all so ridiculously difficult, complicated," he said.

"Which parts?" Lisa offered.

"Every part. Pick one. Why this cat reacts like this to human touch. Why the tail stiffens. Why there are twenty cases of sockeye salmon stacked in your kitchen. Why I'm still with Pamela after all these years."

Lisa sat back on the couch, pulled a blanket up around her neck, made a point to stay quiet, not answer his unanswerable questions. Let him go. She hadn't seen this side of him before. What she wanted to call vulnerability. She drifted back to her nap. Vulnerability had been one of the scrambled words, actually two of them, separated into vowels and consonants. She was glad to see it come to life, make some sense in her real life, her current thoughts.

"Sorry," he said. "You don't need to hear this stuff."

"I do need to hear this stuff. Glad to know I have company."

She saw his lips form a grin. "Misery loves company," he said. She leaned forward, took another sip of beer, wrapped herself up again and rested her head on a pillow, thought carefully about what to say next.

"This feels different, between us. It's a good thing. So, I'm going to tell you something I hate," Lisa said. Michael's eyes opened. "There's not much sense to it. It's just this thing I've had ever sense I was a kid. Something my mom ingrained in me."

"I don't think I've ever heard you talk about her," Michael said.

"She's come back into my life since G died. But the things she taught me to hate were clichés, people who use them."

Michael smiled. "Ah. Got it. Misery and company and the like."

Lisa nodded, took another sip of beer. "Your turn. What do you hate about me?"

Eloise jumped off Michael's lap as he scooted forward in the chair. "Wow! We're diving right into this thing." He got up, walked to the window, pointed at Turks and Caicos prancing around their playground. "Those two are so much better off here than with us."

Lisa didn't disagree but didn't want to let him change the subject. She stayed quiet. Michael came back, walked past the chair, sat on the couch just beyond where her feet rested under the blanket. He got comfortable, which made her a little uncomfortable.

"I've never really thought of you and hatred in the same, I don't know, how would you say it, without creating a cliché, or worse yet, a mixed metaphor."

She stopped him. "Mixed metaphors are much better than clichés."

"Never thought of you and hatred in the same breath, occupying the same sentence together. If I was forced to begin a sentence with 'What I hate about Lisa Hardrock is …' I would have to do a little work to finish it."

Lisa moved her feet away from him, up under her thighs. "That's all I'm asking. A little bit of work, some truth."

Michael continued. "What I hate about Lisa Hardrock is that I don't know enough about her to really hate her. What I hate about Lisa Hardrock is that my brother kept her so tightly guarded that I could never find a way in. What I hate about Lisa Hardrock is that she thinks she knows who I am, thinks she knows who Pamela is, who we are together."

"I'm beginning to hate that myself," she said.

"Which part?"

"That I didn't have much of a life when I was with G." Michael nodded, stayed quiet, pulled the blanket over his legs. "Speaking of which," she continued, "you alluded to something a couple of weeks ago that has bothered me. Stayed with me."

He got up, walked to the window again, finished his beer. "I know. I know. I've been kicking myself ever since. I never should have said anything. It was stupid to bring it up."

"So you know what I'm talking about?"

"Of course I do. I saw the change in your face after I said it and hated myself."

"There we go. Let's add some self-hate into this discussion. But why did you say it?"

"Because it's true. I forget what we were talking about that brought it on, but it seemed appropriate at the time."

"To basically tell me that I was nothing special, that G had headed to Point Reyes Station to find any woman to bring home as his little pot slave, sex slave?"

"That's a little harsh. I never should have said anything. There's more to it, but I can't go there."

"And here I thought we were making a little progress today. Sharing secrets and truths. Working our way into hearts and real topics. Like I want to hear more about Pamela."

"I'm sure you do. But what truths have you shared with me?"

"You know you're changing the subject, and I'm going to allow it, for a minute, but if we're going to be partners, we need to be sharing the hard stuff. As you said earlier, the ridiculously difficult complicated stuff. Like G seeking me or someone out seven years ago, the whys and hows of it. Let me share a truth with you, something I discovered, something I could have kept from you forever. But here you go. Alexa, what are my lists?" The blue-green ring on top of the Echo lit up.

Alexa answered. "You have seven lists. Shopping. Hogs. Zack. For Michael. For Lisa. Hemp seeds. Just in case."

"You're kidding me"? Michael came back to the couch, paced back and forth behind it. "How'd you figure that out?"

"Ben said something about checking out Voicegram. I did. Voicegram no longer exists by itself, is part of a company called Sayspring. And when you go to Sayspring, it says they're now part of Adobe. There's no way in to use it. You have to register and request an invitation."

"That's crazy."

"Yeah. I got an email back from Adobe saying I'm under consideration. Anyway, I just started researching other ways to have Alexa record your voice. Turns out lists are the easiest way."

"This is totally amazing, and totally scary."

"I know. Apparently, Amazon employees can listen to everything we say. I don't know if G knew that. If he kept confidential information on his lists or not."

"What have you discovered so far?"

"The shopping list has five-ninety-two granola, bananas, and almond milk on it."

"What? On seven lists that's all you found?"

"I didn't say that. Why we're even talking about this is trust and truth. I only listened to the least-threatening list. I decided to wait to listen to the others until you were here with me."

"Even the one labeled 'For Lisa'?"

"Even the one labeled 'For Lisa.' What do I care anymore? I'm trying to pry myself out of the past and move on."

"Well, if that's true, you probably shouldn't care about the hows and whys of G's trip to Point Reyes Station."

"All I'm saying is that you asked for truths and I'm giving them to you. Maybe someday you'll return the favor." Michael continued pacing around the room, tilting his beer.

"You want a panini?" Lisa asked.

"What kind?"

"Tuna. Cheese. Whole wheat."

"Whose recipe?"

"Mine."

"Sure."

"One or two?"

"Two. Please."

Lisa busied herself with the sandwiches, waited for Michael to continue the discussion, interested in which direction he would head next. So much stuff, lives disturbed and altered so quickly. She saw Turks and Caicos through the kitchen window. Except theirs. Just feed us, let us run, ignore our slobber, and we're good, not worrying about who's here and who's not here. Nothing mysterious or hidden about a couple of towering bull mastiffs looking to enjoy their lives.

"Alexa, shopping list," Michael said from the couch.

"You have three items on your shopping list. Five-nine-two granola. Bananas. Almond milk."

"That is just beyond me," he said.

"You want Tater Tots with these?"

"I'd love some. Makes me think of Gregory."

"Yeah. I know. I'm not buying anymore. So enjoy them. Ketchup?"

"Yes, please," Michael said. "Shall we listen to the other lists?"

Lisa handed him a paper plate with the paninis. "Tots ready in two minutes. I don't know. Are we ready for this? There's so much else. Do we want to do this first? Or stay with our plan to talk about the greenhouse. Or, to have me show you the inside of the workshop?"

"Damn!" he said. "It's like a candy store."

"More like a little shop of horrors," she added.

Michael laughed out loud. Lisa joined him. He wolfed down one of the paninis before speaking. "These are great. Thanks. Here's what I'm thinking. Before we make any major decisions about what to do with the greenhouse, the property, our lives, we should try to uncover as many of Gregory's secrets as possible"

"Makes sense. How about this? You sit here and finish your food. We listen to a couple of the lists that might be safer than the others. Like maybe you want to listen to 'For Michael' without me in the room."

"No way. I have nothing to hide, want to move forward together on all of this stuff." She wanted to say, "Then tell me about the Point Reyes Station part," but didn't. He was right. That was the past, and did it really matter anyway? It did to her, but she'd let it go for now.

172

"I agree. Let's start simple, with the Zack list. He's in Big Sur until tomorrow. I don't know if we need to tell him about the list. Maybe just details that may be important to him."

Michael nodded. "I say we listen to it, take notes, then delete it." Lisa went to the kitchen, grabbed her computer, opened her journal, typed "Zack's Alexa List."

"Go for it," she said to Michael.

He scooched closer to Lisa, looked at her computer screen, said, "Alexa, read Zack's list."

"You have thirteen items on Zack's list. Things to talk to Zack about. I use Moore and Sons when I need something small. They're over on East Cliff Drive. For the bigger stuff I go to West Coast Harley Davidson in Salinas. The handle-bar bushings are worn out. Need to replace them soon. Bit of a rough idle lately. Adjust the carburetor to get desired fuel flow. Battery hasn't been holding charge well. Have Moore check it out. There are oil leaks on the drain plugs. I've been wrapping them in Teflon tape to delay the leakage, but it's an ongoing task. The plastic on the cam chain is wearing out again. Needs to be replaced soon. I've still got the stock horn on this thing, and it sucks. Need to eventually replace it. Ask Zack for more salmon. Ask Zack about smoked trout. Ask Zack about investing in hemp seeds. Ask Zack when he'll move to Santa Cruz. Get to Alaska to visit Zack."

Lisa typed rapidly. "Say it again? She talks too fast. I missed some."

After the second time through, she looked at Michael, said, "No rocket science there. I say we let him listen to it."

"Wait. Two things," Michael said. "Do we trust Zack? I mean, if he hears us invoking Alexa's lists, he might hunt for other lists when we're not around."

"Okay," she said. "I get it. I'll just print my notes out for him. What's the other thing?"

"Hemp seeds. What's that about?"

"Oh, that. Do you want to keep going with the lists, or shall I take you out to the workshop and show you something about hemp seeds?"

"Definitely the workshop. Let's do it now. Lists later."

"I haven't spent much time out there yet. Not much that will interest you. But there's definitely hemp-seed stuff."

• • •

Inside the workshop the first thing Michael went for was the Harley, rubbed his hands over the body and fenders like it was a prized horse. "We're really going to let Zack walk away with this?" Michael asked.

"It's what G wanted. It's the right thing to do. And I've been thinking, having Zack in the house for a while won't be so bad. There's things he can help with."

Michael stared at her, went quiet.

"What?" Lisa asked.

Michael shook his head, moved away from the Harley, looked at the easel pad. "Just that the two of us have enough to figure out without a third person ringing in with ideas."

Lisa's cell phone pinged. Cody. *Landed at SFO. Ben picked me up and we're headed for the penthouse! See you in a couple days.*

"Who's that?" Michael asked.

Lisa didn't like Michael slipping into that possessive tone, that feeling-left-out attitude he wore around Gregory. But they were doing this thing together, so she let him in. "It's Cody. She's in the city with Ben."

"Right. And speaking of folks ringing in with ideas. Now we've got Ms. Codyrocks and her attorney heading to town, for … how long?"

Lisa hesitated, walked to the easel, flipped a page. "Two to three weeks. You can never be sure with her. But let's get on with this stuff."

Michael looked at the easel, shook his head. "I've been cranking away examining the legal side of pot growing, you've been working on the orchid angle, but even now, from his grave, Gregory is thinking way ahead of us with some new scheme he hasn't shared with anybody? Controlling motherfucker."

"I know. Kind of looks that way. But it's just something else to consider. Looks like he's done most of the research on this one. I've looked at it twice, and don't completely understand it." She turned one page at a time, and they read everything out loud to each other. When they reached a blank page at the end, Michael plopped himself down in a chair, body crumpled and slack.

"I mean, hemp seeds?"

"I know. How could he not even mention this to us?" Just one more thing to rack up against him. In her head she added it to the

174

Disappointments column. Way too early to even consider it possibly being an accomplishment. "Tell me where you are with the legal pot idea."

"Okay. Every path I've looked into suggests that the small pot farmer is dead. Prices have come down. Licensing and legalization make it restrictive. Cost of materials too high against the lowered price per ounce. The hybrid idea of mostly orchids, with a handful of individual plants with a medical marijuana card, or a collective with five folks, might be an idea worth considering. But it's still not completely legal, and even if the state lets you slide, the feds could come after you. What about the orchids idea?"

"I joined an orchid club. Newsletters. Have books coming. Have read every website available. It seems like there are really two choices. You get into it as a hobby, small scale, give plants away to friends, or you're a monster farmer with mega-greenhouses and employees and bills and income. While the idea of a hybrid operation along with pot sounds good on paper, the reality is that the cycles, the humidity levels, everything about growing orchids is different, and it doesn't make sense to combine them."

Michael removed himself from the chair, again stood up in front of the easel, flipped over a couple of pages. He looked past the easel. "Hey. What's that stuff?" He walked to the bookcase with the mounted geodes.

"Rocks I brought here from Berkeley when I moved in. They were Alice's. My mom's."

"Rocks, hell! These are geodes. This wood. These stories on the back."

"I know. The man of mystery lives on, in every way he can."

"You didn't know about this?" Michael continued looking at each geode until he got to the bottom shelf.

"You know the answer. I'd never set foot inside here until yesterday. Was never invited in."

"Right. Sorry. These are amazing."

"I know. Just stirs things up a little more."

Michael went back to the chair. "It seems like Gregory was predicting the future of the small farmer before springing it on us."

"Yeah. I'm not saying we've made any decisions yet, but if we ruled out pot by itself so we could stay out of jail, and if we ruled out

175

orchids because it isn't lucrative enough for the small farmer, and if the hybrid idea won't work because of the growing differences, what makes hemp seeds less risky?"

"According to Gregory's notes, there's no legal risk. This law they passed in 2018 makes it legal to grow hemp for fiber, CBD oil, or seeds. And in a thirty-by-hundred-foot greenhouse like ours, we could fit ninety-nine plants."

"Right," Lisa jumped in. "Seems like the risk has to do with the feminization of the crop, making sure identified males are removed. Doing this right is a lot more work than growing pot or orchids. And if you aren't certified at less than zero-point-three-percent THC levels, your finished crop is worth nothing. That means there's a very high risk of losing a lot of time and money for an end-product you can't do anything with."

Michael flipped the chart to the last page. "But, if his calculations are accurate, if you've done everything right, get your certification, you're likely to harvest ten thousand seeds per plant, times ninety-nine plants, times a dollar-plus per seed. We're talking a million dollars per growing season. According to this, the selling of the seeds is a no-brainer, and legal. It puts a lot of pressure on you, though."

"What do you mean?" Lisa cocked her head, looked around the easel to a corner of the workshop, a small desk and chair in a dark corner. She stood up, moved in that direction.

"I mean there's much more weight on the shoulders of the master gardener, making sure you can land this thing the way it's designed."

"Yeah. That sounds right." She pulled the chair out from under the desk. Gregory's Patagonia jacket. She lifted it from the seat, carried it back in both hands like a wounded deer. Hands around the zippered pocket, she felt Gregory's cell phone, the handmade notebook. A couple of pens. "I need to go inside."

"But we just started. So much to hunt through in here. Those cabinets alone."

She lowered her head, showed Michael's G's jacket. "I know. I just need to go inside for now. Give all of this a rest. This is the first I've seen his jacket, since the accident. The phone. His notebook."

Michael nodded. "Got it. Want me to lock up?"

No way Michael was getting his hands on her keys. "No thanks. I'm good."

Inside the house, Michael lit another fire. Lisa sat in G's chair, jacket across her lap. Michael went to the fridge, grabbed two Dos Equis, handed her one, and sat on the couch. "How shall we proceed?" he asked.

She held her palm up, pointed it at him. "I need to do this one by myself. You'll need to trust if I discover anything pertinent, I'll share it with you."

"That's fine with me. What I meant was how shall we proceed with the hemp-seeds idea?"

"I am really wearing down. I might need some time away. How about if you dig into everything hemp-seed related, read things, talk to folks, make the decision for us? I'm good with that if you are."

"What do you mean by time away?"

"Just like it sounds. Away from this house. From Zack. From you. From everybody." The landline rang.

Lisa stared at it. Michael said, "Want me to get that?"

"Sure."

"Hello. Hello. Anybody there?" He hung it up, stared at her.

"It's been happening every couple of days. No clue."

Michael shook his head. "Those Central Valley dicks. They don't know he's dead yet."

"Good point. I was thinking we should write a short obit. Get it in the papers."

"That makes sense. Pamela still thinks we should have a memorial. Maybe we have something small, add the info to the obit. Put Gregory behind us, and any others he might be in debt to."

Lisa smiled, stuck her hands inside G's Patagonia jacket, warmed them against the lining. "We both know he didn't want that, but this is no longer about his wishes. We need to take care of ourselves. You want to write it?"

"I'll take the first stab, run it by Pamela, who is an excellent editor, then you can alter it how you want. What about the memorial? When?"

"New Year's Eve is in two weeks. Let's do it then."

"Okay. But where are you going?"

"Not far. I'll stay within the county. Here's another thing. I know we have to keep meeting, almost daily, to figure out next steps. I mean, if we end up deciding to carve this property up and sell it, that'll take some work for both of us. Either way, we probably need to have daily meetings. But I need to get into my office every day, including weekends, probably from morning until maybe two o'clock, so I'll be available in the afternoons."

"Fair enough. I'll plan on it. When you get back."

"Good. And you can babysit Zack and Cody and Ben in the meantime."

Michael smiled. "Happy to. Ben can take care of himself, though."

When they left the workshop, she brought one geode mounted on zebra wood with her, set it on the nightstand next to the bed, left a candle lit next to it, kept the TV off, allowed herself to sleep deeply without it.

34

TUESDAY
12-17-19

I N THE MORNING, NO RESIDUE OF PARADES or marching words, just a lightness, a relaxation she hadn't remembered feeling since she was very young, maybe at an event Alice and Anita had taken her to at Sigmund Stern Grove in San Francisco. There had been clowns and posters and photographs, everyone was smiling, snapping pictures, her mom and Anita unpacking a picnic lunch, egg-salad sandwiches, potato salad with pickles and olives and potatoes with the red skins still attached. That had been a good day, Cody not quite so pushy, captured by the lives of others depicted in photographs.

Michael would make some decisions on his own, would write the obit, and she could slip away, hide, maybe in plain sight. She had an idea, would check it out today. She was excited about it, glad to have made a decision to dedicate this time to herself, to Alice and her books, to blogging, to trying something new, something Socrates had said about an unexamined life. It was time to examine hers, those around her, quit wallowing in negativity and disappointment and figure a few things out.

Eloise and the boys were gone from her room. She took a quick shower, liked seeing the blue sky blend through the stained-glass window in the ceiling, left her hair wet, slipped into jeans and a t-shirt, headed for the kitchen. Zack was there, scraping a can of salmon into Eloise's bowl.

"Hey. Hi," he said.

"Eloise thanks you for that."

"My pleasure."

"How was Big Sur?"

"Fabulous, again. I didn't see Joan Baez this trip."

She laughed. "As if you've ever seen her, on any trip."

"Doesn't mean I won't someday. But I did meet some fascinating folks. Learned some things about myself."

"Wish I had time to hear the stories, but I have an appointment downtown."

"Yay! With who?"

She shook her head. What made people think it was okay to ask such questions that invaded one's privacy? No. She didn't want to go there today, simply answered, "With myself."

"Ah. Good company. Have some fun!"

"I intend to. By the way. The Harley is yours, and you're welcome to stay here if you like. For a while."

"That's great news! Thank you."

"I still have the only key to the workshop, so we can deal with it when I get back."

"Where you going?"

More questions. "To spend some time with myself."

"Again, great choice! Don't worry about the Harley. I've got a key to the workshop."

"You what?"

"Oops. You didn't know? Gregory gave me one last summer."

"Like I said. You're welcome to the Harley, welcome to hang for a bit, but I'd really appreciate it if you don't go into the workshop without me."

"Makes sense. In fact," he pulled a keychain from his pocket, removed a key, and set it on the kitchen counter. "There you go."

This guy was being way too kind. Didn't make sense to her. Not how she had remembered him. Maybe it was the lack of meat in his bloodstream. The Mr. Clean head shave. He popped two halves of an

English muffin into the toaster. She thought about his daughter. He had shown her pictures during last year's visit. Maybe it was just a custody issue. Maybe not cancer or leukemia or something else that had carried her away on his northern lights. When the toaster popped, Zack dabbed peanut butter on the halves, put them on a paper plate, wrapped them in foil, handed them to her.

"For your road trip."

She still didn't believe this change in him was real and would stick. "Where's the fresh-squeezed juice?" She tried to withhold a grin, unsuccessfully. He opened the fridge, grabbed a quart of Nob Hill orange juice, set it on the counter.

"Best I can do."

Lisa was glad he didn't say sorry, offer an apology for something out of his control. She went back to the bedroom, found her backpack, filled it with some clothes, grabbed her computer bag off the couch, and headed for the front door. "By the way, my friend Cody and her friend Ben are coming down. They'll stay in the guest room you're in, probably through New Year's. You should switch to the spare room across the hall."

"Perfect!" Zack said. She walked to the kitchen counter, picked up the key, headed for the front door, grabbed G's Patagonia jacket off a chair.

Hand on the doorknob, she turned back to Zack, who had Eloise's taut tail in his hands.

"Your daughter?" she said.

"Another time." She watched him turn away, walked down the hallway, slip into the spare room she knew was overgrown with Gregory's possessions, a mattress somewhere under the piles.

•   •   •

First to arrive at the office, she opened the laptop, leaned back in the chair, stretched, twisted her torso, breathed in deeply before placing the earbuds, starting the meditation music. There were over a hundred comments to read through on Pious Rebel. Most were one- or two-liners that she could buzz through quickly, but some were looking for best friends, wanted to form long-term relationships through electronic dialogues. Even though many of those were sincere, she was reluctant to accept them, as they weren't just comments, they posed questions, got personal, and she wasn't sure this was a good venue to do so. The number of unique visitors was growing. It was like a virus — exposure begets more exposure. Bianca's corps of dedicated online friends each had their own networks. If she built a Venn diagram, there would be a percentage of overlap among Bianca's friends, but they each had another dozen nodes that overlapped other friends. As long as she could keep them interested in her topics, in her, as Bianca had been saying, who knew where this thing could lead?

After the vetting, Lisa made out a new to-do list in her journal:

- Write a new blog post
- Finish Rocks and Rolls
- Call Land of Medicine Buddha
- Open the Patagonia jacket, cell phone
- Research geodes
- Research Zack's daughter
- Research hemp seeds
- Figure out where to spread G's ashes
- Take a trip to Berkeley – (maybe wait for Cody)

She typed:

My mother, Alice Hardrock, was an independent woman. She was an editor by profession, read nonfiction manuscripts for professors and politicians around the world. They knew she was good, would wait in line for her services, paid her well. She would lock the door to her office, leave my friend Cody and me with ears to the French doors, listening to her pound away on her electric typewriter. Upon her death last year, I discovered that she was also a writer of fiction. Buried away in a dilapidated shed on the back of her property, I discovered a banker's box containing five manuscripts. This flabbergasted me. She never talked to me about it, kept it a well-hidden secret. I've yet to tell Cody about it, haven't even told her about this blog site yet. I'm almost through reading the second book, Rocks and Rolls. When I found the box of manuscripts, I also found a box full of geodes that Alice kept scattered around her writing desk, until she had so many they leaked out into the living room, the dining room, all over the house. I hadn't been able to find them at my current house in Aptos until yesterday. Seven years without them in my life. But yesterday, I discovered them locked away in a room I had never been given access to. When I found them, I was pleased and pissed. My partner, who had kept them hidden, had taken each one, mounted it on a piece of sanded and polished fine hardwood, engraved fictional stories on the back, and built a bookshelf that housed them all in his private workshop. That he did this told me more about him than I'd learned during seven years with him. That he never shared it with me confirmed the sinking feelings I'd been having about him. The good news is Alice's geodes have returned to me. The bad news is ... I'm not sure at the moment there is any bad news, at least around this discovery. But there are more discoveries to come. Hang around. I'm sure some bad news, or at least disturbing news, is lurking. As well as the Holy Grail!

She reread it once, didn't edit a single word, hit Publish, moved to the next item on the list.

The dog-ear in *Rocks and Rolls* brought her to the final chapter. Back in Point Reyes Station, many of her friends in the Sunday-afternoon reading salon had unique idiosyncrasies about how they read books. One would flip straight to the last page and read it before going back to page one. Similar to the way John Irving writes his books, that friend had once commented to her. Another would get to the last chapter, and if she had loved the book so much she didn't want it to end, she'd never finish it, had a whole shelf of unfinished books that she loved, looked forward to someday completing.

Neither of those techniques were shared by Lisa, especially with Alice's novels. She wanted to be as surprised as she imagined Alice was when she first wrote them, would never zoom ahead to the end. And, she absolutely wanted to get to the last page, the final sentence, the period that punctuated the end, because she had more of Alice's books to read. Number three in the series, *Love Muffins*, was in the queue. But first, to finish the final chapter of Book 2.

The women who wanted William to help them learn how to bake were quick to volunteer their assistance as Celia

grew closer to full term. They took turns working the
front counter, helping William mix and bake and glaze as
Celia spent more time sitting, in bed, resting. Celia was
of two minds about the help. Justin had quit coming by
with the rocks. Celia would see him walk past their
window with high school girls, holding hands, arms
around shoulders, him carrying their books. First it was
one girl with brown hair, then another with blond hair,
until he had been through the rainbow with them. Also of
two minds. She couldn't fault him for it, any more than
she could fault William for enjoying attention from his
volunteers.

On November 10, early in the morning, her water
broke. William hurried her to Children's Hospital on
Pill Hill, wheeled her into the maternity ward, and by
noon he and Celia had an eight-pound daughter, cleaned
and swaddled and ready to begin her new life as the
baker's daughter. With the baby asleep on her chest,
Celia turned and saw three geodes sitting on the
nightstand. She looked around the room for William,
thought he must have taken them off the coffee shelf, but
found Justin, leaning forward on his elbows, watching
them both.

"Well, hello," she said.

"Well, hello back at you. I bet you thought I
abandoned you."

"Absolutely not. As expected. You simply graduated."

Lisa was enthralled with Justin, remembered the fifteen-year-olds
in her life when she had gone to Piedmont High School in 1998. They
were a bit upscale, held their noses a little too high, thought they could
get away with acting like dicks, and usually did. Her first didn't bring
her rocks. Arnold had brought her greeting cards, way too many, two a
day for the whole month of February, cards with syrupy sentimentality,
used the word love way too often for someone who couldn't even drive
yet. She wanted to know where Alice had gotten the rocks, who had
given them to her. She thought about Anita, who would be around
seventy-five if she were still alive. Anita would know. There was no one
closer to Alice than Anita. When Lisa had moved out in her early

twenties, she wondered if Anita and her mom were lovers. Is that why Anita applied the turkey baster? Were they creating this baby together with the help of their close-knit group of male friends? She added "Find Anita" to her to-do list. Made her think about when Sam Shephard died in 2017. It made her cry. Made her speculate again.

•   •   •

It was too early to call Land of Medicine Buddha. She skipped to the next item on the list — G's jacket. He must have left it in the workshop before heading to the oak stand with his chain saw. She reached in the side pockets. Tissues in the left — he had a chronic runny nose — receipts from Home Depot and Ace Hardware in the right.

Finally she unzipped the pocket on the front, the one that held things over his heart, removed his cell phone and pocket notebook he had traded pot for with a friend who made handmade journals and books. The cell phone was dead. She used her power cord to begin the charge, then opened the notebook. It was fairly new. The first date was October 1. There were only a handful of notes:

October 1 – (A scribble of a light bulb next to a quote):

"Don't be afraid to ride alone and don't worry about liking it. Sometimes you need to lose yourself to find yourself."

It wasn't like him to be philosophical. But the quote was mostly about riding his Harley. Ironically, it felt like a metaphor for Lisa's whole life.

October 7 – Another light bulb and another motorcycle quotation: "Money can't buy you love or immortality, but it can get me a Hog, so what's the difference." That was a little closer to G's mentality.

October 13 – No light bulb, just a dash. "Dreamweaver ready for delivery. Find her a card." There was a mystery solved. Partially.

October 17 – 30-year anniversary of Loma Prieta earthquake. Stay off the hog and under doorways.

October 24 – Another meeting with Pamela at Gayle's
Bakery.

October 29 – Codyrocks coming to town for Thanksgiving!
Ask her about Colorado hemp seeds.

Why was he meeting Pamela at Gayle's? Apparently more than
once. She had never known him to meet Pamela anywhere for
anything, rarely mentioned her. The Codyrocks thing popping up
again. Who was this man? Who *is* Cody? On and on these mysteries
plagued her. Still too early to call Medicine Buddha.

The cell phone needed a full charge given its weeks of non-use.
Lisa was patient, would let it fill up before digging for the next treasure,
the next nest of brown recluse spiders waiting to devour her whole.
She added to the T-chart Accomplishments "Found G's jacket and
phone" and added to the Disappointments side "Other women, as if I
hadn't already known."

Inside Pious Rebel she opened the Comments page to see over two
hundred waiting for her. She laughed. None of the management folks
were in yet, so she laughed louder, cackled over the wall for no one to
hear but herself. HotMama had been right. She was developing a
following, and she had no idea why. Her posts were not rocket science,
weren't especially gossipy. She didn't understand the attraction, hadn't
spent enough time in that world to translate the motivation and
psychology behind bloggers and blog viewers. She accepted almost all
comments, noticing that they were beginning to arrange themselves into
a handful of categories: 1) friends of Bianca who would respond
positively to everything, 2) friends of friends of Bianca, who, again, didn't
appear to be critical about anything, yet, 3) people who loved orchids and
wanted to purchase them as soon as they were ready, 4) folks who were
falling in love with Alice, 5) those who wanted Lisa to post the full text of
Alice's manuscripts, 6) bakers, 7) geode freaks, 8) random visitors with
specific interests, 9) wackos and perverts, and 10) Michael.

Luckily the wackos and perverts were limited, and she could lock
them out forever as needed. She was starting to allow the Bianca folks in
without much vetting. So far, they were proving to be safe. It was Michael
she had to watch, and the obsessive types with personal agendas who took
a sideways approach, to their lives as well as her posts, she was guessing.

The geode folks were amusing. She liked what they had to say. They were providing her with information and insights that she didn't have to research herself. But could she trust them? At this point she was beginning to think that trust was overrated. She had trusted G. She had trusted Cody. On the other hand, Ryan had trusted her. They were all at fault, she included. She banned three perverts who made suggestions about what she could do with Alice's rocks. What makes depraved people tick? She didn't care. They were gone. The new category of random visitors that appeared today were twenty folks who had responded to her query about books to read. She opened the to-do list, added the book titles:

- *The Overstory* by Richard Powers
- *The Moons of August* by Danusha Laméris
- *Little Fires Everywhere* by Celeste Ng
- *Eleanor Oliphant Is Completely Fine* by Gail Honeyman
- *Talking to Strangers* by Malcolm Gladwell
- *How to Do Nothing* by Jenny Odell
- *The Art of Voice* by Tony Hoagland
- *500 Social Media Marketing Tips* by Andrew McCarthy

She thanked all the commenters who had recommended books, would stop by Bookshop and pick up one on the way home.

9:03. Now she could call.

"Land of Medicine Buddha. How can we help you?"

"Hi. I'd like to find out about accommodations."

"Certainly. We have many options, depending on the size of your group, and when you'd like to come."

"I'd like to come as soon as possible, even as soon as tonight if you have something."

"We do have availability. There's a two-night minimum at the rate of two hundred and fifty dollars."

"Is that two-fifty per night?"

"That's for both nights. How many in your party?"

"That depends. Do you allow dogs?"

"Why, of course. We believe that dogs are sentient beings, too. In order to maintain harmony, dogs must be on leashes at all times."

"Is there an extra charge for the dogs?"

"Dogs are free."

"These are very large dogs. Bull mastiffs. I'm not sure I could manage them on leashes. I need a little R and R during this stay."

"That's completely up to you. You don't have to decide now."

"Great."

After providing her credit-card information, Lisa came back to G's cell phone, now fully charged. She opened it. It wanted the four-digit password. Of course it did. She banged her head lightly against the desk, not hard enough to do damage, just enough to remind her how tired she was of G and his world. She tried HOGS. No. She tried ZACK. No. She tried LISA. No. She tried WEED. No. She keyed in CODY, and was in. "Fuck me!" she screamed over the walls into a still-empty room. She clicked on the phone icon, selected Voicemail and perused a list of read and unread messages over the past six weeks. It looked as if all calls received before the day he died had been erased, not keeping any info that would divulge anything to anybody. But, since Halloween, there were fifty-three messages. She recognized some of the names: A few from Zack. A Dreamweaver. A Goldenrod. Others she didn't recognize. Her energy was waning. A stiffness in her neck working its way down her back. A resistance to play. She didn't want to listen to these right now, stuffed the phone and the notebook back in the zippered pocket.

The bell to the outside office rang twice.

"Holy shit!" Bianca didn't wait to enter Lisa's office. "You are skyrocketing. Here's what we need to do next." Lisa raised her palms to block Bianca's face.

"Stop! Slow down. I'm fried."

"With what?"

"With everything. Way too much bombarding me right now. I'm going to get away for a couple of days. Unplug."

"No! You can't. This is a critical time. I need you to sit down, for just ten minutes, so I can talk to you about the advertising and marketing end of this game."

"I don't care. I can't do this right now."

"Trust me. Just ten minutes. You've seen the ads on my page, right?"

Reluctantly, Lisa flopped into her chair, drooped her shoulders, held her forehead in her hands. "Of course I've seen them. I hate them."

"Hate them all you like. Every time any of my followers visits a page with ads, I make money. Every time a follower clicks on an ad, I make even more money."

"I don't care."

"Right now it's up to five hundred a month, and rising."

Lisa sat up. "What?"

Bianca nodded. "That's right. At some point I won't need this shit job anymore. Dealing with these whiny wet-nosed tenants and property owners."

"Did you say five hundred a month?"

"I did indeed. But you, with your content, and the flavor of followers you're attracting, you'll surpass me in a hurry. We can have you set up over lunch. Forty minutes max."

"I like the idea. But I don't want to do it right now."

"You need to get it up now while the traffic is zooming."

"Can you do it for me?"

"Of course I can, but it's better if you understand it, can manage it on your own."

"I get it. I want that. But I'm taking a retreat in about two hours, and my head won't be able to deal with this stuff right now."

"Okay. Give me your password. I'll set you up. This means you owe me another dinner. Alderwood this time."

Lisa knew nothing of Alderwood. "Sounds fair." She wrote down *eloiselovessockeye* on a scrap of paper and handed it to Bianca.

"Ah! Isn't that sweet. Okay. Consider it done. When you get back, change the password, and get ready for me to destroy a monstrous porterhouse steak and eat a couple dozen oysters. Where you going? Carmel? Up the coast?"

She really didn't want anyone to know, but Bianca wouldn't bug her. "Land of Medicine Buddha."

"What? That hippie-dippie place?"

"It's peaceful."

"But no Internet access. No Wi-Fi. You'll fall behind on comments. Unless you want to trust me to that, too."

"That's fine. But just vet them. No responses."

"You got it. Before this whole thing is over, I may end up your employee."

"Funny. I'm shutting this door now."

"Gotcha."

•   •   •

Lisa opened up *Rocks and Roll*, finished reading the final chapter, read it slowly, reread it twice. Remembered Francine Prose's book *Reading Like a Writer,* thought about slowing down, understanding the underlying thread, the subtext, what it was that captured a reader and made them want to read more. The bitter and the sweet. A baby girl to love. A growing trust between Celia and William. Painting the nursery together at the end of the day, tired, sweating, a hungry daughter tugging at Celia's breasts. Love and stability fighting it out with each other. It made her think of Gregory, who was only about stability. Love never complicating the formula. But the rocks? The mounted rocks and the engraved stories? She really knew nothing about anything.

She replaced *Rocks and Rolls* in its box, slid it into a desk drawer, scooped up the two boxes containing *Love Muffins* and *Waiting for Good Dough.* She couldn't keep from laughing again. Alice and her puns. Torturing Samuel Beckett's classic play and title. She couldn't wait.

On the drive home she texted Michael.

Headed home. Have you got time to meet over lunch? Maybe spend two hours going over a few things before I leave. There's a key under the front mat.

She hadn't gone two blocks before the response came in.

I'll be there when you get home. Can I retreat, too?

She smiled. *No. Single occupancy* — which wasn't true. There were two beds. But she didn't want to share a room or a bed with anybody. Except maybe Eloise.

•   •   •

Zack's truck was gone, but Michael's car was in the driveway. Lisa hurried in the front door, dropped the copy of *The Overstory* she purchased at Bookshop on the kitchen counter, found Michael there cooking.

"Hope you don't mind," he said. "I'm hungry."

"So am I," she said. "Back in a minute." She returned with an easel pad, two colored markers. She wrote a note for Zack:

I'm gone for a couple of days. Will you feed Eloise and the boys for me? ~ Lisa

Michael looked over her shoulder, read the note. "I can do that, you know?"

"Right. And so can he. What are we eating?"

"A surprise. Are we easel-padding today?"

"Yep." She went to the chart, grabbed a marker, wrote:

Lists (for Michael)
Shopping List – I don't care. Delete it if you want.
HOGS – I don't care. Delete it if you want.
Zack's List – Delete it. Give him my notes.
For Michael – All yours.
For Lisa – Listen if you want. I don't care. Don't delete it.
Hemp Seeds – Should check it out.
Just in Case – Definitely need to read this one.

She leaned back, reread the seven titles. This organization thing was feeling better than the passive path she usually chose. Make a choice. Move on.

Michael brought two plates to the couch, Yukon fried potatoes and salmon croquettes,

"Wait! You used Eloise's salmon for these?"

"I did. Take it out of my paycheck." He pointed at the easel pad. "Looks like a lot of things you don't care about."

She nodded. "It's true. I just need to cull right now."

"I understand. Pamela wants to be more involved."

"How? Why?"

"To be honest, there's a bit of jealousy there."

"Of me? That's crazy."

"Maybe more about the situation. Feeling left out."

"It was Gregory who left her out. Not us."

"Are you talking about the will again? Because I'm getting a little tired of that. You want to do battle over the will, I can do that. But it's not my interest."

"Sorry. I am very frazzled. No, I don't want to fight. I shouldn't have said that. But I'm willing to have you take the lead on a lot of this stuff, starting with the lists. And if you're comfortable bringing Pamela into the mix, I can learn to accept that."

"That makes sense for me. There's a good side to her."

"I'd love to see it sometime. But still, you'd better ask her why her name was in G's notebook."

"What are you talking about?" Michael said. Lisa handed him the notebook. He shook his head as he took his cell phone out of his pocket. "Excuse me." He stepped outside onto the porch, raised his voice. She couldn't hear what he was saying, but watched the expression on his face shift from anger to something softer. She took a bite of the croquettes, loved them, as she did the potatoes.

Michael returned. "You like the food?"

"I do. Another family recipe?"

Michael nodded. "Mom's favorite. She won contests with it at the county fair."

"What makes it so moist?"

"Cream of celery soup."

"Oh, yeah. I can taste it."

Michael brought a frying pan back from the kitchen, scooped more patties onto each of their plates. "Are you sure you want me listening to the For Lisa list?"

"Look. You more than anybody know what a wimp I've been, ever since you've known me. I'm tired of it. The old me was literally and figuratively drugged. I'm done with that."

"Yeah. You were pretty wimpy. Except in the greenhouse."

Michael pulled a folded sheet of paper from his pocket, handed it to her. "I had Pam look at it. You should read it, see what you think."

Lisa had never heard anyone refer to Pamela as Pam. It sounded endearing, more affectionate than she could imagine Michael being toward her. The paper was an obituary for Gregory. She read it to herself:

> The family and friends of Gregory P. Daniels would like to invite you to a celebration of his life at his property at 4775 Porter Gulch Road on December 31, New Year's Eve, from 5:00 to 8:00 p.m. Bring something to drink, and if your last initial begins with A through J bring a salad, K through P bring finger food, and Q through Z bring dessert.

> For those of you who haven't heard yet, Gregory met with an untimely death at the hands of a falling oak tree. Death was immediate, no pain, no suffering. He leaves behind his brother, Michael, and his friends Cody, Lisa, Pamela, Turks and Caicos, and Zack.

> Music will be provided. Harleys welcome!

It wasn't lengthy. Got to the point. Served its purpose. Lisa laughed, choked on a bite of salmon. "Cody gets billing ahead of me as a friend?"

"It's alphabetical. Pam's idea. At least you're ahead of her."

"When did she suddenly become *Pam*?"

"Not so sudden. I just asked her about meeting Gregory at Gayle's. Apparently it was a weekly meeting the past couple of months."

"What? How's that possible. Neither of us ever noticed?"

"We were too busy implementing Gregory's plans. Anyway, you know Pam is a marketing consultant, good writer and thinker."

"Never knew that. Why would I?"

"Good point. You know all those rocks Gregory mounted for you?"

Lisa looked up from her plate. "Yeah, so?"

"Did you really think Gregory had it in him to be so, how do you say it, loving, or creative?"

"Not really. I never thought that. Until I read them, then my thoughts changed a bit."

"Well, it wasn't him. I guess in a way it was. It was his idea to do something, but the words were all Pam's."

"Are you serious?"

193

"Afraid so. When I called her on it, she opened her computer, read me her notes." Lisa's stomach rumbled. She carried the plate to the kitchen and scraped the remaining croquettes into Eloise's bowl.

"The obit looks fine to me. Let's run it in the *Sentinel*, the *Good Times*, and probably as many Central Valley newspapers as we can identify. Clovis for sure."

"Sounds good. I know there are folks in Turlock, Modesto, Merced."

Lisa sat back on the couch in front of the easel pad, picked up a marker and flipped to a blank page, wrote:

Submit Obit to Papers
Plan Menu
Identify and Hire Musician
Balloons from Woodworm
Paper Plates and Cups

"Can you take care of this stuff or do you want to wait until I get back?"

"When are you coming back?"

It was none of his business. Yes it was. Fence sitter. "Thursday."

"I'll have Pam deal with this. Pretty innocuous. As opposed to dealing with Alexa's lists."

"That's fine." She closed her eyes, leaned back against the pillows on the couch, tossed a marker to Michael. "I'm tired. But let's get the greenhouse out of the way?"

"Okay," Michael said. He listed the options they had talked about: growing more pot illegally, growing orchids, a hybrid of orchids and legal pot, hemp seeds. "This covers all our growing options. At least the one's we've brainstormed."

"I agree."

"There is one other non-growing option we haven't discussed."

"Tell me."

"Renting out the greenhouse to another grower."

"Grower of what?"

"I don't care as long as it's not illegal."

"Right. How much?"

"According to my sources, up to two thousand a month."

"Wow! That could put a nice dent into property taxes, repairs, the unknowns."

194

"I know. You'd just have to deal with having folks on the property all the time."

"Do you have a preference?" Lisa asked.

"I'm leaning away from pot and orchids."

"Why?"

"Legal risks with the pot. And too much labor for you. You've carried the brunt of that for way too long. So, if we can get all the details on the hemp-seeds venture, I'm thinking if we really want to make money, it may be the best plan. Problem is, it's still a lot of labor."

"Yep. Ten to twelve hours a day."

"I never had a clue you were working that much."

"Why would you? He kept you out of the growing side. Kept me on the inside. Tucked away. But I'm thinking if Zack is serious about staying around, and he stays off me, maybe he'd take care of the operation for us."

"My thoughts exactly. And Pam agrees, by the way."

Lisa took the key Michael had left on the counter, handed it to him. "I figure we should make this official. Spare key to the front door. I would stop short of making one for Pamela, though." No way she could start calling her Pam. Still no affection there. Though the thought of her providing G with the stories about the geodes was grinding away on her.

"Thanks for this." He smiled. "Got one for the workshop, too?"

"Real funny. I still need to do that one by myself for a while. I'll bring the hemp-seed notes in before I go. Oh, and there's this." She reached for G's jacket, slipped open the zippered pocket, handed Michael G's cell phone. "You want to deal with this, too?"

"You bet. Anything else before you go?"

"I don't think so. But one thought. Maybe we should have the memorial in the greenhouse, open it up and show folks, let them see we aren't growing anything they'd care to steal. Nothing to hide."

"Good idea. Got to go. Meeting Pam for lunch. Have fun, whatever it is you're doing." He reached his arms around her and hugged her before he left, something he had never done.

Lisa ran to the front door. "Hey, wait. One more thing before you go. Would you change the message on the answering machine? I don't want to hear G's voice there anymore."

Part of her wanted to strap a pack on her back, walk straight through the trees to Land of Medicine Buddha, but it would be best for her car to be gone with her. Pretend like they had both disappeared to Esalen or the Mesa Refuge. She didn't pack much. Alice's two manuscripts, *The Overstory,* and even though there was no Internet or Wi-Fi, her computer, for two reasons: to keep anyone from snooping in it while she was gone, and to continue writing blog posts that she could post later. Her only worry was getting behind on the comments from her followers, but that was in Bianca's hands for now.

The to-do lists had been well checked. Even if she was completely overwhelmed, she felt like there was forward movement, very little disappointment. She drove down Porter Gulch, stopped in Soquel at Vino Cruz to buy a bottle of Kathryn Kennedy 2012 Chardonnay, weaved her way up Main Street and Prescott Road until she reached the one-lane entrance to the retreat. She parked, sighed. Everywhere she looked there were colorful altars and flags and gardens and people with long hair and shaved heads. After checking in, she found her room. Sparse, reminded her of the lodgings at sixth-grade science camp. The twin bed was comfortable. The lighting was good. The desk was sturdy. Perfect!

.   .   .

Back propped against two pillows in bed, she opened the bottle of wine first, then the manuscript box with *Love Muffins* inside. The wine was perfect. She read the date again: September 2001. It had been the beginning of her junior year at Piedmont. A homecoming game. Floats and royal courts and football players all hunked up in uniforms, she and Cody checking them out, and here was Alice, sitting at home plucking away on her keyboard, making up another story, spreading rocks further into the house, the hallway, both bathrooms, a window sill in Lisa's bedroom. Prying deeper into the lives and heads of Celia and William, and forming the character of their new daughter. Alice as God, creator of life, taking raw clay and baking it in a kiln. Lisa turned to page 1.

If you were to take snapshots of the front of the
bakery, you'd see carefully painted cakes and cookies, a

196

glistening sheen off the faces of rolls, the sparkle of
salt and sugar everywhere, lines of contented customers
thrilled to be waiting for the artwork of William and
Celia, bills overflowing in the cash register.

But if you slipped behind the curtain to the back
room, you might see a young baby trying to sleep amidst
the commotion, the mixing of dough with milk and butter,
the sacred following of recipes, cases of flour and brown
sugar and chocolate chips stacked to the ceiling,
unswept floors gathering dust and spillage, no time for
sweeping or wiping, barely time for feeding and rocking
young Amelia to sleep.

Lisa smiled, closed her eyes. Alice jumping to life again, blending
the names Alice and Celia into Amelia, falling a bit short in real life
with Lisa, but it would do, had done her well. Lisa Hardrock, daughter
of Alice Hardrock.

William slept less, woke earlier to make up for
Celia's lost time to care for their daughter. He was a big
man, bigger as the weeks went on, eating himself into
some masked face of comfort with his own products. His
legs ached. Sciatica came and went as it chose. To make
ends meet, they decided they could increase their profits
by making muffins—blueberry, zucchini, banana nut,
pumpkin—muffins that their loyal clientele quickly
came to love and looked forward to hot every morning.
They didn't need to get clever with their signage and
labeling of food. The flavor alone was enough to sell
them. But the customers themselves came up with the
labels, and Love Muffins took over, occupied all their
lips. Celia made sure William made a few dozen more than
they could sell, so she could walk down the street,
distribute warm muffins to the hungry folks without
homes.

Alice had never stayed at the breakfast table long enough to
actually eat the muffins with Lisa and Cody, hurried back into her
office and began typing. But after the girls had fallen asleep on a Friday
or Saturday night, Alice had managed to color frosting, bake muffins,

ice them with hearts and rainbows, cover them in sprinkles and chocolate chips, and when she called them to the table, it was with "Love muffins ready to be eaten!" That may have been the closest Alice had come to love, the closest Lisa could remember anyway.

It had been a long day. Productive. Packed. She had accomplished a little of everything. A lot of everything. She drifted off with Alice and muffins.

35

WEDNESDAY
12-18-19

T HE SLEEP HAD BEEN EXCELLENT, DEEP. Lisa had never been spiritually-minded, but being in these surroundings may have had an effect. She stayed in bed, eyes closed, thought about feeding Eloise, but she didn't have to. Thought about vetting comments, but she couldn't. Bianca taking care of the blog site. Zack taking care of the animals. Michael taking care of business and a few decisions. Pamela, *Pam*, maybe taking care of everything and everybody. All Lisa had to do was take care of herself for a couple of days, reduce her need for disappointment, give up worrying about accomplishments.

With computer open, she typed in her journal:

I'm away today, in a place where I can't engage in research about growing orchids or hunting geodes, won't be able to post this until I return in a couple of days. I am at once slowing down and refueling, spending time with Alice and the worlds she spun into magic when I was young. Worlds I'm only discovering now. I've shared just a tiny bit with you here, a taste of I Really Knead You, a hint of Rocks and Rolls.

Many of you want more, have asked for Alice's words rather than my interpretations. Beginning Thursday, I will post one chapter a day from I Really Knead You. By mid-January, you'll have had the opportunity to read the whole thing. This is a Dickensian experiment. Or maybe Stephen King, when he charged a daily fee to read ongoing excerpts. No daily fee here. Just your time, to check in and stay current with the life and mind of Alice Hardrock. Let me know if this works for you. I'm going for a hike now.

And she did. She closed the computer, slid it under her pillow, put on G's jacket, and headed out for a walk. The first sign she saw was for the Medicine Buddha Loop Trail, 5.5 miles, rated moderate. It was 7:30 a.m. when she began. She took her time. Stopped and sat on a bench under a tree, took out *The Overstory* and read the first two chapters. It had been so long since she'd read a book. One that had its roots in the mind rather than all the gardening books Gregory had brought her with roots firmly implanted in black plastic squat pots. Even though she had lived in this forest for so many years, she hadn't paid attention, had gone back and forth from house to greenhouse, an occasional jaunt to the blackberry bushes. But she hadn't tuned in. Hadn't really cared. Richard Powers carried her into his world of trees, and she let herself grow into it, listen to his construction of sentences, the implications of his warnings. She closed the book, listened to birdsong, wildlife scraping through brush, the flow of the creek.

Three hours later she found her way to the dining room, famished, loaded a plate with a vegetarian scramble, nine-seed toast with strawberry jam, fresh melons and grapes, and a tall glass of freshly squeezed orange juice. A couple at a neighboring table talked of a *Qi Gong* workshop at 11:30. After two plates of food, she found the Pine Room and entered. Ten others were there, waiting quietly. The leader appeared, introduced herself as Briege, told them of the day's exercise, *Ba Duan Jin*, translated as Eight Pieces of Brocade. On their feet, they inhaled and exhaled in a steady rhythm, moved their hands and arms gently with intent.

Lisa had tried yoga a few times in her life, mostly with Ryan. It hadn't worked for her. She was running a bookstore, head occupied with tasks and orders and planning events and readings for book groups, didn't have time or interest to slow down and take care of herself. This was different. Maybe because she was different. No umbilical cord attaching her to the mind and body of another person twenty-four by seven. Even though she was within a thousand feet of her house on Porter Gulch, it felt like she was in Kathmandu, the forests of Bali, maybe on another planet. Even though they were indoors, she heard birds, realized Briege had turned on a recording, but it didn't matter. Lisa closed her eyes and accepted it, the contrived birdsong better than none.

Back in her room, she was pleasantly exhausted, an oxymoron she thought Alice would like. She wanted to pick up *Love Muffins*, dive back in, but found herself with drool on her chin nearly four hours later, almost time for dinner. While on her second helping of eggplant parmesan and garlic bread, she drifted back to *Qi Gong*, to yoga and Ryan, the bookstore that she should have loved but somehow didn't. The locals had been nice enough, those in her book groups, the ones who came to the monthly readings by semi-famous authors. The tourists were another matter. Had expectations about how they should be treated, a me-first all-about-me attitude she hadn't liked. The irony was that Gregory had been a tourist, and she had flung herself at him, let him wrap her up in velvet chains and carry her back to his dungeon.

Dessert was an apple crisp with a scoop of vanilla-bean gelato. She felt guilty opening her computer in the tech-less environment of the dining room. Too bad. This was her retreat, and she'd do it the way she needed to. She almost forgot about the lack of Internet, wanted in to Pious Rebel, but caught herself, went to the journal instead.

Thanks so much to RachelReads for suggesting The Overstory for my reading list. Fittingly, I was sitting under a tree on a trail that wraps around the forest where I'm staying when I read the short opening chapter "Root," before proceeding to "Nicholas Hoel." It's been so long since I've read for pleasure, since I've critiqued anything for anybody. Mostly it's for myself. But now that I know there are so many of you paying attention out there, I'll be careful, try to be mindful and kind with my thoughts. I hadn't known about the fate of the chestnuts before this. I hadn't known about Richard Powers

before this. I'm happy to have met both. I wonder if my old
reading group in Point Reyes Station has read it yet. Wonder
if they were as overtaken with his language as was I. I do
know the story is supposed to grow dark and somewhat
depressing, but such is the planet we live on. And if you're
going to drag me into a quagmire and leave me there to die,
at least do it with language that sedates and explodes me at
the same time.

Because of her afternoon nap, and the sugar rush from two
helpings of apple crisp, she returned to her room wide awake, dug into
Alice's brain by way of Celia, William, and now Amelia.

William was not happy about Celia's choice of Justin
as Amelia's godfather. And it made no sense to him at all
that Margie had been named the godmother, Margie who
would have chosen to have Amelia's life carved from
Celia's womb by a part-time doctor in Vernalis. But he
stayed quiet, was still honest and forthcoming when
Celia questioned him. But Celia wasn't aware of this tick
that had burrowed into William's skin, that slowly ate
away at him. She did notice that William's habit of one
glass of red wine on Sunday evenings had increased to two
glasses each night. He worked hard. An extra hour a day
to prep and bake the highly successful love muffins. For
Amelia's first birthday, William told Celia he was going
shopping, left her alone in the bakery with Amelia and a
horde of customers, showed up at home in time for dinner
with two bottles of wine and a gift for Amelia wrapped in
paper covered with rabbits. He smelled like whiskey.
What Celia knew and trusted was that William was not a
bad drunk, not obnoxious and sarcastic. She classified
him more as a weepy, sentimental drunk. Head in his
hands, rolling his neck on his shoulders. "I'm so sorry to
be so late. I stopped at Ernie's place, and they just kept
buying me drinks to celebrate Amelia. I said they should
be toasting you, so they bought more drinks and raised a
glass to you."
Justin had offered William a shoulder to help him to
the bedroom when he staggered up from the table. He was

snoring into the pillow before Celia opened the packages
for Amelia. Margie had gotten her a book about the
suffragettes. "Someday she'll be able to read it. Until
then, I'll read it to her." William's gift was a doll. Celia
had knitted her a matching hat and gloves. When Celia
opened Justin's box and saw the geode, she had to hide the
tears, quickly faked a sneeze and got up to find a tissue.
Margie put an arm around her shoulder, rubbed her back.
Gave her a light slap on the cheek. "Get on with it."

Lisa had worked her way through half the novel before fading
close to midnight.

36

THURSDAY
12-19-19

THERE WAS NO *QI GONG* OR OTHER DHARMA SERVICES on Thursdays. She spent most of the morning on trails. She had purchased a trail map at the store, found the spot that came within a thousand feet of Porter Gulch Road. She veered off and within minutes was staring through oak trees at the back sides of the greenhouse and G's workshop. She didn't want to be here or see this right now, but it might be useful later, to know she was just a walk away from relaxation.

She was reminded at breakfast that checkout time was 11:00. She packed up Alice Hardrock and Richard Powers and made the short drive home. Home? She wasn't sure. It could be. But for so long it had felt like a hotel, a workplace. There were no cars in the driveway. Turks and Caicos were happy to see her. She went to the fence, rubbed their ears, then quickly into the house, where Eloise rushed to her feet, entangled them with her tail.

Making her way down the hallway, she stuck her head in rooms. Two suitcases leaned against the wall in the guest room. The spare room was spotless. Zack had gone to work, rearranged things and made himself at home. Her room looked the same. G's room. His pillows draped over the bed. His framed motorcycle prints on all the walls. The only thing she could really call her own was the geode sitting on the nightstand. Back in the kitchen she found three notes, each cryptic in its own way, not wanting the writers of the other notes to know too much. Zack's was brief.

Boys and girl already fed today. See you later.

Michael's made him sound mysterious, like his brother:

Lots to talk about. In good shape for NYE. News on HS. CP. More.

Cody had written the third note.

We took the guest room. See you soon.

NYE was easy. Hemp seeds was easy. But CP was eluding her. No need to bog down in the frothy messes yet. They'd all converge on her soon. Something fun first. She went to Pious Rebel. Over three hundred comments, most vetted and posted by Bianca, some waiting. Better check messages first. Phone open, she discovered texts from Bianca, Michael, two from Cody. Cody's first.

We're in town! Headed to El Palomar bar downtown. See you tonight.

The second message began:

Ben here, on Cody's phone. Cody fell off a stool at the bar. We're headed to ER for stitches. Home shortly.

And so it begins, Lisa thought.

Michael's messages were not pushy, not too informative, mostly wishing her well, welcoming her back. Bianca's were pushy, way too informative. She hurried through them.

If I'm going to be working for you, you're going to have to pay me more. On that note, I've made a reservation at Alderwood for tonight. Hope that's okay. I made it for four people at 6:00, knowing your friends were coming to town. Change it if you want. Get online in a hurry when you get

back. Check the Comments holding tank. You've got some
decisions to make. You're over 500 now! Check out the
marketing. Ads are up. Money, money!

Back on Pious Rebel it took her an hour to read through the posts
Bianca had accepted. The same categories of folks were still there,
expanding, Bianca's friends leading the horde. Over twenty of the new
folks had posted about the Holy Grail, the history, the significance,
comparing it to Alice's and Lisa's lives, philosophical ramblings about
the elusive search for meaning. Another whole thread focused on
secrets, men and their secrets. She might have to un-vet some of these,
understood that Bianca probably agreed with them and wanted their
perspectives to shine through, also wanted the potential ad income.
The geode lovers were growing as well, responding not only to Lisa's
original posts, but to each other, sharing their knowledge of locales, of
dealers who sold them, pontificating about their personal collections,
their obsessions, their desires. One post stood out, seemed a bit more
reflective than the others, a cautious interest in Alice and her rocks, in
Celia's fictional collection at the hands of Justin. His handle was
simply RockHound. He must have been at it for a long time to land
that username. Why did she assume it was a he? There were no clues
in the post. No identifying pronouns. She reread the post.

Fascinated by the story of Alice Hardrock. Five manuscripts,
you say? How very eccentric, the writing of them, the hiding
of them, never published. I for one am hoping to read more
of them here. Love the idea of Celia and Justin, though it
does seem a bit tragic. Can you post photos of the geodes?

Good idea. She'd wanted to find her nice EOS 7D camera for
these. Hadn't taken one picture with it while in Santa Cruz.

Lisa didn't understand RockHound's suggestion of tragedy in the
stories. In the holding tank, Bianca had banned a few more perverts, left
a few unvetted that were way off-content, some pointing to other blogs
and websites for marketing purposes, some just wild rants at anything and
everything. She banned them, went to her journal, copied and pasted the
two posts she had written at Medicine Buddha, published them, knowing
there would be a flurry of response almost immediately. She closed the

computer, put on the mediation music, stood and took the *Qi Gong* pose she'd learned. Tires disturbed gravel on the driveway. Zack opened the front door carrying two bags of groceries, whispered, "*Qi Gong*. Nice." They ignored each other while she completed the twenty-minute routine, him setting the bags on the counter, disappearing to his room.

Among other goodies, Zack's bags contained sparkling water and cran-raspberry. She mixed two tall glasses with half of each, dropped ice cubes in each, yelled down the hallway, "Made you a half-and-half."

"Thanks," he yelled back. "Be right there."

Zack appeared, carrying Eloise. "She's letting you carry her? That's a first."

"Yeah. She's very loving. Been sleeping in my room." He let Eloise down and she rubbed past Lisa's legs, went to her bowl in the kitchen.

"Speaking of your room. Wow! Nice job. I hope you didn't throw anything away."

"Nothing of value. Lots of things in the closet for you to check out."

She wondered if their value scales matched. He'd better have left her books intact.

"How long are you thinking of staying?"

"That was fast. I wear out my welcome already?"

"Not at all. Happy to have you here." Part of her was, so it wasn't a lie. But part of her still associated him with the mystery man, Gregory, and she wondered how much he was withholding. Before she proceeded, she wanted to see how much growth he'd really achieved and how much was a mask. "Can you tell me about your daughter?"

Zack took a sip of his drink, rearranged himself on the couch, sighed deeply. "Sure. I guess we're kind of like comrades on this journey, so why not. Last year, I was out on the big boat, working some halibut. Cell phones are dead out there, but soon as we hit the dock, mine starts blaring at me. It's Tanya, my wife. Ex-wife now. She and Rebecca, my daughter, Becs to me, were on their daily bike ride after school. I got to the hospital too late. Her lying there in that bed, mouth open, bandaged up and bloody. Tanya wouldn't hug me, wouldn't even look at me. We buried her. Didn't care about wasting land in a cemetery. Wanted a place to visit her. We couldn't live together with that grief smashing us from all sides like a trash compactor. Tanya finally left. Don't know where she is. Don't really care."

He deserved some affection, a hug, but she couldn't do it. Couldn't drag herself off the couch and reach out. Gregory under that oak tree, Becs next to him in the hospital bed, had temporarily blinded her, froze her ability to speak, to move. Eloise hopped into her lap, demanded she snap out of it, and she did.

There was no appropriate response, but she tried. "Comrades. Right." This complicated life of hers didn't matter much when compared with a dead daughter. "Michael and I are trying to figure out next steps around here. That's why I asked about your plans."

"I'll be out of your hair as soon as you need me to be."

"No, it's not that. Kind of the opposite. Maybe. If we decide to do something with that greenhouse, we might need someone around to help, someone we can trust."

"Good to know," he said. "I'll think about it."

The front door opened, Cody wearing a large bandage across her forehead. Lisa ignored her. "I know," she said. "Frank N. Stein. Give me a hug," she said to Lisa, grabbing her from behind.

"Hi, Ben," Lisa said. Zack moved toward the door. "Zack, you have plans tonight?" she asked.

"In fact I do. Fundraiser dinner at the Resource Center for Nonviolence. Love this town. See you on the flip side."

Cody flopped down on the couch next to Lisa. "But *we* have no plans. We're all yours."

"Good. We're going to dinner at a swanky new restaurant downtown. High price tags."

"Oh, good! I know a wealthy lawyer. And I'm kind of wealthy now."

"Really? How much?"

"Two-hundred fifty K!"

"You're kidding."

"No. I'm not. My lord and master knocked it out of the park. Sent those guys groveling. Threatened them with a million, given the long-term devastation to my name and reputation." Ben walked to the kitchen, poured himself some cran-rasp, tried to ignore them.

"And what happened to your head?"

"Depends on who you ask."

"I'll just ask the lawyer"

Ben held his hands up. "No. I take the fifth."

Cody turned to Lisa. "He'll say I fell off the bar stool after three margaritas, but it was two and a half, and I'm sure that asshole next to me pushed me."

"Welcome back," Lisa said. "Dinner's at six." Her phone pinged. Michael.

> Hi! Hope you had a good rest. We're all set up for NYE. Pamela has it covered. Including the obit to appear in six papers beginning this weekend.

Mixed emotions. They could have one combined vote. A half vote each, but she wouldn't have any two against one stacking up.

> Great. she responded. What's CP?
>
> CP?
>
> In your note.
>
> No clue.

In the kitchen, Cody slipped her hands down Ben's pants. He looked over his shoulder at Lisa, pushed Cody away.

She waited a second before responding to Michael. This was probably not the smartest thought she had recently, but a little buffer from Cody and Ben might be perfect.

> Hey. What are you and Pamela doing tonight?

She backspaced and erased the *e-l-a* from Pamela.

> Want to join us for dinner tonight?
>
> Who is us?
>
> Ben. Cody. My office mate, Bianca. 6:00 at Alderwood.

Having them there might help to buffer Bianca a bit. The Pamela-and-Cody show alone would be enough for strategic diversions.

> Alderwood? That's a step up. Who's paying?
>
> I think this one might be on me.
>
> Let me check with Pamela. I'm pretty sure we're free.
>
> Okay. If you're in, just call the restaurant and make it six instead of four.
>
> Thanks for the invite. Lots to talk about tomorrow. Especially if either of us can remember what CP stands for.

She laughed, felt better when she did. Needed to make a point to watch more comedy, go to that new DNA comedy club by the river and listen to comedians. Watch some old Johnny Carson shows.

Richard Pryor. George Carlin. Work her way out of this twisted shell she'd found herself in. Gregor Samsa on the move.

Bianca's turn.

Great job on my site. Thanks! We are up to six for dinner, including brother-in-law Michael (Peter Rarebit) and his wife/partner, Pamela. Let's keep it low-key regarding Pious Rebel tonight. See you at 6:00.

An immediate reply.

Low-key? Me? Ha! Good luck with that. Can we meet tomorrow morning?

Not sure yet.

Lisa pulled up a stool at the kitchen counter. "Tell me about the settlement."

Cody pulled out her checkbook, showed her a deposit of $250,000 two days ago. "I'm rich."

Ben shook his head. "Not the way you spend. You need to invest it, get it out of reach."

"I know. I know. I will."

Lisa thought about the greenhouse, the next crop, whatever it might be. No. It would be nuts having Cody as an investor, sticking her nose in everywhere. She changed the subject. "I've got some news, too."

"You're pregnant! You and Michael? You and Zack?" Ben shook his head at her. Lisa didn't think Cody would behave well enough to keep Ben around for long.

"No. I have a blog. I've been posting things. I have a following."

"Wait! Why don't I know this already? You've been holding out on me." Lisa wanted to remind her about Ryan. Not now.

"Just started it a couple of weeks ago. But it's thriving." It was a good idea to tell her as much as possible before Bianca started drinking wine and forgetting to stay low-key.

"What's it called? How do I get there?"

Lisa hesitated. Letting Cody in would change things. Another specific audience to worry about. But if she had to, she could lock her out. "It's Pious Rebel."

"What a fantastic name! Not that you've ever been much of either. Alice would have loved it, though."

"Speaking of Alice, you want to go to Berkeley with me?"

"Sure. But why?"

"The storage locker up there. Where I put her stuff. I need to look through it, dump most of it, maybe bring some back."

"I'd love to. When?"

"Maybe tomorrow."

∙   ∙   ∙

Bianca was already seated when they arrived, computer open, glass half empty. Before introductions had been offered, Cody started in on her. "I've been through all of Pious Rebel. You two have been busy."

"It's all her. I'm just the techie," Bianca said.

"And the marketer, the brains. Brought in your networks."

"Like I said, Lisa is the Pious Rebel, and folks are flocking to her as we speak. Those two new posts this afternoon lit up the boards."

"So much for low-key," Lisa whispered to Bianca.

Bianca smiled. "Whole new threads popped up. Chestnuts. *The Overstory*. Richard Powers."

The waitperson brought waters, said, "I know you're waiting for two more. Can I get you anything now?"

"Two more?" Cody said. "Who?"

"We're good for now," Lisa answered. "Michael and Pamela."

"What? Are you crazy?" As Cody spoke, they walked through the door, took seats at the table.

"Hi all," Michael said. "Nice to see everybody again. This is Pam."

Pamela shook hands with Bianca and Ben. "The rest of you I know. Thanks for the invite."

Cody kept her mouth shut as the waitperson returned. "Cocktails? Wine?" Pamela asked, opening the menu. "Can we get shots of Fortaleza Blanco all around?"

"What's that?" Michael asked.

"Tequila," Pamela said, training her eyes on Lisa, waiting for a response, ignoring Cody altogether.

"A bottle of the Big Basin Homestead Block Roussanne," Ben said. "Hands up if you want oysters." Cody, Bianca, and Michael raised their hands. "How about a dozen each of the Kumamoto and Shigoku, please."

"Have you been here before?" Michael asked.

"No," Ben said. "But I recognize the quality."

Cody couldn't keep quiet any longer. "We went to Hog Island Oyster Bar over Thanksgiving. Totally amazing."

"How so?" Pamela asked. "Did they marinate them in Patron?"

Cody had opened her mouth to respond, turning to face Pamela, when the waitperson arrived with the six shots of tequila, set one in front of each of each of them, announced with a light flourish, "Fortaleza Blanco." Cody pounded her shot back, slammed the glass into the tabletop, stared at Pamela.

"Isn't that delicate," Pamela said. Cody started to stand, but Ben pulled her down.

Bianca stepped in. "How many of you saw the new posts today, the hundreds of comments?"

"Me," Cody shouted.

"Pretty impressive," Ben said.

Pamela leaned in, got closer to Bianca, said, "What posts? What are we talking about?"

"I believe the *'we'* refers to those of us who have access to Lisa's new project," Bianca answered.

Pamela stared at Michael. "You know what they're talking about?"

"Lisa is posting to a blog site. I believe Bianca is helping her establish a following."

"Why don't I know about this?"

Bianca again, to the rescue. "It's out of my hands now. This is all about Lisa Hardrock. Two hundred new followers today alone." The waitperson reappeared with the wine, poured a taste for Ben, who nodded, then filled the others' glasses.

Lisa leaned into Bianca, covered her mouth and whispered. "Do me a favor. Take low- key just a little lower. No talk about the ads and income." Bianca nodded.

Ben raised his glass. "To Lisa. May you start anew, and may your followers stay faithful."

"Amen!" Cody shouted, finished her wine, followed it with Ben's shot.

The waiter returned to take orders. "Any questions or decisions yet?"

Bianca said, "I have a suggestion. We order all five first-course items, because it's way too hard to narrow them down. Toss in one of the air-dried Wagyu short ribs from the snack menu. One bite each, then pass them around. Any naysayers?"

"Go for it!" Cody said.

"And for main courses?"

"Eight-ounce filet for me," Michael said.

"Me too," Pamela said.

"Anybody up for sharing the porterhouse with me?" Bianca said. Lisa smiled at her, figured this meal was heading well over a thousand dollars.

Ben said, "Sure." Cody nodded.

Lisa closed her menu. "I'd like the sunchoke risotto and the potato pavé." Slowly working her way off meat, paying more attention to what went in and out of her body. She wanted to stand up and slip into her *Qi Gong* pose, but didn't.

Once more, quietly, to Bianca. "Thanks for toning it down. I don't want to talk money with these folks."

On cue Ben said, "How's it going with the ad campaign? Every page seems loaded up."

Bianca turned to Lisa, letting her know she had to field this one.

"Oh, you know, they just pop up."

"Right," Ben said. "But every time they pop up, *ka-ching*, you're pulling in nickels and dimes."

"Don't know about that. I'd like to make a toast to Cody. Congratulations on settling your suit."

"Yes! Speaking of *ka-ching*. And that's all because of my sweet Ben! Biggest brain on the West Coast."

"That's a little restrictive," Michael said.

Pamela cut in. "Tell me more about your website, Lisa. What are you sharing there?"

Lisa didn't want to be telling Pamela much of anything. She finished her wine, said, "Just little tidbits about my life."

"For example?" Pamela prodded.

"For example," Cody said, "about how her mother Alice was a writer. For example, how Alice collected geodes. For example, how she's going to grow orchids in her greenhouse. Those kinds of *for examples*."

By the time dessert was delivered, apple-pie profiteroles for everybody, Cody could barely keep her head straight, was leaning it against the tablecloth, and Michael and Ben were deep into a discussion about hemp seeds, Ben being an investor in an operation above Marin. "Risky stuff," Ben said. "Got to keep the males out of the mix."

"You got that damn straight," Bianca said, clinking glasses with Lisa.

Pamela was the only one left out of the conversations, but seemed okay with it. Lisa tried to reel her in. "I hear your boss gives you tickets to shows."

Pamela stared at Michael again. Jeez, Lisa thought. Were all topics off-limits with her?" Michael ignored her.

"We went to *The Nutcracker* last month. San Francisco Symphony last week. We had New Year's tickets to *Hamilton,* but had to back out of those given the memorial."

Cody popped up. "What memorial?" she asked.

"Gregory's."

"He didn't want one," Cody slurred.

"Memorials are for the living," Michael said. "And he's gone. It's for us."

"I said," she paused, "he DIDN'T want one! His wishes. Got to follow his wishes."

"You know what I wish?" Pamela started, but Michael cut her off.

"That we move this party out of here," he said.

"No! Let me finish. I wish you'd tell us how you know so much about Gregory's wishes."

Cody reached for her empty wine glass, then went for Ben's and downed it. "Everybody knows that. No big secret."

"Oh, really. How long did you know Gregory?"

"None of your business."

"I'm thinking it should be everybody's business now."

"You shut up."

Michael grabbed Pamela's shoulders, whispered in her ear.

"No," she said, loud enough for the whole table to hear. "I will not let it go. She's gotten away with her crap way too long." She turned to Cody. "Didn't you know Gregory before he brought Lisa to Porter Gulch?"

Lisa wriggled in her chair, stared back and forth between Cody and Pamela. "What are you saying?"

214

"I'm saying your best friend knew Gregory before you owned your bookstore. Before Ryan."

Michael stood up. "Come on, Pam. Let's go."

Pamela stood, still talking. "I'm saying you orchestrated Gregory's coming to Point Reyes Station, meeting Lisa, him swooping her away, leaving Ryan behind for you."

Lisa turned to Bianca, dropped her forehead to Bianca's shoulder, let tears well up. "Are you fucking kidding me?" she whispered to her.

Bianca put her hand on Lisa's. "You need to lock these two out of Pious Rebel. As soon as you get home. Otherwise this stuff will become its own thread." Lisa nodded, still trying to understand what had just happened, what had been said, how much of it was Pamela's residual anger about Cody and Michael at Margaritaville, how much of it was empathy for Lisa, having such a conniving loser as a best friend. No wonder Michael had avoided telling her the truth for so long.

Michael took Pamela's hand and pulled her toward the door. He waved back at the table. "Thanks for dinner. Whoever's paying for it."

Lisa waved her credit card to the waitperson. Ben shook his head. "Taken care of already."

"By ME, you're welcome very much!" Cody said. "What a loon bird she is." Cody grabbed at Lisa's arm. "Hey! We still on for Berkeley tomorrow?"

"No," Lisa said, releasing herself from Cody's grip.

In bed, her head rotated around the ceiling lamp. Damn that Cody! She needed to get to Berkeley, but not with her.

Pam came to mind. She liked the single syllable rather than the three required by *Pamela*. It was cleaner, more direct, seemed less threatening. She didn't have her cell-phone number, couldn't text her. But WhamPam was in the Pious Rebel system. She dug in, found her.

Michael tells me you have a flex schedule in your job, mostly work from home. I'm wondering how flexible your day is tomorrow. I need to go to Berkeley, check out my mom's stuff in storage. Maybe even take a diversion north to Point Reyes Station. I could use the help, and the company. What do you think? I could pick you at noon.

She hit Send.

Under her covers with the heated blanket turned up to ten, Lisa started a new post. She attached the photo of the geode bookshelf.

> Here they are. Alice's geodes. Celia's geodes. Amelia's geodes.
> My geodes. At the foot of my bed. Within reach when needed.
> Ready to occupy any dreams that may wish to include them.
> Some things are really bad. Others are this good.

She was so disappointed in Cody, in herself for trusting her for so long, loving her for so long. She wanted to keep this disappointment out of her head, out of her posts, but in this phase of her life where truth and honesty were trying to establish a foothold, it was nearly impossible.

Zack. Damn! She had forgotten to ask him if she could borrow his truck tomorrow. All the lights were off in the kitchen and dining room. She knocked on the door to Zack's bedroom.

"Come in," Zack said. He was propped up on a pillow, lamp on, bare-chested, holding a book on his lap.

"Hi. Sorry to interrupt. I was wondering if there was any chance of trading vehicles with you tomorrow. I'm going to Alice's storage locker in Berkeley and I need to haul some stuff."

"You bet. I'd love the opportunity to drive a Prius. Much healthier for the planet than my guzzler."

The book cover now in clear view, she read the title, *Zen and the Art of Motorcycle Maintenance,* by Robert Pirsig.

"Great book," he said. "Have you read it?"

"Twenty years ago in grad school."

"Me too. Didn't really settle in then as it does now. It's all about quality, values. How you choose to live your life."

Lisa nodded. Part of her wanted to cuddle up next to him under the covers, wrap her arms around his shoulders, pretend he was G, have him read to her. But G had never read her anything, was wrapped around his own shoulders.

"Thanks," she said. "I'll leave my key on the kitchen counter."

Back in bed, she hurried back into Pious Rebel. Pam had already responded.

> Totally flexible. I'd be honored. I probably need to be back by
> Christmas Eve, though. Shall I come to you or vice versa?

216

Lisa laughed. She assumed it was a joke about Christmas Eve. She replied:

I'll come to you. See you at 12:00. What's your address? All these years, I've never been to your house.

She closed the computer, watched the light from the last quarter moon glaze the surface of the geodes, each one blinking as she turned her head. It had been nearly three months since G had died. Was it too soon to have thoughts about someone else? Probably. It was probably written in chapter 1 of some book titled *The Dummies' Guide to Grieving*. But her thoughts were not about passion, more about holding someone close, feeling the warmth of skin against skin, something about the possible merger of heartbeats. The shared loss. A daughter. A partner. Too soon. Way too soon.

37

FRIDAY
12-20-19

E LOISE WAS LICKING THE KNUCKLES ON LISA'S RIGHT HAND. Or was it one of those fake dreams? Lisa opened one eye to see it was 5:55. The wine and tequila had pulled her down. Plastered her head to the pillow. A steady parade of people carrying Alice's geodes through downtown Point Reyes Station. Holding the mounted rocks above their heads. Posing for cameras. Crowds lining the streets, shouting and cheering. Michael was supposed to be here at ten. The cell phone pinged. She didn't want to focus on any of them. Didn't want to bring her thumbs into play so soon this morning. She picked it up, read the first of two messages. Bianca:

Lock them both out. Trust me. Pamela's already been through the whole site last night. No comments yet, but I'm certain they're coming. Nothing from Cody yet, but she was so shitfaced I'm not surprised. Good luck with the comments today. They're mostly sane, but there are a ton of them.

The next message was Michael's:

Can I come earlier? I'm wide awake. Up all night with Pam. Still at it

218

this morning. She's pissed I didn't tell her about Pious Rebel. I'm sure you're mad at me, too. Hell, you're probably mad at most of the dinner party. Maybe not Ben. I'll try to be there by eight, if that works. Oh, I hear you and Pam are going to Berkeley this afternoon. How the hell did that happen?

She replied to Michael: Eight is fine. See you soon.

She wiped her wet knuckles against the sheet. Eloise rubbed up against her face. She smelled like salmon. Somebody had fed her. Maybe Ben. Probably Zack. She stretched, made her body long, twisted her joints to bring them back to life. Her head wasn't too bad. A pulsing at the base of her neck. She looked around the room. Gregory's room. Still his room. His Harley posters defining it. Dressers full of his clothes. Closets full of his toys. In the shower, she made the water hotter than usual, stood under the flow, thought of cleansing herself from last night's battles, revelations, letting the heat steam it out of her. Poor Michael had been carrying ugly secrets around way too long. So had Pam. Lisa was back at that place of knowing so much less than she thought she had known. She wanted the hot water to restructure her DNA, erase her memories, let her walk out of the room dry and clean and empty-headed. As she stood there, water streaming down her back, an idea dripped into her pores, coursed its way around and through her body.

Zack was already in the kitchen cooking, orange peels scattered around the counter, no sign of Cody and Ben. "Good morning," she said. "You're up early."

"So are you. Are you hungry?"

"A little. Just something to coat my stomach." He handed her a glass of orange juice. "How was your fundraiser?"

"Excellent. Raised a lot of money. Met a lot of very nice, caring people who try to make a difference."

"How do they do that? Make a difference."

"They donate. Volunteer their time. Work on projects. I joined one last night."

Lisa sipped the orange juice, looked at this man who seemed so comfortable in his body, in her kitchen, with her animals. Thought about his daughter, his wife, his friendship with Gregory, remembered the long curly locks that used to fall down Zack's back, the bushy beard that smelled like the Pacific Northwest. Not that she had ever been there. But thought it should smell like him.

"You're a different man, aren't you?"

He laughed, stared at the ceiling, rolled his head around his neck, cartilage and bone twisting and cracking. He dropped three eggs into boiling water, broke pieces of nine-grain bread into a bowl, pushed a button on the microwave to melt a slab of butter. "Yes. I suppose I am. If you're a sentient being, you'd better be ready to change, to adapt to what gets tossed your way. Or to seek out what it is you should be doing."

"My whole life I've never heard *sentient* said out loud. Now two times this week."

"What was the other one?"

So far she hadn't told anyone the details of her retreat. Now felt right. She told Zack about the Land of Medicine Buddha receptionist's comments about dogs.

He didn't pry, ask for more information about the stay, just nodded his head, said, "Turks and Caicos would agree."

"What project did you join at the Resource Center?"

"It's called the Coalition to Overcome Racism."

"Why that?"

"Why not? If we can solve that one, as a species, we can solve anything. Might as well start at the top. Most of my crew are immigrants. I see how they're treated. Makes me sick to my stomach. Last night we read an essay written by a poet named Tony Hoagland."

"I know him. Well, knew him. A Berkeley poet. Died of pancreatic cancer. My mother had all his books. Invited him to our house once."

"Really? I would have loved to have met him. The essay is titled 'The Cure for Racism Is Cancer.' First published in *The Sun* magazine in September 2018, a month before he died."

Lisa reached for her laptop on the counter, opened her journal, repeated the title as she typed it in: "The Cure for Racism Is Cancer."

"Highly controversial piece. *The Sun* allows readers to comment online. Dozens in agreement with his ideas, just as many hating it."

The comments. She should open Pious Rebel and get to work. Zack didn't know about it yet. Time to let him in. "Speaking of seeking out what you should be doing, let me show you something."

"Just a sec." He drained the poached eggs, slid them on top of the bread chunks, poured the melted butter over the top, sprinkled a little salt and pepper, and set it in front of her. "To coat the stomach." He pulled a stool up next to her, looked over her shoulder at the screen.

While switching from the journal to Pious Rebel, she turned the screen to face him. "I started this blog site a couple of weeks ago. I'm kind of starting to love it."

"Ah. That's a tall order to fill."

"I get those comments like Tony Hoagland did with that essay. Look." She clicked on the holding tank for comments. "Holy Shit!" she said. There were 511 comments since her two posts yesterday.

"Wow! This is huge." Zack moved closer to the screen. "Do all of these comments automatically go up?"

"No. I have to accept or deny them."

"So, if I go to Pious Rebel, I can see everything you've posted, all the comments you've allowed in, but if I write a comment, it won't appear until after you've decided whether or not you like it?"

"Mostly. But I don't know that 'liking it' is one of my criteria. I mean, I do like to read positive posts, know that people are enjoying what I put up, but I allow lots of comments that I don't especially like or agree with, because I appreciate the debate, the different points of view that pop up."

"That's perfect."

"I've been so isolated for so long it feels good to have some exposure to the world."

"You mean isolated as in Gregory keeping you tucked away up here in his kingdom, using you for his own purposes?"

Lisa was surprised how quickly Zack went there, would have expected him to defend Gregory. "Yeah, kind of like that."

"I loved him to death. Miss him every day. But he was kind of a selfish guy. I was sorry to watch you living in his shadows over the years. So thrilled now to see this new you emerging."

"Yeah, me too. Kind of on the subject, I had a brainstorm in the shower this morning. I want to switch rooms with you."

"I don't get it. What do you mean?"

"I mean that room I'm sleeping in is Gregory's room. Most of what's in there is his stuff, his life, as you say, his selfishness. I'm done with that. My plan is that you move your stuff to the big bedroom. I'll move mine to the spare room."

"Your place. Whatever you want."

"My day has rapidly changed. Can you take care of moving our stuff around?"

"Glad to be of service. By the way, working in the greenhouse sounds fun."

He really was a new person. Had shed the old skin like a snake. She was trying to do the same.

"Thank you. Need to focus on Pious Rebel before Michael gets here."

Alice was making her resurrection, commenters from every category loving the first chapter from *I Really Knead You.*

More please, some said. Faster. More chapters.

Lisa opened the manuscript, typed in the next two chapters, split it up into two posts, Published them both.

This was crazy, she thought. Had to be a better way. She went to the comments before reading more of *Love Muffins.* Quick acceptance of the regulars who were weaving their own interpretations of the lives of Celia and William, offering their own "what ifs" as foreshadowing alternatives.

Lisa called Bianca, who answered before Lisa could speak. "God! What a night! I need aspirin. Coffee? What do you want so damn early?"

"Just need to check in. I can't come in today. Anything new?"

"As a matter of fact, on an earlier post you said something about living in Aptos. You can't do that anymore. I went in and erased it. Which reminds me, change your password. Seriously, you'll end up like those celebrities on star maps. People will want to know where you live, see how you live. Same thing with this office. Don't give folks specifics. Rhonda and Sarah are liable to get irked if folks start showing up here. I know your nut-job friend, Cody, hasn't chimed in yet, but she will. Lock her out. You can read her stuff, but don't put it up live. Two more chapters of *Knead* up. Good job."

Now was the time to jump in. "About that, I need some help."

"Shoot."

"Is there a way to get the chapters up without me having to retype them all by hand?"

"No electronic files, right?"

"Right."

"Here's what we do." Lisa liked hearing Bianca use "we," felt like she was a teammate, was joining a faithful tribe, something she'd never had or been in before. "Give me the manuscript. I'll take it to Kinko's. They have an OCR machine that will drop it into text files from the hard copy."

"That's great. Never heard of that. What's OCR?"

"Optical character recognition. It's totally cool. And fast. And fairly cheap. Maybe I should take all five manuscripts down there, get a head start."

"No way. You can take *Rocks and Rolls*, too. But I need to read the others first. I might not want to share those."

"Yes, you will. Have you read the two comments I highlighted?"

"Not yet. Soon."

"Now! Open them now so we can talk."

"Yes, boss." Lisa found the comments, opened the first one, read it out loud:

> Dear Pious Rebel, love your handle! Love your site! Love the writing of your mother Alice Hardrocks. I'm the publisher of a small press in the Bay Area. I like Alice's stories. They might be a nice addition to our lineup of books for late 2020. Give me a call or schedule an appointment.

Email, phone, cell, and address in Berkeley were at the bottom of the post.

"You're kidding me!"

"The other one's basically the same. Someone from L.A. A little bigger press. You're going to need a lawyer. Someone who can guide you through this stuff. Or a lawyer/agent. They usually take ten percent of any deal they put together, but it's worth it. We've got a couple of great women lawyers we work with here. I would steer clear of Ben. He seems sharp, would probably give you a rate, but given his connection to Cody, it's probably a bad idea."

"Wait a minute. You think somebody's going to offer money for Mom's stuff?"

"I know it. Just have to be ready for it. Think it through first. Talk to folks who have been there. This will far surpass your ad income."

"This is all way too fast," Lisa said.

"Seize the day," Bianca said. Lisa wanted to say something about clichés, but decided to keep her mouth shut. "The joke I made the other day about becoming your employee, may be some truth to that. But there's going to be way more here than what I can deal with. Might need to bring in a trusted friend to handle the growing avalanche of comments and followers."

Trusted friends. Did she have any? Not really. "I'll get back to you on that."

"Okay, but hurry. This stuff will get out of hand if we don't get organized."

"I understand."

"Put the manuscripts on my desk when you can."

"Thank you! See you Monday."

Lisa read one more comment before losing herself in Love Muffins. It was RockHounds. The post was related to the geodes thread, but didn't really feel connected to it, more like it was a direct link to her. There had been others like that, orchid growers who wanted to teach her tips and tricks. Women who were tired of men and who wanted Lisa to join their organization, stand up and be heard in front of women who cared, women who needed to be empowered. And at least three folks had invited her to Christmas dinner with their families. This one was different. Softer. Less insistent, an obsession that felt closer to the center than the fringes.

> Looking forward to seeing photos of those geodes. Lucky women, Alice and Celia. And now you, to possess these magical rocks formed by who knows what. Seeds from misplaced dreams? Spit from geysers and volcanoes, scattered around the world, lucky to be found by hounds like me who cannot live without them. And I'm loving reading Alice's stories, getting inside her brain.

She would not post this one live, would leave it in its holding-pattern status, but she did reply.

Dear RockHound. Thanks for your thoughts. Glad you're liking Mom's stories. I'm liking them myself. More chapters coming.

Onward to an installment of *Love Muffins* before Michael arrived.

For her second birthday, Amelia requested daddy's love muffins. "The big ones with the funny faces." William got up earlier than usual, made a huge batch of her favorite chocolate-chip macadamia muffins, enough for everyone at the party to have two each. Celia hid the wine and whiskey William had scattered around the bakery and house. She rented tables and chairs and tablecloths and set up a banquet table in their living room, enough to hold all twenty-four guests. They closed the bakery early at 5:00, folks arriving as early as 5:30. Margie helped make the punch. The volunteer ladies' club helped decorate the muffins. Friends from the neighborhood and preschool filled the table, brought Amelia gifts. Celia saw Justin enter a little late, not one interested in making an entrance, staying quiet, preferring to slide up the staircase and stay hidden in the floral design of the wallpaper. She saw him set a package on the gift table, wrapped in newspaper.

Margie hugged him, handed him a glass of punch. "How's life at Cal? Are you a sophomore now?" Celia listened to his answer.

"Yes. Just turned nineteen. I love it there. Love geology. Just perfect for me. Next semester I'm headed to Ireland to study the Cliffs of Moher. Can't wait." Celia resisted the impulse to interject herself into the conversation.

"How exciting for you!"

William entered from the stairway, a drink in his hands. Celia wondered if he'd found the hidden stash or if he'd just come back from Donny's Place at the corner. "Happy birthday my sweet!"

Amelia ran up to him and hugged him. "Thank you, Daddy, for the exquisite muffins."

"Such a big word for a little girl," he said.

"Mommy taught me that word. Just for your muffins."

Amelia raced through the gifts until she saw the one wrapped in newspaper. She knew it was from Justin. They all did. She worked slowly, untied knots, saved the twine in a little pile next to the box, took a pair of scissors and slipped it under tape, removed the newspaper, folded it, set it under the twine, and opened the box. She knew it! Another geode. Her eyes lit up. "Where's this one from, Uncle Justin?"

"It's called Cinnamon Geode Beds."

"Where's that?"

"It's in Southern California at a place called the Colorado Desert." For the rest of the party, during Pin the Tale on the Donkey, Balloon Burst, and Musical Chairs, Amelia held the geode close to her chest, until every guest had gone home, until she fell asleep in Celia's lap. When Celia tucked her in bed, she opened an eye and lifted the geode up to her nightstand, where the other geodes greeted the new one from Cinnamon Beds.

•   •   •

Ben and Cody were still in bed, Zack was off on his run, when Lisa and Michael approached the workshop. He carried a small can of WD-40, squirted the lock, and Lisa slid the key in, much easier than before.

"Good idea. Thanks." She walked to the bookshelf, stared at the geodes. "Can we start here?"

"Sure. What do you have in mind?"

"I want to get the wheelbarrow from the greenhouse, the clean one, and haul these all into my room." They emptied the shelves, and Michael pushed the wheelbarrow up the driveway and through the back door. He started wheeling it toward the big bedroom, but Lisa stopped him.

"No. I'm in here now. Just set the stuff outside the door."

"Why?"

"Why not?"

"Are you hooking up with Zack, already?"

Lisa laughed. "God, no! I switched rooms with him. I want my own space. My own walls. Pictures. Rocks."

Back in the workshop they sat in front of the easel pad. Michael said, "There's no question in my mind now. If we decide to grow something, it should definitely be hemp seeds. It's legal. It's potentially lucrative. There's lots to it, though. The feminization. Keeping the males out of it. Spraying the crops with colloidal silver. Lots of work. Not sure if you're up for it."

"Thanks for thinking of me. I've mentioned the possibility to Zack. He'd be willing to help, maybe run the operation for us."

"And you're okay with him being around that much?"

"I don't think it's going to be a problem."

"Shall we venture into the cupboards? The ones without locks first."

Lisa stood up, went to the closest cupboard. "To be honest, I'm more interested in the locked ones, but sure, let's go."

The first one was loaded with Harley parts. The second had a library of books and magazines about Harleys. The next one was a catchall for odds and ends, trinkets, what looked like gifts from folks, a few jars full of marbles.

Three cabinets remained. All locked. Yale locks securing metal hinges.

Michael shook one. "Sturdy. Any idea about where the keys might be?"

"I'm not going on another one of his idiotic scavenger hunts." She went to G's toolbox, removed a hammer and a chisel, set the chisel underneath the first lock, and smashed it. The parts fell quickly to the ground.

"Well, then," Michael said. "Here we are."

Lisa pulled the cabinet doors open. She had not known what to expect, but she didn't expect what she saw. One full shelf of porn DVDs. Another shelf with a wide variety of condoms. Another with oils, magazines, accoutrements. A small travel bag, one she recognized from his trips south.

"My, my, my," Michael said. "Who knew?"

"Not me," Lisa answered. "But I won't say anything surprises me anymore. We watched a little porn together occasionally, but nothing like this."

"What do you want to do with this?"

"You want it? Maybe Pam would like it."

"Hilarious! By the way, are you okay with what happened last night?"

"What did happen last night? Why wouldn't I be okay? At least Pam was being honest. It's you who's been a chickenshit for so long. Never mind. Let's load this stuff into the wheelbarrow. Trash it." She felt like she should get in her car, drive to the Sutter Clinic on Soquel, get tested for AIDS and every other possible STD. As Michael emptied the shelves, she leaned over the turtle on the porch and threw up.

"Two to go," Michael said. He smashed the hammer into the chisel, twice, both locks tumbling away. The first cabinet they opened had more boxes, but they looked like completed projects, dioramas and assemblage combined with collage. It really was quite impressive, artistic.

"This doesn't look like his style. Like I said the other day, he was not this creative or interesting," Michael said.

Lisa slammed the doors shut. "Next!" This one was full of portable file cabinets, papers, invoices, business-related stuff. One plastic file was full of the names and transactions of the Central Valley clients.

Michael grabbed the one labeled *Locals* and thumbed through it. "Yep. They're all here. What do you think?"

"I think we're positive we're out of this business. Let's take it all to G's furnace." Gregory had built an incinerator between the workshop and the greenhouse to burn the slash from his oak cuttings and the finished pot crop.

"Shouldn't we read this stuff first?"

"Maybe save the Central Valley papers. Not the local stuff. Let's burn it now. You take it to the incinerator and I'll look through the rest."

Michael loaded up the wheelbarrow with four file cabinets, pushed it out the door. Lisa grabbed a box of papers labeled *The Pot Plan*, set it on a table and rifled through it. Receipts and pictures of greenhouses and catalogues. Boring. She was done with it all, tossed it out the door. Another box was labeled *Hemp Seeds*. She set it aside for Michael. The final box was labeled *The Property*. A folder titled "Past Bills." Another titled "Property Taxes." Another, "Mortgages." She pulled that one out, flipped it open. There was a spreadsheet in front that showed withdrawals from local banks and credit unions. It looked like there were at least five mortgages against the property. Four of them were small, totaling a little over $50,000. But the fifth one? Was this really possible? A balloon payment of $250,000 due the first week of January?

When Michael returned, she was sitting with her forehead leaning against her palms.

"What? What's the matter?"

She handed him the folder. He fell into a chair. They stayed silent for a long time. Lisa finally spoke. "Maybe we *should* sell the whole place?"

"Maybe. This kills us. How could he do this? So unlike him. We could amortize. If we leased it out we could pay down two thousand a month. But that wouldn't touch the principal."

Lisa grabbed the hemp-seeds box, handed it to Michael. "That's why Gregory was moving into hemp seeds. The million dollars looked good to him."

"Right. And he'd rely on his master gardener to make sure the crop came through as it should."

"Yeah. Killing all the little males. Feminization of the greenhouse. Of the world. Here's the bank account info. I'll dig through it when I'm up to it. We need to figure this out."

"There is another option. You won't like it."

"Tell me."

"Wasn't Cody bragging about her windfall last night? Picking up that monster tab."

Lisa still wasn't sure what she was going to do with Cody. Punch her in the nose. Kick her out of her house.

"Not thinking I could be partnering with her right now. Unless I wanted to ensure her failure and make sure males inhabit the greenhouse."

"Cutting off your own nose. Sorry," he said quickly.

She smiled. "Thanks for thinking of it."

"And then there's Zack."

"What about him?"

"He's rich. Entrepreneurial. He might be interested."

"I don't know. He did say he'd be willing to help with the greenhouse. But I don't know about being a financial partner."

•   •   •

Zack was cooking lunch when they came in from the workshop. Lisa carried the box with the financial information, down the hall, opened the door to the spare room. Zack had already switched the rooms, her stuff neatly arranged, her camera sitting on one pillow, his Zen book on the other. She stuffed the box on top of the closet, went back to the kitchen where Michael was setting set a box on the counter. "Harley stuff in here," he said to Zack. "It's yours if you want it. What are you cooking? Smells great."

"Thanks. Made friends with some of the guys out on the wharf. Got some halibut right out of the water. Shiitake risotto. Fresh spinach and peas. Francese rolls from Gayle's." He nodded to the box. "Anything fun in there?"

"Not to me. Maybe to you."

Lisa handed Zack his key to the workshop. "There's one whole cabinet in there with Harley parts. Knock yourself out. Alexa, open Zack's list." Zack turned from the stove.

"Opening Zack's list. Reading thirteen items." Zack leaned in, paid attention.

When Alexa finished, Zack said. "That's wild. Sounds like I won't have it on the road until 2020. Thanks for the key."

She went to the couch, wrapped herself in a blanket, opened her computer screen.

Michael walked toward the door. "I'm headed home. Have fun in Berkeley. See you whenever."

"Thanks. Talk soon."

Ben appeared from the bedroom.

She smiled at him. "Is it still Thursday?"

He grumbled. "I have no idea. All I know is I can't keep up with your friend."

"Nobody can."

"You moving forward with the hemp-seed idea?"

"Not sure yet. Something."

"I represent two of the best growers on the West Coast. Let me know if you want me to set up a meeting."

"Good to know. Thanks. Cody still in bed?"

"She's in the shower now." He turned to Zack. "Damn. What are you cooking, man?"

Lisa went into Pious Rebel, opened a new post. Wanted to go on a rant and bash Gregory. Bash Cody. Bash the sycophants and users. She took a deep breath, stood up and stepped into a couple minutes of *Qi Gong*, sat back down, started typing:

> I've been feeling more and more like an ostrich with every new thing I learn. Like I've been one, I should say. Head buried so deeply in other people's sand, I didn't know I wasn't breathing. You'll be glad to know that phase of my life is over. I'm not exactly sure what the next phase will look like, but you and Pious Rebel are leading the charge. Thanks to my friend HotMama, all chapters of *I Really Knead You* are digitized and ready to be posted. I won't put them up all at once, will continue to tantalize you, have you begging for more. Just kidding! You'll be happy to know that all of Alice's geodes are now sitting in my new bedroom on a bookshelf, so I can wake every morning and stare into their mesmerizing eyes. I've never been to a geode bed before. One of these days.

It was a short post, but it was all she had. Time to prepare herself for Cody's eventual appearance. She was hating Cody right now. Pulling plates and napkins from the cupboard, Zack called from the kitchen. "How many for lunch today?"

"You, Cody, Ben. I've got to leave soon to pick up Pam." she said. Ben sat on the couch next to her.

"Cody's oblivious, you know."

"I've known that for a long time."

"Right. But I mean about last night."

"You mean convenient selective memory?"

"Not sure how selective it is. But I believe she goes into brownouts, especially with tequila. She has zero memory about most of last night, especially Pam's revelations."

"I understand that. Have known that about her for a long time. But that doesn't let her off the hook for what she's done. By the way, what do you see in her? A successful guy like you who can pretty much have your choice. I don't get it."

"Come on. You guys have been best friends for how long?"

"Forever."

"So you know the good parts about her. How she loves her work, kids. How she stands up for herself and her friends."

"Excuse me?" Lisa glared at him.

"Well, in general, you know she does. You guys have some specific issues to deal with."

Cody appeared, Eloise in her arms, petting her forehead. "This is such a sweet kitty. Jeez, I haven't slept that long since —"

Lisa cut her off. "Since you drained the last bar of tequila?"

Cody chuckled. "Yeah. Something like that. Last thing I remember was that final bite of porterhouse. That was so good."

"Lunch is ready," Zack said.

"Where'd you find this guy?" Cody joked. "Better be good to me, Ben. Or I may have to dump you for Chez Zack." Ben said nothing. Zack passed the platter of halibut around the table. Lisa pulled out her cell phone, snapped a picture.

"Not much chance of that," Zack said.

"Whoa! What? Are you previously encumbered?"

"Not encumbered to any one person. But to a lifestyle. And from what I understand, you're a bit of a train wreck," Zack said as he dug into the risotto. Lisa took another picture, which triggered a thought of RockHounds. She got up, went to her room, snapped a photo of the geodes on her bookshelf, returned to the table.

"What'd I miss?" Lisa said. "Any head-on collisions? I do so enjoy hearing truths spoken around me."

"You didn't miss anything," Cody grumbled. "Just waiting for you to get back so I could understand who's been saying things to Zack about me. I did just win a defamation-of-character lawsuit. I'd be happy to do it again. Right, Ben?" He ignored her.

Lisa stood up, walked to the door. "I'll be out back for a while. See you shortly."

In the workshop she thought about Zack being unencumbered. The loss of a daughter would explain that. The loss of a marriage. An errant oak tree. She wondered about the roots of encumber, if it had anything to do with connection, with twisting around each other like she had done with G's bare legs after sex. She looked it up on *Dictionary.com*. The core of the definition dealt with restricting or burdening. Is that really what it meant every time she'd used it incorrectly and out of context over the years? Gregory had definitely encumbered her, given this definition. She and Michael were encumbered by the mortgages Gregory had levied against the house. That Zack used the word so quickly and casually made sense. Forging a life with minimal restrictions and burdens was what he needed now. Trying to heal from the loss of a daughter. Heal from a life that had pretty much gone unexamined.

Cody barged in, carrying a bottle of wine and two glasses. "What are you doing out here?"

"Working."

"Are you avoiding me?"

"Why would I be avoiding you?"

"I haven't the slightest idea. But Ben says there was some kerfuffle last night at dinner. I don't remember any of that."

Lisa reached for the bottle. She opened the workshop door, leaned out, and dumped the wine onto the ground.

"What are you doing? That's good wine."

"So what. I'm no longer supporting this habit of yours. It screws up lives."

"What is with this goody-two-shoes mother protectorate bullshit? I can't believe you threw that wine away!"

"What I can't believe is what a rotten two-faced friend you've been. Do you not know how snockered you were last night?"

"I have a pretty good idea."

"But you have no recollection of what was said. Of Pam?"

"Oh, there was some blabber coming out of her. I don't know anything about it."

"Let's back up, *friend*. First of all, we go for seven years with you never saying a word about you and Ryan until I happen to hear about it elsewhere and bring it up. And you tell me that was all my fault, for abandoning you both, and that Ryan never cared about me, had other women interested in him. I'm guessing you were the only other woman."

Cody opened her mouth to interrupt.

"No. I'm talking right now. Not too long ago, Michael accidentally blurts out something about Point Reyes Station and you, but he won't give me any details. I ask him numerous times, but for some reason he's feeling more protective of you than me. Although I'm guessing it was really more the memory of Gregory he was protecting."

Cody sat down. "Then, finally, last night a little more truth leaked out. Mainly because of Pam."

"She is such a bitch. And when did you start calling her Pam?"

"What you were too drunk to remember is her sharing that you knew Gregory before he ever came into the bookstore."

"She said that?"

"That you two were an item before I ever knew him. That you orchestrated the whole meeting that night at the bookstore, that you enticed him to haul me away to Aptos. I'm not exactly sure why, but it's starting to become clear. I'm sure Pam only knew about it because Gregory had talked to Michael, and Michael had talked to Pam because he felt guilty about not telling me. The whole damn tangled mess slowly becoming untangled."

Cody stood. "This is crazy talk. So, you don't want me in Berkeley with you?"

"Absolutely not."

"Fine." She walked out.

Lisa locked the workshop, followed her. Cody stopped, turned around. "Are you kicking me and Ben out?"

"No. I kind of like *him*."

"What's that supposed to mean?"

"It doesn't mean anything. He's a nice guy. One who could turn your life around. But I'm sure you'll drink yourself into oblivion and screw it up."

Inside Lisa grabbed her pack and headed for the door. "I wish I'd had time to eat. Smells great."

Zack bowed his head. "Another time."

•   •   •

Michael and Pam lived on Linden Street. Lisa had never seen it before, a quaint street with ranch houses. Pam looked surprised when Lisa pulled up in Zack's truck.

"Jeez! I may need a ladder to get in."

"I know. There's a handle here, and here. Grab those one at a time and it's easier. I was thinking Los Gatos for a late lunch. What do you think?"

234

"Perfect."

"I looked up a place this morning called Southern Kitchen."

"That place is great. I love their chocolate-chip pancakes. Or the Nova Scotia Benedict."

Traffic was light going over Highway 17. They arrived in thirty-five minutes, were seated immediately. They avoided any heavy topics on the way over. Lisa mentioned *Zen and the Art of Motorcycle Maintenance*, told her Zack had left it on her bed. Pam had also read it in college days, remembered that it had a strong effect on her then, though details were fuzzy. "Maybe we should have a two-person book group," Pam suggested. "Dig back in. Pretend like we have brains again."

At the restaurant they both ordered chocolate-chip pancakes. While waiting, Lisa said, "About pretending like we have brains again, that pretty much applies to me. But not you. What you did with the geode stories was pretty amazing."

Pam squirmed in her seat, rearranged her silverware, pushed the syrup aside, like making moves on a chessboard. "I'm sorry you had to hear about that. You weren't ever supposed to know."

"Like I was never supposed to know they existed, hidden away on a bookshelf in G's workshop."

"Right. That's weird, too. But you were never supposed to know about my involvement."

"I've been wondering about your involvement with G. Whether or not you were one of the many with whom he had flings."

"Oh, god, no! I would never. For so many reasons."

"I'd love to hear them."

"He was a selfish pig. I mean, he was brilliant in his own way. But it had to be about him. I helped him because he was Michael's brother. Michael felt insecure around him, like he couldn't live up to him. So, I helped Gregory with ideas for marketing, distribution, and of course the geodes that were supposed to be for you."

"They're mine now."

"I read the posts this morning. And I'm caught up now with Alice's stories. So marvelous. I love them. Love her. Love all the characters. But I had zero interest in Gregory beyond helping Michael, helping him do something nice for you. I've felt so sorry for you, the way he treated you."

235

"That's done." Lisa took a bite of her pancakes. "Why has it taken us so long to connect? I felt like you were distant, in some ways kind of a snob."

Pam smiled. "I *was* distant, intentionally. Hated that Michael was selling pot for a living. I didn't want to have anything to do with it. And you were at the core of it. So good at the growing and harvesting. It's what kept them in it for so long. I secretly hoped the whole thing would fail. Sorry if it came off snob-like. I was just angry. Fearful. I didn't want Michael to go to jail."

By the time they reached Oakland and headed toward Berkeley, they had thoroughly discussed Pam's disclosures at Alderwood, which didn't take long. They were both in agreement about Cody and G's despicable behavior. Lisa brought up Pious Rebel again, told Pam about Bianca and how she was helping with the site. About the ad placements, the publisher interested in Alice's books. About the need for help with management of the comments, the site.

As they pulled into the storage facility, Lisa said, "Would you have any interest in helping me out? For pay, I mean?"

"Interesting proposition. My skills do fit your needs. But part of me is reluctant, you know, the family part, the mixing business with friends. Not that we're friends. Yet. But you know what I mean. Then there's the other part."

"What's that?"

"You know. The greenhouse. The danger. The risk. The Central Valley bozos. And now this stupid balloon payment. What does this whole package look like for the short- and long-term future?"

"I know. It's so braided. But it seems like hemp seeds are in. Either way, I'm continuing with Pious Rebel and need help."

Lisa pulled Zack's truck in front of Alice's storage space. They stepped carefully from the truck, stretched their feet to the ground. It took both of them to raise the sliding door, not having been touched in over a year. The light from outside reminded Lisa of the contents, of pasts crammed into boxes, lives stacked neatly inside a ten-by-ten room, floor to ceiling, spider webs and rats and fading memories.

"Remind me when your mom died."

"Last year, Labor Day. I had to hire local folks to move things. Gregory wouldn't help."

"Of course he wouldn't."

"It was harvest time, and he didn't want me spending time up here, too much work to do in the greenhouse. I found the box of manuscripts, the geodes, and that's all I brought home. Everything else got shoved into this space by people who didn't know what they were carrying and didn't care."

"Have you got a plan of attack?"

Lisa chuckled. "Sounds like a battle. A war. I guess it kind of is. But, yes. Most of this stuff I want to give away. There's a place in Oakland called the East Bay Depot for Creative Reuse. We'll load up the truck and deliver it there. We'll leave the things I want to keep and pick them up on the way home. When do you have to be back?"

"Like I said, Christmas Eve."

"Good. Maybe we stay in Point Reyes Station tonight, come back tomorrow." Lisa hadn't even thought about Christmas, that it was a holiday, that it would be here soon. That it usually involved presents and a big meal. Zack would probably love to plan the meal. But the presents. She didn't care right now. She was hoping there were buried gifts for her in Alice's boxes.

"I need to open every box, look for treasures before I toss them. There's two box knives in the backpack. Let's see what we can find." They sliced open box tops, put containers of dishes and kitchen supplies and wall hangings and knickknacks in the truck. Every box brought back memories of life with Alice, Cody with them, as if Alice had adopted her, invited her into the family. In one corner there were ten boxes full of Alice's books, half of them full of poets like Tony Hoagland, Josephine Miles, Gary Snyder, Robert Hass, Philip Levine, Gary Young.

"These need to go home with us. Put them in tomorrow's pile."

"Great stuff. Where you going to put it all?" Lisa had the germ of an idea forming, but didn't want to say it out loud, didn't even want to think about it yet.

"I'll figure that out later. But it will involve those three bookcases." They dragged them from a corner, set them near the door, ready to haul back to Aptos tomorrow.

"I'm taking this desk, too." It was the desk where Alice had conducted her work for hire. The desk where she had written her manuscripts. The one that had been off limits to Lisa and Cody for most of their lives.

Pam had her hands inside a box. "You'll want to look at this one." Lisa joined her. Photo albums, loose pictures, recipes. Pam held one up. "Is that you and Cody?"

"Oh, my god. Science camp. We were twelve. They brought us down to Big Basin that year, Camp Hammer. The snake wrapped around Cody's neck was called Jasper. Yep. This box goes home with us."

In another corner Pam lifted a blanket, said, "You want this old thing?" The IBM Selectric looked brand new, as if it had never been used, polished and cleaned daily by Alice.

"I can't give that away. You know she never touched a computer in her life. Used this for everything. Drove her clients crazy, but she was so good at what she did. They kept coming back."

"Will you ever use it?"

"Probably not. But I have to take it."

They worked fast, blasted their way through boxes, jammed the truck bed full of furniture and lamps Lisa didn't want. There was one wall of boxes left they hadn't touched yet. They were all banker's boxes like the two she had taken last year. Most of them were full of magazines, *The New Yorker*, *The Paris Review*, *Ploughshares*, *New England Review*, *Harper's Magazine* and others she didn't recognize.

"Damn! I should keep these. Literary relics. No. I can't do it. Let's toss them."

There were two boxes left. In unison, they slid their blades through cardboard and packing tape, lifted the flaps. Lisa's box contained five more manuscript boxes, reminding her of when she'd found *The Baker's Quintet*. She teared up a bit, a rare occurrence for her. She quickly closed the lid, didn't want to look inside yet. A treasure, maybe. A Christmas gift from Alice to her. Maybe. She slid the box to the Aptos pile, watched as Pam removed books from her box.

"What have you got there?" Lisa asked.

"This could be the Holy Grail." She handed a notebook to Lisa. Lisa thought about her Holy Grail blog post, how folks had flocked to it. Once she opened the notebook, she knew what she had in her hands, knew what this box contained. The one she held had *September 1998* written across the top, underlined. Journals. Alice's journals. Eight of them. She skimmed through, replaced them, put the lid back on the box, carried it like a case of eggs to the truck, placed it on the front seat of the cab, locked it. She knew it made no sense, no one within miles, but she wasn't letting that box out of her sight.

They pulled the sliding door down, fought their way into the cab, and headed for the Reuse Depot. Once the truck had been emptied, Lisa sat quietly, almost catatonic.

"What now?" Pam said.

Lisa wasn't sure. Part of her wanted to curl up on the seat and fall asleep. She was excited to get home and work her way through the photos, the books, the journals, possible new manuscripts. But part of her was terrified. It was all so fast. Almost overwhelming. Maybe she needed to book a week at Medicine Buddha. Maybe head down to Esalen and force herself to get further away from home than a thousand feet.

She snapped out of it. "I'd planned on heading straight to Point Reyes Station, if that works for you."

"Sounds like an adventure."

"Yes. But I'm thinking I've got one more stop to make first. Would you grab my computer case from under your seat?"

Pam handed her the bag, and she opened the computer and found the address for the publisher in Berkeley. In seven minutes, they were in an elevator taking them to a third-floor office. Their unexpected visit was met with enthusiasm and excitement by the woman who was the executive director, publisher, and editor of the small press.

"We love Alice and her stories!" she said.

Lisa wondered if she was using the royal 'we', as it didn't look like there were any other employees, the office just one room.

"What are the next steps?" Pam interjected. Lisa didn't feel this was the work of pushy Pamela, but rather of helpful Pam.

"Ideally, I need to get copies of the manuscripts, read them, decide if we want any or all of them. If so, I'd work up a contract with details of publication rollout, royalties, everything you'd need to know."

"Any advance payment toward royalties?" Pam asked. The woman looked carefully at her.

"I'll need to read them first before we make those kinds of decisions."

Lisa leaned forward. "We also just located a box full of Alice's journals."

"Really!" The woman's eyes widened. "One thing I love about this project is that she's an unknown and she's local. Having access to the journals could be a huge marketing tool."

"One other thing. I'm guessing you're following the site," Lisa said.

"Oh, yes."

"Then you've probably seen that I started posting chapters from the first book."

"Right. We usually like to have first North American publication rights, meaning you can't post it online. But, because your following is zooming past all expectations, it's a marketing technique I'm liking at the moment."

Lisa left her contact information; told the woman she'd be in touch.

Pam finished the conversation saying, "We do have a couple of other presses from L.A. and New York interested. Just so you know."

"Thanks for sharing that."

They made their way up 580 and past Point Richmond.

Lisa said, "Have you ever been to the Rosie the Riveter exhibit?"

"No."

"It's worth a visit. It's a national park so it's well funded. Movies, books, artifacts, great photos. Ryan and I went there a couple of times. They have the Codex Book Fair right next door in the Craneway Pavilion. That's another cool place to visit. Hundreds of handmade books from around the world."

"Speaking of Ryan," Pam said, "I've never heard much about him, from anybody. Is that why we're headed to Point Reyes Station?"

"It's mostly just a wild hair. A bit of remorse has worked its way into my head lately, thinking about how I just left and haven't talked to him since."

"I don't get it. He never came after you, no email, no phone calls?"

"Nothing. But according to Cody, he was ready to dump me before I left."

Pam shook her head. "No way you believe anything that begins with 'according to Cody.' You need to let that remorse go."

"I know. I will. I also want to see my old bookstore."

"Sounds good," Pam said. Lisa looked over, saw Pam's head rested against the seat, eyes closed. "See you there." She was happy to have her along, a calming influence. So glad it wasn't Cody yammering away nonstop.

·   ·   ·

They passed San Quentin and continued up 101 until they got to Lucas Valley Road, cut their way over to the coast and landed in Point Reyes Station. Lisa made her way to one of her favorite places in town, the Cowgirl Creamery on Fourth Street, an old hay barn turned into a creamery and retail store. She let Pam sleep and went in, the aromas carrying her back, the dozens of times she'd walked through these doors smelling and tasting the latest cheese.

Her basket filled rapidly with house-baked cookies, two bottles of house-made lemonade, two of the ready-to-go roasted turkey sandwiches with house-roasted turkey cooked on the property, complete with herbed Cowgirl Creamery fromage blanc, savory onion jam, and greens. Everything was all about the house. The home these two women had created. She missed that. Wondered if she could find that hominess in Santa Cruz or Aptos. She was working on it, would dig a little deeper now and see what she could uncover. She saw Pam coming through the door. Maybe she could help, show her the ins and outs of local life that Gregory never had. She picked up a wedge of Brie and a Gouda she'd never seen before, tossed a package of rustic crackers in the basket, and wheeled toward Pam.

"Anything else?" Lisa pointed at the basket.

"This looks good. I do need coffee, though."

They sat outside in a shaded picnic area.

"God, this Brie is to die for."

Lisa almost forgot to think about the cliché. "I know. Straight into the veins. Clog me up. Death by cheese."

Pam smiled, pointed back toward the Creamery. "What's that?"

"Are you talking about the Susan Hayes sign?"

Pam nodded, pushing a cracker with Brie into her mouth.

"That's an amazing store. Susan Hayes Handwovens. They've been in town for thirty years or more. High-end designers."

"Looks like maybe a good place to find Christmas presents."

Lisa put down her sandwich, looked at Pam. "What's the date today?"

"The twenty-first. Why?"

Too much else going on to consider it, hadn't even thought about gifts for others.

"Christmas is in four days?"

"It certainly is."

"Oh, jeez." She took her cell phone out of her purse, punched in a few numbers. "Zack. It's Lisa. Hi. Can you do me a favor? Christmas dinner. It completely slipped my mind. Can you handle it? I'll reimburse you when we get back. The 'we' is me and Pam. Probably late tomorrow afternoon. Thanks. Bye."

She ignored the text messages, needed to be away from them for a day.

Pam stood up, tossed her sandwich wrapper in a trash can. "Nice to have those kinds of resources living with you."

"Yeah. He's great. So are you. Thanks for coming with me."

Pam ignored her, nodded toward the building. "We need to get some Christmas shopping therapy in. What do you say?"

Lisa had no clue what to buy for whom, but it made sense. "Absolutely."

An hour later, three clerks helped them carry bags and boxes to the truck. They crammed everything in the cab behind the seats.

"That was quite an unexpected hit," Lisa said.

"It's a good thing my work pays well."

"What do you mean?"

"I mean right now there's not much income for Michael, and given that you're getting out of the pot business, which you know I highly applaud, there's going to be even less."

Lisa thought about the current state of her and Michael's financial balance or lack of. She'd be running into this wall soon herself. Maybe she shouldn't have indulged in this spree.

"We'll figure something out."

"I know Michael has mentioned it to you, but have you carefully considered the possibility of selling, or splitting the property?" Pam said.

Lisa didn't want to think about this now, didn't want to have this conversation with Pam. Things had been good between them so far.

This could turn that. "Not carefully, yet. Come on. Let me show you the bookstore. It's around the corner."

They fought their way up into the cab again, grabbing handles, thrusting themselves in.

"We ought to name this beast," Pam said.

Lisa laughed. "Good idea. Like the Blue Monster, or Shrek."

"Good ones. What about Paul Bunyan's blue ox?"

"Babe! That's perfect."

"Babe it is."

They turned the corner and pulled Babe into a parking place in front of the hardware store across from the bookstore. Lisa looked for the sign. "Wait a minute! Where is it?"

"What do you mean?"

"I mean it's gone. It was right there. Where that real estate office is."

Inside the office Lisa walked up to one of the agents. "Do you know where the bookstore moved?"

"The bookstore? That was a long time ago. I don't think they went anywhere. Closed down just before we moved in."

"When was that?"

"Let me see. Six, seven years ago — 2013 or 14."

Lisa thanked him, though she wasn't sure for what.

Back in Babe, Pam said, "What's that all about?"

"I have no idea."

"What now?"

"Our farm. I mean Ryan's farm."

They took the Shoreline Highway toward Tomasina Canyon, passed Point Reyes Country Inn and drove down a hundred-foot driveway toward a small farmhouse surrounded by gardens.

"My gardens," Lisa said. "Used to be, anyway."

A woman who looked to be in her late twenties, digging weeds with a hoe, watched them drive in, walked toward the truck to greet them. Lisa rolled down her window.

"Are you here to pick up the berries?" the woman said.

"No," Lisa said. "But how are the berries doing?" It was a strange question. Why would this woman answer such a question?

She looked over her shoulder. "Thriving. Like always. Are you here to buy something?"

The woman was attractive, sturdy. Ryan had done well, found a good replacement for her.

"I'm actually looking for Ryan." She stopped short of entangling things more, of saying she was the ex, ex-partner, ex-lover, ex-keeper of the blackberries.

"Ryan's not here anymore. My partner and I rent the property from him."

"What do you mean he's not here? You mean here on the farm, or here as in Point Reyes Station?"

"I mean he moved to Aspen. We mail him monthly checks."

"Aspen? When?"

"Three, four years ago."

Lisa turned to Pam, who shook her head, stared out the window at the gardens.

"Did he go by himself?"

"I have no idea. If you give me your name, contact info, I'll include it with the next payment."

"Oh, no thanks. I'm good. Great place you've got here."

Back down the driveway, Lisa sat at the edge of the highway, both hands gripping Babe's large steering wheel, head resting against the horn. She didn't know whether to turn left and head back to Aptos, or right toward Tomales Bay.

"What now, my friend?" Pam said softly.

Was she her friend? Maybe eventually. Just accept it. Allow it in and let it be. Consider it an accomplishment. Head into the office tomorrow and write it on the T-chart. Ignore the disappointments of the day. Rejoice a little. In the finding of potential new treasures in Alice's boxes. At the Brie still lingering on her taste buds. At the gifts they'd found at the hands of Susan Hayes.

"We could head back to town, or not," Lisa said.

"Which town?"

"Good point." Her head was spinning, not thinking clearly.

"Minimally, we need to go back to Berkeley eventually, load up Babe with what you're bringing back. Do we have time to do all that tonight?"

"Only if we plan on getting home by midnight, and I don't like driving in the dark. Especially in a strange vehicle."

"Shh. I don't think Babe would appreciate being called strange," Pam said.

Lisa laughed. She liked having Pam around. A little saner version of Bianca.

"How about this for a plan? We drive back to Berkeley now, find a place to spend the night. I have a couple of things I'd like to accomplish in the morning before we load Babe up. We should get home by early afternoon tomorrow."

Pam had her cell phone in hand, typing as she answered, "I'm game. Do you like theater?"

"I used to. When I had a life."

"Come on. Quit whining. You've got one now. Or getting one. There's a play at the Berkeley Rep called *Becky Nurse of Salem*, at eight p.m. tonight, written by Sarah Ruhl."

"I love Sarah Ruhl! MacArthur genius. I saw *In the Next Room* when it opened there in 2009."

"Shall I buy these tickets?"

"Yes!"

"Excellent. Done. Now about lodging. We can go Airbnb. The Claremont. Or we can stay at the Hotel Shattuck Plaza, two-tenths of a mile from the theater."

Lisa turned onto the highway, headed southeast. "I'm open to persuasion. But I do like the idea of walking out of the theater and plopping into bed within a few minutes."

Pam punched keys on the phone. "Two hundred fifty-nine dollars. We're all set."

It was hard to find a spot on Shattuck big enough to fit Babe. They parked in a garage around the corner. Lisa waited in the cab while Pam checked in, returned with a hand truck she'd borrowed. They stacked the box of photos and journals up, and Lisa grabbed her computer bag from under the seat, strapped it around her shoulder, with just enough time to make it into the theater.

38

SATURDAY
12-21-19

L ISA WAS UP EARLY THE NEXT MORNING, reading a text from Bianca. Books 1 and 2 are both digitized. I set them up for you as separate posts. They're in holding tanks with the titles of the books. I called our lawyer friend. She wants to help. Have fun!

She crouched into her *Qi Gong* pose, tiptoed to the bathroom, and returned to bed. After the twenty-minute routine, Lisa opened the computer. The threads on *I Really Knead You* had doubled overnight. Of course, there were a few naysayers who grumbled about recipes and baking and how to glaze muffins, but ninety-nine percent were loving Alice's stories. There were two more messages from the director of the small press in Berkeley, gently prodding her to send the manuscripts. The second one included a sample contract.

"Are you awake?" Lisa whispered.

Pam whispered back. "I am now."

"Sorry. I was wondering if you could help me find somebody. Actually, two somebodies."

Pam rolled over on her side. "I'm here to serve."

"No you're not. But I'm very thankful you're here."

"I wake up a little cranky in the mornings. And that play has my head spinning a bit."

"I know. Makes me ponder a little deeper about witchcraft and magic. Pretty different than her other stuff."

Pam sat up, reached for her phone on the nightstand. "Yeah, it's a different face for her. A different vehicle, but the same message. Finding power inside oneself outside of what society gives you, or expects from you. Who do you want to find?"

"Right. I'm understanding that message."

"Hell, you're living that message."

"Anita is her name. Anita Ortiz. My mother's best friend."

"Where does she live? How old? Is that a maiden or married name?"

"Same age that my mom would have been, seventy-five. I'm hoping she's still alive, in Berkeley or Oakland. I believe she went by Ortiz. Never married that I know of. Made me wonder if she and Mom were lovers."

Pam grabbed her wallet, removed a credit card, punched in numbers on her phone.

"What are you doing?" Lisa asked. "Are you having to pay for that?"

"Not much. Don't worry about it. Okay. I'm in. Four Anita Ortizes in the Bay Area. Only one who fits all your criteria. She lives in an assisted-care facility in Piedmont."

"Wow! That was fast. How about breakfast downstairs, then we head to the storage unit, then Piedmont?"

"Breakfast sounds good, but I'd go to Piedmont before loading the truck and having it exposed on the street for anybody to break into. Even if it is Piedmont."

At breakfast Lisa spent time on the computer reading posts and vetting. RockHounds:

Thank you so much for the pictures of the geodes! I can't
describe to you how seeing them makes me feel, so I won't try.
The story of Celia, William, Justin is precious. Makes me cry.

Uh-oh. RockHounds was turning a little weird. Not wacky or perverted, but one to watch.

The waitperson arrived with their food, placed a coffee in front of Pam. The large juice for Lisa landed on a fork, the whole thing smashing into the keyboard, drenching everything, liquid drizzling between the keys, into the touch pad, behind the screen, large clouds and shadows forming behind windows and text, lemonade dripping off the table into Lisa's lap. Lisa and Pam froze. The waitperson grabbed unused napkins from other tables and attempted to sop up the mess, dabbing the keyboard, the screen.

"I am so sorry." More napkins, more dabbing. "But I really don't think it was my fault. I mean, that computer on the table is a little precarious."

Lisa wanted to take a fork and run it through the waitperson's eyeball. Just one. Leave her enough sight to know what she was missing from the other eye. The T-chart sprung into her head. She'd need to flip the page, need more room, more markers, different colors to show the multiple shades of disappointment and anger crushing in all around her.

She felt Pam's hand rubbing her back. "Would you please have the manager come over?"

When he arrived, Pam said, "We'd like to have this incident written up. I'm certain you have insurance to cover these types of accidents."

He cleared his throat. "Was the computer sitting on the table?"

"Just like it is now. It hasn't moved," Lisa blurted out.

"I'm sorry, but our insurance won't cover accidents that have been precipitated by the customer's choice of placing items of value on the surface of the table. The best we can do is comp you the meal."

Lisa wanted to cry but saw that Pam was about to become unglued. She grabbed Pam's hand, and pulled her away from the table, stuffing the drenched computer into its bag on their way out.

"I'll take care of the bill," the manager called after them.

"Fuck you, moron!" Lisa shouted back.

•   •   •

Lisa drove under the speed limit toward Piedmont, energy drained.

"Most of my life was on that computer. All the Pious Rebel stuff. I did not need this right now. Maybe we should stop at the Apple Store in Los Gatos on the way home. See if they can save it."

"The bad news is they can't save this. You're completely fried. The good news is that all the Pious Rebel stuff is online. You just need another computer."

At the retirement home, Lisa jumped to the ground without using the handles, texted Bianca as they walked to the front door, told her about the computer, Pious Rebel on hold for now.

As they walked to the door Pam said, "This might be futile."

"What do you mean?" Lisa asked.

"HIPPA regulations. Might not tell us much. Might not let us in. Let me deal with this."

At the front desk, a receptionist with a name tag reading *Sheila* asked how she could help.

"We're here to visit my aunt, Anita Ortiz," Pam said.

"Do we have you on file?"

"No. I've been abroad for a few years in Haiti. Doctors Without Borders. I'm just back for a week to see Auntie Anita."

"What's your name?"

"Sally Ortiz. This is my wife, Dawn."

"Okay. I'll need you both to sign in." She handed Pam a clipboard and pen.

"Down the hall and to the left. Room 113. Have a nice visit."

"Thank you," Pam said. "I love her so much. Can't wait to talk with her."

Sheila took the clipboard from Pam, rested her hand on her wrist, looked in both directions, then whispered, "I shouldn't be saying this." Another look in both directions. "Sweet Anita's thoughts come and go. So be patient." She handed them visitors' badges.

"Thanks."

Anita's thoughts mostly did not come during their visit. She lit up when Lisa mentioned Alice's name, mumbled something about desserts or deserts, asked about her tapioca pudding, wanted to hold Lisa's hand the whole time, wouldn't give eye contact to Pam. Lisa knew it was absurd, but she said, "Did I really come from a turkey baster?"

Anita laughed, slapped the bed with her hand, said, "Oh, that Alice. Such a caution. I remember that Thanksgiving when she wanted duck instead of turkey. I resisted. Drove her down to that little park below campus and made her look at the mallards. So lovely. I refused. What's your name?"

"Lisa. Lisa Hardrock, Anita."

"What a lovely name. Nice to meet you Lisa Hardrock Anita."

Pam fiddled with her cell phone, turned up the volume and pointed it toward Anita, "Goodnight Irene" playing. Anita turned to the phone, big grin on her face, "Oh, my, my, my. I love Gordon Jenkins and the Weavers." She closed her eyes and nodded her head. "I loved Alice so much." She opened her eyes and stared at Pam. "Do I know you?"

•   •   •

Back in the truck, Pam said, "That's a pretty high-level concept, 'such a caution.'"

"Or just a mind so used to flinging out clichés that she doesn't even know what it means anymore."

"What did you think you might get from her?"

"Oh, just the thing about the turkey baster. Never had a father, biological or otherwise. Thought maybe she could confirm Alice's explanation."

"Like the receptionist said, maybe another day she'll be more lucid."

"What a crapshoot."

At the storage facility, they loaded up the desk, the bookshelves, the boxes full of Alice's books, the typewriter, checked into the front desk to cancel the lease.

"What next, oh fearless leader?"

"Miki's paper on Fourth Street."

Pam stayed with Babe while Lisa went inside. She returned with a round package wrapped in brown Kraft paper.

"What's this?"

"Decorative papers. For Christmas presents."

"Cool. Your phone's been pinging."

It was Bianca. *Call me. Now!* Lisa didn't want to talk to her. Didn't want to be chastised for losing access to Pious Rebel. Best to get it over with, though, not have it hound her all the way home.

"What?" Lisa said before Bianca could speak.

"Ha!" Bianca said. "Orange juice! I did mine with Kahlua coffee. Sticky, gooey mess all over everything. Where are you?"

"Leaving Berkeley."

"Perfect. My nephew works for Apple. He can get you a twenty-five-percent discount on a new MacBook Pro. You can pick it up today on the way home if you want." Lisa leaned over the steering wheel and wept. What had she done to deserve people like Bianca and Pam in her life? Not a thing. Not a damn thing. Blind luck. She tried to shake the cliché out of her head.

"Thank you! But, I can't afford this right now."

"What can you afford?"

"Not much. Let me think about it. Can you handle any Pious Rebel emergencies?"

"Sure. See you Monday at the office?"

"Maybe."

They got through Oakland, past Fremont and Milpitas, before Pam said, "Who's the second one?"

"Second one what?"

"Person you want me to find."

"Oh, I'm just curious. About Ryan. If he's really in Aspen."

"Do you care?"

"Not so much about him. More about the ongoing mystery of Cody. How many more layers to be uncovered."

"I say you forget about her for a while. But if you want, I'll check on Ryan."

"Will you have to pay again?"

"That doesn't matter. It's like buying a puzzle, sitting down for a day until that final piece slips into place. I'd pay ten bucks for that any day."

"Not yet."

·   ·   ·

At home, Lisa carried the two banker's boxes to her bedroom. Zack unloaded the truck while Pam opened her computer.

"You want to use mine to get onto your blog site?"

"No. I need to not think about it. Do something else."

Lisa walked outside to find Zack unloading the desk and bookshelves, boxes already piled up, leaning against the playground fence, Turks and Caicos sniffing for potential food.

"What's your plan with this stuff?"

"That's a good question. I have an idea, though."

"Care to share it, or is that privileged information?"

"Let's go to the workshop."

Zack used his key to open the door. Lisa noticed the Harley had been moved, polished, cleaned up. "I emptied that cabinet of the Harley stuff. Moved it in boxes into the greenhouse. Hope that's okay."

"Your jumping into my brain. That's perfect. Any chance of moving the Harley out as well? I'd like to take over this space."

"If it's okay with you and Michael, I was thinking I could start the repairs on the Harley in that back section of the greenhouse that doesn't seem like it's used much. I can wheel it out there today."

"That's good. Anyway, this is where I want Alice's stuff to go. We can just leave it outside for a couple of days while I clean up. Maybe drape a tarp over it."

Back in the house, Michael had arrived and was talking to Pam about the computer.

"Some good news," Pam said to Lisa. "We were able to get a shadow of a screen on the old Mac. If you get another one, we should be able to get into Migration Assistant and transfer over your existing data. Could blow up and lock us out at any minute, though. But for now, I think you're okay. Fingers crossed."

"I can't deal with it right now," Lisa said.

"Michael, can we talk?"

"Uh-oh. What now?"

Pam smiled. "Always worried about being the bad boy."

Lisa and Michael went to the couch.

"Anything new on your end?" Lisa said.

"Some. But you called this meeting. You first."

"So much. Where to start?" Lisa said.

"How was your trip? Did Pam stay in line?"

"I don't want her to stay in line. I want her to step out of line."

"Wait. Didn't you steal that line from what's-her-name from *The Marvelous Mrs. Maisel* when she accepted her award?"

252

"I love her so much. I want to be her."

"She seems like a pious-rebel sort."

"I wonder? I question how much of those acceptance speeches are rehearsed scenes. The trip was okay. Drama. Tons more drama."

"You talking about the orange juice?"

"For starters. We found stuff in Alice's locker. Not sure yet what to expect with that, but she had saved journals from when I was a kid. Maybe up until the day she died. I haven't dug in yet."

"What about Point Reyes Station?"

"That is a long and ugly story. More on that later. But this computer thing is causing me major stress. I'm getting near the bottom of my resources. I'm wondering if we can draw some cash from the safe."

"Funny you should mention that. I'm short, too. Pam has enough for most of our needs, but I'm having some guilt about not contributing."

"But you know she doesn't want you selling pot anymore, right?"

"Right. Even to our friends. Would a thousand each work for you?"

"For now, yes." Lisa said. "And I have an idea for cutting back one expense. Zack wants to work on the Harley in the greenhouse. Given that we don't have a definitive plan yet, it's fine with me. I'm thinking of cleaning out the workshop, using it as an office. That way I could save three ninety-five a month on my office rent downtown."

"I thought you loved that office?"

"I kind of do. But they are off-the-charts noisy."

Michael smiled. "Would that be classified as a cliché?"

"No, more of an idiom. Anyway, is it okay if I take over the workshop?"

"If you're willing to clean up the rat shit, why not."

"I'm willing. I brought some furniture and books that belonged to my mom."

"By the way, I sat with Ben yesterday and discovered more about growing hemp seeds. If we want, he'll send his partners down to talk next steps."

"Makes sense. I need to dig through all the receipts and bank statements. Try to figure out where we are. What we owe. How we're going to deal with this mortgage deadline."

"I know. On that topic, I'm planning on looking for a job, find some steady income. Are you sure Zack would run the hemp seeds for us?"

"Pretty sure. What kind of job?"

"I'm going down to Watsonville to talk to Giant. A couple of other corporate growers."

"What would you do for them?"

"Marketing. Distribution. I've got a pretty good idea given what we've done with our crops. Pam says she'll help me understand the lingo."

Bianca texted.

That lady from Berkeley keeps sending you stuff. They really want Alice's books.

I know. Lisa texted back. More later.

"Pam, you have any time tomorrow to look over that contract with me?"

"Sure."

Bianca again.

Don't forget about those lawyers I mentioned to you. They're eager to help out a fellow woman. Hey. Sounds like another oxymoron. Talk soon.

"What do you think? Can we do this without the lawyers?"

"It's not my field of expertise, but let's take a look and decide whether you need them or not."

Cody and Ben weren't home when she went to bed. She carried the trashed computer with her, propped it up on a pillow. The events of the last two days should have been enough to let her pass out as soon as she slipped into the sheets. But her brain wouldn't let her close her eyes. *The Overstory* rested on one nightstand, *Zen and the Art of Motorcycle Maintenance* on the other. She felt obliged to RachelReads to dive into Powers' next story, find out what else he had to say about trees and people on this planet. She also wanted to understand what it was about Pirsig's book that attracted Zack to it, other than the word *motorcycle* in the title.

Lisa opened the lid to the computer, saw the cloudy, washed-out image of her screen saver in the background. It still looked waterlogged, but was usable. She opened Safari and tested the Pious Rebel password.

She was in. It was ugly, but the computer still worked. Would save her $3,000 if it kept working. She couldn't afford it now, was thankful, felt lucky that it kept chugging away. She closed the lid, picked up *Zen*, fell asleep before completing the first chapter.

39

SUNDAY
12-22-19

T HE NON-DREAMS BEGAN MARCHING THROUGH HER HEAD, her bed, sometime after two in the morning, when sleep was interrupted by a key in the front-door lock, what sounded like stumbling against furniture, a male voice hushing an obnoxious female. Her lamp was still on, book open and resting against her chest. It fascinated her how little she moved during the night, that she could lay flat on her back without turning, open her eyes and stare at the ceiling. She closed them, let the carousel of images and thoughts spin in front of her, a lazy Susan showcasing platters of moo shu pork, spicy eggplant chicken, walnut prawns, books and journals, desks and bookcases, for-sale signs on farms, blackberries, a Harley in the back of a big blue truck. It was definitely not a dream, and she was definitely not awake.

By 4:00 she kept her eyes open, picked up *Zen*, completed the first chapter, but would need to read it again, too many interruptions between the pages to have any kind of understanding of the context Pirsig was trying to construct. Zack was usually out for a run before she got up, but not today. She chose not to knock, turned the knob to

Gregory's bedroom quietly, entered carrying clothes for the day, slipped into the shower without Zack hearing her. Too dark to enjoy the view through the skylight, she boiled herself in the hot flow, stayed longer than usual, twisted kinks from her neck, hoped the heat would help dissipate the throb working on her forehead.

In front of the floor-to-ceiling mirror Gregory had installed, she dried herself, looked at her thirty-seven-year-old body almost as if she'd never seen it before, through her own eyes, had been in existence only through G's, was only alive because he wanted her to be. She was still attractive, had always liked her own breasts, the slight curve of her hips, though they were slighter now, not having eaten much since G died. She thought about the three meals with Pam and smiled. That would help. She spent time caressing herself, hadn't been aroused like this in over two months. Clothes on, she stepped back into the bedroom.

"Good morning," Zack whispered.

"Good morning."

"Have you read any *Zen* yet?"

She needed to get her hand on the doorknob, get ready to eject herself from the room, avoid running to the bed and jumping on Babe's owner. "One chapter. I'll need to start again. I don't quite get it. It's difficult for me."

"The good things usually are."

"Okay, got to run. Bye."

"You're running now?"

He was dragging this out. Wanted her to stay. Wanted her warm body next to his. "I mean leave. Got to leave. Now." She closed the door, a little too hard. What did she know about his wants and needs? He was a grieving father. What did she know about her own? She was grieving, too. About so much, so much that she couldn't track it all.

Needing to get out the front door, before she changed her mind, did something she knew she'd regret, she opened the fridge, grabbed a full quart of orange juice, made her way to the greenhouse where she grabbed a wheelbarrow full of cleaning supplies, and pushed it to the workshop. Zack had wrapped the furniture in tarps, tied it down, neat, organized, unlike either of their lives, a transfer of one thing to another.

In a few large gulps, she was done with the juice, unlocked the workshop door, turned on the lamp, stood with mouth open. She hadn't asked him to do this. Not sure if he was trying to please her or himself. There was no way to know the truth. Probably some of each. The Harley was gone. Gregory's tool chest was gone. Boxes had disappeared. The floor swept clean. She could see through the windows now. The finished and unfinished boxes still lined the cabinets, along with a few containers of receipts and papers she hadn't gone through yet. But the space was mostly empty, ready for her. She wheeled the supplies back to the greenhouse, walked to the other end where she found the Harley, the tools, a space Zack had temporarily claimed as his own. They'd have to watch that, make sure he didn't overstep, make himself too welcome.

Within an hour, she had the desk and bookshelves in place, Alice's books on shelves, cardboard boxes flattened and shoved into G's incinerator. Alice's IBM Selectric sitting on the desk. Not that she'd ever use it, but it was nice seeing it there. This place was cold. Zero heat. The sun was up now, and Home Depot was open.

She brought back three space heaters and plugged them in. That was better. This would work. The room felt larger now with the Harley and accoutrements gone. There was still a long table in the middle that would come in handy. She hauled the easel stand and pad with the hemp-seed information to the greenhouse, where it would be more useful to Michael and Ben today. Thinking that, she realized she was making the workshop her space, a private space, for her thoughts and work, accompanied by Alice and others she invited in, this space that had been off-limits and mysterious now ready to open and ignite.

Swiveling in G's Herman Miller chair, she could see the future of this room, with each rotation a new addition, a white board, a lamp, a bulletin board full of multicolored pushpins, posters and prints, not motorcycles but real art she picked out, speakers playing classical music. Pious Rebel and Alice and Celia and William and Justin and Amelia, companions, not ghosts but guides, and although she was sitting by herself, for the first time in a decade, she didn't feel alone.

A knock on the door.

Although it seemed absurd to do so, she said, "Come in."

"Hey. Looks good in here. I'm headed for my run. This was in the cab." Zack handed her the rolled paper from Miki's.

"Thank you so much. For this, and for this." She spun around in the chair. "You are something else."

"Trying to become. I hope you give Pirsig another chance. He's worth it. Is this going to be your office now?"

She shrugged. "Headquarters. Let's call it that."

"You've got room for a bed in here. May never have to come up to the big house again."

"Too damn cold to sleep out here. But a daybed might be nice. By the way, the Harley looks good out there."

"I hope to be riding her by New Year's."

"Her? Does she have a name?"

"Not yet. But it's definitely a her."

"Which reminds me, Pam and I named your truck. Babe."

He laughed. "That is so perfect. Paul Bunyan would approve. Before I forget, we're all set for Christmas dinner."

"I keep forgetting about that. What's the date today?"

"Twenty-second. Wednesday is Christmas."

"What do I owe you?"

"You owe me nothing."

"You can't be doing that."

"You're giving me free rent. A Harley. Maybe a job. I can definitely be doing this. And happy to do so. Do you know how many guests yet?"

"I hadn't even thought of that part. I haven't mentioned it to anybody yet, except you. And you're welcome to bring someone if you want."

"Probably not, but maybe. Getting close to some folks at the Resource Center."

"Michael and Pam, if they're not already busy. Cody and Ben, if I don't strangle her first. Bianca, but she probably has multiple other offers. So, maybe around eight or so."

"Perfect. And what time?"

Lisa had never been responsible for a gathering like this before. G was in charge, or Ryan, and even Alice. She remembered Alice's standard phrase, used it now.

"Gather at one. Eat at two. Oh, one other thing. Michael is meeting with Ben and a couple of his friends about the hemp-seed idea. If you're around, you want to be in on that?"

"I'm around, and it seems like I should be there."

"Great. I'll check with Michael first. Make sure we don't step on any toes."

Back in the house she opened the computer, sent emails to Bianca, Michael, Pam, Cody, and Ben about Christmas dinner. Same message to everybody.

Chez Zack is cooking. Gather at 1:00, eat at 2:00. Bring others if you like. Just let us know.

She cc'ed Zack.

Time to get back into Pious Rebel. So much. The comments. Reading *The Overstory*. Finishing *Love Muffins*. Responding to the Berkeley-press woman. Restarting *Zen*. She didn't feel like prioritizing right now. Knew she had to. Ignored them all, pulled her camera off the bookshelf, dusted it off, cleaned the lens, took the mounted geodes one at a time from the bookshelf in her room and set them on her pillow, snapped shots of all of them. After uploading the images to her computer, she attached the first one to a new post.

I'm learning more about my mother all the time. Just cleared out her storage locker and found boxes of her books, her journals, possibly more manuscripts. I've just taken individual photos of all the mounted geodes. Here's the first one. I visited two of my old haunts yesterday: Berkeley and Point Reyes Station. Mixed emotions. Happy Sunday!

With *Love Muffins* in her hands, ready to continue the story, the cell phone pinged. Pam.

Michael is coming out at 1:00 to meet with Ben et al. in the greenhouse. Thought I'd come with him so you and I could talk contracts, etc. Does that work for you?

Lisa replied.

Yes, that's good. See you then.

and went back to Alice.

Justin sent letters to Celia and Amelia from Ireland. In the first months of his stay, he made his way to Scotland a few times to hunt for hollow geodes with amygdale linings that he sent across the Atlantic on a slow boat, which eventually made its way to Berkeley.

Celia asked William to build a bookshelf for Amelia's room where they could store the new arrivals. Because Justin was 5,000 miles away, William's jealousy waned, and he built a sturdy and attractive piece of furniture for his wife and daughter. He might need to have a direct conversation with Justin when he came back.

But for now, he was focused on muffins. Local supermarkets were purchasing nearly a hundred a day. The volunteer ladies in the community were no longer enough. He recruited some would-be chefs from the culinary school in downtown Oakland to work a couple of hours a day each morning, bought a shrink-wrap machine to package them. He continued to drink more than Celia would like, often sleeping on the couch in front of the television. When he smelled of whiskey, Celia was happy to leave him on the couch, glad he wasn't stinking up her bedroom, pulling sheets off her all night long.

The money was better with the sales, the bakery crowded and sold out by the end of the day, the supermarket orders increasing as more learned of the quality of William's muffins. Stability. At what cost? Celia waited at the mailbox every day hoping to find something from Justin. The letters and packages grew scarce. At first they showed up weekly, than maybe once a month. And for the past six months, nothing. The bookshelf was half full.

Amelia missed Justin less than Celia did, busy with new friends in preschool, but when the geodes did appear, she took them to school, shared them with her teacher, her classmates, made up stories about them, stories that she rehearsed with Celia at breakfast, Celia helping with the fictional details, pronunciation of made-up words like geoplastinate and cystallagtite.

The thought of living without William in her life only came late at night when he hadn't made it to bed. They were brief little chunks of emptiness that she quickly rubbed out with all his good qualities. He didn't mess with the volunteer ladies, had really stepped up with the love muffins, was a good teacher to the chefs-in-training, and was a wonderful father to Amelia.

261

Sacrificing a little bit of love in trade for a little
bit of stability was just fine, would get them through
another year, a new cycle.

Lisa posted two more chapters of *I Really Knead You* along with
a new post.

Friends of Alice — FOA. I'm guessing you'll have read most of
the two new chapters before I even tell you about them
being up, but they are up, six more to go. To help you plan
your upcoming reading schedule, I'm posting two a night
over the next few days. On a related note, there is a small
press interested in publishing Alice's books. Given that I've
been letting you read them online, how many of you would
purchase a copy of *I Really Knead You* if it was readily
available? The publisher is paying close attention to the site
and your responses, so let her know what you think, and let
me know what you think. I'm reading through a contract
tomorrow with a friend, trying to figure out what I should do.
Thanks again for all your support!

Ben and Cody were late risers again. Lisa had just finished vetting
another batch of comments when they appeared in the kitchen, both
in sweats and Ben's t-shirts, his a *Grateful Dead*, hers a *Bonnie Raitt*.

"Nice shirts," Lisa said, hoping to set the tone before Cody rang in.

"It's Ben's," Cody said. "Not really my style, but comfortable."

"Are you a collector, Ben?"

"I sure am. Both these concerts were held in the early nineties.
Snazzy Productions. I go to every concert I can."

"What were you, ten?"

"A very young teen with parents who didn't care where I was at
night."

"How was Berkeley?" Cody said, refusing to give Lisa eye contact,
a hint of disdain in her voice.

"Productive."

"I hear Pamela went with you. That must have been a shit show."

"It was good. Very helpful. Especially when we got to Point Reyes
Station."

Cody choked on a glass of water. "What? You drove all the way up there? How was that?"

"Informative." She let Cody squirm, let her worry about one lie connected to the next. "Did you know the bookstore was gone?"

"You're kidding! No, I didn't."

Lisa cocked her head, amazed at how smoothly and quickly Cody delivered deceit. "And that Ryan doesn't live there anymore?"

"Really?"

Lisa didn't want to bury her with truth right now. Would hold onto it for a while, let it stew in both their heads. Maybe she would let it dissipate. What did it really matter? That was the past. What she cared about was now and the near future. Forging a new office. Having a Christmas dinner. Getting Alice's name and work out into the world.

"Are you guys in for Christmas dinner?"

"Wouldn't miss it. Will *Bianca* be here?"

"Yes. With a friend. And Michael and Pam."

"Whooptiedoodles!"

"Zack and maybe a friend or two."

"He made friends already? Didn't think he had it in him."

"Can't wait," Ben said, when he could get a word in. "What can we bring?"

"You'll need to ask Zack. He's the boss on this one."

Ben stood. "My Marin guys will be here shortly. I'm going to get a shower in first." He left Lisa and Cody alone at the dining-room table, Cody sipping a coffee, Lisa with her orange juice. They were quiet.

Cody picked up the newspaper, dug in and found the crossword puzzle. Lisa opened Pious Rebel.

A new message from RockHounds:

I would buy multiple copies of *I Really Knead You*. Pass them out to my friends. And thank you for the geode photo. I believe that one comes from a geode bed near the Colorado River near Blythe. I'll have to check my *U. S. Encyclopedia of Geodes* to be sure.

She opened another Google window, searched for 'U. S. Encyclopedia of Geodes'. Nothing. He was toying with her. Just one more fabricator in her life. She wondered what it was about her that attracted them. Some strange pheromone that invited folks to tell the biggest lies they could design. Maybe she should banish him. It didn't matter that he'd buy Alice's books for all his friends. It mattered that he was one of them.

"What's a five-letter word for 'fatty acid' with a 'p' in the middle?" Cody asked, without looking up from the paper.

Lisa began a post to RockHounds:

There is no *U. S. Encyclopedia of Geodes*. Why lie?

She stopped to consider Cody's question, "Lipid, maybe."
"Perfect! Thank you."
"You're welcome."
Lisa continued typing.

I mean, you may be the first follower I've found to be dishonest so far on Pious Rebel. Why is that?

She had never written a response like this, engaged like this so directly over a comment. *Erase it. Get over it.* But, no. On she went.

I'm not in a mood right now to read posts like this. I'm glad you like Alice's books. But don't pretend to know about her geodes, and don't lie to me.

She sent the reply.
"Eleven-letter word for lucidity, beginning with that 'p' in 'lipid'?"
"Perspicuity." That was an activity Lisa had loved with Alice, sitting at the dinner table, working on the *New York Times* puzzle. Alice had been such a word freak. She wasn't sure, but Pious Rebel may have been one of Alice's oxymorons.

Even if Lisa didn't want to help Cody complete the puzzle, even if she wanted her to fail miserably at everything she would ever do again in her life, she couldn't resist the answer. The words. The way her brain puckered in on itself, almost sizzled, until the word squeezed out.

Cody set the puzzle down. "You still mad at me about Alderwood?"
"So much more," Lisa said.
"What are you talking about?"
"I can't do it right now. Another time. Too fresh. And never-ending."

"Ben told me what Pam said the other night, and how drunk I was. This is about my drinking, right?"

"I said I didn't want to do it now. But fine. We could start there. I'm sure it influences everything else that defines who you are. I remember it all the way back when we were twelve."

"What are you talking about?"

"Mom was out, up at the campus delivering an edited manuscript to some professor. I remember the title. She read it to us. *The Uncertainty of Silk Road Manifestations and Productivity.*"

"I kind of remember that. That we were bored stiff."

Lisa refused to point out the cliché, just added it to her reasons to hate Cody.

"We knew she'd be gone for an hour or so. We were packing for science camp, leaving for the Santa Cruz Mountains the next day. You hauled me into her study and found the key to the liquor cabinet hidden underneath the Selectric. You grabbed one of those pint-sized plastic containers with a lid from the kitchen cupboard. There must have been a dozen bottles in the cabinet. Vodka, gin, Drambuie, Kahlua, Southern Comfort, Jack Daniels, crème de menthe."

Cody laughed. "I remember. She was quite a drinker."

"She was not!" Lisa yelled. "Those were for guests. She rarely drank. As opposed to you. So you filled up the container with a half-inch from each of the bottles, thinking Alice wouldn't notice, took a piece of duct tape and wrapped the lid on tight, buried it in the middle of your sleeping bag."

"So, I was a risk-taker. What of it?"

"What of it? The decisions of a risk-taker affect those around them more than the risk-taker herself. I had to clean up your vomit. I had to tell the naturalist that you'd had the flu. Even then, when you couldn't open your mouth to lie, you had others do it for you. I had to dump the remaining alcohol into the toilet and flush it five times. Had to pour mouthwash into the bowl to cover up the smell."

"What's your point?"

Lisa shook her head. "My point is you have a serious problem you've never been willing to admit to yourself."

Ben walked in. "What serious problem?"

"She thinks I'm an alcoholic." Cody cackled, picked up the crossword. Ben stared at them both, waited.

"Well, aren't you?" Lisa asked.

"Of course not. So I like to drink, bury my woes sometimes. No big deal."

"Do you drink every day?"

"Maybe. But not because I have to. Just want to."

Lisa turned to Ben, stared into his eyes. Ben put his hands up to ward her off, clearly not wanting to play. "Ben, you asked what you could bring to Christmas dinner."

"Yeah. And?"

"And I'd like to ask you what not to bring. No beer, wine, tequila, nothing with alcohol." She turned to Cody, looking for a reaction. "That okay with you?"

"Of course it's okay with me. Why wouldn't it be?"

Michael and Pam came through the front door.

"Looks like your two seed guys are sitting outside in the driveway. Nice Tesla."

"Great! Let's go get them," Ben said.

"We'll be in the greenhouse. Show them what we've got to work with," Michael said.

"Sounds good." He put his hand on Michael's shoulder. "Seems like you've got a bit of a thing for cars."

Michael chuckled. "Just the cars I could never afford to own."

Pam joined Lisa and Cody at the table. "Nine-letter word for isopods."

"Woodlice," Pam said.

"Yes! How do you know that?" Cody asked.

"I finished the puzzle two hours ago." She looked at Lisa. "So, we ready to look at that contract?"

"What contract?" Cody asked.

Pam waited for a response from Lisa. "None of your business," Lisa said calmly.

"Well that's just rude. Especially when I've got two hundred and fifty thousand dollars burning a hole in my pocket. Damn it!"

"What's that have to do with me?" Lisa said.

"Ben and I have been talking. He wants me to invest. Maybe in this seed thing, if it goes the way they want today."

Lisa didn't want Cody anywhere near her business anymore. Maybe her life. Maybe needed to boot her after Christmas, or at least after the memorial. She stood up, grabbed a folder off the table. "Let's go to the workshop."

"Fine!" Cody said. "Leave me by myself. Where's Zack?"

"Running. And you leave Zack alone."

"What do you mean? Why?"

"He's a good guy. Just stay away from him."

In the workshop, Lisa turned on the heaters.

"What happened here?" Pam said. "Very impressive. One step closer to having the aura of Gregory out of your life."

Lisa nodded. "Yep. It's all mine now."

"We need some paint out here."

Again, someone including her in a "we" statement. She liked it. Could get used to it. Lisa looked around the room. "We certainly do. White on the cupboards?"

"Maybe an off-white. Desert sand."

"What about the walls?"

"Something a little darker."

"Ceiling the same as the walls?"

"Hmm. Let's get radical. How about a bright white?"

"Can we head over to Home Depot right now, get some paint, accouterments? Bring the contract along with us?"

"I'm game. But I prefer King's Paint. Support the local guy."

"Right. Something I haven't had to think about much."

"Something you weren't allowed to think about."

•   •   •

Pam read the contract out loud as they made their way down Soquel Drive. "I did some research on royalty rates. These numbers look like they're in line with industry standards. The biggest question is whether or not a small press is the best way to go. Their marketing and distribution policies and abilities should be examined before you make a decision."

"Is there any mention of advance payment toward royalties?"

"There's a blank placeholder here for that. Like she told us, she needs to read the manuscripts first so she can calculate how fast she thinks the books might sell, which would determine if and how much of an advance can be offered."

"I'm just thinking about cash on hand, or lack of. If we decide to pursue the hemp-seed idea, a decision I'm guessing could happen soon, and we might have to put money into that. No idea how much yet, and I imagine it takes months for that crop to come in and begin paying for itself."

"Yeah, all that stuff."

"The other factor is that because this is a Berkeley press, and Mom was born and lived there her whole life, I like the connection. Like you say, supporting the local guy."

"You could just give her the first book, see how it goes. See if those followers of yours come through and help to sell out the first edition."

"That makes sense. Then there's the other thing."

"The balloon payment?"

"Yeah. This little contract doesn't come anywhere near touching that thing."

"No. You and Michael have some tough decisions over that one."

They wheeled a basket to the car, full of three gallons of paint, stirring sticks, brushes, rollers and rolling pans, gowns and hats, light tarps to cover furniture.

By the time the men finished in the greenhouse, Lisa and Pam were putting the final touches on baseboards, the room jumping to life with a brighter, warmer feel. They all converged on the house together, the Marin growers easing their Tesla out of the driveway.

"I'm starved," Michael said. "Anybody for takeout?"

"How about Carpo's?" Lisa asked. Pam took orders. Lisa got back on the computer, was having those pangs of remorse after having done something she shouldn't have. Calling RockHound a liar was a mistake. He'd already replied to her message:

I understand why you might be leery of folks who aren't straight with you. I've had those feelings most of my life. I'm sure you have, too. I've attached a photo in a subsequent message. Maybe it will explain.

She opened the second message, no text, simply a photo of a very thick handmade journal with a handwritten cover: *U. S. Encyclopedia of Geodes.* This was another one of those times where she felt sick to her stomach, had clearly stepped over a line and had no way to take it back.

Michael looked over her shoulder. "Lots to talk about."

"Can we wait until after the food gets here? I need to rest for a minute."

"You okay?" Pam asked.

"I just piss myself off sometimes. Back in a while." She looked for Eloise, needed some comfort, but Cody and Ben's door was shut, and Eloise was spending a lot of time with them. In her room she laid flat on the bed. It was cold. She pulled half the bedspread over her body, snuggled up to a pillow. She'd need to make amends to Rockhound, would continue to feel terrible until she did. Bad ideas that she pursued too quickly. Like going to Point Reyes Station Why had she thought that would be a good idea? Even if Ryan had been there, no way would she have considered returning, starting up where they left off. No way. Then why go there? Why stir things up? Why inhabit the tiny corner of her brain with the idea that there was no longer a bookstore to return to, a Ryan, a farm with blackberries, a reading group and books and something she once called home? She'd successfully gutted her past, at least segments of it. There was no longer a house or storage facility where the memories of Alice might be living. Most of her possessions were probably already being sold from the Reuse Depot, organs harvested from a cadaver, being doled out to others in need who could make use of them.

Becky Nurse of Salem drifted into her brain, ricocheted off the walls, a spiritual Frisbee with no place to land. "Help me, Alice. Show me the way," she said to herself, drifted off.

She heard a knuckle knock, pictured Bianca barging in with some loud critical piece of information she had to address immediately. Instead a movement and depression in the bed next to her. She opened her eyes, saw Cody curled up, head on pillow, staring at her. "They asked me to come get you. For dinner."

Lisa closed her eyes, didn't want to see her, think about her.

"How long are you going to be mad at me?" Forever was the word that came to Lisa's mind, but she locked it away. "I haven't had anything to drink today." Cody got closer, opened her mouth, breathed in Lisa's face.

It was true. Smelled like garlic and salmon, but no booze. That was something. An accomplishment for Cody, who might not have gone one day in the last five years without a drink.

"That's good," Lisa finally said. "I can't really talk to you about this stuff right now. I'm too frazzled."

"*Frazzled*. I love you and your words. You are your mother's daughter."

That she was. She remembered Alice's journals sitting in the box at the foot of the bed. "I brought the Selectric back from Berkeley."

"You did! Oh, sweet Alice. So many good memories."

"And her some of her books." Lisa pointed to the box.

"What? You're kidding. Let's read them. Me to you, then you to me. Like the old days."

The old days had been mostly good. Alice would go out for the evening, leave the two girls in front of the fireplace with popcorn and soda pop and books to read to each other.

"Remember when we did *The Wonderful O,* by Thurber?"

Lisa nodded, smiled. "And *The Phantom Tollbooth,* Norton Juster."

"Oh, my god!" Can we go back to those days?"

Lisa wanted to tell her about the journals, wanted to tell her but not show her, rub her nose in it. But, if Cody knew of their existence, who knew what she might do.

Another knuckle knock. They saw Zack's shiny head through a crack in the door. "They've sent in backups. Fries are getting cold."

Cody sat up. "We'll read the journals later."

"No *we* won't." This 'we' club had no members, nothing to talk about. "Let's eat."

"Who had the veggie burgers?" Ben asked.

Pam raised her hand. Lisa said, "Me."

"Regular fries or sweet-potato fries?"

"Sweet potato," Lisa and Pam said together.

"Isn't that nice," Cody said. "Like the twin sisters neither of you had."

"What is wrong with you?" Ben said.

"I'm just saying," Cody said.

Lisa knew what was wrong with her. The smart-aleck loudmouth she'd been since they met as youngsters. Combined with going on eighteen hours without booze.

"So tell us. What did the Marin mega-minds say?"

Michael said, "Ben, you want to start?"

"No way. This is your thing."

"Well, *our* thing, but sure. I'm convinced that we should move ahead with the hemp-seeds plan. But it's an expensive and time-consuming operation, depending on how we go about it."

Lisa shook her head. "Two things we want to avoid. The cost and the time-sink."

"Right. That's why we have some options."

"You talking about leasing it out or selling the property?" Pam asked.

"No. Those are down-the-road options. These are options right now with the hemp seeds. We can buy seeds from Ben's friends and plant this week. If you'd be up for that, Zack."

"Up for anything."

"Or we can buy plants from them and same thing, have them in the ground by this week. Quicker harvest but more expensive."

Lisa swallowed a bit of her veggie burger. "I like the quicker-harvest idea."

"The next option is pretty interesting. If we'd like, the mega-minds would become partners with us. Instead of buying all our seeds and plants, and the necessary lighting fixtures and regulators from them, they would send a crew of four guys in, as early as tomorrow, bring the feminized plants, sterilized pots, fertilized soil, lights, watering system, everything we'd need to have those little girls growing toward the roofline."

Pam spoke up. "What does partnership translate to in real dollars?"

"Right. I'm getting to that. Zack would still have some daily work to do, but not as much given that these guys know what they're doing and would set it up correctly from the get-go." *Was "get-go" one?* Lisa asked herself. Maybe not, but it was annoying. "Their guys would come out once a week to check on things, make sure no males were trying to sneak their way in, and would come back before harvest and spray the plants with the silver solution to keep them in line. And they would distribute and sell the seeds for us. Thus, a fifty-fifty partnership."

"Million-dollar crop, they get five hundred thousand?" Lisa sat forward, elbows on the table, hands under her chin.

"So do we," Michael added. "There was one other option suggested. Ben, you take this one."

"Okay. I'm partners with the Marin guys in their greenhouses up the coast. I helped with the original financing. I get a percentage of net profits. As you know, Cody has some cash she needs to invest, so do I. I offered that as an option. Not a fifty-fifty, but more of a seventy-thirty. More potential income for the two of you."

"And a lot more work and risk," Michael said. "We didn't make any decisions yet, Lisa. I figured you needed to hear all the options first. But I'm against the final option."

"You guys did a great job. I'm impressed. I agree, Michael." She hesitated, didn't want Cody's money anywhere near this thing. Nor Ben's. But she didn't want to say it out loud. Thought it might be rude given the circumstances. "I don't think we should be greedy. Let's have the pros do what they do. If we see five hundred thousand out of this, just break even maybe, pay our debts, I would be amazed and thrilled."

"I completely agree. There's one more piece. Ben."

Ben sat up straight. "Right. The balloon payment Gregory strapped you with, due after New Year's. This seed crop doesn't come in probably until early spring. You can't wait that long. You either have to pay it off or amortize it. As you already know, monthly payments on an amortized loan won't pay the principal down much."

"Come on," Pam said. "Get to the punch line."

"Right. Cody and I would pay off the balloon payment, and the other four small mortgages."

Lisa stood up, paced around the room.

"In exchange for what?" Pam continued.

"We become part owners in the property, with non-voting rights, and if you ever do decide to, or need to, split the property, we would get our choice of parcels, after Lisa and Michael. We'd agree to market value, minus the amount of the mortgages we cover."

Lisa folded her arms across her chest. "I said I don't want Cody's money anywhere near this place."

"Why?" Cody finally spoke up. "What's wrong with my money?"

"It's not your money. It's you."

"I told you I haven't had a drink all day."

"Yeah. And look at how your hand's shaking."

Pam turned to Lisa. "How do you expect to deal with the mortgage?"

"I don't know. Don't have any idea yet." She thought about Alice's books. The ad income. Wondered if the woman in Berkeley would agree to an advance. But even if she did, it wouldn't come anywhere near what they needed. Then there was Zack. He was being strangely quiet through this whole discussion. He might eventually offer to be a partner himself. Bottom line for her, no Cody.

"What do you think, about the greenhouse?" Michael asked.

"Good question. I'm thinking the less risk the better. How about you?"

"I agree. It seems like the Marin folks are experts at this and make money at it."

Lisa said, "I say we let Ben's friends set it up. Better chances of having a cash crop than if Zack and I are having to handle more than we should, especially being novices at this." Zack nodded, still keeping quiet.

"Okay, then," Michael said. Ben, you want to set that up with the Marin boys?"

"Sure, Michael. Expect them to work fast. I wouldn't be surprised to see them here tomorrow. Probably takes them a couple days to set everything up. Not sure how Christmas will affect things."

Michael and Pam put on coats to leave. "We need to prep for Michael's interview tomorrow."

"Good luck with that," Lisa said.

"I'm heading downtown to a movie at the Resource Center," Zack said. "See you folks tomorrow."

Ben said, "Bye, Zack. Thanks for being here today."

"I need to get out of here," Cody said. "Look at this." She held up a shaking hand to Ben. "I don't think I can do this."

"Come on," Ben said. "Get your jacket on. I've got an idea." Cody went down the hall.

Lisa stared at Ben. "You're not going to let her drink, are you?"

"I can't stop her if that's what she wants. But I won't enable her. You think that art store in Capitola is still open?"

"Palace Arts." She opened her computer. "Yeah. For another hour." Art had been Cody's salvation, in school, getting a job as a teacher. She was good. As an artist and a teacher.

Cody returned wearing her Aspen clothes: furry jacket, warm gloves, hat and scarf. "Let's get out of this place."

Saying something now about not drinking wouldn't make sense. Lisa said, "Have fun!" one of her favorite phrases, so much so that it had almost become a cliché. She meant it when she said it, but it was starting to sound worn out, as if it was connected to an old joke that no longer had teeth, in this case possibly interpreted by others as a slap in Cody's face, that her lame attempt to stop drinking wouldn't last another half hour.

"Back soon," Ben said.

Lisa was suddenly by herself, not even Eloise curling around her legs, now that she was spending most of her time in Zack's or Cody's rooms. It was strangely quiet. She built a fire, brought *The Overstory*, *Zen*, and her computer to the easy chair in front of the fireplace, and pulled her socked feet underneath two blankets. She liked having options, keeping busy on her own projects, rather than running out all day long to tend to a crop, snip leaves, buds. She was happy to have that behind her, have Pious Rebel in front of her. Her mind drifted to the box of journals in her room. More than a hesitation kept her from jumping in and reading them all tonight. It was almost fear. That the magic of Alice she was currently enjoying might fizzle up, wear down, blow away.

Thinking of Alice, she opened the computer, opened a new email. Time to make a decision, get this thing moving forward. She'd forgotten the name of the woman at the Berkeley press. Penny? No, Peggy.

Dear Peggy — I've attached an electronic copy of Alice Hardrock's first manuscript, I Really Knead You, for your perusal, to help you fill in the blanks in your contract related to advance payments. So you know, I'm ready to move forward with having you publish it as per the stipulations of the contract you sent, depending on whether you are able to come up with an advance payment that makes sense to me.

She backspaced, erased the period after "me," changed it to:

me and my agent, Pam.

It wasn't a threat, it wasn't exactly saying the advance payment was a deal breaker, but it was close. She was definitely going to need the income soon, but she wanted to treat Alice's legacy with respect, be careful with how she moved forward.

RockHound was also hanging around her neck, an unexplainable tightness. Maybe it was the painting of bright white ceilings. No. It was RockHound's last response, a fairly kind response to her suggestion that he was lying. She reread his post, opened a new one.

Mr. Hound.

It sounded corny, but she was feeling the need to be a little corny, less serious. Move on. Let go of these cascading disappointments.

Hope it's okay to call you that. But wait. I'm making an assumption that you are a man. Why is that? Are most rock hounds men? Am I shoving you inappropriately into a stereotypical hole? What I'm really trying to say is that I'm sorry for my earlier assertions about your character. Thanks for the clarifying photo. It's clear you are serious about your avocation. Or is it vocation? Pious Rebel.

The logs on the fire snapped, sparked, but it was still too quiet. She thought about letting Turks and Caicos in to romp, but they were happier in the playground. No need to affect their lives to appease hers. She wasn't ready to plow into a book. She saw the Amazon Echo sitting on the table next to the chair. They still hadn't taken, or made, the time to listen to the other lists. Not that it mattered. This was a good time with the house empty. She opened her journal to take notes, said, "Alexa, what are my lists?"

Alexa answered, "You have two lists. Shopping. For Lisa." The other five — Hogs, Zack, For Michael, Hemp Seeds, and Just in Case — were gone. She recalled telling Michael he could do what he wanted with them, but this felt awkward. Listening was one thing, but deleting them before she had a chance to hear them? Was he hiding something from her? Just as she was starting to trust him.

"Alexa. Read Shopping list."

"You have fourteen items on your Shopping list. Twenty-four-pound turkey from Fish Lady. Prime rib from Shopper's Corner. Wines from Soif. Stuffing mix, gravy, and dips from Gayle's. Pecan pie and lemon poppyseed cake from the Buttery. Yams, marshmallows, macadamia nuts, fruits, whipping cream, etcetera, from Nob Hill."

It made her stomach growl. She was happy, on one hand, that Zack had the menu under control, but unhappy, on the other, that he knew about and how to use Alexa's lists and still was not sure about who to trust with what anymore.

"Alexa. Read For Lisa."

"You have one item in Lisa's list. Michael here. Didn't want to give access to lists to anyone else who could figure it out as easily as Zack did. I've recorded For Michael, For Lisa, and Just in Case on my phone for you to hear when ready. Cut the others, as nothing of value there. Hemp Seeds was restatement of what is on easel pad. Talk soon." It made her feel better. About Michael. About herself. It was strange, though, hearing this electronic woman's voice speaking Michael's words.

She heard Turks and Caicos barking, looked out the kitchen window. With dog bones in hand, she turned the porch light on and walked to the playground, handed one to each through the fence. A single headlight flashed through the trees, followed by the familiar sound of a hogs's engine starting up, and a not-so-quiet exit through gravel onto Porter Gulch. Gregory's bike? Had someone stolen it? She ran to the greenhouse. Gregory's hog was still there. She corrected that. Zack's hog. Gregory was almost gone from this property. Voice disappearing from answering machines, Amazon devices, his name on accounts and fingerprints on the women he'd left behind fading. But who was on that hog? Probably just a random rider not knowing that Porter Gulch dead ended a few hundred yards up the road. Or was she being stalked?

Back inside, she got comfortable under the blanket, readied herself for "Mimi Ma," the next adventure Richard Powers was preparing to navigate her through in his tree-lined *The Overstory*.

It was the first time in ages she'd been able to finish a story without falling under its ether, reading the final period on the final page as Cody banged her way through the front door, Ben propping her up, a lit cigarette dangling from her mouth, both arms wrapped in bag handles.

"Get that cigarette out of here! I'm serious. Outside." She jumped off the couch, grabbed the bags from Cody, nudged her into the front yard with her shoulder, slammed the door. She turned to Ben, still fuming. "This is your big idea! Cigarettes and ..." She fumbled through the bags. "Art supplies!"

Ben sat down, waited for her to calm down. "Are you saying you'd have preferred me to stop at Sir Froggy's Pub like she wanted? Or the liquor store on Soquel Drive like she wanted?"

"Gregory hates cigarette smoke in the house!" Lisa heard what she'd just said, shook her head. "And so do I."

Cody reentered. "What is wrong with you? You want me to give up food, too?"

"I want you to smoke outside if that's what you need to do."

"Can I smoke out the window of the bedroom?"

Cody was pushing it, but Lisa needed to calm down. It appeared that Cody was still sober. That was something. "You can stick your head out the bedroom window. I'm going to bed."

Ben came down the hall after her. "If you want her to have any success at this thing, she's going to need some encouragement. Where can she set up her art supplies? The workshop? The greenhouse?"

"Absolutely not the workshop. I'll need to check with Zack about the greenhouse. Tomorrow."

She had brought the mirror from Zack's room to her bedroom, stood in front of it now naked, in *Qi Gong* pose, relaxing into herself, trying to empty her mind. She became Mimi Ma, slipped inside her skin, heard her listening to her father saying, "Then the bears get top bunk again." Knowing he meant that humans were failing, would fail, and nature would revert. She didn't know if she believed it, but it was possible. She thought of the three jade rings carved in the shape of trees, a family legacy hardly understood, Mimi Ma "left with the thin trunk of things to come." Lisa felt as if she had inherited Mimi Ma's ring, her trunk of things to come as thin as the ancient jade ring. Thought of the dead chestnut trees, the fading mulberry, the fallen oaks.

40

MONDAY
12-23-19

I T HAD BEEN A LONG, RESTLESS NIGHT. Lisa swore she could smell smoke make its way from the guest room around the back of the house and slide through her window. Pervasive Cody, pushing herself and needs on her, on everybody. But Lisa didn't know addiction, had never allowed herself to obsess on anything that would harm her. She'd walk away first. Like leaving Ryan in Point Reyes Station. Like leaving Alice in Berkeley. She was close to leaving Cody, because of her obsession with self-gratification and what appeared to be a lifelong trail of lies. Gregory had left her before she'd had a chance to leave him.

Maybe Ben was right. Give Cody a little encouragement. Try to understand what it was like to be her. Ease up a little. When they were kids Lisa used to imagine that she was Cody, and vice versa. Lisa would be the one with the famous opera-singer mother who traveled around the world to perform, paying Alice a monthly stipend to act as her surrogate mom, Cody included in the package as a stepsister. At five years old, Lisa had had a mother who was rarely available to her, working on her editing and bakery manuscripts, a one-in-five shot of a father from a mixed-sperm solution, and now a stepsister, twin beds, sharing a room, a stepsister who was more confident, made friends more easily, and was happy to have Lisa buried in her shadow.

Lisa knew all that. Nothing new. The new part was now. Pretending to be adults in a world too complex for either of them. Guided by events and habits forged in a different century. The two boxes she and Pam had retrieved from the storage facility sat stacked against the wall at the foot of the bed. Her trust in Cody at a low, she worried that invasion of privacy was a concept Cody couldn't comprehend right now. That she might sneak into Lisa's room, open both boxes, rifle through them, discover more about Alice than either of them knew before Lisa had the chance to do so herself.

Wrapped in a robe, stepping into untied tennis shoes, Lisa carried the box of journals down the hall, found Zack on the couch, reading. "Good morning. New book?"

"Hey. Old book. Lydia Davis. *Can't and Won't,*" Zack said.

"Love the title," Lisa said.

"Me too! Some editor telling her she was lazy because she didn't spell out cannot and will not. Too absurd. What are you up to?"

"Taking my mom's journals out to the workshop. Putting them behind sturdy locks."

"I understand. Need help?"

Her normal response would be to say, "No. I'm good," whether she was or not. But there was another box in her room. Why make two trips? "Sure," she said. "Another box like this at the foot of the bed."

At the workshop, Lisa opened the door, Zack carrying both boxes inside.

"Holy shit! What a transformation!"

"Yep. That Pam is a real go-getter. We did this instead of meeting with the seed guys yesterday."

"I was wondering about that. It's always been your greenhouse. Your genius that created this successful venture for Gregory."

"Between you and Michael, I trusted we were covered. And Ben. Nice to have a lawyer on your side."

Zack shook his head. "Sharp guy, but, I'm afraid Ben is on Ben's side. This paint job looks great. Love the white ceiling."

As they spoke, Lisa took the journals from the banker's box and set them inside one of the cabinets. She did the same with the other five manuscript boxes.

"What are those?" Zack asked.

Lisa grinned. "Christmas presents. From Alice to me. I haven't looked inside yet. But I'm guessing five more manuscripts. Maybe I'll open them New Year's morning."

"Good plan."

On the way back to the house, they stopped to watch Turks and Caicos playing with each other. "Can I ask you a question?" she said. "Maybe two questions. Unrelated."

"Fire away."

"What do you think of Cody?"

"Hmm. Not sure I want to be in the middle of this."

"Just your impressions."

"She's a bundle of fireworks, waiting to explode at will. The drinking doesn't help. She's smart. She's attractive. Is that what you're after?"

"I guess. Would you date her?"

"She's with Ben."

"I mean hypothetically."

"You mean is she my type?"

"Right."

"No. Not at all. I don't like the way she treats people. Real mouthy and a me-first demeanor. Sorry. I said too much."

"That's fine. I'm just looking for confirmation. One more question."

"Okay."

"Yesterday, last night. You were quieter than usual."

"Seems more like an observation than a question," he smiled.

"What was going on?"

"There's the question. Becs. Yesterday would have been her eleventh birthday."

"Oh. Sorry."

"It might look like I'm cool and calm, but when it comes to her, I'm like a puddle of mercury, slipping away."

Inside, Ben was making breakfast, Cody rifling through her art supplies. Zack stoked the fire. Lisa sat down with Cody. "You have plans for this stuff?"

"To make some art. Ben's idea."

"What kind of art?"

"Don't know yet."

"You smell like an ashtray."

Cody laughed. A good sign, laughing at herself. "I'm guessing that's better than smelling like a brewery." She held out her shaky hands to Lisa. Lisa took them.

"I've got a thought. Come on."

Cody followed her down the hall to Gregory's office. Lisa opened the door, looked around.

"Let's gut this place."

"What are you talking about?"

"I don't care about any of this stuff. Let's rearrange. Take his stuff to the incinerator. I have leftover paint if you want." Ben would be proud of her. Encouragement. Inclusion. Burying the hatchet. Stop it. Change that one. Forgive and forget. No. Another one. Be original. Like Alice. Get on with one's life and move forward. Better, but not great. "You can use it as an art studio while you're here."

Cody hugged her, sobbed. "I don't deserve you."

"I know you don't."

"You know that Ryan's in Aspen?" Cody said.

"I do."

"That we sold the bookstore when you left?"

"I figured there was a connection. Did you say 'we' sold the bookstore?"

"Yes. Sorry. When you left, I became his partner. Well, you know, and his lover."

"My blackberries are still there. Thriving."

"He took care of them, when you left. As if he was taking care of you."

"Why did he never try to contact me?"

"Me. I wouldn't let him. Why didn't you try to contact him?"

"Gregory. Ball-and-chained me to this place." They loosened their embrace. Cody wiped her eyes.

"Let's do this," Lisa said.

"Where do we start?"

"There are a couple of empty Costco boxes in the laundry room. Why don't you grab those? Then get the hand truck from the greenhouse." Cody didn't wait. Lisa enjoyed this deconstruction and reconstruction phase of her life. Like she was removing Gregory's limbs, one at a time, burying them in the yard for Turks and Caicos to gnaw on later. She caught herself, tried to remove the dark thoughts, pushed his desk up against the wall.

Cody returned with the boxes on the hand truck.

"I'll deal with the boxes," Lisa said. "I have another task for you. Erase that computer."

"Seriously? Nothing important in there?"

"I'm done with it. Reformat it, please. You can use it while you're here."

"Are you sure?"

"Positive."

"No paint. I'll have the walls covered with stuff soon. Can I smoke in here?"

"Out the window," Lisa said.

Cody went to work on the computer, and Lisa tossed files and folders and wall hangings of motorcycles, half-empty bottles of aspirin, magazines, post cards. Ben brought them plates of fried eggs and toast with blackberry jam. She saved anything that looked like a bill, would need to deal with those and the others from the workshop soon. Figure out where they were, moneywise. G had loved his old eight-track setup, shelves full of old music. She tossed it all in the box, smashed the deck, ripped out the tapes. By noon, the room was void of Gregory, full of Cody's art supplies.

Lisa left Cody on her own in the room, went out back to the workshop, spun in circles in the Herman Miller chair. She lifted the lid of the computer, Pious Rebel waiting, a cursor blinking, *Tend to me, show me that you love me.* Messages from Bianca, Peggy, RockHound. Bianca first.

> Looks like you're still at full strength with the murky
> computer. Will I see you today? Things are crazy here. Three
> noisy conference calls today. Angry tenants. Angry owners.
> Catch you later.

Lisa snapped a series of pictures in the workshop, attached them to the post she wrote to Bianca.

Check out my new digs. I'm calling it Pious Rebel headquarters. Which means I will probably let Rhonda and Sarah know soon that I'll leave the office end of January. I'm hoping that won't affect you and me. More on that soon. Which reminds me, it might be good to talk to your lawyer friends. Soon!

Peggy was next.

Dear Lisa — I am in love with your mom's work. Based on the one manuscript you sent me, I'm willing to offer a cash advance and finalize the royalty schedule. However, if I could read more scripts sooner than later, and think of this as a long-term package deal, I could possibly offer a larger advance. Let me know.

Lisa hadn't started reading the fourth manuscript yet, but was certain that *Waiting for Good Dough* would offer the same quality of writing and endearing story as the others. She switched to email.

Hi Peggy — Good to hear your review of Mom's work. I've attached the second and third books, which I've completed. I would be happy to have you include them in a package deal, as you mentioned. My prediction is that I would also eventually include the final two books, but I need to read them first. I'll hope to have them done by New Year's.

Now to RockHound.

Pious Rebel, does it matter whether I am a man or a woman? Nothing about our exchanges would change. No identifying pronouns have been used to clarify one way or the other. You have never posted a picture of yourself on the website, so I also have no way of knowing your gender, either. Again, not that it matters, given the nature of exchange we engage in. In answer to your not-so-direct question, it is by vocation that I am so enamored with geodes, rocks, anything and everything to do with geology and the formation of the earth. In the beginning, I would say it was avocation, a youth obsessed with a love of the intricacies of geodes, of the hunt,

of the mapping and driving and hiking to uncover beds of
glorious rocks for the taking. For the sharing. With friends,
with family, with loved ones. For the record, in my vocation,
I've noticed there are as many women as men.

Lisa pondered Rockhound's response. He may be the most
interesting of her Pious Rebel fans. She liked what he was saying about
gender, but she was also curious about how an avocation related to
geodes eventually led to a vocation. She wanted to know more.

Pam and Michael showed up before dinner with bags from
Gayle's Bakery and Rosticceria.

Lisa saw the bags, said, "Their stuff is so good! And so expensive!
Can we afford to eat like this anymore?"

Pam pointed at Michael. "This one can."

"What? So fast?" Lisa said.

"I start day after Christmas. With California Giant blueberry
farms, managing marketing and distribution. Good salary. Benefits.
Profit sharing."

"That is great!" Lisa said.

Ben and Cody entered the room.

"What's great?" Cody asked.

"Michael got a job," Pam said.

Ben patted him on the back. "That didn't take long. I guess no
hemp seeds for you."

"Nope. We'll leave that up to Zack and your buddies."

Cody spotted the bags, stuck her nose in, started pulling boxes
and containers out. "You are kidding me! I love their mac and cheese,
and the twice-baked potatoes. You guys shop well."

Zack came in from outside, hands and arms covered in grease and
smudge. "Hey, everybody." He raised his head, sniffed. "I smell chicken.
Ribs. Even if I don't eat it anymore, I still love the smell." He saw the
green and white bags. "Gayle's! Perfect." He held his hands up, wiggled
his fingers. "Need to clean up. Back in a minute."

Ben brought plates and forks to the table, large spoons for
serving.

Pam helped Cody empty the bags. She leaned into Cody. "Are you
smoking now?"

"I know! I know! It's disgusting and I smell like a fireplace. But it helps. Two days without booze. Baby steps." She lifted a large box from the last bag. "What's this one?"

"Oh. Michael's favorite. Large chocolate-and-vanilla-soufflé cake."

Cody slipped her fingernail under the taped edges, lifted the lid.

"Gorgeous!" Lisa said. Written across the top in lavender icing was "Congratulations, Michael! A Giant of a Man!"

They devoured the food — chicken and ribs, twice-baked potatoes and penne d'Alba, fruit salad, marinated mushrooms, garlic cheese bread, steamed vegetables, polenta casserole, salmon slices, and bow-tie salad. Cody excused herself to Gregory's former office. Lisa curled up on the couch, opened the computer. Instead of responding to RockHound's earlier post, she read the next chapter of *The Overstory*. So far behind on her reading. Needed to read a couple of Lydia Davis stories. They were short, Zack had told her. Two to ten minutes. And they were. They'd be perfect before falling asleep. She also needed to open the manuscript box for *Waiting for Good Dough* to see if Alice had kept the magic alive in Book 4. But Bianca first.

Sorry. Got bogged down here today. Maybe I'll get in tomorrow, but not sure. Otherwise, see you here on Christmas. With your hot date!

While Ben was stoking the fire, his cell phone rang. "Hello. Hey, Pete. That's great. Okay. Very good. That should work fine. See you then."

Zack turned to him. "So?"

"They've given their whole crew Christmas Eve day and Christmas off. They'll be here early Thursday morning to start with the pots, soil, plants. Back on Friday to install the lighting. Finish up on Saturday with the watering system. Give you hands-on training throughout the three days."

Zack nodded. Lisa watched him. He was engaging a little more today. Maybe the work would loosen his thoughts about Becs. Give him a reason to sweat and grow something of value. Not only the $500,000 value to Lisa and Michael, she thought, but the value of the hemp seeds to propagate more crops to create CBD oils and products that were greatly enhancing the lives of cancer patients and others. She had never been sure of the value of THC. Knew how it affected her personally, slowed her down, caused her to read less and eat more, happy to hole up and watch TV.

She switched to RockHound.

Good point! Doesn't matter at all about your gender. I'm glad
to hear women strike a balance with men in your chosen
profession. Here's another photo of an Alice geode.

She hit Send. Even though she'd said gender didn't matter, she
wondered, made up her own answer, envisioned a woman clad in
khakis and boots, dirt under her fingernails, tanned skin, hiking
through a desert to a geode bed, loading a backpack with them, a
woman about her age, another "we" club to form. Maybe someday
she'd ask, seek a buried truth that stepped over the lines of comments
on a social-media site. Or maybe RockHound would offer the
information unasked. Did it matter? Probably not.

Peggy the publisher had responded to her last post

Dear Lisa — I've done a quick skim of *Rocks and Rolls* and
Love Muffins. They are as good if not better than the first
book. I am thrilled to offer you two options for advance
payments. If the contract is based on three books, I'm
prepared to give you $3,000 per book, for a total of $9,000. If
you were able to part with all five right now, I could raise
that amount to $3,500 per book, for a total of $17,500. Both
options include industry-standard royalty rates of 8.5%,
regardless of which option you choose. The one final
consideration is your posting of chapters on Pious Rebel, in,
as you said when we met, a Dickensian fashion. I'm still
thinking about this from a publisher's marketing perspective
and am not sure I want to lock myself into a hard answer yet.
That means I would include language in the contract that
would allow me to determine whether or not to support the
continuation of the chapters as I have the opportunity to
determine their effect on sales. Which, by the way, would
also affect your royalty payments. I've attached copies of
both contracts. When you make your choice, please print out
and sign two copies, and send a hard copy to my Berkeley
address. So glad to be representing you and Alice as
members of our Berkeley tribe.

Damn! Hard numbers. Back to Bianca.

Hey. I've received final contract options from the Berkeley
publishers. Can you see if your lawyer friends have time to
meet with me? I'm available tomorrow. Will take them to
lunch, their choice!

Michael sat next to her on the couch. She rubbed his shoulder.
"Congratulations on the job. That is so great."
"Yeah. Mostly the benefits. Do you have a little time to talk?"
She closed the computer. "Sure. Shoot."
He looked around the room. "Maybe somewhere more private
than this."
"Come on. Let's go. I don't think you've seen the latest iteration
of Pious Rebel headquarters." To the group, "Back in a bit. Giving
Michael a tour of my new headquarters."
Cody appeared from down the hall. "Can I come?" Cody asked.
"No thanks. I'm good."
Lisa unlocked the door, turned on a lamp.
"This is amazing!" Michael said.
Lisa saw a daybed in the corner, complete with sheets, handmade
quilt, designer pillows, a poster hanging on the wall of Anaïs Nin's
quotation about writing to taste life twice. Had she mentioned it to
Zack? Must have. Or he'd been slipping into her head at night. Or had
she posted it on the website? It didn't matter. Whatever it was, he'd
been paying attention, continuing to do nice things for people without
being asked.
She sat in the swivel chair, one of the few things left that had G's
imprint on it, his DNA still clinging to the rubber wraps around the
arms. Michael pulled up a chair next to her, took out his cell phone.
"Oh, right," Lisa said.
"Sorry I went ahead without you, but I figured it'd be best to get
this stuff out of Jeff Bezos's hands."
"You sound like your brother."
"This is one of the few things I agreed with him about. You ready?"
"Do I need to prepare myself?"
"I don't think so." He pushed the button for Voice Memo. "Alexa,
play For Michael."

Alexa's voice answered. "You have eight items on For Michael. Talk to Michael about hemp seeds. Talk to Michael about cutting back on local clientele. Talk to Michael about balloon payment. Talk to Michael about Pamela. Talk to Michael about Cody. Talk to Michael about property taxes. Talk to Michael about the thirty-five pounds of pot owed to the Central Valley folks. Apologize to Michael about being such a shit to him when growing up, especially the berry-farm incident."

Michael pushed the Pause button. "So there's that."

"Most of it we already know," Lisa said. "Not sure about the Cody and Pamela comments."

"I asked Pam about it. She said it probably had to do with her helping him with marketing, or the geode quotations. But who knows. The scumbag he's turning out to be, maybe he was sleeping with her, too."

"No. That would put her in the scumbag category, too, and we don't want that. We don't want to live with that."

"I agree. You want Just in Case or For Lisa next?"

"Just in Case."

He pushed the Play button, his voice again, talking to Alexa. "Alexa, play Just in Case."

Again, she answered. "You have three items in Just in Case. Lot split plan located in bottom of Turks and Caicos food bin. Use local pot to pay Central Valley debts. Get a gun."

Lisa shook her head, held up her hands.

"I know. So glad I got a job and can put this place behind me."

"Excuse me. You *are* still half-owner."

"Sorry. I'm just so tired of him, his residual slime oozing everywhere."

"Have you seen a gun?" Lisa asked.

"No. I'm guessing that means you haven't either."

"No way. We ought to clear the safe out. Hide the cash and pot somewhere else."

"I don't know where else is safer than a safe."

"Damn it. And what about the lot-split thing? Looks like he was ahead of us on that one as well."

"I dug into the boys' food bin yesterday and found the plans. He'd been working with the county already on a possible land split in the future. That must be part of why he got the mortgage, to help pay for costs. I've got the plans at home, made a copy for you. I'll bring them when you're ready to see them."

She shook her head. "Too much else going on now. Don't even want to think about that one. One list to go."

"Right. You want to do this one by yourself? Happy to leave my phone with you."

"No way. We're in this together. Even if you do think you're walking away from everything."

"Give me a break." He pushed the Play button. "Alexa, play For Lisa."

"You have three items in For Lisa. Talk to Lisa about Point Reyes Station. Show Lisa the geodes when finished with story engravings. Apologize to Lisa about Cody, the others."

Lisa sat quietly for a minute. "No terrible news in this one. One could even make a case for good news."

"How's that?"

"He could have said 'Apologize to Lisa about Cody, *Pam*, and the others.' At least he left Pam off that list."

"Unless she was just one of the others."

"Is that it?" Lisa said, walking over to the bed, rolling over and putting her head on the pillow.

"Except for the other thing. You know, the balloon payment."

She rammed the butts of her palms into her temples. "I don't even want to think about that."

"We have to figure it out by January second. Ideally before then, in case there are any kinks."

"Maybe we sell one parcel off. Sounds like G has us pretty far along that road."

"Pretty far, but not that far. That still takes a couple of months to complete. And money."

"What kind of money?"

"Lots. Septic tanks. Sewer lines. Electrical. Water. Inspections —"

"Enough! I get it." She paused. "Can you believe that Zack?"

"What? Working the greenhouse for us?"

"That too. The other day he says a daybed would be nice out here and next thing I know he's done all this."

"Yeah. He kind of likes you."

"I kind of like him, too. But not like that." What was it like? Like the brother she'd never had. No, just someone who cared. A kindred spirit who was grieving. Or at least that's as much as she would let herself believe for now.

"Can't put off this mortgage-payment thing."

"Can too," Lisa said. "I want to hear about the berry-farm incident."

"What?"

"What did G do to you at the berry farm?"

"If I tell you, can we finish with the balloon payment?"

"I don't know about finishing, but yes, we'll talk."

"I was twelve, he was fourteen. We were picking olallieberries for the summer. Off Buena Vista Road in Watsonville. Near the old dump. They have one outhouse, and I needed it drastically. Ran down one of the berry aisles, made it there just before dropping a deuce in my pants, closed the door, pulled my pants down, and sat, just in time." Michael paused.

"That's it?"

"No. Next thing I know the outhouse is shaking. I hear wood against wood. I finish my task, stand up, try to open the door, and it won't open. I look out through a knothole and see that Gregory and two of his older friends have blocked the door with a large plank of wood. Then before I see or hear anything, I smell gunpowder, see the firecrackers tossed inside, a whole package going off under my feet. I hop up on the toilet, my foot slips and falls into the mounds of shit. When the firecrackers stop, I pull my foot out of the muck, my shoe staying there, me in one shoe and one shitty sock, the plank now gone, me smashing the door open, ready to kill them."

"That's terrible."

"We never talked about it. He was probably worried I'd tell our parents. But I didn't. Kept it inside. Had mostly forgotten about it until I heard his note. Enough of that. Balloon payment."

"I don't want her involved."

"I understand. I agree with you in principle, but we're in it deeper than principle. I don't see that we have any choice."

"Can we get a loan against the property?"

"You mean other than the six liens Gregory took out already? And you have no income. And I have no income to show for the past seven years."

"What about the new job?"

"Doesn't count. Not enough time left. We've got to solve this within the next five or six days."

"We could ask Zack." She hated the idea.

"Would you really do that?"

"No. You'd have to do it."

Michael shook his head. "I don't like it. He's already done so much. What if things went wrong? You want Zack in it, or Cody and Ben?"

"Good point."

"Like Ben told us, he's already thought the whole thing through, has it all mapped out. Knowing him, he could have the paperwork all drawn up as well, just waiting for our signatures."

"Give me the quick version again."

"They pay off the three hundred thousand in debts. They each become ten-percent owners in the whole property. If and when the hemp seeds sell, we pay them back their investment plus ten percent, and they retain right of first refusal to purchase one parcel each if we ever split the property."

"And if the hemp seeds don't make as much as we hope?"

"They retain their ten-percent ownership in the property, which gives them the right to identify their parcels of choice after you and I pick ours."

"Fuck! Let's keep Zack out of it. Tell Ben to get it done."

"Let's go tell him together. Partner."

•   •   •

"Great news," Ben said. "I'll start crafting the paperwork. We'll have a signing party on New Year's Day. I can have the debts paid off by January second."

"Where's Cody?" Lisa asked.

"In the art studio."

Lisa walked down the hall, knocked. "Can I come in?"

"Absolutely not!"

"Why? Are you smoking?"

"Only out the window."

"Okay. Just thought you'd want to know, Ben's drawing up papers."

"For what?"

"For the two of you to pay off our mortgages, become ten-percent owners in the property."

Cody opened the door a crack, inched herself out before closing it behind her, gave Lisa a huge hug. "I am so happy about this! Partners. Property. Couldn't be a better Christmas for me."

"Right. I'm going to bed now."

41

TUESDAY
12-24-19

CHRISTMAS EVE MORNING. It didn't mean much to her now. Hadn't in quite some time. On her drive downtown, KDFC was playing Pachelbel's *Canon in D Major*. She had always liked it, the calming effect it had that reminded her that calmness was achievable. Even when the piece had been overused in movies and advertisements, made fun of in *New Yorker* cartoons, she still enjoyed it, as she did now, driving over the river, not caring if she landed the premium parking spot, taking the one in front of Lenz Arts instead.

Waiting for the light at the crosswalk to change, she thought of Christmas Eve rituals with Alice. And Cody. Because Alice had worked at home and had control over her own schedule, and because she and Cody were out of school for two weeks, Alice made a big deal out of December twenty-fourth, made up stories about angels and fairies and gold dust they sprinkled on pancakes at breakfast, really just cinnamon and light brown sugar mixed together, as they mapped out the rest of their day. It started with a drive over the Bay Bridge to San Francisco all the way to China Beach, where they would ramble for hours, hike out to

Mile Rock Beach at Lands End, where they'd walk to the center of the Eagle Point Labyrinth, a rock maze all three of them loved. Alice would get them back to her car in time to head over to Greens restaurant in Fort Mason. Cody would manage to order the most expensive thing on the menu, every time, even as an eight-year-old who shouldn't know anything about that. "I want the vegetable masala curry with Hodo tofu, spinach, carrots and cauliflower, served with Lundberg basmati turmeric rice, pickled okra, and house-made Capay organic chapati." Alice would chuckle, Lisa would roll her eyes, say, "Do you even know what that is?" Cody would straighten her back, say, "What I just said." What Lisa knew is that she simply ran her finger down the menu until she found the highest-priced item. After the chocolate pudding with crème-fraiche caramel, they'd load back into the car, work their way to Golden Gate Park, where they'd spend the rest of the afternoon split between the de Young Museum and the Conservatory of Flowers. Alice would sit on benches in the conservatory, marveling at the flowers for hours. Cody had her colored pencils and pad and would draw them. Lisa had a book, head buried, attached at the hip to the main character, Dicey in *Dicey's Song,* Willie Beech in *Good Night, Mr. Tom.* Cody would fall asleep in the back seat as they took the bridge back to Berkeley, passed through Treasure Island, took the drive up into the Piedmont Hills, where two blocks of fancy homes all had Christmas lights and decorations, Alice driving under five miles an hour, taking it all in, Lisa waking Cody, who would be mad if she missed it. At home, Anita would be there, dinner prepared, the traditional taco bar set up, homemade flan, José Feliciano singing "Feliz Navidad" on the record player.

It had been a long time since she'd remembered that story. What would she do on Christmas Eve tonight? Probably nothing different. Maybe help Zack prep for tomorrow's meal. The traffic light changed. As she crossed, she saw the crowds of street people standing in front of San Lorenzo Lumber. She went back to her car, drove to The Bagelry, ordered three dozen, mostly poppy seed and sesame because that's what she liked, along with pints of egg salad, tuna salad, and pink flamingo. She pulled into the parking lot, rolled down her window and handed the bag to the woman she had seen so many times against the Lenz Arts wall. Her friend was with her. Lisa held out her hand, said, "I'm Lisa. Merry Christmas Eve."

The woman grinned, showed a gap in her teeth. "I'm Lela. This is my friend, Art. And a Merry Christmas to you."

· · ·

When she entered the office, Bianca saw her first. "Hey, stranger." Lisa raised a palm and high-fived her. She went straight to the open area where Rhonda and Sarah had their stand-up desks. After *cordial-but-I'm-busy* greetings from both, Lisa spoke. "I'll need to use my deposit for the month of January, as I won't be able to afford the space any longer. A lot's going on at the property, which will tap me pretty hard."

"So sorry to hear that," Rhonda said. "We'll miss you."

Sarah flipped a calendar page to January. "That means your final day will be January thirty-first."

"Right," Lisa said. "But I'll have my stuff out of there well before that. Let me know if you need me out sooner."

"Thanks. Will do."

Bianca followed Lisa into her office. "Lunch at eleven thirty with the lawyer work for you? Liz is out of town with her daughter at a volleyball tournament, but Felicia will join us. Gabriella Café."

"That's good. I don't think I've ever eaten there. Don't even know where it is."

"Just down the street from Alderwood. I'll take you. Why don't you send Felicia copies of your contracts, so she can read them in advance?" Bianca handed her Felicia's business card. "I don't think she'll charge you, but you never know. What can I bring tomorrow?"

"Pretty sure Zack's got everything covered."

"A couple bottles of wine, maybe?"

"No. Please. Cody's been dry for a few days. I'd like to keep it that way."

"Really? That's a big deal. She driving you crazy?"

"Not too bad yet. Smells like smoke all day long. Just bring your hot date."

"This one is definitely hot. But not a date."

In the outer office Lisa heard the nameless receptionist setting up a conference call. She slipped on her earbuds, covered them with the headset, opened the computer, and turned on the meditation music before she lifted the *Waiting for Good Dough* manuscript from its box, *January 2005* written on the cover. Second year at Cal, still living with Alice, still young and curious. She had never read the play, but she and Alice had gone together to see it at the Rep, probably in the year before Alice's version was written. She decided to dedicate the rest of the morning to the story, hopefully finish it by end of day tomorrow, give her one more piece of information to guide her discussion with Peggy.

The bakery business had grown more competitive. Chain stores on every corner offering folks more and more product. Amelia had just celebrated her twelfth birthday. William achieving new heights, tipping the scale at over 225. Celia was taking night classes, hoping to get her AA at Berkeley City College. Statistics. Accounting. Contemporary literature. She wanted to take a mix of things, no focus yet, test things out, see what she liked, see if something might move her, make her want to change her life.

They hadn't heard from Justin in years, the geode shelf still sitting half empty. Margie had married her third husband in an Elvis chapel in Las Vegas, seemed happy enough for now, but Celia knew it wouldn't last, Margie never satisfied for long.

William continued to use chef interns from the local institutes to lighten his load, to give him more time to perfect a recipe for a cookie dough that would blow his competitors away. He experimented daily, asked the interns for their opinions, especially the newest two, the ones who philosophized about everything, about the shades of dye used in the icings, the proper amount of vanilla to add. Mirdival was the talker of the two, made up stories and was on his feet all day long. Tragones could pull his weight, but had a bad leg and needed to sit down more often, take a rest when needed. Their families had both immigrated from Czechoslovakia, made their way to New York, baked their way through the Midwest until Mirdival and Tragones found jobs as kitchen helpers at the St. Francis Hotel in San Francisco. When they had saved enough money, they found the culinary school in Oakland, and moved to the East Bay.

Lisa stopped, laughed at her mother. Within the first two pages, she had laced the text with echoes of Beckett's characters, names transformed, lightly veiled behind Mirdival and Tragones.

At 11:20, Bianca yelled over the wall, "Time to go."

Lisa yelled back, "One minute."

She was on page 110, a third of the way through, wished she could just lie back in the chair, keep reading until the sun went down.

· · ·

Gabriella Café was a surprise to Lisa, very French and bistro-like. She would have liked to sit on the outside patio, pretend she was in some Parisian back alley, but it was too cold. Bianca was a friend of Paul, the owner, and he escorted them to a nice table with a window overlooking the sidewalk.

"Felicia likes to get her steps in, so she's probably walking over."

"From where?"

"They have an office on Seabright."

Their heads were buried in menus when Felicia arrived. Lisa was surprised when Felicia gave her a big hug instead of a handshake. "I love Pious Rebel and Alice. Great job!"

"Thanks. It's all Bianca's fault."

Felicia punched buttons on her Apple Watch.

"How many steps?" Bianca asked.

"Ten thousand five hundred seventy-two."

"Jeez! Before lunch! That's great."

"I've got a one o'clock, so let's dive right into this thing." Felicia distributed copies of both sets of contracts to Lisa and Bianca. "This is all very clean, well-written, fair. I did some research into Peggy Nelson as a person. Seems to be on our side." Lisa wondered what that meant, wondered if she had a side. Just one more notion of belonging to a club. "She donated money to the Hillary Clinton campaign in 2016. She belongs to a health club two doors down from her office. She's a member of the Spiritual Women Leaders Network, along with three-thousand-plus other Bay Area women. Never been sued or sued anybody herself. Both contracts are fair and make financial sense, to her, and to you, especially given that Alice started writing her books

297

probably in the late eighties. So, three thousand dollars a book for three books is a good deal. If I were you, I'd take the second contract, give her all five books for the increased price of thirty-five hundred each, because I doubt you're going to be displeased with books four and five. As much as I loved I Really Knead You, I'm certain they'll only get better."

Lisa nodded. "You're right. *Rocks and Rolls* and *Love Muffins* are really good. I started *Waiting for Good Dough* this morning."

"That's the title?" Felicia said. "How brilliant is that? In my opinion, the only downside is that as a small publisher, she won't be able to market it as well as someone from L.A. or New York. But, this is income you'd never imagined, and the turnaround with Peggy is quite quick given the usual publishing-industry delays."

Felicia looked at her watch. "I need to order."

"My only concern is if I run into something that feels too personal," Lisa said. "So far Celia and William and Amelia don't feel like they're directly related to my life with Alice. Maybe a little, but not much."

Bianca said, "Well, maybe the geodes."

"That's true. But not the rest. In these last two books, I'm at Berkeley, the empty-nest syndrome comes into play, and who knows where Alice may take the stories. Given the titles, sounds like they're still in the bakery business."

They each had the beet salads and focaccia bread, San Pellegrino.

"I understand," Felicia said. "It's your life and your call. By the way, my username on your site is FelineLover."

"Oh! That's you? You have Lorraine."

"I do have Lorraine! Love of my life."

"Thank you so much for the advice. Can you just send me a bill to Bianca at the office?"

"No way. No charge. You're just finding your way in this game. When you become rich and famous, then we'll talk."

At the office, Lisa signed the five-book contract and mailed it to Peggy before heading home to meet Pam to review Gregory's preliminary lot-split plans. The house was quiet, Zack off for the day with his anti-racism group, Ben and Cody spending the day in Half Moon Bay, and Michael home studying manuals for his new job. Pam was in the playground with Turks and Caicos, throwing a Frisbee like she knew what she was doing. Lisa stood by the fence, quiet, impressed with Pam's athletic ability.

"Hey," Pam called. "Want to play?"

"I'm no good at it. Where'd you learn to throw like that?"

"Ultimate Frisbee team at UCSC. Went to state finals."

"Who knew?"

"Mostly nobody. These days, just Michael."

Lisa walked toward the house. "I'll be inside when you're ready. Need to lie down for a minute or two."

"Rough day with the lawyer?"

"No, that part was easy. Although I learned she'd already walked ten thousand steps before lunch. That made me tired just thinking about it."

Eloise greeted her at the door. Lisa wondered how she would act if she met Lorraine. Would it be an immediate attraction? Kindred spirits? Or would there be a hint of territoriality? She grabbed The Overstory from her bed, brought it back to the living room, started reading the next story on the couch. When she opened her eyes, Pam was sitting at the table, marking the property map with a yellow highlighter.

"How long was I out?" Lisa asked.

"About an hour and a half."

"That's crazy." She twisted her body long, pointed her socks toward the ceiling, wiggled her joints back into place, before standing and taking a seat next to Pam. "What do you think?"

"To be honest, it looks like he knew what he was doing. Or at least was working with others who knew what they were doing. I've highlighted the proposed property lines between the five parcels, each parcel a tad over five acres. The greenhouse is on a parcel by itself, here. Just south of it down Porter Gulch is a fairly flat five-acre piece with no building. North of the greenhouse is this house on a five-acre parcel. Behind that one is a parcel with the workshop. And the fifth parcel is farthest north, almost butts into Nisene Marks. No buildings. I hope we don't have to deal with this. But if we did, this looks pretty good."

"If we had to pick today, what do you think Michael would want?"

"We talked last night. He had rationales for each parcel. But if he had first choice — by the way, he thinks you should have first choice — but his choice would be the house."

Lisa grinned. "Perfect! Because I don't want this house. I want the workshop, and I like nudging up to Land of Medicine Buddha. I'd probably take a machete and carve a path over there."

"I'd love seeing you with a machete in your hand. Maybe not with Cody in the room."

"You're funny. She hasn't been quite as bad lately."

"It's only a matter of time."

"Do me a favor?"

"Okay. What?"

"The second person."

"Seriously? I thought you didn't care. Didn't need to know."

"It's been creeping into my thoughts. Just curious is all."

Pam opened her cell phone. "What's the last name?"

"Arthur. Ryan Arthur."

While Pam hunted, Lisa calculated the distance from the back of the workshop to Land of Medicine Buddha property, 976 feet.

"Yep. He's there."

"Are you sure?"

"I'm sure there's a Ryan Arthur there. It's a common name, though. It may not be your Ryan Arthur.

"There is no *my* Ryan Arthur."

"You want the address?"

"Of course not! Maybe the phone."

Pam wrote the number in pencil on the parcel map.

"Do this. Hunt for Cody."

In less than thirty seconds, "Yep. Same address, different phone numbers."

•   •   •

Other than Lisa and Eloise hunkered under a blanket on the couch, the house was empty. The light was fading outside when the boys started growling and barking. Again Lisa went to the front door, heard the motorcycle engine start, saw a headlight flash on, slip quietly down the road. She didn't feel like checking the property this time, was nearly three-fourths finished with *Waiting for Good Dough* and was anticipating the final eighty pages, Alice having hooked her from page one, pulling her through to the end riding a taut thread, a few diversions along the way but working her way up to a landing, and Lisa couldn't tell if it would be rocky or smooth.

Thirty pages later, she heard the key in the front-door lock. Zack was hauling in three bags of groceries.

"More?" Lisa said.

"I had a few more ideas. Got some recipes from friends at the Center."

"How's that going?"

"What?"

"Curing racism."

"One bigot at a time. What are you up to tonight?"

"Finishing one of Alice's books. Fifty pages to go. How about you?"

"I need to prep a few things, do some chopping, marinating. I was wondering if you'd be up for a ride."

"What kind of ride? Did you finish the Harley? I won't ride on the bike."

"No. A few more days. I was thinking of taking Babe for a ride to see some Christmas lights."

"I haven't done that since I was a kid. Where would we go?"

"Two possibilities I know of. There's a neighborhood in Scotts Valley off Mount Hermon. Or we could drive over to Los Gatos to this amazing display at Vasona Lake."

Surely he wasn't thinking of this as a date. Just a sort-of roommate trying to keep occupied, keep grief at a distance, finding something to do on a Christmas Eve. And she just happened to be the one around to invite. Why not?

"I need about an hour and a half to finish."

"Which is exactly what I need to get ready for tomorrow." He looked at his watch. "Six thirty, then. It's a date."

No it's not, damn it. I don't date. It's too soon. Way too soon.

"By the way," he continued, "did you happen to hear any bikers up here?"

"In fact, I did. About an hour ago." She filled him in on the details. "Why?"

"When I turned up Porter Gulch, there were five of them clustered in a circle at the Temple Beth El parking lot."

She chose to let it go and dedicate her thoughts to her mom's clever words. She pulled a headset from her backpack, slipped it on, dulled most of the sounds coming from Zack's knives in the kitchen. But she could smell the minced garlic, and it did not mix well with brown-sugar cookie dough. Over the top of the pages, she could see his lithe body organizing, piling, wrapping, putting bowls in the refrigerator, task-oriented, keeping his head full of little jobs. She had to leave, walked down the hall to her room, closed the door, left the headset on, and dove back into the current scene.

The rain hadn't stopped in a week. William had Mirdival and Tragones place sandbags in front and back of the bakery. Business was slower. Folks didn't like to go out and get wet, fight the battles with umbrellas. Celia didn't mind the weather, found it refreshing to point her face to the sky, open her mouth, stick out her tongue, and walk the few blocks to the college three nights a week.

Before she left for her accounting class, William handed her a new bag of cookies. "Mirdi came up with this batch today. I kind of like it, but it's still not quite right. Let's have your unfocused focus group tell us what they think again."

Celia had been taking experimental batches to her classmates throughout the semester. Of course they had loved everything, but she forced them to be more analytical. Taught them how to take the dough on their tongues, tap it into the roofs of their mouths, separate it into disparate piles, identify tastes, and determine what was missing, or what was heavy-handed, and mostly, what their ideal vision of the perfect cookie would be. As she prepared to step over the sandbags, one of their regular customers, who called himself Bozo, after the clown, because of his constant red and runny nose, raced down the sidewalk, holding onto a leash, being tugged by a dog they hadn't seen before. He managed to get out, 'New dog. I call her Happy. Yikes,' before the dog dragged him past the bakery. After Bozo left, being pulled down the sidewalk by Happy, a boy stepped in through the door,

```
water dripping down his hair, over his ears, drops
falling off his chin. William saw him. Asked him if he
was hungry.
     "Yes, sir."
     "Do you have any money?"
     "No, sir."
     "Were you here yesterday?"
     "No, sir. Maybe it was my brother."
     William put six cookies in a bag and handed it to the
boy.
     "Run along now."
```

Lisa stopped, closed her eyes, smiled at her mother who was using everything she could from Beckett's masterpiece.

The downpour still strong, Celia left the covered hallways of the accounting building, splashed her way home, happy, thinking of it as a baptism, nothing she had ever known as a child or any other time in her life, but had learned about in her philosophy-of-religion class. She yelled into the darkness of the storm, "Hallelujah! Cleanse me." She laughed as she entered the bakery, laughing on each step as she ascended the stairway.

William and Amelia were at the kitchen table, Amelia cooking most of the dinners when Celia was at school. Tonight was meatloaf with green olives perched on top. Mashed potatoes drenched in slabs of butter, and a bowl of succotash, heavier on the corn than lima beans, the way William liked it. A large bottle of ketchup stood upside down, its contents ready to slide out on command. Her plate had no food on it, instead a package in the middle. Neither William nor Amelia greeted her. Neither asked how her classes had gone. She sat down, moved the package from her plate without looking at it, tried to keep her heart from racing, her face from flushing. It could only mean one thing.

"Pass the meatloaf, please." Amelia handed her the bowl. "Nice touch with the green olives."

William was clearly unhappy, a habit he had drifted into more than she would like these days. Amelia had a scowl on her face. "Succotash, please," Celia said. The mashed potatoes were close enough to reach. She spooned a large pile onto her plate, stuck in her fork and ate. "Great potatoes." They would not relent until she finally addressed the package. It had to be from him. Amelia jealous that it hadn't been addressed to her. William just jealous.

The package was about the size of a box of Ritz crackers, wrapped in brown kraft paper. No return address. Addressed to *Ms. Celia Livingstone.*

She paused again. It was the first time in four books that Alice had given William and Celia a last name. Why wait so long? Why do it at all now? Was it significant, or had she become lazy, letting threads fall unattended? Lisa read on.

When they were married, Celia had taken William's last name, was proud to do so, had never thought it might be important to keep her maiden name, was happy to be considered as an accessory to William and his life, and his bakery. Now Amelia had his name. And so did this package, with Justin's handwriting, Justin having to write William's last name on this package he sent from . . . from nowhere. Why no return address? If she didn't have a place to associate with him, maybe it was easier, maybe he was less real, a ghost sending ghost packages. It was the first in years. And all the others had been sent directly to Amelia. Had William said something to him, warned him off? Not really William's style. Instead he'd eat and drink himself away from his thoughts, bury himself in fat and clogged arteries.

"Well, what have we here?" Celia tried to smile as she stuck her knife under packing tape, ripped it open, raised the lids, pulled out pieces of crumpled newspaper. She could look at the heading, easily figure out where he was. Had he wanted that? Had he expected that she would use her investigative savvy and know exactly where he was the minute he sent it, the minute she opened it? Maybe. But she wouldn't play. Wouldn't give him the satisfaction, even if he never knew the truth.

There were three packages in the box. The first said 'For William' across the top, wrapped in the same newspaper. Celia handed it to him. He seemed surprised, as if he had been hoping it would be all about Celia so his

anger could be justified. The second package was labeled
'Amelia,' and she ripped it open the minute Celia handed it
to her. A beautiful geode. A spot waiting for it on her
incomplete bookshelf, Celia thought. The final package
had Celia's name on it. She wanted to walk away from the
table, lock herself in the bathroom, savor it, take her
time to enjoy the gift from Justin. Justin who must be
married by now, have his own children, a life he was
unwilling to divulge in a return address. You want me,
figure it out. Read the newspaper. Come find me. William
opened his package. A knife from Germany. He lit up.
"This is quality stuff. Wow!"

Celia put on her best nonchalant face. "My turn." She
closed her eyes as she tugged at the newspaper, tossed it
on the floor out of her vision. It was a book written by
Samuel Beckett. Collected Poems in English and French.
No inscription. No note. She had only vaguely heard of
Beckett, had never read him or seen his plays. She held it
up across the table so Amelia and William could get a
closer look at the benign book. See, she thought to
herself. Nothing special for me. I'm just the addressee.
Ms. Celia Livingstone. Wife of William. Mother of Amelia.
Former friend of Justin. Who wants her to learn French.

Lisa opened her computer, found Amazon, found *Collected
Poems in English and French.* She should wait. Should buy it local.
Well, order it local. An obscure book of poetry by Beckett in English
and French would take forever to arrive. She didn't have time. Correct
that. She didn't want to wait, ordered it.

Zack was wiping down the sink, setting out the dishes and
silverware for tomorrow's meal when Lisa came into the kitchen, a
scarf wrapped around her neck, pulling on G's Patagonia jacket.

"Still wearing that thing, huh?"

She zipped it up. "Yep. I guess so."

"Why?"

"I don't know. It's black. Dark."

"You need some light in you. In your life."

"Then let's go see these Christmas lights of yours."

"They're not really mine."

"You know what I mean."

When they passed Temple Beth El the parking lot was empty.

Zack pointed Babe onto the freeway, turned toward Scotts Valley. "What do you think?" he asked.

"About what?"

"Scotts Valley or Los Gatos?"

"Oh. Let's stay local."

"Sounds good. We'll save Vasona for next Christmas."

She leaned against her window, turned toward him. "How long are you planning on being here?"

"Like I said before, I'm not much for planning these days. A drive to Scotts Valley. A Christmas dinner. That's about it."

"Sorry. I just finished one of Alice's books and I'm feeling a little out of sorts. Can I tell you the last sentence of this book?"

"No way! I don't roll that way. Loving what you post chapter by chapter."

"You're reading it?"

"You bet. Can't wait for *Rocks and Rolls* to appear."

"Soon."

•   •   •

Zack slowed Babe as they made their way through the upscale neighborhood, each house outdoing the next on lawns and rooftops and mailboxes, large blow-up Santas and reindeer, small generators and pumps keeping everything up and running through New Year's. They stayed quiet, observant on the first street. By the second street, Zack spoke. "You know, if you'd like me out of there it wouldn't be a problem. I've had a few other offers."

"I don't want you gone at all. It was just the thing you said about next Christmas. I haven't allowed myself to think that far ahead. It's all I can do to get up every morning and open my computer to Pious Rebel. Post and respond. On the fly."

"On the fly seems to be working quite well for you. I'm hooked."

"Anyway, I'm sorry about what I said. If you weren't there, who would cook dinner tomorrow?"

Lisa's cell phone pinged. Cody.

We're up in Half Moon Bay. Staying at the Ritz-Carlton tonight. Don't worry. Perrier and cran-rasp. No booze! Day four, but who's counting. Back and forth between jumping in the ocean and the hot tub to keep myself sane. See you tomorrow. Stay out of my art studio! I'm working on Christmas presents in there.

Damn, Lisa thought. The Christmas presents. She had taken care of all the shopping with Pam the other day but had stuffed the bags in the big closet in G's room, Zack's room.

When they returned, Zack went straight for the kitchen to craft a cheese ball. Lisa took the opportunity to retrieve the Susan Hayes Handwoven bags from Zack's closet and pile them on her bed. In a kitchen drawer she found scissors and tape, a ball of twine. With the bags emptied into a mound against her pillows, she sliced open the roll of paper from Miki's. The paper alone was nice enough to be a gift. Seemed a shame to wrap gifts in it and have it be torn to pieces. She'd tape it lightly, give those who cared to a chance to save it, reuse it, make something else out of it. First she had to remember who got which presents. Cody was easy. The furry snow boots for the Aspen winters. Because Bianca worked on computers all day long, in that freezing cold office, hers were the handknitted wrist warmers, fingers open for keyboard work. She had gotten both Michael and Pamela scarves, but couldn't remember who got which. Didn't matter. They were both warm and beautiful. There were a number of other pieces still on the bed, mostly because she didn't know who would show, and she preferred to be heavy rather than light in these situations. Better heavy than light in every situation. She didn't know if she should wrap something for Bianca's date. Lisa was still calling the person a date even if Bianca refused to acknowledge it. She made no assumptions about Zack's guest, or guests, dates or otherwise, but she thought it too strange to give them something on first meeting. Zack was the other easy one. The large coat with fake-fur lining, perfect for breaking the wind while riding a Harley. Ben was the one she couldn't figure out. Didn't have a reading on him. There were extra scarves, a pair of gloves, two hats. She wanted to give him the fedora, not so much because it was a fitting gift, more to show the diversity of Susan Hayes. But giving a hat to someone felt too personal. Hats made a statement, a statement that only the wearer was able to make for him or herself.

No hat. She liked the fedora. She'd wear it. The gloves made most sense for Ben. Now the fun. Matching the right paper with the right gift, the right person.

She liked this part. Alice had started it, before Cody had come to live with them. They'd drive over the bridge, find little paper stores all over San Francisco, buy scraps and rolls, bring it all home, and talk about who deserved what. "What do think for Auntie Anita?" Alice would ask. Lisa would take her time to answer, turning every piece of paper over in her hands, rubbing her fingers in the weave, touching them to her face, until finally she'd say, "This one for Auntie Anita."

"Not until you tell me why," Alice would toy with her.

"Because," Lisa would say. "She has a cat with a blue collar with bells, like these bells on this paper, and because of the blue border around the edge of the gold stars."

What would she have given G for Christmas this year? She knew which paper, the one with golden dragons spitting red flames, fire in their eyes, ready to burn their way through to the end of a battle. What would Zack have given Becs? Everything, all of it, the whole world wrapped up in silver chains, small salmon boats, books about rainbows, a new bike, a new mother, a town to live in without big trucks and careless drivers. She would have given G advice, advice he would ignore. "Stay away from the oaks. Come make love with me. At least sleep with me."

The matching done, the packages wrapped, she carried them to the living room, set them under a Christmas tree she hadn't looked at. Zack had chopped it down back near the Land of Medicine Buddha property. Had popped popcorn, bought cranberries, strung and wrapped the tree with no help, mostly no one even noticing that it was there, that it was Christmas. He must have found tinsel and balls and lighthouses and golden apples buried in a box in the hall closet, because they were all there, and Lisa knew, without question, it was all for Becs, all for his memory of the expression he would have seen on her face had she been around to see it. What he had done for her.

She was making it all up and it still made her cry a little. Enough to remind her of the salt flavor of grief, of how it slid sideways through a sinus cavity and ended up in a small puddle on the floor.

It was time to address her following. She laughed at herself. Her following. Careful now, don't let this small-time stuff go to your head. It was time to push all the other gifts off the bed and onto the floor. She opened the computer, wished her bevy of new friends a happy new year. Told RachelReads she was happy to have *The Overstory* in her life. Told Peggy she liked book four. Thanked FelineLover for the help. Got more personal with a few more followers. Posted more pictures of geodes for the fanatics. Put up the first chapter of *Rocks and Rolls*. When finished, she knocked softly but hard enough to be heard on Zack's door.

"Yeah," he said.

"Can I come in?"

"It's your house. You need a shower?"

"Probably, but no." She twisted the knob, shut it behind her without looking at him. "Will you read to me?" She climbed up onto the bed, rested her head on one of her old pillows.

"I'd love to. What would you like to hear?"

"You pick. I trust your judgment."

The book in his hands was Lydia Davis, the one he had mentioned the other day. He read a short piece, stopped. "You want to get under the covers?" Yes, she wanted under the covers. The heat. The smell. The cuddle.

"No! But thanks. I'm good. I liked that one. Blunt. To the point. Bit of a surprise ending."

42

WEDNESDAY
12-25-19

W HEN SHE OPENED HER EYES, she was still on top of the bedspread. Zack had taken two blankets from the living room and covered her body, toes to chin. She carried them back to the couch, said, "Good morning. Merry Christmas."

Zack was unwrapping bowls, heating water, slicing mushrooms. The whole house smelled of roasted turkey. "Merry Christmas to you. You know Lydia doesn't usually put people to sleep that quickly. She's going to want a rematch."

"Fair enough. I'll bring toothpicks for my eyelids."

"Ahh. No prosthetics allowed. She demands focused attention."

"What can I do to help?"

"How about setting the table?"

"How many are you bringing?"

"They're bringing themselves, but I'm expecting two." He was starting to get a little spunky, a little mouthy, interpreting words too exactly. Alice would have liked him. Might still like him yet.

"And do these two expectants have names?"

"They do."

She waited but knew what he was up to. "And what are their names? Tell me some stories."

"One is Walter. Walter is very intelligent. Probably a bigger brain than everyone else in the room combined."

"You mean if we were to scoop the brain matter from every head, put it in a bowl and weigh it on the bathroom scale, it would weigh less than Walter's?"

"That's exactly what I mean. You can use the melon baller."

Lisa nodded. "And number two?"

"Number two is a complete mystery. A friend of Walter's."

"Male or female?"

"Does it matter?" Lisa was enjoying the light sparring, something Gregory had never allowed himself to participate in. Too serious. Knowing more about everything than anyone in the room. Or at least that's what he wanted folks to think by sucking in all the air in a conversation, making it difficult for others to breathe.

"Oh, it absolutely matters. I have one set of napkins for males. A separate set for females. A hybrid set for females with females, and something completely different for males with males." She was amusing herself. Had been too serious most of the time as well, or too stoned. She'd try to avoid both today. Maybe forever. Wait a minute. Slow down. One day at a time. Forever was way too long.

"So which napkins does Bianca's guest get?"

"Like Walter's guest, I have no idea. All I know is that he, or she, is hot, and not a date. According to Bianca."

Alice would have loved this conversation. She'd have corrected both of them multiple times by now. Would have sliced their smugness into small pieces of flesh that only the cat or dogs could remove. Why had she not brought Alice to live here with her in Aptos? She could have done so years ago. Because Alice would have hated Gregory. Because Gregory would have hated her. They would both have expected Lisa to make a choice. But hadn't she made that choice by not even inviting Alice? Letting her die by herself in Berkeley? By not even bringing it up with Gregory? Living the quiet, simple, unexamined life. Lydia Davis wouldn't stand for it. Alice would have lashed out at everything, everybody involved in the cover-up, in the refusal to invite Socrates to the party, guilty of the crime of refusing to speak and stand up for oneself. The way Celia was starting to do in book four. But look how long it had taken her. And she wasn't there yet. It also wasn't clear yet if Amelia was her father's daughter or her mother's charge. It was all hanging on the words of book five. On how Alice chose to string words together to mold her readers into the followers she expected them to become. Imagining the whole thing out of cookie dough and brown sugar. Because in truth, Alice had never had readers. Or that was Lisa's first thought. But maybe Anita. Maybe professors and politicians whose words she had crafted into something more brilliant than they were when they first brought them to her. Maybe they had returned the favor, had provided critique and direction for Alice's fictional worlds. And maybe not. Most likely Lisa was the first reader Alice had had. But not the last. Lisa had made sure of that. Or Bianca had made sure of that. This blogging thing that sprang out of cracks in concrete. Grew wildflowers without water or soil. Simply with the light behind eyes, the heat from well-spent breaths. Alice had readers now. Had them forever, as long as that might be.

"Hello? Can Lisa come out and play?" Zack jogged her back to reality. "By my count that's ten of us. And if I remember correctly, we are gathering at one, eating at two."

Lisa shook the water from her ears, didn't want to trust her ability to count, listed everyone off by name: "Ben and Cody. Michael and Pam. Bianca and somebody. Walter and somebody. You and me." She hadn't planned on landing at "you and me." Sounded so coupled, along with and following the others. "And anybody else who might show up."

"Which reminds me. Have you had more phone hang-ups?"

"Not for a while."

"I'm worried about those bozos."

"What good will worrying do? We know they'll show up eventually. I'm guessing minimally at the memorial."

"We should be prepared. Get ready for them. Not worry."

"I agree."

Pam came through the front door, Michael behind her.

"I know. I know. We're early. I forgot to buy wrapping paper."

Michael had bags hanging from hands and shoulders.

"On my bed," Lisa said.

"Do you have any paper left?"

"You mean my good Miki's paper?"

"Isn't that what you used?"

"Yes, but ..." She stopped. "It's on the bed. At least pair it well."

"Do what?"

Lisa smiled. "Never mind. Use what you need."

Michael reappeared. "Back in a minute. More in the car."

"Want help?"

"Uh. Hmm. I guess it doesn't matter."

"What does that mean?"

"You'll see. Come on."

They walked outside, saw Turks and Caicos with noses through the fence.

"Let's take care of the boys first." He reached into the back seat, pulled two dog bones out of a sealed pouch, handed one to Lisa, then walked to the fence, rubbed Turks' ears. Lisa did the same with Caicos.

"You're kind of a good guy, sometimes."

"Yeah, you just have to land on the right sometime."

He opened the back end of the car, slid out a four-by-six-foot flat package wrapped in butcher paper with doodles and designs all over it.

"Take an end," he said. He grabbed the other side, said, "Follow me." At the workshop they stopped, and he leaned the package up against the wall. She opened the door and they carried it in. "Merry Christmas. Go ahead and open it."

Lisa looked at the wrapping paper, remembered what her mom would say. "Don't screw with the paper. Paper is easy, cheap. Get to the given gift, acknowledge it to the giver. Make them feel good about themselves. Feel good about yourself." Lisa had never agreed with her, cared about the paper, cared about this paper with the handmade designs.

She removed it carefully, as if she might save it and frame it. With the paper removed, she saw the whiteboard, "Merry Christmas from Pam and Michael!" written in multiple colors.

·　　·　　·

Cody and Ben arrived a little before eleven. He carried a small bag, Cody barely able to carry herself in, hands rammed into her coat pockets, eyes hidden behind sunglasses. She went straight to the art studio.

"Did she drink?" Lisa said.

"No," Ben said. "DTs kicking in pretty badly. It smells great in here, Zack. Anything I can do to help?"

"I'm sure I can find something for you."

"Okay. I need to do a little wrapping first. Back shortly."

Lisa was on Pious Rebel when Pam appeared, arms full of packages, set them under the tree.

"Thank you so much for the white board! It's just perfect."

"You are so welcome. It's been hard over the years to figure out what to get you. That made sense this year. Who strung the popcorn and cranberries?"

"That would be Zack."

Pam shook her head, whispered to Lisa, "If only I were single."

"You're kidding, right?" Lisa said.

"Of course I am. Where *is* Michael?"

"Filling Turks and Caicos's food bin. Is he excited about tomorrow?"

"Seems like it. And nervous. It's been so long since he's had a real job. Getting up to eat breakfast before noon. Packing a lunch. Punching timecards." She chuckled. "But he'll be fine."

Ben returned, a handful of small packages in hand that he placed under the tree on top of Pam's packages.

"How was the Ritz?" Lisa said.

"Exceptional," Ben said.

"You stayed at the Ritz-Carlton? Which one?" Pam said.

"Half Moon Bay. It was part of my present to Cody."

Ben found the card table Lisa had put out for the lot-split documents when she'd set the table for Zack.

"This is perfect," Ben said. "I need to include these details in the contract language. Have you and Michael identified your preferred parcels yet?"

"Isn't that jumping the gun? We don't need to worry about parcel splits and boundaries if the hemp seeds come in. Which is the plan."

"I understand," he said. "But from a lawyer's perspective, it's best to have it all laid out in advance, just in case. Have the dominoes in place before they start tumbling."

"In fact," Pam said, "we have talked about it. Michael and I want parcel C, with the house. Lisa wants parcel D, with the workshop. The

314

other three are up for grabs. But we aren't looking forward to it landing that way."

"That's why you pay me to do the looking forward for you."

"Wait? We're paying you?" Lisa said.

"That's just a figure of speech. My work is gratis. I need to head up to the city for a couple of days tomorrow. I should have the paperwork ready for signatures by New Year's Day."

The landline rang.

"Shall I get that?" Pam asked.

Lisa stopped her. "No. Lots of hang-ups. Let's see if this is another."

After the third ring, Michael's voice came on. "Please leave a message for Lisa or Michael," followed by the beep.

"Hello, Michael and Lisa. This is an RSVP for Gregory's memorial on New Year's Eve. We'll be coming. A lot of us. This is Goldenrod. Merry Christmas. Really, a *lot* of us. We'll be hungry," the steady male voice said.

"What's with those guys!" Zack said. "Back in a minute. Looking for Michael."

"Apparently they saw the obituary in their local paper," Pam said.

"Yeah, but we didn't give a phone number," Lisa said.

Bianca and her non-date arrived a little before one. "Hey, everybody, this is Quinn. Quinn identifies as she/her." Bianca had certainly undersold her friend by only saying she was hot. This person was a god, or goddess. Lisa had never been physically attracted to women, but this was different. A designer haircut, blond and tight on the sides, longer on top with a swirl of teal. A body out of magazines, tanned, buff, confident in her movements. Tight black pants, light blue suede shoe tops, white rubber bottoms, a beige Patagonia sweater on top of a pink dress shirt.

"Welcome, Quinn," Lisa said.

Zack returned with Michael, both of them stopping in the kitchen as if encountering an invisible wall when they saw her. Cody appeared, hair wet after a shower, without sunglasses, looking much more presentable than earlier.

"What have we here?" she said, big smile across her face. She approached Quinn, offered her a cupped handshake.

Lisa watched. Cody had never restricted her tastes to one gender or another, had been open to experiencing whatever came her way.

And here was Quinn, right in the middle of her way. Ben watched, pretended to look at the parcel map, nodded to Quinn and waved.

Lisa saw the bottle of wine in Quinn's left hand, stepped in to greet her with a hug, said, "I'll take that for you." In the kitchen she handed it to Zack who hid it in the cupboard. Again she corralled Quinn, said, "Let me show you the house." On the tour Lisa explained to Quinn about the desire to avoid alcohol. Two messages, Lisa thought. The second was that Cody was damaged goods, stay away from her. But who was she to step in the middle? Who wasn't damaged? And maybe damage was Quinn's preference. Who knew? She let it go, gave up the need to control something uncontrollable. Not really her business, except the wine part, but she did watch Ben, wondering how the lawyer would react, if Cody stepped out of line.

All that changed quickly when Walter arrived with his mystery guest. Two new unknowns to round out the party of ten. Walter was white, over six feet tall, slender, dark hair below his neck like Adam Driver. His friend Hidalgo was short, a cleanly-shaved head, tattoos on all visible skin, hands, neck, ear lobes. He looked a little like the Cuban-American singer Pitbull. She wondered if he could sing. The dynamics in the room shifted, Walter talking to Quinn. They knew each other from an anti-racism workshop.

Zack and Hidalgo talked in the kitchen, Hidalgo helping him bring dishes to the table.

"We're just about ready," Zack announced.

"No place cards," Lisa followed. "Sit where you like."

She imagined Cody blurting out that she'd like to sit on Quinn's lap, but it didn't happen. Ben had taken his chair first. Cody didn't wait for Quinn to sit to choose her chair. She sat next to Ben, put her arm around his shoulder, rubbed his back, kissed his cheek. How about that? A bit of territoriality from her friend, her sister.

Zack's food was so good it was a relatively quiet meal, mouths busy chewing rather than talking. The yam-and-macadamia-nut dish topped with oven-roasted marshmallows was more like a dessert than vegetable. Cody was already dipping in for her third helping before trying anything else. The Diestel turkey was exceptional, crisp brown skin on the outside, moist breast and thigh meat inside. Half the table were vegetarians, but the other half devoured the prime rib, lightly marinated in garlic cloves, olive oil, salt, black pepper, and thyme. "I'm spending the night, having this for breakfast." Hidalgo said.

Walter giggled. "You spend the night and somebody will be having *you* for breakfast."

"Pass the gravy, please," Ben said, after heaping a pile of mashed potatoes and stuffing on his plate. Quinn mostly ate the Gambian green beans and fresh fruit topped with whipped cream. The glazed Brussels sprouts and morel mushrooms mixed with real maple syrup and G's famous black truffle oil disappeared first. Lisa was already thinking about turkey sandwiches for dinner. She watched Cody with Ben, feeling sad for the physical challenge she was facing, happy that she was having some success, and not completely over her bad behavior of the past three decades.

Bianca's phone pinged and she looked at the screen. She shook her head, grinned, handed it across the table to Lisa. The *Rocks and Rolls* thread was going viral. Thousands of new followers, chatting with each other, opening new threads, wanting more chapters. She'd need to get to her computer soon, but it would be rude to leave too quickly. And she wanted more yams.

After clearing the table, Zack and Ben brought over the lemon poppy-seed cake and pecan pie. Hidalgo had brought an olallieberry pie. "My dad owns fields over in Watsonville. My mom baked this." Lisa looked at Michael, caught his eye, nodded, thinking about his unfortunate event with Gregory in the outhouse.

She finally got her hands on the computer, dealt with her fans, marveled at the number of new folks pouring in. She saw Ben and Michael looking at the parcel maps. If it came to it, Michael and Pam would be the perfect occupants of the house. Maybe it would be communal. She'd have her daybed in the workshop, come in at nights to sleep. Maybe Zack would be renting a room from them. Maybe he'd still be reading to her. Or maybe she'd be reading to him from Beckett's poems in French and English. But she'd much rather have the hemp seeds succeed, for everybody's sake. Ben needed to go home to Berkeley. Cody needed to go home to Aspen. Zack could stay, for as long as he needed.

"Time for presents," Cody said. When she had entered Lisa and Alice's lives, she demanded to be the distributor of presents on Christmas mornings. Alice would relent, would hold Lisa's hand, letting her know that they were both suffering through the new girl's temper tantrums, neediness. Lisa blocked her out now, let her continue with her self-appointed ritual, as she dug further into Pious Rebel, checked out the explosion in the *Rocks and Rolls* forum. A message from Peggy the publisher.

> This is nuts! I say keep it up. Put up all the chapters of *Rocks and Rolls*, all at once or inch by inch. Your call. Keep up the good work!

Lisa posted the remaining geode photos. Those guys, and maybe gals, were also going nuts. GeodeGeorge had posted ten times. EverybodyMustGetStones was brand-new tonight. Five posts already. CinammonBeds had posted three. RockHound was strangely quiet. She hoped he was okay. He was probably old. There she went again, assuming a male. Assuming age. Maybe he was in a foreign country and their Internet reception was bad in some isolated canyon or desert.

Finally, she uploaded all the chapters to *Rocks and Rolls*, hit Send, wrote a quick post to accompany them.

> Friends, Merry Christmas! Whether you believe in Christ as your savior, as a role model, or as just one other human being who inhabited this planet, I wish you the very best things yet to come in your lives. I have discovered a box full of Alice's journals that date from the early sixties through last year. I haven't had the courage to look inside yet. What I remember of my childhood with Alice is one story, one I'm certain I've altered to make myself feel more wanted, more a part of her life than I really was. If I discover information I think will be helpful to your continuing understanding of Alice, I'll post it. If it's too personal, damaging, or dilutes the integrity of any of us involved in Alice's adventures in the East Bay, I'll keep it to myself. Pious Rebel is keeping me quite busy. RachelReads, still trying to work my way through The Overstory, a very important book with implications for the future of our survival on this planet. I haven't forgotten you or it. It's on the nightstand with Zen and the Art of Motorcycle Maintenance, recommended by my friend Zack, Zack who cooked an

awesome Christmas dinner all by himself, Zack who has been
reading to me from a Lydia Davis book of short stories. If
you're reading this Zack, Merry Christmas and thank you.

She hit Publish. As soon as she did, remorse rode up her arm and
attacked her heart, a slightly irregular heartbeat that straightened itself
out fast. Not just about Zack, not that she had said too much, too soon.
It was more about Cody, about Alice's journals, about Cody's need to
know everything first. She panicked. Ran out the front door to the
workshop, no shoes, no coat, unlocked the door, found the box of
journals safely locked in the cabinet. Not enough. She carried the box
to the greenhouse, opened the safe, lifted a pile of journals and set
them inside. The jars of seeds were there. But no cash. No pot. Damn
that Michael. She shoved the journals inside, locked the safe, ran back
to the house.

Pam looked at her dirty feet. "What are you up to?"

"Never mind. Where's Michael?"

"In the bathroom. We're ready to open presents. Just waiting for
you." Piles of packages were distributed around the living room next
to their intended owners.

She sat on the couch, watching for Michael. When he walked into
the room, she waved him over, made room for him next to her.

"We need to talk," she said.

"Isn't that what we're doing now?" he said.

"I'm serious. It's about the safe."

"Oh," he said. "What are you doing in there?"

"Putting some things in I want kept safe."

"Don't worry about it. I've got it under control."

"Apparently so. But I don't like being out of control."

"I've hidden it elsewhere. When that last phone call came in. Just
in case."

"Just in case what?"

"You know. The creeps from down south. What we supposedly
owe them."

"Supposedly. Why supposedly? Gregory left a message saying we
owed them. Pretty straightforward."

"Are you ready to just hand over all that pot?"

"Are you ready not to?"

"Quit jabbering over there!" Cody said. "Open! Open."

Lisa pulled away from Michael, needed to watch how folks opened their presents. Cody ripped the paper, found the boots in a hurry. Pam and Zack were slow, methodical, understood the quality of the wrapping, both removed the tape as they went along, were careful with the paper, folded it neatly and set it aside as if it had been the gift. The rest were in the middle, they were slow but ripped, pretended like they cared but didn't really.

As the piles shrunk and paper was mostly tossed into trash bags, Cody said, "Mine aren't wrapped. Just a sec." She returned from her art studio with three framed paintings, handed one each to Michael, Pam, and Zack. The content of each painting fit the person. Zack's was Gregory's Harley with Zack sitting on the seat, arms crossed, big smile across his face. Pam's depicted a scene at Alderwood, Cody on her feet, shoving an oyster in Pam's mouth.

"Sorry," Cody said. "I started yours before I quit drinking. It does show me as the bad guy, at least."

Pam smiled. "I love it! I know just where to put it." Lisa was imagining G's incinerator.

Michael's showed him at the fence, a bone in each hand, Turks and Caicos grabbing them. "This is great!" Michael said. "You're good. Never would have guessed it." Pam elbowed him. "I'm serious. I love this."

Cody stood, hands on hips, happy with herself. "Ben already got his. One left for Lisa. Back in a jiff."

She returned with a two-foot-by-three-foot framed painting, wire mounting, ready to hang. "For you, my sweet friend."

Lisa turned the painting around. It was a storefront sign that read "Pious Rebel Headquarters." Cody's identifiable style, intricate details, acrylic ink. It was gorgeous. Lisa had kept her feelings buried so long, this was not the time to betray herself, to burst into tears. She brought Cody close, sunk her face in her shoulder, swallowed three times, held back, refused to let go in this room of strangers and friends. She whispered in Cody's ear. "I love you."

Cody whispered back. "I know you do. Let's go hang it."

"I'll have Michael help. I need to talk to him."

In the workshop Lisa said, "What'd you do with everything?"

"Buried half the pot in the food bin. The rest is in my trunk for now."

"Why?"

"That call from Goldenrod this morning. The safe's the first thing they'll want opened. Need to stay two steps ahead of them."

"We need to stay alive. What about the money?"

"Still eight thousand dollars there. Pam's got it."

They hung the painting behind her desk. Zack had already been there, hung the white board in the perfect spot, had put six colored markers in the tray. Of course he had.

Quinn and Bianca were leaving with Walter and Hidalgo, heading down to the Catalyst to play games at the Orphans' Christmas party.

Ben and Pam started scooping up paper, tossing it in bags, but Zack stopped them. "I'll take care of this."

"You sure?" Ben asked.

"Positive."

"Okay." He turned to Michael and Lisa. "I'll finish the paperwork this week. Have it ready next week. See you in a few days. We have a Boxing Day party on Alcatraz and then we're having a few friends over Friday. See you sometime Saturday."

"Good night," Lisa said. She stepped in to hug Cody. "Thanks again for the wonderful painting."

"My pleasure."

"Hope you're able to stay sober at those fancy parties."

"Me, too."

"Just talked to the Marin guys. They'll be here at eight o'clock. Good luck."

Lisa walked Pam and Michael to their car, looked at the darkness of the road after their taillights disappeared around the corner. It was quiet. No engines, no headlights.

The kitchen table was clear, Hidalgo and Quinn had cleaned everything. Zack sat at the table, an iron in hand, pressing it into one piece of Miki's paper at a time.

"I like your friends," Lisa said.

"They liked you."

"You can never be sure about how these things will go."

"But in the end, it's over, and regardless of the dead bodies scattered around, life goes on for the living."

"That's pretty dark."

"I know. Sorry."

Lisa knew better than to dig into this one. "Thank you for hanging my white board."

"I'm liking the looks of Pious Rebel headquarters. Cody's painting is amazing. Feels just right in there for you."

"I like it. Gave up my office downtown yesterday. Want to spend more time here."

"Love that idea. Let's do lunch." He smiled.

She gave him a soft jab on his shoulder. "You're funny."

"Sometimes. I'm working on it." He pushed the ironed pile of Miki's papers toward her.

"You want a turkey sandwich?" she asked.

"I've been waiting all day for one," he said.

"You want everything on it?"

"Depends on your definition of everything."

"Sliced wheat bread. Mayo, a thin layer of mustard. Evenly spread stuffing on one side. Cranberry sauce on the other. Mostly white meat in the middle."

"All of that, except I want all dark meat on mine. No mustard."

Lisa grabbed two paper plates, took a dill pickle from the fridge, sliced it in quarters, two on Zack's plate, two on hers, a pile of Kettle Chips, and the sandwiches. She sat in the easy chair as he rebuilt the fire. "Alexa, play Tchaikovsky's *Nutcracker.*"

"Playing *Nutcracker Suite* by Pyotr Ilyich Tchaikovsky."

"Alexa, softer," Lisa said, biting into her sandwich

Zack sat next to her, picked up his plate, took a bite of pickle. They listened quietly to the music for a few minutes until the first break. "What do you think the second half of your life will look like?"

She choked on her turkey. "Gee. Just a light little question."

He laid his head back on the couch, stared at the angel on top of the tree. "Okay. Let's start a little easier. Where'd you find that angel?

"I went to Ferrari's after lunch yesterday."

"It's very nice. Okay. Enough with the foreplay. The second half of your life. The camera's rolling." He put his fists up to his face, pretended to be a camera.

"Are we assuming my life's half over? That I'll live to be seventy-four?"

"Give or take a couple of years. But that's close enough."

She pulled one of the blankets over her shoulders. "How about if we start with Cody. The first half of my life has been filled by her, in every imaginable way. I would like it if the second half would be less so." Lisa rocked her head on her shoulders. "What else? My blog work could be huge in the second half. Not the whole time. But for now. That I will meet new friends there. Real friends who care. That Alice's books will become widely read."

"Any kids?"

"Are you trying to determine if I might be a proper host for your offspring?" She shouldn't have said that. Idiot.

He laughed, still had the ability to do so. "No. I'm done with that, but wondered if you were."

"Honestly, I've never considered it. Knew I had no interest in Ryan as a father, nor G. And for that matter, no interest in me as a mother. Alice was my role model, and that was kind of a failure."

"What about your life on this property?"

"I'm truly hoping that hemp seeds are the salvation. If we had one or two crops a year, that would be fantastic. Keep things just as they are. Pay off Ben and Cody. Get them out of here as soon as possible. Wouldn't need to think about splitting up the property."

"What else? By the time you're seventy-four."

"I can't plan that far out."

"What have you missed in your life that you're itching to do? To accomplish"

She couldn't have this part of the conversation with him. No way she could tell him what she was really missing. Every time he recognized a need in her life, he fulfilled it. A daybed. Hanging a white board. Giving her books to read. Reading to her. If she opened up, was completely honest, he'd try to fulfill every need, make an unnatural attempt to make her happy. She knew he would. Had to avoid it. Had to keep it clean, at a distance, away from her chest and circulatory system. Keep it in the head, between the ears, put it in the hands of Lydia Davis and Richard Powers and maybe even Pirsig, if she could get to it. Or Alice, leave it all up to Alice and her ever-expanding audience. Five books with advance royalties, and she predicted there were five more waiting in the workshop. "I believe I will be writing blog posts until I die. Fingers on keyboard, or if they freeze with Parkinson's or something else, I'll turn on dictation and speak into a Word document, have an assistant convert them, publish them. Make sure all the threads are current, one for each of the ten books. The Holy Grail. *The Good Dough. Rocks and Rolls.* And the geodes. Almost forgot them. I need to get them out of my room. Display them." She stopped herself, could see him now in her room taking care of it for her. She didn't want that. "But, Zack. I need to do that myself. I appreciate your attentiveness, but how's a woman supposed to take care of business if others do everything for her?"

He sulked a bit, chin to chest, but nodded. "Sorry. I know what you mean. Since Becs died it's this thing I've slipped into. Making up for lost time with her. Imagining that every good deed I accomplish is really all for her. I imagine it can be a little suffocating. A little like what you suffered at the hands of Gregory."

"Oh, nothing at all like that. Trust me. Nothing. His stranglehold was more about limiting the oxygen intake. Thought control. Yours is nothing like that. Comes from a whole different place."

Zack took their plates to the kitchen, wrapped the food and placed it back in the fridge. "I'm beat," he said as he walked down the hall. "See you in the morning."

"No Lydia tonight?" She was ready to lift the two blankets off the couch and carry them to his bedroom.

"I don't think so. Need to crash. Big day tomorrow."

That's right. She had forgotten about the Marin crew. "Good night. Merry Christmas."

43

THURSDAY
12-26-19

It was another one of those nights, the non-dreams active, Turks and Caicos barking, reminding her she was not completely asleep, that this new parade of images and floats were not figments, but were real translations of her day's activities. On one float covered in violets, she stood at a dais, reading an acceptance speech, on behalf of Alice, Best First Book. "Thank you so much for this. The whole family appreciates your support and recognition. Alice, Cody, and I are honored to accept this award on behalf of Alice's ten novels." There was a float for each novel, complete with cinnamon rolls and geodes and large machines that kneaded ingredients together and colorful iced muffins, mountains of cookies, the titles painted by Cody on plaques mounted to the frames, except for the final five floats, whose titles were blank. After the book floats, there was one covered in black squat pots full of hemp plants, another with a two-hundred-pound Diestel turkey, followed by a Pious Rebel float, Cody's hand-painted sign prominently placed in the middle of Bianca's lap, Bianca waving at Alice's fans, who crowded around the float, wanted a fleeting touch. Two more in the distance, rolling into view, Cody and Ben with red gloves covering their fists, standing in a boxing ring on Alcatraz, and the final one with Zack perched across Gregory's bike, arms crossed over his chest, wearing his Susan Hayes handwoven jacket, trying to look tough, a smile leaking out. The dogs barked. Eloise jumped up onto the last float, landed on Lisa's chest, snuggled up to her chin.

Lisa walked to the front room holding Eloise, looked out the window expecting to see bikers and headlights. It was Ben and Cody pulling out of the driveway, on their way to San Francisco. She opened a can of salmon, scooped it into a bowl, walked into the laundry room where the food bins stood next to the stacked washer and dryer. She propped open the lid, stuck her hands into the Iams, not knowing exactly what to look for, how far it would be buried. About eight inches down she felt a rope, pulled on it slowly, and a heavy-duty black trash bag appeared.

In the bathroom she stepped on the scale, 126 pounds. She lifted the bag, 161 pounds. The door to Zack's bedroom was open, his bed empty. Babe was still in the driveway. He must have stayed local for his run, maybe up into Nisene Marks. By the time she had shoveled the Iams out of the bins into a wheelbarrow and replaced the bag of pot on the bottom, reloaded it, she was sweaty, smelled like dog food, climbed into the shower in Zack's room. She was toweling off as he entered. In the walk-in closet, he slipped out of his jogging shorts and wet t-shirt, and she stepped out of the room. She hadn't seen the sculpted curves of a man's buttocks in a while, almost three months. And Zack's were nice, different than Gregory's, which pooched out a bit, or Ryan, who was small and flat. No, Zack's were just right. She laughed, felt like Goldilocks.

When Zack walked into the kitchen, Lisa handed him a plate of food. This was the better answer, better than the one she had posed last night. She felt bad about hurting his feelings. It was okay for him to do nice things for her, but only if she did nice things for him. She had been so steeped in Pious Rebel and the property and digging out of the messes and mysteries Gregory had left behind, she sometimes forgot about being nice, thoughtful, doing something for others just for the sake of doing it. She wanted to go outside and take the hose to Babe, clean her up for him. Forget that, too cold.

"Thanks," Zack said.

"My pleasure."

She brought two glasses and a bottle of orange juice to the table, sat next to him. He filled their glasses, raised his to hers, said, "Happy Boxing Day." They touched glasses.

"And happy hemp-seeds day." They clinked again.

Zack looked at his watch. "They should be here soon."

"Long trip from Marin."

"What are you up to today?" Zack asked.

"I'm going to spend all day in the workshop. Headquarters."

He smiled, took a sip of orange juice. "I like you calling it headquarters rather than workshop. Makes it your place now."

"This whole day will be dedicated to Pious Rebel. I have lots of reading to do. I'll start book five today, read the next chapters of *The Overstory*, maybe get into *Zen*, but it's taken a back seat."

·   ·   ·

The first truck pulled into the driveway, followed by three more.

Zack jumped up. "Thanks for breakfast." He put his hand against her back as he left.

Lisa carried her computer to headquarters, stopped by the greenhouse on the way. One truck contained the ninety-nine plants and pots. One had the fertilized soil. Another full of lumber, and the fourth carrying the light fixtures and watering system. The Marin guys and Zack were removing all the old growing pots, ripping out the tables with hammers and crowbars. It felt a little like personal surgery, thousands of days of her life sitting in a pile.

Zack came over. "You okay with this?"

"Don't have much choice, do I? But I'm good."

"I'll take the wood to the incinerator. These guys will haul the old pots away."

"Why rip out the tables?"

"They want everything clean and fresh. Control is what they're looking for."

"Yeah. Aren't we all. Have fun!"

In the swivel chair she spun. Eyes closed. Like a ride at the Boardwalk, another place Gregory had never taken her. She stood up, grabbed a green marker, wrote *Visit the Boardwalk* on the white board.

With a blue marker she wrote *Boxing Day*, drew a line under it, started a bulleted list:

- *Vet Pious Rebel comments*
- *Check out new posts to threads*
- *Read 100 pages of This Site Uses Cookies*
- *Read two chapters from The Overstory:*
  - *Adam Appich*
  - *Ray Brinkman and Dorothy Cazaly*
- *Make turkey sandwiches for Zack and the crew*
- *"Maybe" read some Zen*
- *Think about another stay at LOMB*
- *Buy a machete*

It had been a while since she had been so organized, usually only around planting season. Time for Pious Rebel. Quinn, Walter, and Hidalgo had all visited the site late last night. *Rocks and Rolls* continued its surge. She wished she knew more about the math behind how that happened. Permutations and the reproductive calculations of rabbits in captivity. Facebook and Instagram and Twitter had all figured out the formula. She had lucked into it with Bianca, Alice, the manuscripts. Being in an organizational state of mind, she texted Pam.

Need any help with the memorial plans?

Within seconds Pam replied:

All set. Zoccoli's is catering it. I have a classical guitarist named Armando who will play music from 6:00 to 7:00. Michael will make a short speech, as will Zack. You don't have to say anything unless you want to. Lisa responded. Thanks. What about photos? Pam wrote, Scanned photos from albums. Blew them up at Kinko's.

The next text went to Michael.

Good luck today! Have some fun!

RockHound was back.

Fantastic assortment of new geode photos! Went to Dugway Geode Beds in Juab County, Utah, for a few days, with wife, EverybodyMustGetStones. So much for gender neutrality and mystery. Or maybe not. By the way, a good friend of ours owns the rock-and-gem shop on Front Street in Santa Cruz.

> We're coming down tomorrow (Friday) to visit. Any interest
> in meeting us for lunch?

This was new. First time a follower had wanted to make it live rather than virtual. Her first inclination was to say No. Keep things safe, at a distance. Was he really married to EverybodyMustGetStones? Maybe he was both, had created a second account to help carry out his scheme. But maybe not. He seemed to genuinely know more about geodes than any of her followers, had showed the most interest in the photos. Had a *U. S. Encyclopedia of Geodes*! Even if handmade. She smiled. She could be selective, keep it within her control, the meeting place, invite someone to join her, someone big like Zack, or someone assertive like Bianca, or just someone with brains and savvy like Pam.

She wrote and erased her reply three times, settled on:

> Sounds good. How about the Crow's Nest at noon? He
> replied, That works for us. What do you look like?

A safety valve would make sense. Some way to view them from a distance, walk away if needed.

> I'll be wearing a brown fedora. How about you? The response
> was quick. We are both 56 years old. Both with short brown
> hair fading into grey. I have a short beard, greyer than my
> hair. Oops! Probably a male. See you then.

Her first request for backup went to Bianca, who responded:
You can't be doing that! No fraternizing with the followers. First rule of blogging. Let me check my calendar. I'll get back to you.
To be safe, she texted Pam who said:
Are you crazy? Online wackos? I'll be there.
With the fifth manuscript box now sitting on the desk, she reached in and scooped *This Site Uses Cookies* out of its cradle. Lisa was curious about the title, given that Alice had never owned a computer, wouldn't have known about how websites use cookies. The double meaning was clear, but that Alice knew nothing about one of the meanings wasn't.

Written in 2008. Lisa had been living on campus at UCSC, twenty-five years old, majoring in literature, having dropped the double-major in Psychology. She still loved the Psych classes when she had room in her schedule for one, especially the Abnormal Psychology workshop she took because a man she liked was taking it. He didn't last long, but the class fascinated her. She hadn't even thought of Cody during the first three quarters of the class. It was when she learned about the "Four D's" that something clicked — devious, dysfunction, distress, and danger. By the time the professor had shared multiple examples of each, and why they occur, a clear image of Cody was emblazoned in her brain, and it disturbed her. She didn't want that, didn't need that.

Her love of reading far surpassed that of Psychology, so she focused on literature, reading everything she could, but flailed as a student, missing classes, spending more time up the coast at beaches and hiking up Big Creek in Swanton. It's where she'd met Ryan, at the base of the first falls, a glass-like pool, dammed up by a fallen redwood, the whole area covered in wildflowers and moss. She hadn't seen him at first, had set her backpack on the tree, removed her clothes, ready to jump in when his head popped out of the water. They stared at each other, both in shock. "Join me?" he had asked. "Why not?" she answered.

It felt strange, knowing this was the first page of the fifth book of five. She'd check out the new boxes soon. At least get a clue if they continued with Celia and William at the bakery, or if it was a whole new set of characters in a different part of the country, another chunk of the world. It excited her to think about it, so many possibilities. But she was more excited to dig into *Cookies*, see where it took her, find out if Celia graduated, what came next for all of them.

> It was no Tony statuette for best costume design for a musical comedy, but rather an Associate of Arts certificate proving Celia had successfully completed coursework at Berkeley Community College. William and Amelia sat in the front row, standing and cheering and waving their arms as the dean handed Celia her certificate in accounting. As she looked over at William and Amelia, smiled and waved, she thought she saw a familiar face, a man standing in the back. When she climbed off the stage, looked in his direction, he was gone.
>
> She'd thought about taking the sewing classes, but that wouldn't be much help in a bakery. Accounting, however, would. She could take over the books, save some

money by doing it herself rather than farming it out to the old guy who was retiring this year. Profits were soaring, costs were increasing. Mirdival and Tragones were gone, had moved back to San Francisco and landed positions with high-end restaurants. But their experiments had proven fruitful. They crafted a secret cookie-dough recipe that everybody loved. William had already established a foothold in East Bay delis and chains with his iced muffins, but the cookies were better, easier to make in large quantities, easier to package, and easier to distribute.

Amelia was fifteen, playing soccer and volleyball, brought friends home for baked goods. Boys were in the picture now, but nothing serious. Celia helped her keep her head screwed on, found herself talking with her about the delicate balance between stability and love, the sacrifices that come with both. Amelia asked her one day if she still loved William. 'Of course I do!' came the automatic answer, but it was a question that would haunt her for most of the next year.

Celia was accepted into Cal State University, East Bay, and started with a full load the first semester. Justin had disappeared again. After the first package had arrived a few years earlier, he had followed with six or seven more. Without fail, they included three gifts, neatly wrapped in newspaper. Secretly, Celia had saved the newspapers, shoved them away in an empty flour bag, hid them behind cases of oil. After his latest disappearance, going on six months this time, Celia dug out the flour bag, sat on the back porch while William was in the kitchen, Amelia at school, read every newspaper in the order in which they'd been received. Ireland. Scotland. South America. Italy. Utah. Mexico. What a life he was having!

Lisa brought the manuscript and her cell phone to the daybed, crawled under the blankets, set the alarm for eleven thirty, and went back to *Cookies* until the alarm blasted her out of a soft snooze. On her way by the greenhouse, she saw Zack and the boys kneeling over pots, shoving plants into the soil.

They applauded her when she showed up with a platter of turkey sandwiches, spears of dill pickles, a box of stoned-wheat crackers. There was a red toothpick stuck into one of the sandwiches. She looked at Zack. "For you. Dark meat." She understood why he did it, why he was being so helpful. It felt good. An ironic twist to the *all-about-me* syndrome. Stroke others and you stroke yourself.

•   •   •

Back at headquarters, not ready to jump into "Adam Appich" in The Overstory, she grabbed her keys, hopped in the Prius, headed down to Ace Hardware. In the back corner she found a wall full of machetes. She knew nothing about them. One by one, she set them in her palm. It was all about feel. She swung each one a few times, saw the staff at the front watching her in a circular mirror. The first couple of swings were light, but soon she was taking a full-on baseball swing. She settled on an eighteen-inch Fiskars model. She trusted Fiskars in scissors, why not machetes? Still feeling guilty about making Zack feel bad, still feeling the need to overcompensate, she went by Many Hands Gallery in Capitola, found a small assemblage angel by an artist named Marlena Telfor. She placed it in the hidey-hole behind the back seat, went over to Gayle's, picked up two twice-baked potatoes, Francese rolls, a small key-lime pie, a bottle of lemon poppy-seed dressing, and a dozen jumbo shrimp.

After dropping off the dinner supplies in the kitchen, she put on a pair of old gardening boots, walked past the workshop to the thick underbrush, machete in hand. She slashed at branches, shooters. It was harder than she thought. Her muscles had atrophied in the past few months, harvest over and less physical work to attend to. Fifty feet into the project she stopped, went back over the trail, brought the slash to the incinerator, tossed it into the flames Zack had already stoked for the old table lumber. The trail was starting to look good. Another goal, she thought. Fifty feet a day. She needed to find G's old free weights, bulk up a bit. She stopped back by headquarters, wrote *50 feet a day* on the white board.

A hot shower shook the grime and potential ticks loose. She picked up two ten-pound weights from G's closet and brought them into the living room. She heard one of the truck engines rev. Out the window she saw all four Marin guys load into the cab and head down Porter Gulch. Zack was still in the greenhouse.

Butter lettuce, watermelon radishes, endive, and spinach provided the base of her salads. On top she layered slivered almonds, onion rings, green peas, artichoke hearts, crowned with a circle of jumbo shrimp. The poppy-seed dressing was too rich for her, needed to be cut with oil and vinegar. She shook it up and set it in a small pitcher Gregory had traded for. She reached into one of the kitchen cabinets where they had hidden the wine from Cody, found Quinn's bottle of 2013 Rhys Vineyards "Horseshoe" Syrah. She didn't know wines, but this bottle looked special. She'd need to send Quinn a note on Pious Rebel telling her they'd opened it.

Tonight was a placemat-and-cloth-napkin kind of night. She set the salads, dressing, Francese rolls, wineglasses, and wine on the table.

Zack came in and saw the spread. "You expecting someone?"

"That I am."

He hurried down the hall and she heard the shower go on and off. When he returned, he had his jacket and a beanie on.

"Where you going?" she asked.

"I'll just head to town so you can have some privacy."

"It's *you* I'm expecting."

He looked at the bottle of wine. "Is that the Rhys Quinn brought?"

"It is."

"What's the occasion?" He wriggled out of his jacket, tossed his cap to the couch.

"A quiet dinner."

"How nice."

They took their seats.

"Alexa, play Edward Elgar's' 'Salut d'Amour.'"

"Playing Edward Elgar's' 'Salut d'Amour.'"

"Alexa, softer. Alexa, softer."

Zack lifted the bottle, filled their glasses.

"Can I ask a favor of you?" Zack nodded. "Have I told you about RockHound?"

"No. But I've seen his posts."

"I have a private discussion going on with him. He and his wife are coming to town tomorrow and we're meeting at the Crow's Nest for lunch. I'm wanting folks to be there with me. Just in case."

Zack smiled. "Didn't we go to school with him?"

Lisa wrinkled her face, hadn't known Zack, much less gone to school with him. "What are you talking about?"

"Sorry. It's a thing Becs' mother and I used to do. Just in case. Sounds like Justin Case. You know, 'Didn't we go to school with him?'"

"Got it. I like it." In fact she loved it. Alice would have loved it.

"But to answer your question, I don't think I should leave Ben's friends alone. I have too much to learn if I'm going to be a proper tender of the crop."

"That's okay. I've got options. By the way, where'd those guys go?"

"Down to Zameen's for dinner. Too crazy to drive all the way back to Marin tonight and come back in the morning. They have sleeping bags."

"Can I ask another favor?"

"Certainly."

"Will you read to me again tonight?"

He tilted his head, twisted his lips. "Could be dangerous. If we reach the bottom of this bottle."

She laughed. "I have a machete. And I'll bring the blankets."

Zack took a sip from his glass. "This wine is way too good for a stranger to bring to a Christmas party."

"Lucky us. Thank you, Quinn." She swirled the wine in her glass. "Would you sleep with her?" Another sip.

He rocked back in his chair, laughed at the ceiling. "I don't think there would be much sleeping going on. What a specimen. Like she was built in a test tube. The result of years of experiments."

Lisa nodded. "I know. Smart, too. Right up your alley. The anti-racism work."

"Yeah. All the right pieces are there. But there's something a little off."

"Seriously? I didn't catch the off part."

"It's hard to explain. Maybe like a Rubik's Cube. Getting that one last surface to match. Solid colors all around."

"So this is about perfection?"

"Not exactly. The Stepford wives come to mind. But that isn't exactly it, either. Preprogrammed. A distance. Part of her feels unreachable."

"You know, all the years I spent with Gregory, we never once had a conversation like this."

"He had his strengths and weaknesses. Like we all do."

Lisa nodded. "What about Cody?"

"What about her?"

"Would you sleep with her?" Lisa felt the wine warming her cheeks, racing around a track inside her head.

"Didn't we already have this discussion?"

"No. That time I asked if you'd date her. This is different."

"But the same answer. Absolutely not! First off, rarely in my life have I simply slept with someone. Maybe in my teens a few times. I'm kind of weird this way. Context has to be built. A whole world inside my imagination, predicting the future, almost living it in advance. The minute Cody opens her mouth, that whole world is shattered. Way too selfish, at least what appears to be selfishness. Really, more that she's way too fragile and insecure and takes advantage of folks."

"I understand. What about Pam?"

"No. I mean, I could envision the last color dropping into place, but Michael would be there, preventing it. No. I wouldn't do that to Michael."

Lisa emptied her wineglass, swished it around her tongue. "What about me?"

Zack shook his head lightly, a faint smile trying to form. "We can't have this conversation."

"Why not?"

"It's not time."

"Read to me, then."

44

FRIDAY
12-27-19

A T FIVE A.M. SHE FOUND ELOISE PERCHED ON ZACK'S BACK, his face buried in one of G's pillows. She had fallen asleep so fast, left poor Lydia reeling at a lack of attention. Still wearing clothes and shoes from last night, Lisa walked past Turks and Caicos, opened the headquarters, removed the *Cookies* manuscript, headed back to the house. She heard a chorus of snores coming from the greenhouse. Poking her head inside, she saw the ninety-nine pots lined up in three rows, perched on top of freshly built tables, ninety-nine plants pushing their way upward. It stirred something in her, that this had been her domain, the master gardener, Gregory's charge. This was going to work, without her. Zack would take care of the girls, coax them into their outfits, watch them thrive and flourish. Life was good, at least becoming better. Becoming more than just bearable. Looking around the greenhouse, she felt a huge sense of accomplishment. Couldn't remember any disappointments in the last few days.

Back under the covers next to Zack she found her place in *Cookies*. Eloise had shifted, cuddled up behind his thighs. "My turn," she whispered to herself. She read out loud in a soft voice intended to slowly inhabit his dreams, pull him into her world, Alice's world.

"William had aged poorly. Approaching his fiftieth birthday, he had diabetes, no cartilage in either knee, weighed over two hundred fifty pounds, and hadn't made love with Celia in over a year. More accurately, she hadn't made love with him. Amelia was in grad school at UCLA, studying modern dance and costume design. After Celia got her BA from California College of the Arts, she had bought Amelia a sewing machine after she Amelia took to it, was a natural, made all her own clothes, all her own gifts for friends and lovers. With a little jealousy and a lot of pride, Celia knew it would be Amelia standing up on that stage in New York City grasping her Tony.

"In addition to handling the increasingly complicated books for the bakery, as a CPA, Celia now had fifty clients whose taxes and books she handled. Word had spread about her efficient and calm demeanor, especially among the women entrepreneurs who were heading up businesses and firms all over the East Bay. They trusted her, never felt demeaned by her, and she brought them freshly baked cookies that were better than any they had tasted.

"The cookies had changed their lives. William needed more space, so they opened two more branches, one on Fourth Street among the other designer stores, another in Emeryville by the Ikea building. Justin occasionally injected himself into their lives, maybe once a year a package appearing at the original bakery, where they still lived on the second floor. Wrapped in newspaper, three separate gifts, until Amelia went away to college, as if he knew, as if he was tracking her life, then there were just the two gifts, still an offering to William of cutlery and other kitchen tools, what Celia felt had become an attempt to assuage his guilt, the second gift another geode, now for her, one more to place on the bookshelf William had built, almost full now, room for a few more. She flattened the wrinkles out of the newspaper. It was The Daily Californian, the

student-run paper at Cal. She didn't think he had ever
been this close. Maybe that one time at her graduation.
That could have been him, hiding in the back, gone before
she could find him, hug him, gone before William would see
him, seek him out for another reason. He'd be forty by
now, more than half a life gone, half a life drifting in
and out of hers, theirs.

"The latest gift had arrived last week. She placed
William's package on his work desk, carried the geode
upstairs to Amelia's old room, set it on the bookshelf, sat
on her bed, stared at the Bernina sewing machine, the
shelves full of materials and buttons, the place where
she and Amelia had forged a strong mother-daughter
friendship. She had work to do, papers to file,
spreadsheets to complete, customers who were waiting, but
she didn't care, lay back into Amelia's bed. At what cost
had this stability come? She and William had more money
now than they could ever spend, and it would continue to
grow. What she had with William could no longer be
classified as love. He was a good man, a friend, someone
she could talk to, an excellent father. His employees
loved him, he loved them. But it no longer shined, didn't
reach out and grab her by the throat.

"She got up, pulled some fabric out of a bin, buttons,
metal zippers, sat at the sewing machine and went to
work. With no idea what size Justin might be now,
assuming he was still a large, she proceeded to make him
what she imagined to be the perfect jacket for a lover of
geodes. Pockets inside and out that could fit multiple
specimen sizes. It was lined with fleece that was perfect
for winter treks to deserts, a lining that could be zipped
out and removed for summer jaunts over the Atlantic. Now
to hide it, slip it between clothes Amelia had left behind
in her closet. Now to find him, drape it over his
shoulders, hug him, kiss his cheek."

Lisa's voice trailed off. What had Alice been thinking when she
wrote this? How much of this was pure fiction?

Zack rolled over. "Don't stop," he said. Lisa sighed deeply. "How's
she going to find him? How far into the story are we?"

She rolled over and kissed the back of Zack's hand. That 'we' popping up again. She loved it. "I don't know. She might not. I like the clue about the newspaper at Cal." She jumped off the bed, Eloise scrambling to the floor. "I need to go make breakfast for the crew."

"I'll help."

They carried platters of scrambled eggs, fried potatoes, toast, blackberry jam, and orange juice to the greenhouse.

"Breakfast, boys!" Zack yelled. They rolled around in their bags, found their way out, grabbed plates and forks, thanked them.

"You're welcome. What are you working on today?" Lisa said.

"Watering system," one of them said. "Done by tonight. We'll finish up tomorrow, with the lighting and security."

"Security?"

"We'll have the whole place wired, so if anybody who shouldn't be is messing around out here, you'll be notified by cell phone, and bells and whistles shouting into the air."

"That's pretty cool."

"It's very cool."

"Thanks for all your hard work." She pulled Zack aside. "I'm going to my office downtown to get some things, then to the Crow's Nest."

"Have fun with your fan club."

"You're funny. Have fun with yours."

. . .

The line at the Buttery was long, folks stocking up for Casual Friday parties. More muffins for her. What the office mates preferred. She bought an extra bag of zucchini muffins, set them against the wall at Lenz, even though no one was there yet. Inside the office she set the box on the receptionist's desk. "I need to ask you something."

"Okay," she said, as she plucked a blueberry muffin from the box.

"This is embarrassing. I've been here so long, and I don't think we ever got introduced, and I don't know your name."

From across the room, Bianca cackled. "Oh, my god! That is precious!"

The receptionist cocked her head. "It's Lonnie."

"Thank you. Sorry."

"By the way. I can be there for lunch," Bianca said.

"Oh, good. Thank you."

With the door to her office closed, she sat down in the Grey Bears chair, the Outdoor World and Lenz Arts walls providing their continual backdrop. She saw Lela and Art approach the bag, hand a Taco Bell burrito back and forth. Cars stopped at the light, backing up River Street. The orchid woman again, a yellow one in her hands this time, waving at her through the window, big smile on her face. Lisa loved seeing her, looked forward to seeing her walk by, wondering about her mission. Then the two bells ringing at the door, soft knuckles tapping.

Lisa opened it, the woman standing there, outstretched hands.

"For you," she said. "Happy Friday."

Lisa stared at her for just a minute, thinking she was the reincarnation of Alice, or the ghost of Alice inhabiting this sweet woman's body, before she took the orchid.

The woman leaned in, spoke into Lisa's ear, "I've been watching you. You deserve this."

Lisa put her hand on the woman's shoulder. "I've often wondered where you took these."

"Just where they're needed, dear. Just where they're needed most." She turned around and walked out.

"How sweet is that?" Bianca said.

"Oh, wow! I've been wanting this for so long." She wiped away one tear, shook it off, rolled-up the T-chart and the three wall hangings and carried them to her car as Bianca brought the orchid.

They drove separately to the Crow's Nest. Pam was waiting at a table overlooking the harbor.

"So we're triple-teaming him?"

"Right. And I asked Zack, too, but he thought he should stay home with the greenhouse guys."

"How's that going?"

"Looks good. Potential."

Bianca said, "Do we need to strategize before they get here?"

"I don't think so. Just an avid follower."

As they looked at the menu, an employee with a black tie and white shirt approached the tables around them, phone in hand, asking questions of the guests. He made his way to their table, said, "Sorry for the interruption. Are any of you associated with Pious Rebel?"

"That would be me," Lisa said.

"This call's for you."

"Hello," Lisa said. "Oh, no. That's terrible! I'll check my calendar when I get home. I'll get back to you online. Okay. Good luck."

"You're kidding me! He's bailing. What a putz," Bianca said.

"Their car broke down on the summit. He didn't know my cell phone number."

Pam shook her head. "Who even drives cars that break down these days?"

"He wants to reschedule for Monday."

"I'm showing a condo. I can't make," Bianca said.

"Neither can I," Pam said. "I'm in Los Gatos all day."

"Drop this guy. He's a loser." Bianca flagged the waiter. "We're in kind of a hurry. Can we order, please?"

After ordering, Bianca said, "While we're here, can we talk about Pious Rebel?"

Lisa was wishing she hadn't touched the T-chart today, hadn't lauded herself yesterday about accomplishments, now suffering from the fallout of being stood up by RockHound, a meeting she hadn't really wanted to take. "What's to talk about?"

"Oh, how about over ten thousand followers? How about twenty different threads going? How about setting policy about dealing with wackos like RockHound? There's tons of work to do. The ad management takes a few hours a week, and to do it right will take more like ten. Then there's the vetting. That's huge. And now the whole Alice-and-publishing angle. We need a little task management here. And to talk about compensation."

Lisa turned to Pam. "Have you thought about what I asked you?"

"I have."

"And?"

"I'd be happy to help. But as Bianca said, we need to be clear about who's doing what. And I don't need any compensation."

Bianca finished chewing a forkful of salmon. "I need compensation. What are you willing to work on, Pam?"

"My field is marketing. I could take that off your hands. I could do those ten hours a week."

"That would be fantastic! I have to go on my site a few times a day and vet. I'll do Pious Rebel at the same time. Lisa, that leaves you dealing directly with followers if you want. And with the publisher. If you give me copies of the other books, I'll have them digitized so you can post them when ready. And of course, you're going to need to do half the vetting as well. And maybe we just make some decisions about the folks we predict don't need vetting. Let them in directly. If we do that, we may need a volunteer or two willing to read every post and get back to us if needed."

"That all sounds good to me. Zack is reading everything already. I could mention it to him. And he wouldn't charge us."

"I like the 'us,'" Bianca said.

"Me, too," Lisa said. She turned to Pam, "How was Michael's first day?"

"He finished half his dinner, went to bed at seven, slept twelve hours straight. Not even getting up to pee. I think he likes it. The legitimacy. He's got responsibilities, but not with a capital 'R', as in not having to go to jail."

"Hey!" Bianca said. "How'd you all like Quinn?"

"Quite statuesque. Polished," Lisa said.

"Yeah. Like Adonis or Aphrodite."

"I liked her choice of wine."

•　　•　　•

Lisa had not spent any time driving around Santa Cruz since she'd lived here. Now was a good time. She drove along the coast, past the house at the south end of Twin Lakes Beach, the one that had been pink until being recently upgraded to white. It had sold to a Silicon Valley couple for four million dollars. When Alice had brought her and Cody down for day trips from Berkeley, she would stop in the parking lot, engine running, stare at the house, muse to herself, "Someday I'm going to live in that house." She hadn't remembered Alice dreaming or hoping much in her life. More of a get-it-done person, living in the now rather than in some embellished future. But she had done so a half-dozen times in her life in this parking lot.

As she passed Black's Beach and the Cove, the nunnery on the cliff, Pleasure Point and the Hook, she remembered all the places Alice would point out, make up stories about, characters who sprang from her head and into theirs. They'd end up in Aptos at the cement ship, sit on the beach in front of it eating egg-salad and tuna sandwiches, wondering how cement could float. Alice shared another story. It had to do with mixing the cement with sparkling water instead of regular water, so the bubbles would create thousands of air pockets, and the heavy boat would float easily.

Lisa found herself parked in front of the boat, a semblance of its former self, eroding, slipping away slowly. She worked her way across the freeway to Soquel Drive, ignored the turn up her road, and proceeded to Soquel, where she made her way to Land of Medicine Buddha. At the facility she parked, got out, found a quiet spot on a dense trail, dropped into her *Qi Gong* pose, completed the full routine.

•   •   •

By the time she got home, one of the trucks was gone again. Zack had left a note on the kitchen counter.

Having dinner with the boys at that new Bad Animal place downtown. I'll bring you something if you like. Check out their online menu. Text me if you see something specific. Or tell me you're good, or just ignore this whole note.

Different tone for Zack. Felt like he was still reacting to her comments the other night. Trying to dance with her without stepping on her toes.

The menu was rather avant-garde, what with the rabbit pâté and chicken-liver mousse. She sent him a text.

Thanks for the offer. I'll take the ricotta gnocchi. And the smoked almonds.

The landline rang. She left it alone. "Hello. Goldenrod here. Just a reminder, we'll see you Tuesday at five to pay our condolences, and collect what we're owed."

On Google she found dozens of Goldenrod references, none in California. She switched to Pious Rebel, saw the messages from RockHound and EverybodyMustGetStones. She read the wife's first — or supposedly the wife's.

> We were so sorry to miss you today. Our stupid old woody is
> so old. But my husband loves to take it on our treks to the
> desert. We'd love to meet you Monday at the Crow's Nest.
> Best salad bar in town. If you're worried about who we are,
> talk to our friend at the rock shop in Santa Cruz. He'll vouch for
> us. Then to RockHound's post. I could give you my real name
> and you'd be able to find me online, know I'm legit. I apologize
> for my old vehicle. I repair her myself, but with cars whizzing
> by on Highway 17 that was impossible. AAA towed us back to
> Berkeley. We'll bring the Tesla Monday, if you'll still have us.

If she was smart, she'd be done with him, them. Bianca had a sixth sense about this stuff. But the wife knew about the salad bar. And they lived in Berkeley. It also sounded like if she insisted on his name, he'd give it to her. If she went through with this, she'd rather there were no names, anonymity, a meal, a "Hi-how-are-you," a departure, and maybe an online friendship.

It was time to post *Love Muffins*. To save the precious time Bianca referred to, she posted all chapters together, the whole book ready to binge for those who were truly obsessed, for those who preferred to power through to the final page, the last sentence, rather than sleep. She looked through the folders of comments she had not allowed in for one reason or another. There were fewer than a hundred names. All the others looked safe. She switched all those to immediate-posting status. This would save a ton of time. Now it was just the hundred questionables, and the new ones that flowed in every day. This thing was growing huge, but she didn't feel at all like it was a monster. Instead it was the community, the tribe she'd been thinking about forever. The sense of belonging she'd felt missing most of her life.

She wrote a new post.

> By design, I will know very little about you, your lives. And
> likewise, you will know very little about me. You will

occasionally hear some random thoughts from me, to either give you updates about topics that might interest you or things I need to get off my chest and have no other place to vent or rant. Though I'm not really much of a venter or ranter, but you know what I mean. I've just posted book three, Love Muffins, in its entirety. I hope you enjoy it. It gives me pleasure to keep Alice alive and well, if only in our imaginations, escorting us on her ghostly arm, offering advice about how we think and write. I miss her more each day. Have fun!

She hit Publish.

After a quick search for a phone number, she picked up the landline, dialed. "Hi. How late are you open today? Great, I'll be there in fifteen minutes."

This was a crazy time to be heading back into town, the traffic coming back jammed on all the onramps. She found a spot on Front Street, parked, and entered World of Stones and Mystics. She walked up to the counter, said, "I have a strange request."

The proprietor said, "That's good. I have strange things." Lisa looked at the hundreds of jars full of gemstones.

"This is about a person. But before I ask, I don't want to know any names."

"Ah. I know what you want. He called me an hour ago. I don't know what strange game the two of you are playing, but no names. He is the most trustworthy person I know. We went to school together thirty-plus years ago. And his wife is lovely. They have two sons, three or four grandkids by now. I love your website. I just posted something thirty minutes ago. I'm MysticOne."

So many gorgeous things to see in this store. "Thank you for the positive review of the site, and of your friend. I'll just look around for a minute."

"Let me know if I can help."

She could spend a lot of money in here. But she needed to be careful, at least until Peggy sent her advance-payment checks. What she wanted found her. A flash of light bouncing off its surface. An amethyst point for eighty-six dollars.

"I'll take this."

"Excellent choice. Would you like it wrapped?" Lisa remembered the ironed paper from Miki's, which would be appropriate for this gift.

"No thanks. I'm good."

He covered it in white tissue, twisted the ends, dropped it in a small bag with handles. "I hope you, and maybe your nameless friend, come back sometime soon."

"Not a friend, but thanks."

• • •

At home, she walked into Zack's room, placed the amethyst point on top of the Lydia Davis book. It looked good there. "Oh, crap!" she said, hurried down the hall and out to the car, lifted the lid to the hidey-hole, took out the bag from Many Hands Gallery. She set the assemblage angel next to the amethyst point. That was better.

"The drip system is fully functional now. Want to see it?" Zack asked as he walked in the front door.

"I need to eat. I'm starved." She grabbed the bag out of his hand, munched on the almonds as she took the foil off the gnocchi. "What did you have?"

"Sweet-potato pavé and the mussel cassoulet. Good sourdough bread with salted butter."

"This gnocchi's good. Thank you. So, tomorrow we get the lights?"

"And security," Zack said. He walked to the cabinet where the remaining wine was still hidden. "Don't Cody and Ben come back tomorrow?"

"That's what Ben said."

"Shall we drink one of these, hide the rest?" Zack said.

"Are we too spoiled after Quinn's bottle to ever drink wine again?"

"These two I got from Soif for Christmas are pretty good."

"Okay. If you insist. Your pick."

"I insist. The security system they've perfected is pretty cool. I've asked them to connect it to both our cell phones. If somebody's down there messing around, we'll get a ping, and alarms will go off."

"Shouldn't Michael be in on this?"

"It wouldn't help. He lives too far away. We're the front lines. How'd your lunch go? Was he a wacko?"

"Don't know yet. His car broke down and he had to cancel. Rescheduled for Monday."

"Bummer. This package was on the front porch. For you."

She hesitated before she took it, thought about the phone call. "Would you hit the message button on the phone?" Zack pushed and they listened together.

"Wow! Maybe we need two machetes. Let me open that for you, just in case."

Lisa smiled. "Didn't he graduate a couple years ahead of us?"

"Ha, ha." He turned away from her as he opened the box. "A puzzle." He handed it to her.

"I ordered this two weeks before Christmas. For Cody. She used to love puzzles when we were growing up."

"You want to set it up?"

"No. I'm ready for some more Lydia, though."

"You got it," Zack said.

At the bed Lisa removed her shoes, slipped under the blankets, watched him strip to his boxers, reach for the book. He turned around, the amethyst point in one hand, the angel in the other.

She grinned.

"I don't know what to say to you. These are lovely. More than lovely. But it feels a little like mixed messages."

"Not mixed. Just slow, confused, uncertain."

"This amethyst reminds me of the color of a freshly fileted salmon."

"Do you miss being home?"

"Not at all. I've got people who do everything. I don't want to be on the boats anymore. Don't want to be anywhere near that town for now. I like it here. Who knew I'd become a hemp-seed farmer?"

"Read to me," she said, a little too insistently.

45

SATURDAY
12-28-19

Z ACK WAS ALREADY OUTSIDE IN THE GREENHOUSE when she got dressed. She expected the convergence to occur before noon. Michael and Pam were bringing lunch for the boys, wanting to talk about the memorial, other business. Ben and Cody would be rolling in from San Francisco, Ben ready to deal with contracts, the future. Peggy the publisher had left a text saying she and her wife were planning on spending the day in Santa Cruz, and wondered if they could stop by, visit, talk about the future:

I've got the address on the contract. We're early risers, so
sometime before noon.

Lisa hadn't said, "No, we have a lot going on," mainly because she didn't feel like it was an option. The community had expanded. The "us" and "we" stretched its arms across the bay, the mountains, fingered out into worlds she never imagined.

A machete in her hands right now would be nice. She laced up her boots, grabbed a flannel shirt from G's closet, but stopped, threw the shirt onto the bed, then removed all his clothes, his shoes, his jackets, carried them out the front door and tossed them into the back end of Babe. It took her three trips, just enough to get her blood moving. She stopped at headquarters to pick up the machete, headed down her fifty-foot pathway toward salvation and bliss, and hacked, slammed the blade into branches and small trees. She lasted two hours, made a dent twice as far as last time. She still couldn't see Land of Medicine Buddha through the trees, but knew it was there.

Peggy and her wife were the first to show, sitting on the porch as Lisa walked up with the dirty machete.

"What a perfect spot!" Peggy said. "Ann, this is Lisa. Lisa, Ann."

"Pleasure to meet you," Lisa said. She twirled around. "So, this is our chunk of paradise. Greenhouse over there, workshop. Turks and Caicos in the pen. Come on inside."

Lisa invited them to have a seat in the living room, built a fire.

"Oh, we won't stay long," Peggy said. "I just wanted to give you an update on the progress of the books. I brought some sample covers. My photographer found this old-time bakery in San Francisco and got a whole series of great shots. These are the covers for the first three books. Tell me what you think."

Lisa was prepared to hate them, find herself in the uncomfortable position of having to tell Peggy so, expecting disappointment. But she loved all three. Bright, colorful. The photographer had done a great job of capturing the ambiance of life in a bakery.

"I am very impressed," Lisa said.

"Good. Here are a few more images, possibilities for the last two books."

Lisa thumbed through them. "They're all great. I completely trust your judgment."

"Okay. Now let's talk about the rollout. Because of the wild excitement from folks on your blog, I'm expediting production, expect to have an edition of ten thousand copies of the first book available in two weeks."

"What? That's crazy fast."

"Thirty dollars for the hard cover. Nineteen for the paperback. I'm thinking of launch parties here at Bookshop Santa Cruz, and one at Pegasus Books in Berkeley the first week of February."

"Do I need to buy new clothes?"

"I can't answer that. But Berkeley and Santa Cruz are pretty casual audiences. This rollout will be a whirlwind. A book a month from now until June. You ready for this?"

"Do I have a choice?" Eloise jumped into Ann's lap, pushed her paws into her thighs.

"Not really." Peggy smiled. "You are under contract. Just kidding. Don't worry about that stuff. I'm also trying to book Kepler's in Palo Alto, Book Passages in Corte Madera. Maybe even Powell's in Oregon. We'll have to wait and see how the reviews come back. I'm sending twenty copies out to my favorite reviewers. I'll let you know when they return."

"I'm excited," Lisa said. "There's one other thing that may be important for you to know."

"Really? Now you've got me excited, or nervous."

"When I was in Berkeley last week, I found another box of manuscripts, five more."

"What?"

"Don't get too excited yet. I haven't opened them, have no idea what they are."

"Where are they? Let's go look right now."

"No. I have a plan. I'm opening them on New Year's Day. If it looks important, I'll let you know."

"Like immediately, please!"

"Okay. I understand."

"And what about those journals you mentioned?"

"Same thing. Haven't looked yet. Soon."

Peggy stood and Ann followed. "Okay. We're off to Carmel."

Lisa walked them to their car

"Talk to you soon," Peggy said. Lisa thought about the checks, but she didn't want to seem pushy.

•   •   •

Michael and Pam were in the kitchen, assembling smoked-ham-and-provolone sandwiches on Dutch-crunch rolls. Lisa washing the crate of olallieberries Michael had brought. When Cody and Ben arrived, Cody hurried off to the art studio without acknowledging anybody.

"Welcome back, Ben," Lisa said. "How was the Boxing Day party?"

"About five hundred people, a lot of food, a lot of booze. It's just an annual excuse for another party, because nobody remembers why they even have Boxing Day."

"Isn't it British?" Michael asked.

"Pretty much in the beginning. Boxing Day was named for a Christmas box or present. The masters used to give their servants, or slaves, the day off, so they could go home and give their own family Christmas boxes. We brought a box of fireworks. Still have some left if anybody wants to play later." He set the box on the counter.

Pam jumped in. "Not up here. It's way too dense, and illegal."

Ben said, "I know a good lawyer if you get busted."

"Speaking of which, how's it going with the paperwork?" Michael said.

"Slow. Too much partying, but I'll have it ready by next week. Maybe we can look at the parcel map together sometime today. I have a few questions."

"How's Cody doing?" Lisa asked.

"You'll have to ask her yourself. Here she comes."

Barefoot in a change of clothes, Cody came into the kitchen, tossed two berries in her mouth.

"How you doing, Cody?" Pam asked.

"I'm fine! Hunky-dory! Sober as a judge. Who cares, anyway?" The tone was angry, like she was ready to fight if you gave her an opening.

Lisa wondered how much Alice would have hated these clichés, especially out of Cody's mouth. She didn't say anything. The phone rang.

"Don't pick it up!" she hurried to say.

"Goldenrod here. Another reminder, we'll be there to pay respects Tuesday. And expect to be paid what's owed us, with interest."

Michael stopped making sandwiches. "What is that?"

"Fourth one this week. Same message. But the interest part is new."

Pam loaded platters. "Somebody help me carry these out. And there's a cooler in the car with drinks."

"I need to talk to Lisa," Michael said. "Ben, Cody, can you help Pam?" Cody and Pam took the platters, Ben got the cooler.

"What do you think they mean by interest?" Lisa said.

"Who knows. Criminals."

"Right. But so were we."

"*Were* being the key word," Michael said. "We know we owe them the thirty-five pounds, according to Gregory's message."

"Which is still in the dog-food bin, right?"

"Yes. The other ten pounds is now under the cedar flooring in Gregory's closet."

"What are you talking about?"

"You don't know about that?"

Lisa jogged down the hallway, pushed boxes around, found a removable hatch that she had never seen before, lifted it and found another black bag. "Damn it!" She said, kick the closet door and left a dent. She returned to Michael, who was sitting on the couch, sat next to him, said. "Will your brother's surprises every end."

Michael grinned. "Probably not."

"And are these guys going to hurt us?"

"I have no idea. What good does that do them?"

"I don't know. A pound of flesh, for interest," Lisa said. "Maybe we should give them the whole forty-five pounds."

"No way! I need that for my locals."

"You'd rather take care of the friendly locals than get these nasty guys out of our lives?"

"I don't know! I don't know. Goddamn that Gregory for getting us into this mess."

"That we know. Why'd you even take the pot out of the safe?"

"I panicked. The thought of them storming in here at the memorial, taking over the whole property, guns and rifles, I just kind of freaked out."

"Every time I hear one of Goldenrod's phone messages I'm thinking of some greasy guy with a beard down to his navel, chains and knives wrapped around his waist. Freaks me out, too."

Michael leaned forward, put his head in his hands. "Here's what I think we should do. We give Goldenrod the thirty-five pounds, tell him that's all we have left, and see what happens. If we have to, we give up the other ten pounds. Last resort, Pam's got the cash hidden in the car."

"How much?"

"It's up to about fifteen thousand now with the five pounds I've sold the past week."

"Is all that money safe in the car?" Lisa said

"It's hidden in the hidey hole. Nobody knows about the hidey hole."

"Except for the other ten million people who own a Prius."

They sat quietly for a couple of minutes.

"The hemp seeds look good," Michael said.

"Real good." Lisa said. "We'll be fine. How's the job?"

"All the berries I can eat. No, it's good. Nice to know there's a paycheck coming every two weeks. And I can finally get this hernia taken care of?"

"You have a hernia? Why don't I know this?"

"Because we didn't know very much at all about each other until this juggernaut took over."

"Nice word. Mom would have liked you."

"I pretty much like her, too. Glad to see the new book go up. Pam reads it to me when I get home.

"Really?"

"Yeah, why?"

"Being read to is nice."

Cody blasted through the front door, Ben behind her. "That's really impressive out there. You guys aren't going to need *my* money."

"We need it for the balloon payment."

"Not really. Your crop comes in, you pay us off, and we're out of it."

"With ten-percent interest," Michael said

"I don't care about that. I kind of wanted to be your neighbors. Living here on the *commune*."

"Isn't that kind of what you're doing now?" Lisa said.

"Yeah, but I don't own anything."

Pam entered with the empty trays. "It looks so nice out there. Those guys are pros."

"They make me a lot of money," Ben said. "Hope they do you as well. I'm tired. Nap time." He held a hand out to Cody. "Care to join me?"

"I guess so." Still with the pouty tone and pissy face, Lisa noticed.

Lisa stood, picked up her computer. "I'm going out to headquarters for a while." She listened to how she said it, as if it was a real corporate office with elevators and employees and glass windows that looked out over a cityscape.

She stopped at the greenhouse to check the progress. Zack and two of the guys were hanging light fixtures. The other two were wrapping and connecting wires to a master security box.

"Looks good," she said.

Zack saw her. "And I see you got a hundred feet closer to enlightenment this morning."

A big grin on her face. "That I did."

Lisa spent most of the day gathering receipts from the cabinet in headquarters and from Gregory's old office, along with ones she had stored in a box on the kitchen counter. She laid them out on the daybed, the table, and the desk. Finance had never been a strength, mostly because others had stepped in and handled things. Alice had covered the tuition fees and other school-related costs at Berkeley. Ryan had managed the bookshop in Point Reyes Station, and G had managed everything here, if poorly. She could do this. She could do anything. Once tallied — gas bills, pharmacy bills, magazine subscriptions, utilities, Waste Management, the solar panels — the past-due bills were over two thousand dollars, not counting the late property taxes. The taxes would take all the cash Pam had, plus some. It'd probably have to come out of Lisa's advance-payment checks from Peggy.

She found Gregory's checkbooks, made out checks for every bill, stuffed envelopes, didn't lick them shut yet, not knowing whether there was any money in the accounts, if she and Michael could get in. They'd try on Monday. She took one box of trash to the incinerator, carried the other toward the house. The Marin guys and their trucks were gone. She walked to the greenhouse, found it locked. She stuck her face up to the wall, placed her hand on it, heard the alarms blare, felt her phone vibrating in her pocket. She backed away, covered her ears, Zack and Michael appeared, out of breath, Michael carrying a kitchen knife, Zack a baseball bat.

"Oh, jeez! It's just you," Zack gasped. Michael bent over, hands on knees, breathed deeply. Zack punched a few numbers into his cell phone and the alarm stopped.

"As you've just discovered," Zack said, "the security system's live. Anybody touches anything, comes within six inches of it, well, this happens." They walked back to the house, Michael carrying the box of bills and weapons. Zack showed Lisa how to reset the alarms.

"Holy crap! That is loud? What about animals? Will they set it off?" Lisa asked, as they walked up the stairs to the house.

"They say a mountain lion will. But not deer, or anything smaller. Mostly just humans."

Ben and Cody were at the table with Pam, looking at the parcel map.

"Pretty good alarm system," Pam said.

"You think?" Lisa said.

"Everybody's too tired to cook tonight," Cody said. "We're thinking Bella Roma in Capitola. I called, made a reservation for six at six."

"We can all fit in the Navigator."

"Thanks, Ben, but Michael and I will head home after dinner, so we'll take our car, too."

•　　•　　•

Another restaurant Lisa had never seen before. Even Zack had been there, said Gregory had brought him a few years ago. It was nice, authentic, with statues and décor. No wonder G had liked it.

"According to Gregory, the best Italian food in town," Zack shared.

"No way! What with Ristorante Avanti and now Lillian's? No way!" Pam was adamant.

"His opinion was based on the real Italian chef, how the food was prepared, that it was authentic."

Lisa smiled. G and his brainwashing, his know-it-all panache that pervaded all conversation and thought.

When the waiter brought the wine menu, Zack handed it back to him. They ordered communally, everybody getting something different so they could get a taste of everything, vote later to determine if Gregory was right, or, as Michael said, "Just blowing hot air as usual."

Three types of bread in the basket, a bowl of oil with big chunks of roasted garlic, but no balsamic, Ben pointed out. They started with the three salads offered — spinach, Caesar, and house — passed them around the table until they were gone. Then came the main courses, Linguini tutto mare for Pam, ravioli pesto for Michael, gnocchi al ragu for Zack, lamb shank for Cody, the special filet mignon for Ben, and the risotto misto mare for Lisa.

Heads nodded, indicating the quality of the food.

"Remember when Mom would drive us down here, take us to that old Italian place near downtown? I think it was on Market Street." Cody said.

Lisa had never heard Cody refer to Alice as Mom before. It felt awkward, almost obscene coming out of her mouth, more fabrication, more world building. She knew it had to do with the withdrawals, going almost a week without alcohol after being pickled for most of her adult life. Part of Lisa wanted to blast her about the comment, rip her to shreds verbally, like Alice could do if she slipped into a mood. But she let it go, closed her eyes and saw herself on a trail at Land of Medicine Buddha, a *Qi Gong* state of mind washing over her. Trying to bring forgiveness into her mind. Replace disappointment with the small accomplishments Cody was working on.

Lisa raised her hand, flagged the waiter. "Do you have a dessert menu?"

Instead of handing them a physical menu, he recited to them: "Profiteroles in chocolate mousse with crème fraiche, chocolate torte, and tiramisu."

"One of each, please," she said, then turned to Cody. "It was called Adolph's Restaurant. On the corner of Water and Market." Funny how she knew so much more about this town twenty-five years ago than she did now.

"Yes! That was it. They had those great French-fried raviolis. We got double orders every time, stuffed ourselves on them."

Lisa laughed. "And you managed to talk her into getting an order to go, so we could munch on them as we drove home."

By the time the owner delivered the desserts, announcing them with his thick Italian accent, Lisa was ready to cast her vote in favor of G's pronouncement, as did all the others, only Ben reluctant, and only because of the lack of balsamic with the oil and garlic.

•   •   •

At home Ben dug an old chess set out of the hall closet, set it up for a game with Zack, Cody took Lisa's hand and pulled her to the art studio.

"I've been working on some stuff. Just wanted to show you."

356

The walls were full of canvases, from miniatures to one that looked like it was four by eight feet. Lisa had to sit down. It was overwhelming. Cody was a good artist, had been forever. But this was something different. She was tapping into something new, something she'd never been able to express before. She had been technically strong, but never emotive, like these. The medium was the same, the signature bright acrylic paints outlined in black ink. The paintings were laid out like a retrospective at the de Young or MOMA. Scenes along Shattuck in Berkeley, La Note Restaurant, the Berkeley Rep, interior and exterior views of their house, of the French doors to Alice's office, of the inside of the office that they were rarely privy to, the Christmas Eve jaunts to the city, China Beach, profiles of Alice, a close-up of a man she didn't recognize, the day excursions to Santa Cruz and Aptos, all of it, their whole lives together. Cody had been busy, a spirit free of booze finding itself in remembrance.

Lisa's chest and face welled up. It took a major effort to hold it back, keep it behind thick skin, not fall apart in front of Cody.

"You've got it all in here. Except no men. No Ryan, Ben, G. Just that guy there I don't know. Who's that?"

"Don't know. Just some guy standing in front of a bookstore on Telegraph Ave."

"I love my headquarters sign. And all of this. You are a very special person. Thank you."

Cody threw her arms around Lisa's neck, kissed her cheek.

Lisa said good night to the chess players, saw Zack tilt his head sideways, a slight shrug, unrecognizable to Ben, who was studying his move.

"Good night," Ben managed.

She knew Zack didn't want to say it, would rather be in his room with her, one of them reading to the other. But this was okay. She had a headful of paintings to help put her to sleep. But she didn't sleep, at least it didn't feel like sleep, one of those non-dreams that appeared snakelike, wrapping itself around the hills of Aptos, past the Temple Beth El parking lot, up and around Cabrillo College, through the Horticulture Center, back down Soquel Drive to Soquel and Capitola, all in one long procession of Cody's paintings now inhabiting the returning floats, one painting per float, no live humans standing and waving, draped in flowers and crowns, just the two-dimensional ones represented by Cody's paints, Alice and Cody and Lisa and unknown strangers, stone-faced and flat, a Ken Burns documentary attempting to resurrect a past fraught with mystery and fatigue.

46

SUNDAY
12-29-19

L ISA COULDN'T SLEEP PAST FIVE A.M., the parade still twisting its way around her head, the surrounding roads, the property. A hot shower would help, but she didn't want to wake Zack. He'd been working so hard, he deserved to sleep in. She laced her boots up tight, found Zack's coat in the living room, wrapped it around her shoulders and walked to headquarters, where she picked up the machete. It wasn't a frenzied pace, rather steady, persistent, a clear goal in mind. She went for three hours without stopping for water or food, managed over two hundred feet, could start to see signs of existence through the thicket. As she approached the end of her energy, she envisioned a truckload of yellow bricks being delivered, of carving out a pathway, setting them in place one by one, clicking the heels of her red shoes, the connection made.

She could only imagine what Zack saw as she walked through the door, his coat a mess, her a bigger mess, wet with sweat, dirt and grime stuck to her face. He was laid out on the couch, no socks, watching her. Not ready to speak yet, she went straight for the fridge and downed a quart of orange juice, barely thinking to swallow.

A big sigh. "That's better. How late did he keep you up?" Lisa asked.

Zack turned on his side to face her. She sat across from him in the easy chair. "I beat him the first game. I thought we were only playing one game. Wanted to come find you to read. Then he said two out of three. And when I won the second game, he said three out of five. I was distracted in the third and fourth games, didn't want to be there, but I trounced him in the fifth game, well after one o'clock. He's very competitive, but not a very good chess player. I'm tired."

"Are you good?"

"Better than him. We play on the boats when it's too stormy to go out. The guys from Russia and Czechoslovakia are masters. Live for it. How far did you get this morning?"

"Pretty far. Over halfway there."

"You know I'd love to help."

"I know you would. It feels good to do this one by myself. But I am missing Lydia. And I'm sure she's missing me. Do you need to do anything in the greenhouse today?"

"Minor stuff. Biggest thing is to teach you about the security system, how to deactivate it when you want to go in. Other than that, I'm free. I do have a thing later this afternoon and evening."

"The anti-racism stuff?"

"Yeah. At that Villa Maria place over by Seventeenth Avenue. Overnight retreat."

"How about I shower and come back?"

He nodded, smiled. "I'll put my coat in the laundry."

"Sorry. Can we read in my room today?" she said.

"Okay. Why?"

"I don't know. Change of scenery, maybe."

"Gotcha."

She was getting better at losing the vision of Gregory in Zack's room, had tried to forget that G had installed the stained-glass window above the shower. Tried to forget that his clothes ever occupied the closet. But now something new, a hiding space in the floor. Sometimes it felt as if Zack were reading to both of them, Gregory sandwiched in the middle between them. She was tired of that.

After six of Lydia's short pieces, she stopped him. "Hold on a sec. I need to make a call before it's too late."

She used the landline, put it on speaker.

"Land of Medicine Buddha. How can I help you?"

"I'd like to reserve a room for tonight."

"Number of guests?"

"One."

"Name?"

"Lisa Hardrock."

"It looks like you stayed with us recently. Same credit card information?"

"Yes."

"We still have a two-night minimum stay."

"I might not stay the extra night. But that's fine."

"Okay. You're all set."

"Thank you."

Zack shifted on the bed. "That'll get you there quicker than a machete."

"I figure if my reader is gone tonight, I'll go somewhere where it's quiet and read to myself. No phone calls or pushy roommates."

"Good idea. Shall I read one more before I need to pack?" Lisa nodded, rolled into him, rested her head on his shoulder. "Lydia calls this one 'Dinner.' 'I am still in bed when friends arrive ...'"

Zack was gone when Lisa came out with her backpack loaded. Ben and Cody were playing chess.

"I'll be gone for a night or two," she announced.

"Where are you going?" Cody asked.

"None of your business. Play," Ben said.

"She is my business. Forever."

"To a retreat. Esalen," Lisa lied. Didn't know why she'd lied. Maybe being in the presence of the master. Wanted her privacy. "Not sure when I'll be back."

"Can I come?"

"No. It's a silent retreat."

"What's that supposed to mean?"

"Bye. Have fun."

•   •   •

She tossed the backpack into the Prius, walked down to headquarters. She picked up the *Cookies* manuscript, thought about bringing one of the new ones, but decided to save it, the New Year's present she'd been promising herself. Instead she locked up headquarters, deactivated the alarm system at the greenhouse, opened the safe and removed all of Alice's journals.

Halfway to Soquel she remembered about the lack of Wi-Fi at Medicine Buddha. She had Pious Rebel work to tend to. Vino Cruz was open, so she parked, ordered herself a glass of Martin Ranch pinot noir, opened the computer, shook her head at the number of new folks tuning in, reading Alice. New threads had opened up: *Wonderland, B. Toklas,* and *Looking Glass.* People were so clever, had so many interesting ideas to share, stories to tell, fantasies to make up. If she were only half that clever, she'd write her own book, cash in on her genes, Alice's fertile mind.

She opened a new post and wrote:

Just a heads up. I'll be on a fact-finding mission at a hidden retreat for a couple of days, a magical place that refuses to offer Internet access, but offers a precious silence that can be so hard to find these days. I have good news for those of you who have shown early interest in the publication of Alice's books. I Really Knead You will be available for pre-orders by Valentine's Day. The other four books will roll out once a month from March through June. While the books will be available from the usual large outlets, some of whom you might see in our ads, we do want to remind you to support your local independent bookstores. We will post click-throughs to as many of their sites as we can. If we're missing one of your local favorites, let us know, and we'll work on it. Speaking of working on it, because of your tremendous support and our rapid growth, HotMama! and WhamPam are joining our team to help provide quick and easy service as needed. Thank you so much! Pious Rebel.

She vetted new followers, made sure the questionables were staying in line, accepted a few hundred new posts. In the half hour it took her to do so, both RockHound and EverybodyMustGetStones had responded. RockHound first.

> I do hope you still have time to meet for lunch Monday. My wife so enjoys the peas and hearts of palm at the Crow's Nest salad bar, not to mention the homemade croutons from their leftover brown-bread rolls. So looking forward to it, to meeting you after all this time.

Lisa was not sure about following through with this lunch. Getting just a little too clingy for her. And it hadn't been that much time. Just two months now for Pious Rebel. On to EverybodyMustGetStones.

> My husband was quite sad when he read your post. Not that he wasn't happy about your retreat, about the notion of retreating. He loves his retreats. Loves to be alone with his mountains, hunting for rocks. But sad at thinking maybe you had forgotten about the lunch. I won't say he was heartbroken about missing lunch with you Saturday because of his stupid old car, but he wasn't worth spending time with the rest of the day. Hope we still have a date.

People definitely overused the notion of a date. Not a date, folks. Just a lunch. If she shows. A one-time event which she will most likely never agree to again with any of her followers.

She sent a joint message to Bianca and Pam.

> Let me know if it's okay that I mentioned you both in my last post. I'm guessing you'll get more direct pings from folks, but I believe it's best to give them access. Let me know. Learning as we go. Lisa.

One more. To Zack.

> Thank you so much for Lydia. She deepens my life. As do you. XO ~ Lisa.

She took a long pull from her wine, one that rolled around her tongue and mouth, expanded her throat. She couldn't remember one time ever in her life when she'd used an XO in a closing to a letter or email. Not to anyone, certainly not to Alice, who would have laughed at her for being so sentimental. She had sent daily letters when her eighth-grade history class visited Washington, D.C. Many parents had chaperoned. Not Alice, who had work to do for clients, needed to stay home with Cody to make sure she didn't cause any mayhem. One letter a day for a week, no XO's. Just Lisa.

Okay, one more, to alleviate the potential for unneeded angst. To both RockHound and EverybodyMustGetStones:

My retreat is just a stone's throw from the Crow's Nest.

She immediately backspaced, changed it to:

My retreat is very close to the Crow's Nest, and they don't serve lunch! I also am looking forward to the peas, the croutons, the view, and meeting you both.

Before shutting down Pious Rebel and closing the computer, she waited, eavesdropped on discussions at nearby tables, listened for something of interest, but it was all of interest, if she were willing to pay attention, care about what made people say the things they did. The waiting was about Zack, hoping he'd respond to her post before she was out of range. But the eavesdropping pulled her away from desire, caused her to open her journal, write down the next thing she heard the sixty-plus-year-old woman say to her table mate: "Of course I love him, but he's just too much of a pussy to commit." She typed it in her journal, bolded it, put a colon after the last word, invited herself to continue. But she could do that later, didn't need Wi-Fi for this. Nothing yet from Zack. She closed the computer, wound her way up the road and into the hills, parked her car where Prescott Road dead-ended at the retreat.

•   •   •

The backpack and a water bottle were her only possessions as she entered her humble lodging, a different room than last time but identical contents inside. She clipped the bottle to her belt, found the 5.5-mile trail, walked slowly, without specific intent other than paying attention, observing a slice of life she hadn't witnessed before. Two hours later she arrived at the dining hall, hungry, tired. There were no empty tables, which would have been her preference, so she found one with another woman.

"May I join you?"

"Certainly."

Wherever Lisa went, wherever she was, Alice found her. Anything to do with certainty was fair game with Alice. She would often tell both girls to beware the person who was certain about everything, that most likely they knew nothing of importance. That if you were certain, you weren't open to discovery, to persuasion, to learning anything new about yourself or the person you were with. This woman's "certainly" was a distant relative, not intended in the same vein as "certainty." It was more along the lines of "This is a community table and I look forward to communing with you." Lisa set her pack and water bottle on the table and then filled a plate with potato salad, coleslaw, pureed yams, and triangles of homemade bread.

When she returned, the woman didn't speak, sat with her eyes closed. Lisa took out her cell phone to look for messages, remembered about the Wi-Fi, saw the link on her screen to the greenhouse security system. Damn! Both she and Zack were gone for the night. Hopefully Zack had given Ben or Cody a quick training on how to deal with emergencies if needed. She could just walk up over the hill, find the macheted trail, hand Ben the phone. Or she could just relax, let it go, take advantage of this quiet time, of communing with people who did so with their eyes closed.

With a full water bottle and two brownies, she returned to the room. Before deciding what to read, she stepped outside the door, breathed deeply, fell into twenty minutes of *Qi Gong*.

Alice's *Cookies* and *Can't and Won't* were off-limits, to be read only in the presence of Zack. She'd packed *Zen* and *The Overstory*, but was resisting both. Not yet ready to tackle the nuances of quality and value in the life of the protagonists. Not ready to transfer it to her own life and the life of every person alive. Similarly, she wasn't prepared to continue further into Powers' angst about deforestation, especially now that she took her machete to knock down saplings and branches for her selfish needs of creating a pathway from her personal headquarters to a would-be Shangri-la. The journals. Part of her still wasn't quite ready to lunge into Alice's brain. It felt like a voyeurism well beyond the boundaries of eavesdropping. But part of her couldn't wait. She opened the first journal, recognized Alice's handwriting, or chicken scratch, as she used to call it, so addicted to the Selectric that she had forgotten how to write cursively. It was mostly single letters, with an occasional attachment between two or three that felt like they should naturally merge.

January 15, 1990. It's Martin Luther King, Jr., Day today. He was born 32 years ago. I was four years old. It's a good day to start this journal. I've been threatening to write one for years, ever since Lisa was born, seven years ago. I just completed my first novel, I Really Knead You, about a couple who own a bakery, smothered in the crosshairs of love and stability, so it's time to track my thoughts, about the novel, the characters, my own life, and the lives of Lisa and Cody. Oh, yeah. We have an addition to the family this year. Cody came into our lives on a whim. She is Lisa's friend from school, her mother an opera singer who travels around the world on a ridiculously busy schedule. Lisa and I have sort of adopted her. While her mother travels, she stays with us. Is ours. Which so far has been all the time. I worry about what Lisa thinks of this, but it's the right thing to do, for Cody and her mom, and the monthly stipend her mother provides me helps pay the bills.

June 18, 1990. The girls are finally out of school. Today we will drive to Santa Cruz again. Spend time at the beach. I'll write some, just beginning the new story, tentatively titled Rocks and Rolls. Lisa will bring a book to read. Cody will draw. It's a fun family adventure. Maybe stop at the Sno-White drive-in for a hot dog on a stick laced with mustard. Head south to our favorite cement boat. Spend time up at UCSC. Even though she's only seven, Lisa has declared that she will go to school there. We'll spend time in the McHenry Library, the girls up and down the elevator, Lisa searching for books, Cody just pushing buttons, constantly pushing buttons.

Lisa stayed awake, read straight through from the first page through the last. The final entry on the last page was written more than five years after Alice had started the journal.

June 25, 1995. Another summer trip done. Cody is a pain in the ass. The good news is I've finished Rocks and Rolls, have moved ahead to book three of ten. I'm thinking the first five will be clustered together, called The Baker's Quintet. Not sure yet about the next five. My geode collection continues to grow. Another one appeared last month, on my doorstep, unwrapped, no note. Anita is a godsend. I don't know what I would do if she wasn't in my life. We keep it low-key, best friends. She cooks, I write.

Lisa closed the journal. It was strange to be reliving her youth through the words of Alice, her voice sliding off the page, speaking directly to her. There hadn't been much new in the first journal, no surprises. Maybe the suggestiveness of the relationship with Anita, but not really. Lisa knew that, never from facts observed, but from behaviors watched. She was excited about the final five books. She was excited to wake in the morning and read the second journal. She was excited about Pious Rebel, and Zack, and the headquarters. She was excited that in a few more days, the memorial would be behind her, that Gregory would slip further away.

47

MONDAY
12-30-19

N O SNAKES OR MARCHING BANDS OR PARADES OR FLOATS. She had slept straight through. At six a.m. she went for breakfast, brought two large orange juices back to the room, opened the second journal.

April 11, 1997. Book three is rolling along, a steady but slow pace. Seems to take me five or six years per book. That's fine. Hopefully ten under my belt by the time I die. I wish Lisa were here. She'd catch the 'under-my-belt' cliché, make me erase it, come up with something fresh, something like 'Hopefully ten occupying the bookshelf dedicated to the work of Alice Hardrock." Something like that. She's in Washington, D.C. History class visiting historical monuments and museums for a week. First time Lisa and Cody have been apart since Cody moved in. It's a strange feeling. Lisa has sent daily letters. Signs them with only her name. No love. That's my fault. I've been careful with my own expression, or lack of it. Kept it hidden away, don't even speak to it in my journals. Especially since I caught Cody nosing around in my office, found her holding the key to my locked cabinet, where I keep my manuscripts, my journals, everything of value, my secrets. My work continues to go well. More new clients every month. Need to head up to campus next week to deliver a finished document to a professor in the archaeology department.

April 15, 1997. Taxes due today. Actually they're delinquent today. No Darn Fooling Around, as my dad used to say. The CPA clichés burned into his head, his language. N for November, as in due in November, D for delinquent in December. I usually wait until the delinquent date to file mine, self-employed as I am, waiting until the final minute, thus here we are. I'll drop the returns at the post office, pick Cody up from school before we head up to Cal to deliver my final copy edits on Sam's manuscript.

Shit! Shit! Shit! Bumped into Jason in the hallway outside Sam's office, gave him a cursory handshake, though he tried for a hug, which I diverted, told Cody to sit down and wait while I talked with Sam. A half hour later, Jason was still there, sitting next to Cody. I'm certain all the blood poured out of my face into my ankles. I saw Jason hand Cody a slip of paper as I approached. Jason stood, said, 'Nice talking with you, Cody.' He turned to me, not the usual smile I'd seen on him in the past. 'Good bumping into you, Alice.' I watched him walk down the hallway, enter another office. Cody told me he works there, so does his wife, they share an office in the geology department. Needless to say, I am never taking Cody up there again, will be avoiding Jason's end of the hallway when I visit Sam.

Lisa was not sure what to make of all this, but she didn't stop, read through all eight journals until she reached the end. She'd need to read it all again, especially the section about Cody and Jason. The rest of it was reminiscent, like the long list of oxymorons Alice had kept on the inside back covers of each journal. She took a couple minutes to look through the list, found Pious Rebel. The Cody information is what stuck, needed to be read more carefully. But it was 11:23. She had paid for the second night, but wanted to get home and talk to Cody about this, something that neither Cody nor Alice had ever shared with her. She had to meet RockHound and EverybodyMustGetStones first.

．　　　．　　　．

She took a quick shower, grabbed the water bottle and pack, found her car, made her way through town to the Crow's Nest. She was fifteen minutes early. She wished Pam and Bianca hadn't been busy today. They could have run interference if necessary. Because it was associated with football, she was pretty sure that using the phrase "run interference" to refer to a blockage of sorts probably classified it as a cliché. The fedora was sitting on the back seat, where she had put it the day she'd agreed to meet them.

She chose a table by the window, waited until she was seated, then put the hat on her head. She had eaten here once with Alice and Cody in 2000. It was her sixteenth birthday. The world was in a fuss about Y2K. But it passed. The world didn't end. Her sixteenth year passed too. High school with Cody had been almost more than she could handle. Life of the party, mouthy, knew everything about everything, everybody.

The couple approaching her table looked like normal people, graying hair, as RockHound had said in the post. They looked to be in their mid-fifties. He was tall, lanky. She was short, like Alice. RockHound shook her hand, cupped it with both of his, said, "Hello. So, we finally meet, in person." Such an odd thing to say. EverybodyMustGetStones moved in and hugged her, hard and long, way too long. Lisa pulled away, had to push her out of the clench, took her seat, as did they.

RockHound stared at her, was quiet. EverybodyMustGetStones spoke right up. "We stopped to visit our friend at the rock shop this morning."

Lisa said, "I talked to him the other day, bought an amethyst point for a friend of mine."

"Oh, his stuff is so lovely. He used to be in one of our hiking clubs, until he blew his knee out."

Lisa opened her menu, needed to divert her eyes from them. EverybodyMustGetStones leaned in across the table, a stage whisper, "We already know what we want. Cobb salad, cup of clam chowder, those brown-bread rolls."

"Me, too," Lisa said. It was becoming difficult to keep thinking of them with their Pious Rebel usernames. "Because of our virtual relationship, we don't know each other's real names. Maybe we should share them."

RockHound smiled. "Oh, we know your name, Lisa."

EverybodyMustGetStones grabbed his arm, shook it, got close to his face said, "Too soon! Too soon! You'll scare her. Make her think we're weirdos or something."

That's exactly what she was thinking. How did they know her name was Lisa? She had been careful to conceal her real identity on Pious Rebel. Maybe they knew how to locate the real names of folks who registered domain names. She hadn't paid the extra fee to have WhoIs hide it. But why would they care? Why would they make the effort?

The wife, that was easier to say, focused on Lisa, looked too serious when she said, "I'm Dottie, short for Dorothy."

"Pleasure to meet you, Dottie." She turned to RockHound, waited. His eyes were glazed, looked like he was staring at someone sitting at a table behind her.

Dottie said, "Honey? He does this sometimes, disappears for a few seconds."

"Oh, sorry. I was thinking about Alice."

"Which book?" Lisa asked.

He shook his head. "No book. Just about Alice."

Lisa was thinking now might be the time to leave. Not even say goodbye. Just walk away, lock them out of Pious Rebel, turn her back and be done with them.

"Tell her your name, honey."

"Oh." He held out his hand again. "Sorry. I'm Jason."

The Tilt-a-Whirl stomach found her, messed with her balance. At a Boardwalk visit when they were both ten, she and Cody had been in the bucket, and Cody had yanked at the bar, spun it, twisted it, made Lisa throw up. She was close to that now. She took a deep breath, righted herself.

"Your name is Jason?"

He nodded. "Why?"

"Do you work at UC Berkeley?"

Dottie smiled. "We both do. We've shared the same office for over twenty years. Why do you ask? How'd you know that?" she said.

Jason said, "Cody must have told her." He shook his head. "I told her never to tell you."

"Did you say Cody?" Lisa said. Jason nodded. Can you excuse me a minute? I need to show you something."

Lisa stood, walked away from the table, found her car, sat in the driver's seat, reached over and opened her pack. She removed the second journal and brought it back inside with her.

Dottie and Jason looked flustered when she returned. Lisa sat down, found the spot in the journal, turned it around and handed it to them.

"Oh, my god! This is Alice's journal!" Jason said. "Right. That was the day."

"It certainly was," Dottie added.

"What are you talking about?" Lisa said.

"We were thirty-three years old," Dottie said. "Had twin boys, two years old. Jason hadn't seen Alice in years."

Jason nodded. "I kept sending the geodes, though, until the boys were born."

"All of Alice's geodes were yours? You gave them to her?"

"I can only assume they're all mine. My gifts to her. All the pictures you posted were mine. Started when I was in high school. Met her at a bakery over on Shattuck. I was fifteen. She was twenty-five."

"That's why it's so eerie reading Alice's bakery stories now. Not sure whether it's art imitating life or the other way around," Dottie said.

"Wait. Can we back up a bit?"

"I know, dear. It's very confusing and complicated." She lovingly hit Jason on the shoulder. "Men!"

"Well, and women. Come on. I was nineteen. She was twenty-nine."

"What are you talking about?"

"He's talking about when Alice seduced him. The vamp. I still like her writing, though. But she used my Jason."

"I wasn't your Jason back then. I wasn't anybody's Jason. And nobody got used."

Lisa took a long drink from her water. "You're telling me you slept with Alice?"

"Yes. For a few weeks, back in '82."

"You and Dottie weren't together yet?"

"Oh, no. I didn't come to campus until 1986. Straight from Alabama. Hayseeds still in my hair. Got accepted to grad school in the geology department, and there he was. He loved rocks almost as much as me."

"But hold on," Lisa said. She pointed at the journal. "Back to this. So, you met Cody in the hallway outside your office in 1997?"

"Alice brought Cody with her that day. She had a meeting with Sam Robbins, a professor colleague of ours. Sam told me later she was editing his current book. She went in to talk with him. I sat down with Cody."

"That thirty-minute discussion changed his life," Dottie said.

"How so?" Lisa asked.

"I put two and two together. I asked Cody if she was Alice's daughter. She said, 'Yes I am, and I have an adopted sister, Lisa, who lives with us most of the time.' She said you were away on a trip to Washington, D.C., and that your mother was a famous opera singer."

"God damn her!"

"I don't know why you're saying that, but she sure messed with Jason's head."

"I don't understand," Lisa said.

"Cody and I agreed to never say anything about each other to Alice or you. We saw each other once a week until you were juniors in high school. Then she decided she'd had enough of me. Told me one day she was done with me. I was boring. Me and my rocks."

"They never had a paternity test done, but Jason knew Cody was his daughter. The timing was too perfect to be coincidence."

"Un-fucking believable!" Lisa grabbed her water glass, threw it hard into the carpet, glass shattering, ice cubes flying, waiters rushing to clean up the mess, patrons gawking in amazement. A manager in a tie hurried to the table. "Is everything okay here?"

Dottie spoke up. "Yes, fine, thank you. She just learned some bad news. She'll be fine."

When he left, Dottie put her hand on Lisa's. "Now what was that all about, dear?"

"Cody kept you a secret from me and Alice for, what, five years?"

Jason nodded. "And then I'm out on the net hunting for like-minded geode lovers and find your website. Then the Alice part, and her books, her stories, a whole lot of it really about me."

"You are *not* Cody's father!

"What are you talking about?"

"Cody is not Alice's daughter. Cody's mother is the opera singer. Cody's my adopted sister. She hid you from me for twenty-three years. Alice, is *my* mother."

Lisa couldn't control her thoughts. She was no longer blazing the pathway to enlightenment as she envisioned the machete strong in her right hand, swinging at Cody's neck, her arms, slashing into her ankles and hips, blood everywhere.

Dottie stared at Lisa, turned and looked at Jason. Back again to Lisa. "The bridge of the nose. The eyes. Well, I'll be damned! Another chapter."

When the waitperson brought their food, they weren't hungry. Lisa said, "Let me pay for this. Just bag it up, please." She found a cluster of street people sitting near the harbor, handed them the bags, before accompanying Jason and Dottie to their car. Lisa pulled out her cell phone, snapped a picture of them. Maybe a hint of Sam Shepherd there. The hands, the long fingers. They exchanged emails, phone numbers, but no hugs, no tears. Simply a "We'll be in touch" from Jason. Dottie leaned in, whispered to Lisa, "We'll be in town until Wednesday, if you want to check in."

Lisa turned back to them, said, "Can we not mention any of this on the blog site?"

She wanted to drive her car down the fishing-boat ramp, into the harbor, sink to the bottom, all windows closed, let herself go. Better yet, she'd like to push Cody and her car in. She drove around town, turned KDFC up, listened to Beethoven and Mahler. Went up the coast to Davenport, made a U-turn across the highway and headed back. Going home was not an option. She might hurt somebody.

In Soquel, she stopped in the Vino Cruz parking lot while she still had cell reception, texted Zack.

Not sure when your thing is over. I can't go home. Long story. I have another night at LOMB. Care to join me? If so, bring wine and Lydia. Room 22.

She sent a second text to Pam.

I'll be home tomorrow before noon. Let me know if there's anything you need me to do. Thanks.

Zack texted back: Be there by 6:00.

•   •   •

Together on her twin bed, after she'd filled him in on the Crow's Nest news, Lisa and Zack reread Alice's journal entry for April 15, 1997.

"This is truly disgusting," Zack said. "How'd she manage to be so sneaky and not get caught?"

"I don't know. In high school, she hung out with the jocks and cheerleaders. I was with my friends who liked to read and go to plays. We'd often go for days without talking much."

Zack looked at the entry again. "But to steal someone's father. That's gutsy. Demented."

"Hold on. I don't know he's my father. Just because he thinks the timing was right doesn't make him anyone's father."

"Except for his twin boys."

"Just because he slept with Alice a few times doesn't mean anything. She might have had lots of male friends at that stage of her life." She remembered the photo she'd taken at the Crow's Nest, took it out and showed it to Zack.

"I don't know. Maybe some similarities in the eyes. The nose," he said.

"That's what Dottie said."

"Only way to be certain is a paternity test," Zack said.

"I don't want that. What difference does it make? To clarify what an evil person Cody is? No more proof is necessary."

"Jason as Justin. Very clever of Alice. Hey! There may be one good reason for the paternity test." Lisa glared at him. "I'm serious. The twin boys are how old by now? Thirty-something. That means you might have two half-brothers, maybe even nieces and nephews."

She remembered the owner of the rock store. He had said they had grandkids.

"On a related front, what are your plans for Cody?"

"This from the man who doesn't believe in plans," she said. "I have no plans."

"Really? You're going to walk in tomorrow as if nothing happened? Pretend that Jason doesn't exist? Are you going to let her keep living there?"

"I really don't know yet. No idea."

"Well, I have an idea. But I'm starving. Can we go get some food and I'll tell you my plan? Kill two birds with one stone. Sorry. Let me restate that. Solve two problems at the same time."

Back in the room Zack said, "Do you want to drive down to Soquel, get some Internet access and deal with it now?"

"No. Morning is soon enough. They said they were in town until Wednesday. What I want now is to get into that bed and have you read to me." She undressed in front of him, slowly, and he watched. Socks, underwear, bra, all came off this time. Zack stepped out of his Levi's, slipped the boxers over his hips, slid in next to her. This was the first time their bare skin had fully touched under covers together. It reminded her of G, which was not what she wanted. But G had never really snuggled or cuddled, would just climb on and take care of business. A business he knew well. But when it was over, it was over. Zack put his arms around her back, pulled her close, big hands leaving fingerprints on her skin. She didn't want him yet. Wanted Gregory completely out of her thoughts. Wanted to be read to.

"Lydia, please."

48

TUESDAY
12-31-19

L ISA WOKE WITH ZACK'S ERECTION POKING HER. She wanted to roll over, grab him, push him onto his back. But today was a memorial. At least for the rest of the day, she should stay as focused as possible. Remember the good parts of Gregory. Try to put Cody out of her head. Which reminded her, she needed to contact Dottie and Jason.

As she dressed, she nudged Zack awake. "Got to go."

Driving away from Land of Medicine Buddha, she maneuvered her car into Soquel, Zack in the passenger seat. He said, "Red Apple Café's got Wi-Fi. What do you think?"

"That sounds good. Stay away as long as I can."

Another menu and restaurant Lisa had never seen. Zack ordered the king-salmon Benedict, blackened in exotic Caribbean spices. Lisa got the Hawaiian French toast, piled high with fresh local fruit, grilled bananas, almonds, coconut, and raisins.

"It's like we're traveling around the world," Lisa said.

"Next year. After the hemp seeds come in." Zack's cell phone rang. He answered, said, "I'll call you back."

"Everything okay?"

"Yeah. Alaska stuff." He smiled. "What makes you think I'll be around next year?"

"Touché," she said. "I'm assuming Lydia has more books, or maybe we'll tackle *Zen* together. That could take six months."

"Right. And your snail's pace in *The Overstory* could take another year."

"I know. It is such good writing, language that wraps around your cortex, sometimes with a stranglehold. But the trees. Keeping the light out. Hard to focus and work my way through. I need to apologize to RachelReads." Which reminded her. She pulled out her computer, then her pack to find the strip of paper Dottie had given her. Instead of logging into Pious Rebel, she inserted their addresses into a joint email.

Dottie and Jason — We're having a memorial for my partner, Gregory, today at our property. I'd really like it if the two of you could come by. It'll be from 5:00 to 8:00 at our house at 4775 Porter Gulch Road in Aptos. Turn left at Temple Beth El from Soquel Drive. Hope you can make it. Sorry for the last-minute notice, but this is all so new.

She let Zack read it.

"Looks right to me," he said.

"Shall I mention Cody?"

"I don't think so. That could scare them away. It's you they'll care about now. I predict they'll be there. It'll just be whether or not you can keep from saying anything to Cody today."

"The longer I stay away the better."

She hit Send, looked at a message from Pam.

Everything's in motion. If you show up by 4:00, that's fine.

Lisa replied: I'll be there sooner. Need to fill you in on the latest Cody fiascos.

"Do you know what you'll say about Gregory at the memorial tonight?" Lisa said.

"It'll be short and sweet. What about you?"

"I'm not speaking. Just you and Michael. Probably a few open-mic folks, though I don't know who they would be."

"Shall we kill some time?" He caught himself. "Shall we find a way to spend the day together other than in the presence of Cody?"

She laughed. Alice had influenced so many in her life, with her certainty about what was okay and not okay with the use of language when communicating with others.

"That would be nice. I have an idea. One of the ads Bianca added to Pious Rebel last week is a click-through to the Picnic Basket on Beach Street."

"I've been there." Zack said.

"Let's start there."

•   •   •

They stuffed their packs with water, sandwiches, chips, and followed West Cliff Drive along the ocean until they reached Highway 1.

"Left toward Davenport," Lisa said.

They stayed quiet along the eleven-mile drive, enjoyed the sun on crops, the light traffic for a New Year's Eve day.

"Turn right on Swanton Road. Up a few miles on the right is a gate with No Trespassing signs."

"Why do you know all this?"

"College. Up here instead of classes."

At the gate, Zack pulled in and Lisa jumped out, held it open as Zack drove through.

"Park across from the little stone house on the right."

She led him into a backyard where a small table sat near the back door, a guest book and pen perched on top.

It took them twenty minutes at a steady pace to reach the waterfall, the fallen redwood tree, light from above reflecting off the surface of the pool.

Why had she brought him here? This was supposed to be Gregory's day. And here she was now with Zack at the place she had met Ryan. That's okay. She could let them both drown here. Be rid of them. Claim it with Zack. A cleansing.

She removed her backpack, stepped out of her clothes, and jumped in. Her head was below the water when she felt the concussion of Zack's splash. Heads popped up and they found each other, lips and tongues and skin, so different than she had felt with G, Ryan, the guys in college. They spun together in the pool, unencumbered, flexible, taking turns with the control. They made their way to the grassy shore under the redwood tree. She mounted him, drove his hips into the ground, palms against his chest, his hands around her waist, guiding her, balancing her. He rolled her over, cupped her back with his palms, a few quick thrusts before wriggling his tongue down her neck, through her breasts, stopping between her legs, taking his time, savoring her. Nothing like anything she had experienced, or even envisioned. She exploded and heard the scream echo up into the trees, slide up the waterfalls like salmon going home. He returned to her mouth, salt and musk, as he found her again, a mixture of gentleness and abandonment, back and forth, until finally his scream followed hers, into the pool, where the falls splashed and gurgled.

They stayed naked, clothes spread out as a makeshift blanket, munching Ruffles potato chips and ham-and-cheese sandwiches.

"I could live here. Every day for the rest of my life."

Zack ran a hand through her hair. "What about the lack of Internet?"

She laughed, as if it didn't matter, then sat up, stiffened. "Oh, crap!" She dressed rapidly, started packing her bag, and Zack followed her lead.

"What's up?" he said.

"My computer. I left it in the car but forgot to put it in the hidey-hole. Too easy to break a window and steal things up here."

They raced down the trail and creek until they reached the car, windows intact, computer bag sitting in the back seat.

"I'm so sorry. To wreck that perfect moment like this."

"It's okay. I'll sign us out."

Lisa rested her body across the warm hood of the car, stretched her arms out.

Zack returned, said, "Would you like me to drive?"

"That'd be nice. Don't forget we need to get your truck from Medicine Buddha."

"It's kind of hard to say all four names. Land – of – Medicine – Buddha."

"When I write about it on Pious Rebel, or in my journal, I just use LOMB."

"Will you write about this?"

"You mean the frantic, paranoid run back to the car, or the sex?"

"I mean all of it, any of it, and I like to think of it as lovemaking rather than sex."

"Sorry. With G, it was just sex. With Ryan it wasn't much of either. With you, it was definitely both. I doubt I'll write about it. Not really sure. The posts kind of blow their way in and tend to go where they want. What I won't write about is what happened at the Crow's Nest yesterday. We agreed to keep it off Pious Rebel."

As they approached Davenport, she asked Zack to pull over in the Cash Store parking lot.

"They've got juice in there. Need to find out if Dottie and Jason are coming."

Thank you for the invitation. Wouldn't miss it. J & D.

Lisa looked at her watch. "Two thirty. Should be back by three fifteen. Gives me time to fill Pam in."

"Gives me time to take care of a few greenhouse chores."

•　　　•　　　•.

Lisa pulled in first, followed by Zack in Babe. A Zoccoli's delivery truck was parked by the greenhouse, two women hauling platters and boxes inside, Pam guiding them. She waved.

"To save time," Lisa said, "why don't we shower together?"

"Just to save time?" he grinned. "Might take more time."

"I think I can resist you."

Inside she found a package on the counter addressed to her from Amazon Prime. She looked at the box containing G's ashes on the mantle. Of course he'd have hated this personal invitation she had made to Jeff Bezos into her house. She laughed before opening the box, finding the Beckett book of poems, placing it on her nightstand with Lydia Davis, *The Overstory*, and *Zen*.

They both chose colorful outfits, avoided the traditional dark and drab funeral garb. It wasn't a funeral. It was a memorial, a celebration. Mostly a celebration of the living, of what was to come. Zack wore the Hawaiian shirt he had purchased when he and Gregory had gone to Maui to surf for a couple of weeks in their late twenties. It was worn out, a couple of holes, but Lisa liked it. She wore a dress G had bought her that rested just above the knees. Bright flowers and fruits, a white belt that bunched it together at her waist.

Ben was at the kitchen table when they came out, working at his computer, parcel maps spread out, a partial box of fireworks on top of the maps. "I've got the contracts almost done. I figure we can sign tomorrow, get them notarized soon, pay off the balloon by end of week."

Lisa avoided the contract issue, said, "What's with the fireworks? You can't use those here."

"I know. I had them down in the greenhouse, but Pam told me to get rid of them."

"Where's Cody?" Lisa said.

"In the art studio. Painting. Where else? I've created a monster," he laughed.

"She created her own monster." Lisa touched Zack's arm. "Pam needs you to move the Harley out of the greenhouse. They're setting up tables on that end. There's plenty of room in headquarters."

"If you don't mind. That'd be great," Zack said. "I'm going to take her for a spin first."

"She's ready?"

"Not sure if ready is the right word. But I need to test her. Want to join me?"

"No way. Never have. Never will."

"What time is it?" he asked.

"Four thirty."

"I'll be back in fifteen minutes."

"Are you taking her on the highway?"

"Oh, yeah,"

"Can you hold on a second?"

"Sure."

She went into the house, grabbed Gregory's box of ashes from the mantle, walked it down to the greenhouse. Michael was taping photos to poster board. Pam was adjusting food platters and bowls of chips.

"Michael. I want to give G's ashes to Zack. He's taking the Harley out for a spin. Thought G would like to waft off the back of the bike at seventy miles per hour. Is that okay with you?"

"Perfect!" Michael said.

She handed the box to Zack, watched him push the bike into the driveway, pump it once, heard the rattle of an engine. He followed the Zoccoli's truck out of the driveway.

"Looks great," Lisa said to Pam and Michael. "Thanks for doing all this."

"So tell us the long story," Pam said.

"Not enough time. Short story is that there may be a father in the picture. Cody knew about it, for over twenty years. Never said a word to me."

Pam stopped what she was doing, put a hand on Lisa's shoulder. "What do you mean a father? The opera singer's husband?"

"No! Possibly my father. RockHound."

"RockHound from Pious Rebel? I don't get it."

"I mean I don't really know if he is." Lisa saw the Tesla pull into the driveway. "But you can give me your opinion."

"On what?"

"That's RockHound, and his wife, Dottie. EverybodyMustGetStones."

"You're kidding me!"

"Why would I do that? His name is Jason. Gee, that sounds a lot like Justin, doesn't it? Tell me if he looks like me. There's more. I need to go greet them. Shit will be hitting proverbial fans soon."

Pam hugged her. "Can you use that one? So trite. Your face looks flushed. You okay?"

"I'm very okay."

As she gave Dottie and Jason a tour of the property, a trickle of cars started filling the driveway, mostly local clients, friends of Michael's there to support him.

"That's our greenhouse."

"Those don't look like orchids," Dottie said.

"Long story. They're hemp plants. For seeds." She opened the door to the workshop. "This is what I'm calling Pious Rebel headquarters."

Jason looked at the desk. "That's Alice's typewriter!"

Lisa didn't say anything at first. "It's my typewriter now."

Jason sat in the swivel chair, spun. "This wasn't hers."

"No. That was my former partner's."

"Alice had an old wooden one with the engravings scratched underneath."

"Of course," Dottie said. "This must all seem so surreal to you, Lisa. I know it does for Jason."

"It's more than surreal. How do you know about the engravings?"

"The wheels came loose one day. I went down to repair them, looked up under the chair, found the etched sentence, told her to come down and look. That's when it all started." He turned to Dottie. "Sorry, honey. Didn't think you'd ever have to hear that story again."

"What do I care? Ancient history. I've heard you tell the boys."

Lisa had forgotten about them. "How old are your boys?"

"They're thirty. Two kids each. Grandkids are precious. Worth all the other distractions and bombardments along the way."

Jason stayed quiet, stared at the Selectric.

Dottie continued. "The boys were excited when they learned they had a half-sister. But Cody never showed any interest in them. When she was out of the picture, they asked about her a few times, but eventually forgot about her."

"What was the engraving under the chair?"

Jason chuckled. *"Those who think they know everything annoy those of us who do."*

Lisa heard the rumble up Porter Gulch. She saw Zack return on his Harley, but the sound was wrong, too loud. Thirty feet behind him she discovered the answer. Nearly three dozen hogs following him in, cramming their bikes into any space they could find.

Zack pushed his Harley into the workshop, came out, said, "Look what I found. In the parking lot down the road, as if they were waiting for me to show them the way."

As they removed their helmets, Lisa could see that they were mostly not the long-haired and bearded stereotypes she was expecting. They wore leather chaps, had a few tattoos, but other than that, looked like they could be Silicon Valley executives out for a New Year's Eve jaunt with friends.

The one with the black bow tie and crewcut walked up to Pam. "Are you Lisa?" Pam shook her head, pointed at Lisa.

Michael moved next to Lisa, said, "I'm Michael." He held out a hand.

"Goldenrod," he said, swooped in and gave Michael a deep hug. "I'm so sorry about your brother. He meant a lot to us. To all of us."

The woman who'd ridden in with him hugged Lisa, then Michael. "I'm Dreamweaver." Lisa stepped back to get a good look, imagined Gregory with her. Didn't matter.

Pam ushered the rest of the crowd into the greenhouse for refreshments, pointed out Gregory's photos.

Cody and Ben arrived from the house, Cody with paint smeared on her hands and arms. Lisa watched her make the rounds, introduce herself to each one of the Central Valley crew, the handful of Michael's friends. Dottie and Jason stayed by Lisa's side. She waited for Cody to circle around. Eventually she saw Lisa, rushed over to hug her. "I've been so productive. You're going to love the new paintings."

"Cody, this is Dottie, a new friend of mine. I don't think you know her. She goes by EverybodyMustGetStones on Pious Rebel."

"Wow! You invited followers. I'm surprised folks aren't backed up to Soquel Drive."

"I only invited these two. This is her husband. RockHound. You might know him better as Jason."

"It was a long time ago," Jason said, "but I'm sure you recognize me."

Cody's mouth fell open, blood disappeared from her face. "You must be confusing me with someone else. Nice to meet you both. I need to go finish a painting." Lisa stepped behind her, held both arms firmly, turned her around to face Jason.

"Do you recognize him now? You've got a painting of him in the house. You've known about him for twenty years! And never told me!"

"You'd better let me go or I'll start kicking." Lisa remembered her security training from when she worked in the classroom. She grabbed one of Cody's wrists with each hand and scissor-locked them across her chest. Immovable. Jason came closer, within inches of her face.

"Do you recognize me now? Remember, you told me I was your father. For over twenty years you've tormented me."

"Lisa, goddamn it! Let me go. Do you believe this lunatic?" Ben shoved his hands in his pockets, cocked his head. "What's this about, Cody?"

"Crazy people and crazy lies! I have no idea," Cody said.

"You have every idea. You put the lies into their heads. Made Jason think you were his and Alice's daughter. You are a sick and twisted person, and I want you off this property as quickly as you and

Ben can manage it." Lisa loosened her grip and Cody twisted away, hurried toward the house.

Ben looked at Jason. "She did that?"

"Yes, she did."

Ben shook his head

Lisa said, "You'd better go get her. She's probably heading for the booze, and will most likely want to drink herself into a stupor. I'll tell you more later. One more thing. Rip up those papers. I don't want her money, I don't want her anywhere near me or my property." Michael came up next to her. She turned to him. "I mean our property."

"I understand." Ben headed for the house.

"What about the mortgages?" Michael said.

"I don't care. We'll figure something out. Let them foreclose. We'll split the difference."

Goldenrod and Dreamweaver joined them. "Is there someplace private we can speak?"

Lisa was beginning to understand how and why nerves break down. She breathed deeply, took a mental *Qi Gong* pose, steadied herself.

The four of them walked up to the house. Ben and Cody were in their room, muffled shouting from behind closed doors.

They sat at the kitchen counter, Goldenrod fiddling with the box of fireworks

"I think you have something of ours," he said.

"I believe you're right. Let me get it for you," Michael said.

Dreamweaver stood up. "I'll go with you." She put her hand on her side, as if she was hiding a weapon. Lisa wasn't sure. Dreamweaver was so muscular she probably wouldn't need a weapon to overcome Michael.

Goldenrod plucked some fireworks out of the box, stuffed them in his pocket. "Good stuff. These make a lot of noise and color, and shoot up a hundred feet or so. We sell these as well."

"You mean as well as pot?"

He nodded. Michael returned with Dreamweaver, her holding the bag of weed.

"Thirty-five pounds," Lisa said.

"That's correct," Goldenrod said. "Then there's the interest."

Michael said, "I don't understand the interest part. What's that all about?"

"It's about the fact that we are business folks, trying to keep our customers happy, used to what they're used to. Gregory was supposed to deliver this to us on November first. Tomorrow, we're two months past that. We've been losing money, and clients, every day for sixty days now. We expect to be compensated."

"What does compensation look like to you?" Lisa said.

Dreamweaver said, "We were hoping you'd have some suggestions."

Goldenrod continued. "Which is why I've left the phone messages, to help you remember, to think about how we can solve this unfortunate series of events which has left us without a friend, you without a brother, you without a lover, and most importantly, us with a very late payment of product that we rely on for sustenance."

"I don't know what to say," Michael said.

"If you were still growing pot, I'd say give us another ten or fifteen pounds, gratis, when the next crop comes up. But we have zero interest in that hemp in your greenhouse. Does us no good. We're in it for maximum THC content, not CBD garbage."

Zack entered and took a seat.

Goldenrod glared at him. "Who are you, and why are you here?"

"These are my friends. I live here." Zack looked at the bag of weed in Dreamweaver's hand. "Did you guys get what you came for?"

"We're close. Just haggling over the loss of revenue without product for the past two months."

"I see," Zack said. "Any solutions yet?"

"Dollar-wise, we're thinking in the neighborhood of ten thousand, whether cash, product, or something else."

Dreamweaver opened the bag of pot, stuck her nose inside one of the pouches, sniffed. She nodded to Goldenrod.

"As expected," Goldenrod said, "it's the same high-quality product we've come to expect at the hands of our mistress gardener. Thank you, Lisa."

"Back to the compensation," Zack said. Lisa liked how he was assuming the role as uninterested mediator, something which neither Michael nor she could do in this situation. He spoke to Michael and Lisa "Do you guys have cash or pot that you could afford to part with to these dedicated business folks?" Lisa and Michael shook their heads. He knew they had both if it came to it. They knew he knew.

"I have a suggestion," Dreamweaver said.

Goldenrod tilted his head, Lisa noticed, as if this was something the two of them hadn't discussed yet.

"Love to hear it," Zack said.

"That bike you were on as we followed you up. That's Gregory's."

"Was Gregory's."

"It sounds like you've completely rebuilt it."

"Spent the last month with it."

Dreamweaver nodded. "I'd say it's worth in the neighborhood of ten thousand."

"I'd have to agree with you."

Goldenrod looked at Michael and Lisa. "Does this sound like fair compensation to you?"

Michael turned to Lisa, who was about ready to speak when Zack stopped her.

"Don't ask them. She's my bike. Gregory left it to me. Legally. In his will."

"That's correct," Lisa said.

"But, I think I'm done with Hogs," Zack said. "Not worth the effort. So, Lisa and Michael. How about this? I give Dreamweaver the pink slip to the bike. The two of you owe me ten thousand dollars. You pay me when the hemp seeds come in."

Dreamweaver stuck her thumb in the air. Goldenrod nodded, "Deal." He offered his fist, which Zack, Lisa, Michael, and Dreamweaver bumped.

Zack's cell phone rang. Lisa watched him turn away from the group, whisper into the phone, third time this week. "Talk later."

Zack pulled a key ring out of his pocket, removed the Harley key, handed it to Dreamweaver, who took it as she gazed around the room. "I don't see any of my boxes in here," she said. "Did Gregory not give them to you?"

"I'm not sure what you're talking about."

"I make assemblage boxes and collage. Every time Gregory made a delivery to us, I presented him with one to bring back to you."

"I've never seen one," Lisa lied, thinking about the cabinet in headquarters stuffed full of them.

"How strange," Dreamweaver said. Lisa didn't mind that this bothered Dreamweaver, was happy to think of her imagining Gregory tossing them in a trash bin along Highway 99.

Goldenrod stood up, said, "Thanks for your generosity. Time to celebrate the life of our friend Gregory."

•   •   •

The party continued in the greenhouse until well beyond eight. Armando played some classical guitar. Michael said a few words about his brother, Zack about his friend. Goldenrod even spoke. Even though Pam had intentionally avoided providing alcohol, the bikers all had their own flasks. Pam sat with Dottie and Jason for much of the evening, getting caught up on the recent discoveries. The local friends departed first, most with their allotted stashes that Michael had fished out of Gregory's closet. The bikers left in clusters. A handful were still outside when Lisa, Zack, Michael, and Pam went into the house.

The first thing Lisa noticed was Ben's papers, still in neat piles on the kitchen table, with Post-it notes scattered throughout for signatures, sitting under the box of fireworks. Pam found one of the hidden bottles of wine, filled four glasses and passed them out. Michael fell into the couch. Zack lit a fire.

"What now, my friends?" Pam said. She raised her glass, clinked with the other three before sitting down next to Michael.

"Happy New Year's," Zack said. Lisa came over, sat on his knee, kissed him. Michael kissed Pam.

Pam said, "Can we talk balloon payment?"

"Absolutely not," Lisa said. She went to the kitchen, brought two more chairs into the living room, moved swiftly down the hall to the art studio. She opened the door without knocking.

"What?" Cody said. "Can you leave me alone? Can't you see I'm painting?"

Lisa looked around the room, found the painting she was looking for, picked it up, said, "Can you join us in the living room, please?"

"I'm right in the middle of a painting. Maybe later."

Lisa yanked the brush out of Cody's hand, stuck it in a jar of water, grabbed her wrist and pulled her out of the room. She knocked on Ben and Cody's bedroom door. "Ben. You got a minute?"

"Sit," she said to Cody when they reached the living room.

"What's going on?" Ben said.

Pam said, "I'm guessing Lisa thinks Cody might be wanting a lawyer in the room. To make sure 'the whole truth, so help me, God' is pursued correctly."

Lisa set the painting on the mantle.

"I'm guessing everyone here met this man tonight. He's maybe fifteen or so years younger in the painting, but quite recognizable. Cody is an excellent painter, depicted him quite well."

Michael shook his head. "I can't believe you did this to her, Cody."

Lisa stopped him. "I'm done with all of this. This man may or may not be my biological father. However, I am seeing the resemblance the more I look at this picture, and Jason's face. Jason whom Mom disguised as Justin in *The Baker's Quintet*. No. I'm done with talk." She walked over to Ben's neatly stacked piles, picked them all up, walked to the fireplace, fed in one sheet at a time. "There will never be a partnership connected to this property with Cody's name on it. The two of you can spend the night if you like, but be gone tomorrow morning, and never come back."

"What about your precious balloon payment? How are you going to manage that without me and Ben?" Cody said.

"That's none of your business."

"Hemp seeds," Michael said.

Cody hurried toward the front door, scooped up the wine bottle and firecrackers on her way out.

"I'm going to bed," Ben said. "Tired of her drama."

"Took long enough," Pam said.

"I'm going outside, try to get the stragglers to head home," Michael said.

Lisa moved to the kitchen window, sighed deeply, thought of the changes so far in her life, knew there were more coming. Pam joined her. They saw Goldenrod standing in the middle of the driveway surrounded by cars and bikes, lighting fireworks, saw them shoot into the night sky and explode high above the tree line.

"Idiot!" Pam said, as she hurried outside.

Lisa looked at Zack. "You gave her Gregory's bike. I mean your bike. What are you thinking? What if the hemp project fails?"

Zack smiled. "When I got to the freeway, cranked that sucker up, it fizzled. That engine is crap. The only thing that bike was good for was distributing G's ashes. I'm glad to be rid of it."

•　　•　　•

The shouting was next. Out front people were running, hopping on bikes, yelling at each other. Seconds later, the greenhouse lit up like a giant Duraflame log. The walls were solid sheets of flame, the newly forged tables crackling. The black squat pots melting. The plants withering, disappearing into the soil. The whole place obliterated within minutes. Lisa stared, that roiling stomach returning. She looked at headquarters to make sure it was okay. Cody was there on the front step, standing next to the turtle, watching the walls of the greenhouse tumble to ash, a smirk twisting her lips.

All the bikers had fled. Nobody had called the fire department, neighbors too far away to hear or see anything. Lisa hurried to the greenhouse, found Pam, watched the walls crumble in on themselves. One more thing. One more layer of absurdity and grief. She doubled over, threw up on the ground, remembered when she did the same on Gregory's body under the oak tree, the horror then, anger now. In some sick way a sense of freedom. She turned and stared at Cody on the porch of headquarters.

"It was that Goldenrod guy," Cody yelled. "I saw him toss something in there."

Lisa walked back to the house, looked one more time at Cody. Cody yelled at her. "Now how will you pay your debts?" she sneered. "And another thing. I'm the one who cooked your precious dinner at the Olema Inn. That was *my crème brûlée*. How did you not recognize it? I cooked it for you and your *mom* for thirty years!"

It all flooded back to her now. The professor had used a PowerPoint presentation to clearly build a case for every "D". Devious was first. Everything she had known then about Cody should have alerted her, from the first day she met her when her mother dropped her off. No kiss goodbye, no hug. Then came Dysfunction. The professor switched slides. Every bullet described a characteristic of Cody. Distress. Slide three. It wasn't so much Cody who suffered the distress, but everyone around her. Slide four. Danger. Lisa looked at the Greenhouse, thankful that no one had been injured. One other concept came to mind from her Psych classes. Selective memory, which had clearly had a hold on her for most of her life. She leaned over, put her hands on her knees, and retched.

49

WEDNESDAY
1-1-20

I T WAS 2020. A NEW YEAR. A new vision becoming clear. Ben had forced Cody out of the house last night, before anything else could burn down. Nobody was blaming the fire on her. It could just as easily have been Goldenrod's dangerous play, or maybe just a little more interest than they had bargained for. There was no way to be sure, but Cody's face in the headquarters' window was etched in Lisa's mind. Michael officially had the day off but went to work anyway, to study up on crop management and marketing.

Zack had stayed up half the night watering down the ashes, making sure sparks didn't hop over to headquarters. He was still in bed.

Lisa opened a can of salmon for Eloise, took a large tub of Iams out to Turks and Caicos, didn't mind the slobber on her pants, continued on to headquarters.

It was forty-one degrees in the room. She placed the three heaters in a triangle facing the desk, buttoned up Zack's down jacket to her chin, opened the computer, started a new post.

Dear friends — I hope your 2020 visions are within reach. I have to say I am mixing the glorious with the devastating in my personal life. I prefer not to share details of the devastating in such a wide-open forum. And to be honest, I should change "devastating" to something less dramatic, let's say "unfortunate" or "bothersome," all of which grow moss and lichen with time, become green with life and flourish. Likewise, I won't spill forth with details of my glory. It will be enough for you to know that I am loving much of my life, myself, for the first time in almost forever. This is due to the people I have chosen to be with, in whom I place my trust, people who have made the same choice with me. That includes all of you Pious Rebel devotees who continue your daily, in some cases hourly, vigil with me, with Alice, with her colorful characters who encourage us to compare our own lives and aspirations and motivations to theirs. I was so lucky to have Alice as a mother, a mother who taught me lessons that would take me thirty-seven years to understand. I promise to stay with you, not fizzle out of existence, to dedicate myself to moving forward, to supporting Alice's work. Do know that I am now reading through Alice's journals, learning more about her, about myself, about secrets and magic and the unknown, about how to live each day anew. Pious Rebel.

RockHound had added a new posting to the Geodes thread.

Hi all. I'm putting up some photos of geodes I've taken over the years. They are mostly ones I've given away, some that I've kept for myself, or given to my wife, sons, grandsons, old friends. I hope you appreciate them as much as we do. The next one was from EverybodyMustGetStones. I love you, RockHound. What a special person you are.

They had kept their promise. Nothing openly personal. No secrets revealed. She looked at RockHound's photos, downloaded all of them to her desktop so she could blow them up in Photoshop. They were Alice's geodes, without wooden mounts or engravings on the bottom, but they were identical matches. Jason was offering her evidence, not that she really needed any more. What would it hurt for her to know, or at least think, that she had a living father, brothers? Blood match was overrated. She didn't need to do that. Might appreciate the accomplishment of a match, but would hate the disappointment of a mismatch. Lisa sent a joint message to them.

Very glad to have you both in my life.

A quick response from RockHounds: We'd like to take you rock hunting. To Hauser Geode Beds, where I have found the majority of my geodes. Your geodes.

She wrote back: When?

Dottie wrote: Soon!

Lisa again: How soon?

RockHound: Next weekend. Or the next.

Why not? Lisa thought. Will I have Internet access from there?

Immediate response from Jason: We have satellite equipment we carry with us.

One more, Lisa thought, but she needed to stop this, expend some energy. Can I bring a friend?

Dottie quickly: Anybody but Cody.

The machete lay alongside the Selectric. Outside, she headed to her pathway, imagined herself in *Qi Gong* pose as she sliced her way closer.

Two hours later she was exhausted, leaning forward, hands on knees, breathing deeply, when she heard Zack's voice behind her.

"Care for some company?" He waved a silver blade at her. She wasn't ready to talk, still breathing hard, but nodded her head, and together they blasted their way through.

After a long, hot shower, Lisa dressed in layers for the coldness of the downtown office. "I'm going to clear things out of the office today."

"Want some help?" Zack asked.

"I'm good. I'm going to do a little writing there before I strip it."

"Good. I'll be at the Resource Center." He paused. "It was nice sleeping in your room last night."

"Yes," she said. "No ghosts. What time will you be back?"

"Two-ish?"

"Can we plan a date?"

"Sure."

•   •   •

Lisa pulled up to the office and claimed the prime parking space. Inside she sat in the chair in front of the Levenger desk. The office was empty, closed for New Year's. The chair was still uncomfortable. The heater was still not working. She had worn her gloves, but had to take them off to work the keyboard properly. It was no headquarters, but she wanted to sit here one last time, look across at the Lenz Arts sign, wonder what the interior of Outdoor World looked like, make up stories about every homeless person who walked by, give them backstory, make up times in their lives that had been better for them, when they had jobs and income, wives and children, friends who they weren't afraid might stab them in their sleep for a pack of cigarettes or piece of jerky. By the time she finished in the office, she had counted fifteen, some traveling in pairs, a man and a woman, two men, never two women. Some carrying nothing. She entered it all into her journal, as well as the woman with the orchid, wondered where she was delivering it today, who the lucky recipient might be. She had been lucky in her life, had been born into privilege that put her far ahead of most residents of the planet. Plenty of food to eat, warm clothes, hot showers, roofs overhead. It was time she understood that privilege. How it affected her and others.

•   •   •

Zack had the incinerator flaming, was carrying charred wood from the greenhouse, tossing metal pieces into a large trash bin attached to the back of Babe. She pulled the Prius down the driveway close to headquarters.

"Hey," he said.

"Hey yourself." She walked straight up to him, put her arms around his neck, kissed him, turned around and started unloading the office supplies into headquarters, door open so she could watch Zack work.

"I'll have this cleaned up by tomorrow, right down to the foundation. Ready for a fresh start."

"What are you talking about?"

"We'll talk. I'll be in shortly."

Lisa erased everything on the white board. Drew two columns, not like her T-chart full of disappointments and accomplishments. This one was empty. Fresh. At the top of one column she wrote The Property, and the other she labeled Pious Rebel.

She opened the cabinet with Dreamweaver's boxes. Each one was an amazing, high-quality piece of artwork, gallery-ready. She carried an armful at a time to the incinerator until they were gone.

Zack came in with two sparkling waters, handed her one.

"Thank you."

"You're welcome." Zack looked at the white board. "Well, look at this," he said. "I have an idea for The Property column."

"I'm usually liking your ideas. Fire away."

"I've got a friend through the Resource Center who has a big pile of lumber from barns he tore down on his property in Happy Valley to grow vineyards. It's all ours if I'm willing to haul it away. I can't do it myself right now, but I have two other guys who need the work."

"What guys?"

"Bill and Jeff. Also from the Resource Center.

"And why can't you do it yourself right now?"

"I'll get to that in a minute."

Lisa pushed her chair away from the desk, created a little distance between them.

"Here's what I'm thinking. Bill and Jeff say they can have a new greenhouse built in a couple of weeks."

"Do I want a new greenhouse?"

"Why not? The foundation's already there. Free lumber. Kind of a no brainer. And, remember, I'm now a *trained* hemp-seed grower." He smiled.

"How would that work?"

"Those Marin guys and I got pretty close. Instead of a partnership with Ben's friends, I'd front the funds to buy the plants, the materials, tell Bill and Jeff how to put it together. Get an electrician to help with the wiring and security. I think this hemp-seed idea is a good one."

"But?" Lisa said.

"But what?"

"You can't do it yourself right now."

"Oh. That. I've been getting calls the past few days," Zack said.

"I've noticed."

"From Alaska."

"Uh-huh." Lisa stood, unlocked the cabinet containing the new manuscript boxes, stacked them on the desk between them.

"Becs' mom. Tanya," Zack said.

"Your ex-wife?"

"Technically, estranged wife."

"Oh, I didn't know that."

"The calls were from her sister. Tanya had a breakdown. Needs someone to take care of her for a while."

"How long is a while?"

"Good question. Hard to predict. But I need to head to the airport in two hours. Uber will pick me up."

Lisa unstacked the five boxes, set them side-by-side, avoided eye contact with him, swallowed and breathed slowly.

Zack nodded toward the boxes. "Is this the official unveiling?"

"I guess so. Don't you need to pack?"

"Yeah. But that won't take long. I'll still have a half hour, if you want to keep that date you mentioned."

"Absolutely. You go pack, I'll be in shortly."

"I want to see what's in these."

Lisa sat in front of the manuscript boxes, pushed her feet against the floor to spin her chair, watched the white board and cabinets and boxes and Zack rotate in and out of view until she planted her feet. She shoved a box toward Zack, pulled one toward herself.

"Now?" Zack said.

Lisa nodded, and they flipped the lids, saw stacks of empty pages inside. Lisa's face sagged; her mouth fell open. They each took another box. Same thing.

"This is certainly anticlimactic," Lisa said. She opened the fifth box. Another ream of blank paper, except one page on top, typewritten, a letter and an outline.

She handed the paper to Zack, sat back in the swivel chair, spun. "Will you read to me?"

"I will," Zack said. "It begins with a letter."

Dear Lisa – If I had ever had the wherewithal to
publish <u>The Baker's Quintet</u>, they would all have been
dedicated to you. And if I had finished the next five,
they, as well, would have been my gift to you. What I have
left you here is also a gift of sorts. It's not an outline,
not a map, but simply a hint, a suggestion, of something I
was hoping to write, of something of such importance that
it has never been done well. Below you'll find the title of
another series, five more individual book titles, a line
of description for each. This is not the way I normally
work, prefer to have the ideas fly into my head based on
what I see, hear, touch, feel in my daily life. But I'm
tired, fingers slow on the Selectric, can't sit up for
long. And just for fun, one final cliché to hate: I'm
passing the torch to you. Asking you to continue my work.
Helping you to forge a meaningful future. An offering. I
know it's not much of an inheritance.
Love ⌢ Alice.

Lisa poked her index fingers into her eye sockets, rubbed them in the corners, massaged the eyelids. "More, please."

Zack continued. "'The name of the series is *The Sweet Sorrow of Home.*'"

Lisa chuckled. "Oxymoron."

"'The first title: *Heart is Where the Home Is,* a tale about life on the streets, as seen through the eyes of Sally and Mitch, modeled after folks I know who occupy the streets below campus.'"

"'The second title is *Tight Sleep,* more of Sally and Mitch, the continual hunt for a few hours of comfort.'"

Lisa leaned forward. "You see what she's doing. Bastardizing the clichés. Standing them on their heads and watching them dance."

Zack nodded. "More?"

"Yes."

"'The third title is *Lay in the Bed You Make.* Have Sally and Mitch show what it takes to survive in the world of the homeless.'"

"Notice the intentional bad grammar," Lisa said. "Emphasis on 'lay' instead of 'lie'. Double meaning."

"'Number four: *Bound Homeward*, the nightly hunt for a place to sleep.'"

Lisa laughed. "She loved Simon and Garfunkel. Twisted that one up."

"'The last one: *A Hard Man is Good to Find*. Sally and Mitch dealing with the hunger for affection, comfort, the closeness of skin.'"

Lisa shook her head. "I like the idea, but the title's weak. She stole it from Mae West."

"What do you think?" Zack asked.

"Not quite sure yet. All I know is that we finally get Gregory behind us, but Alice refuses to stay dead. Let me read you something. I wrote this yesterday at the office." Lisa read the paragraph about the homeless folks downtown. "I mean, this came out of nowhere. I'd been watching it out the window for a couple months, never really thinking about it. Now this. Alice invading my privacy."

"Do you really think it's five separate books? Looks like chapter titles to me."

"I have no idea. You should go pack."

"Yeah. See you shortly," Zack said as he left.

She felt it start to creep in, refused it. No more disappointment. She was appointed now. Self-appointed.

Lisa stared at her computer screen, watched the steady blink of the cursor asking for a password. "Ha!" she said. She picked up her cell phone, dialed Michael.

"What's up?"

"I figured out CP."

"What are you talking about?"

"The cryptic note you left me a few weeks ago. The one about NYE and hemp seeds and CP. Neither of us could remember what it meant."

"Oh, yeah. So?"

"Computer password."

"Doesn't ring a bell. But, good work. Got to go. Big truckload of berries headed my way."

"Bye."

Lisa took one blank piece of paper, scrunched it into a ball in her hands, threw it at the whiteboard. She continued, page after page until a small pile covered the floor. She laughed, out loud, loud enough for the guests at Land of Medicine Buddha to hear, loud enough for Bianca to hear.

She unwound the cord wrapped around the Selectric, plugged it in, flipped the switch, the familiar hum coming back to life, silent since Alice's death.

She took a blank page from one of the manuscript boxes, slid it into the platen, rolled it in, adjusted the height, typed:

THE SWEET SORROW OF HOME

at the top of the page. Beneath it she centered

by Lisa and Alice Hardrock

There was no way she could do this, wrap her mind around the scope of a long story with characters and scenes and drama, how to begin, how to end. And she hadn't touched a typewriter since high school. It was crazy, but she imagined Alice's DNA merging with hers, fingertip to fingertip on the keyboard.

No. This was wrong. Gregory was dead. Alice was dead. Zack was heading to Alaska to tend to Becs' mom. She ripped the page out of the typewriter, scrunched it up, threw it into the pile on the floor. She loaded another blank piece of paper, retyped the title, then wrote:

by Lisa Hardrock

She typed the first sentence:

Lela lived on the streets. Art was her friend.

ABOUT THE AUTHOR

Jory Post is an educator, writer, and artist who lives in Santa Cruz, California. He and his wife, Karen Wallace, create handmade books and art together as JoKa Press.

Jory is the co-founder and publisher of *phren-z*, an online literary quarterly. His first book of prose poetry, *The Extra Year*, was published by Anaphora Literary Press in 2019, and was followed by a second, *Of Two Minds*, in 2020.

His work has been published in *Catamaran Literary Reader*, *Chicago Quarterly Review*, *Rumble Fish Quarterly*, *The Sun*, and elsewhere. His short stories "Sweet Jesus" and "Hunt and Gather" were nominated for the 2019 Pushcart Prize.

Made in the USA
Monee, IL
04 November 2020

46715748R00239